LIVING

WITNESS

THE GREGOR DEMARKIAN BOOKS
BY JANE HADDAM

Not a Creature Was Stirring

Precious Blood

Act of Darkness

Quoth the Raven

A Great Day for the Deadly

Feast of Murder

A Stillness in Bethlehem

Murder Superior

Dead Old Dead

Festival of Deaths

Bleeding Hearts

Fountain of Death

And One to Die On

Baptism in Blood

Deadly Beloved

Skeleton Key

True Believers

Somebody Else's Music

Conspiracy Theory

The Headmaster's Wife

Hardscrabble Road

Glass Houses

Cheating at Solitaire

LIVING WITNESS

A Gregor Demarkian Novel

JANE HADDAM

MINOTAUR BOOKS

NEW YORK

This is a work of fiction. All of the characters, organizations, and events portrayed
in this novel are either products of the author's imagination
or are used fictitiously.

www.minotaurbooks.com

Library of Congress Cataloging-in-Publication Data

Haddam, Jane, 1951–
    Living witness : a Gregor Demarkian novel / Jane Haddam.—1st ed.
            p. cm.
    ISBN-13: 978-0-312-38086-1
    ISBN-10: 0-312-38086-0
    1. Demarkian, Gregor (Fictitious character)—Fiction.   2. Private investigators—
Pennsylvania—Fiction.   3. Pennsylvania—Fiction.   I. Title.
    PS3566.A613L58   2009
    813'.54—dc22   2008036059

First Edition: April 2009

10   9   8   7   6   5   4   3   2   1

For Edelweiss—

because fame is another way to go on living

Man by nature wants to know.
—Aristotle

The world changes, and truths cannot be embalmed.
—Richard Hofstadter

PROLOGUE

So, what is evolution, anyway? It's survival of the fittest, right?

—question from student,
Post University, 22 April 2008

Biological (or organic) evolution is change in the properties of populations of organisms or groups of such populations, over the course of generations. The development, or ontogeny, of an individual organism is not considered evolution. Individual organisms do not evolve. The changes in populations that are considered evolutionary are those that are "heritable" via the genetic material from one generation to the next. Biological evolution may be slight or substantial, it embraces everything from slight changes in the proportions of different forms of a gene within a population, such as the alleles that determine the different human blood types, to the alterations that led from the earliest organisms to dinosaurs, bees, snapdragons and humans.

—Douglas J. Futuyma, *Evolutionary Biology, 3rd Edition*

If Ann-Victoria Hadley had been forced to tell the truth—and she never had to be forced; she always told the truth—she would have had to admit that this was not the first time she had been the most hated person in Snow Hill, Pennsylvania. In fact, for most of her ninety-one years, she had made something of a hobby of it. It had started in 1926, when she was ten. That was the first and last time she had ever entered the Snow Hill Historical Society's annual Fourth of July Essay Contest. The winner of the contest got to read her essay from the reviewing stand at the end of the Fourth of July parade.

"Right in front of everybody!" Annie-Vic's fifth-grade teacher had said, as if that was the most important thing in the world—doing whatever you did "right in front of everybody." The teacher was old Miss Encander, a creaking wreck of medical problems held together by nothing but her own smugness. It had seemed to Annie-Vic, at the time, that everybody in Snow Hill was held together by smugness, and that not even the oppressive June heat that always accompanied the last week of school could excuse Miss Encander for *requiring* her class to enter that contest. Besides, it wasn't fair. In elementary school, the hill kids were still mixed in with the kids from the town. They sat at the back of the classroom in stolid, silent rows and stared at their hands if the teacher called on them. The essay that won the contest was always called something like "Today We Thank Our Founding Fathers." What did the hill kids have to be thankful for? There was no plumbing up there in those shacks, and no electricity either, and once or twice a year one of the men died from drinking the stuff they made in a still they kept out of sight in an abandoned mine.

"It's better when they die," Annie-Vic's father had said, at the dinner table, to Annie-Vic's mother. "It's worse when they go blind or crazy and there's nothing you can do for them."

Annie-Vic's father was the one "real" doctor in town, but he had wanted to be a lawyer. Then his older brother Thomas had decided to be a lawyer himself, and *their* father, Annie-Vic's Grampa Hay, had decided that there wasn't enough room for two lawyers in Snow Hill.

"It would never have occurred to him that I could pack up and move away and be a lawyer somewhere else," Annie-Vic's father said. "It never even occurred to me."

Annie-Vic called her essay "Patriotism," and that was accurate. It was an essay about patriotism. Mostly, it was an essay about why patriotism was bad for you, and why they should give up celebrating the Fourth of July until they'd cleaned up everything that was wrong with the country. Annie-Vic had mentioned the hill kids, but she had also mentioned Music and Art and Learning, which were so much more advanced in Europe. That was why old Miss Encander had ended up calling her not just a Communist, but a snob.

These days, people were calling Annie-Vic an atheist, or—worse yet, in the eyes of most of them—a *secular humanist.* Annie-Vic had never heard the term before all this fuss started, and she'd ended up having to look it up on the Internet. Annie-Vic had a cable Internet connection on her computer at home and a wireless card in her laptop, for when she was traveling. She did a lot of traveling. Her last trip had been just last July, to Mongolia, to see a total eclipse of the sun. She had gone with an AAVC tour group and had her picture taken with her arms around a yak.

"Asinine," Annie-Vic thought now, looking down the long straight line of Main Street. She was thinking of the now, of course, but she was also thinking of that long-ago fuss with Miss Encander. She had known even then that she could have written a much more insulting essay. She could have written one entitled "Snow Hill, Pennsylvania, The Town with the Stupidest People in the World," or "Miss Encander Should Learn Something Before She Tries to Teach It." It was a testament to Annie-Vic's mother that Annie-Vic could never force herself to be that rude.

Main Street had stores on it—and churches. There were half a dozen churches, even though Snow Hill was a small place. The churches were

3

not the same ones Annie-Vic remembered from her childhood. The buildings were the same—except for the Holiness Church, which was new, and all the way at the end of the street—but the denominations in them had switched around. The Congregationalists were gone. They had become the United Church of Christ and then just sort of disappeared. Their building had been taken over by the Assembly of God. The Baptists had moved into the church that had once belonged to the Episcopalians. The Mt. Sinai Full Gospel Church had moved in to the Baptist's old building. Only the Lutherans had stayed where they'd started out, and almost nobody went to the Lutherans anymore.

Annie-Vic leaned over and checked the laces on her running shoes. She did not run—she was ninety-one, and she hadn't even liked to run when she was at Vassar; it was a new thing, this driving need to race about everywhere and be athletic—but she did walk every day, up and down Main Street if she were in town. In Mongolia she had not walked because she had hiked every day with her group, but on another AAVC trip, to China, she had risen every morning and paced three or four times around her hotel. The Chinese police were not happy with the idea of an American walking around the streets on her own, for what looked to be no reason of any kind at all.

There were people on Main Street who were waiting for her and Annie-Vic knew it. They'd waited for her when she'd come home on her first vacation from college. In those days it was strange for a girl to go to college at all. It was an affront that a girl would go away to a place like Vassar, which was for people who were richer than the Hadleys were, for people who were not Folks. It was important to almost everybody in Snow Hill to be Just Folks. Annie-Vic had always wondered if they had waited for her on Main Street when they found out that she wasn't coming home after college, that she had enlisted in the Navy instead. That was in 1937, and four short years later America was at war. That time, Annie-Vic had managed to stay away for damned near a decade. She still thought of it as the happiest time of her life, in spite of the fact that she'd spent two years of it in a Japanese prisoner of war camp.

"Asinine," she said again. Then she started off down the sidewalk, moving more quickly than most people twenty years younger than she was could have managed, staring straight ahead as she did. The people who were waiting for her were not going to slow her down, or change her mind. If they weren't all boneheaded stupid, they'd know it.

The first stretch of Main Street was clear of people. It was a working day in the middle of the week, and most of the people who lived in Snow Hill were away at jobs in Harrisburg. Yes, Annie-Vic thought, even Snow Hill was changing. Even Snow Hill couldn't stay stuck in the mud of provincial ignorance forever, although it sure as Hell intended to try. Annie-Vic was an imposing figure, and she knew it. She was tall for a woman, even these days, and so spare she could have served as a flagpole with very little alteration. Her arms and legs pumped, the way she had been taught to make them in the cardiovascular health class she'd taken at the community college. Her hair was thick and wild and gray as dirt. Her eyes were clear of cataracts and in no need of glasses except when she wanted to read. Her spine was as straight as a metal rod.

"Use it or lose it," she whispered to herself, under her breath.

That was just the moment she was coming up on the Snow Hill Diner, and on Alice McGuffie, standing right outside.

"Filthy little bitch," Alice McGuffie said, in a voice loud enough to carry all up and down the street. "You're going to burn in Hell."

2

Nicodemus Frapp saw Alice McGuffie come out onto Main Street just as old Miss Hadley was about to pass, and he knew—even standing all the way up at the other end of town—that it was not a situation likely to end in an exchange of "Good mornings." At least, it wasn't going to end that way for Alice. Annie-Vic was polite to a fault. She was polite in that way that highly educated, highly sophisticated people often were, with such a meticulous dedication to detail that she seemed to be insulting you in a way you couldn't put your finger on. It was the

5

kind of ability Nick had envied endlessly when he was growing up. He had even envied it in old Miss Hadley, since he had grown up in Snow Hill. Now he knew that it was not the kind of thing he would ever be able to do, and that it wouldn't be good for him if he could. There were people in his congregation who thought Nick was highly educated himself. He'd been "away at school" long enough to have figured out the difference between the Oral Roberts University and Vassar.

Main Street was bright and hard this morning. It was too cold for this late in the winter. Nick watched Annie-Vic on her walk, the upright posture, the heel-to-toe "power foot" execution. He'd grown up in the hills. His people were miners and farmers. His own father hadn't lasted but a few months past his fiftieth birthday. Nick could remember himself coming down to school every day with his lunch packed into a plastic beach bucket. All the hill kids had beach buckets to carry their lunches in, because the buckets went on sale cheap at Kmart at the end of the summer, and because it was much too expensive to buy lunch at the cafeteria at school. Nick was willing to bet that Annie-Vic had been able to buy her lunch when she was in elementary school, or—if the cafeteria didn't exist yet; Nick was only thirty-six; some parts of the town's social history still confused him— able to walk home and have it served to her by her mother. Nick's own mother had had a job at a package store most of the time he was growing up. The package store would have killed her, if his father hadn't gotten around to doing it to her first.

Nick took one last look at Annie-Vic, going by the hardware store, and Mr. Radkin stepping out to talk to her. *That* ought to be a conversation, he thought. But there was no conversation. Annie-Vic didn't stop moving. Nick looked up at George Radkin and back at Annie Vic and then around at his own new church, built from scratch less than ten years ago, from money made by the people who had once had to send their children to school with beach buckets. Then he turned his back to the town and went inside. There was a time in his life that he'd thought that he was turning his back on this town for good. He'd thought he would get himself ordained and go to work in a church in a place he'd never seen, an exotic place, like Florida. He didn't know why he'd decided, in the end, to come back home, but he had this to hold on to: he believed in God the way most people believed in their own left shoulders. He could feel the presence of the Almighty with him at every hour of the day and night. He knew that God understood him better than he understood himself, and that God wanted only good things for him. Nick was not the kind of preacher who promised hellfire and destruction. He wasn't even the kind of preacher who believed in it.

Inside the church, two of the men from the Men's Study Group, Harve Griegson and Pete DeMensh, were painting the front of the new choir box. Nick hadn't been sure about putting in a choir, but some of the women had really wanted it, and he didn't think it would do any harm. Still, it was a lot different from the Holiness Church he remembered from his childhood, which had been in the old minister's ten-by-twelve-foot living room in a house where the "driveway" was nothing but mud ruts dug by the minister's big pickup truck. It had been a blessing to get to the summer and be able to worship in a field, no matter how hot it was. It had been a blessing when no more than two people had to be taken to the hospital, too, and not just because there was a legitimate worry about somebody dying from the rattlesnake venom. Dear Lord, the way the nurses at the emergency room had looked at them, every time.

"Nick?" Harve Griegson said.

"I was thinking about the snakes," Nick said. He had turned his back on the two men while he was thinking, and he didn't turn around now. He was looking at the row on row of shiny wooden pews, every one of them planed and sanded and stained and waxed so that they looked like something out of a Hollywood movie about church. Was there something wrong with that? America had moved on since the days when his father had been a boy. It had moved on in the days since he himself had been a boy. Wasn't it right that the hill people should be moving on too?

"You're not thinking about bringing back the snakes, are you, Nick?" Harve Griegson asked. "Because, you know, I thought that was one of your better changes. My daddy died from one of those snakes. You got to wonder what people were thinking."

"They were thinking that God keeps his promises," Nick said, but then he was sorry he'd said it. Harve Griegson had a house with indoor plumbing, two trucks, and a big flat-screen TV, but he'd still never gone beyond his sophomore year in high school, and he barely got through that. It was one of the few things that could make Nick really angry after all these years. It was a joke, what the town used to call an "education" for the hill kids. It was worse than a joke. The only way Nick himself had been able to overcome it was that he was a natural reader. He read everything and anything, and he sat in the library one afternoon for six hours until they broke down and let him have a library card. The hill kids he'd grown up with had barely learned to read at all, and barely learned to figure, and as soon as they got within shouting distance of their fifteenth birthdays they'd gotten the message that everybody would be glad if they would just go.

"Nick," Pete said, sounding worried, "are you all right?"

"He's thinking about bringing back the snakes," Harve said. He sounded worried.

Nick turned around to look at them. "I'm fine. I'm not thinking about bringing back the snakes. I just saw Annie-Vic have a run-in with Alice McGuffie."

"Annie-Vic," Harve Griegson said.

"I still don't get it," Pete said. "I don't get why we aren't part of that lawsuit."

"We've got no reason to be part of that lawsuit," Nick said. "Our children don't go to the public school. We've got our own school."

"She thinks she's better than everybody," Harve said. "Just look at her. Fancy college. Going off all over the place. She thinks the rest of us are brick stupid."

"Which doesn't change the fact that we can't be part of a lawsuit against the teaching of anything at all at the public schools, when our children don't go to the public schools." Nick walked all the way down the center aisle and looked at the choir box. Some churches had choir lofts, but they hadn't planned for that when they built the building, so the choir was going to be in a small boxlike enclosure at the front, to the left of the pulpit and a little ahead of the first lefthand pew. It looked nice, Nick had to admit, even though he was sure there had never been anything like it in any Holiness Church anywhere.

"Somebody's going to do something about that woman someday," Harve said. "She doesn't have any children in the public schools, either. She doesn't have any children. She's a radical feminist. Why's she even on the school board?"

"She's on the school board because she ran for a place and the people elected her," Nick said firmly, "and that's the essence of democracy. We've got to learn to live with it. We've also got to learn to live with what's about to happen in this town come the trial starting up in a couple of weeks. Have any of you talked to the Hendersons like I asked you to?"

Pete and Harve both looked away.

"They're not easy to find," Harve said.

"Well, we'd better find them," Nick said. "Because as sure as the sun rises and the moon sets, they're going to be the first citizens of Snow Hill, Pennsylvania, to hit the cable news networks, and you know it. There's going to be no monkey trial in Snow Hill without the media trying to make Christians look bad."

"Monkey trial," Harve said. "You got to be an intellectual to be stupid enough to believe this crap."

Nick went past them into the vestibule in the back. It was a good, solid building, after years in the shacks and shifting arrangements of the hills. It was a good thing they'd done, too, getting so many of their people into better jobs, and building a school so their children could get real educations and not be forced out by the snobs on the public school faculty. All the things they'd done were good, Nick was sure of it, but there was no getting away from the fact that they were who they were, they were Holiness, they spoke in tongues, they got slain in the spirit, and some of them—some of them—handled snakes.

Oral Roberts University wasn't Vassar, but Nicodemus Frapp had seen how the outside world lived. He didn't give a flying damn whether the public schools of Snow Hill taught evolution or intelligent design or creation or the origin myths of H. P. Lovecraft, but he did mind what was about to happen here, because it was about to happen to him.

Sometimes he thought he couldn't be angry enough at Annie-Vic.

3

Henry Wackford had always wanted to like Ann-Victoria Hadley, just as he always wanted to like anyone he could consider an ally in his life-long war against Ignorance, Stupidity, and Unreason. He thought of the terms in just that way, with capital letters, as he thought of the term Reason itself. He didn't know where he'd picked up that habit, but he was sure he'd had it for a very long time, at least since the days when he'd been in high school in Snow Hill. There were teachers still teaching at Snow Hill High School who remembered him. There were even some who remembered his greatest local triumph, when he'd received his scholarship to Williams and become the first local person since Annie-Vic to go off East to college. Maybe there was something about Snow Hill that made people come back after they'd gone off, and after they knew better. Henry didn't know. He only knew that this last thing had also been the last straw. There was just so much crap he could put up with. Then he couldn't put up with anything more.

He was standing at the window of his office, looking down from the second story of his building onto Main Street. He could see Annie-Vic pumping along, her arms and legs moving like a robot's, with too many angles to be human. Henry wanted to like her, but he couldn't, even if she was crucial to this lawsuit. She was a publicity hound; that was the trouble. And what was worse, she didn't know what to do with publicity when she got it. When Henry had first decided to file this lawsuit—and yes, it was his decision; he even had children in the system to give him standing; nobody else would have thought of it in a million years—he had imagined himself as a sort of spokesman for science. He had seen himself standing up in front of a bank of microphones at press conferences, or at single microphones held by reporters he'd watched on television, laying out the case for keeping "Intelligent Design" out of the Snow Hill public schools.

"Backwardness and superstition cannot be allowed to strangle the advance of science," he would say, or something like that. You had to be careful when you went before the cameras. Reporters were good at making people look like fanatics, and they especially liked making nonreligious people look like fanatics. It was a conspiracy, Henry had always been sure of it. People had laughed at Hillary Clinton for saying that there was a "vast right wing conspiracy" dedicated to taking her husband down, but she'd been absolutely right. Religions wouldn't survive for a minute if they depended on what people actually believed. Nobody could believe that tripe for five minutes if they thought about it. That was why the conspiracy had to keep people from thinking about it. It had to keep people from focusing on their fantasies of God and Heaven and get them focusing on their neighbors, especially the ones they could hate. Henry Wackford was sure he was one of the most hated people in all of Snow Hill, even though the town had elected him to the school board six terms running—right up until it had defeated him, this last time.

Underneath his window, Henry could see not only Annie-Vic, but the storefronts on the north side of the street and the reflection of his own firm's sign in the window of the hardware store. WACKFORD SQUEERS, the sign said, just as it had in his father's time. Henry had no idea why he'd never changed the name of the firm. Old Gander Squeers had been dead for a decade before Henry had graduated from the law school at Penn State, never mind passed the bar. For a while, Henry had thought his father would change the firm's name to "Wackford and Wackford," or even "Richard Wackford and Son," but he never had. He hadn't named Henry after him, either. Henry had asked him about that, but he would never say. Richard Wackford never would say much. After Henry's mother died, he barely said anything at all.

Annie-Vic was passing the Baptist Church now. Henry half-expected one of the theocrats to come rushing out to threaten her, but nothing happened. They were all theocrats, all the religious people in Snow Hill, all the religious people everywhere. They wanted power, and when they got it they wanted to kill all the people who dared to breathe the truth about the world. It was true. Look at history—look at the witch burnings, and the Inquisitions, and the reigns of terror from one end of Europe to the other. It wasn't just Europe, either. Henry had read enough to know that Islam was as bad, or worse, if you looked at the right places in the right centuries. It wasn't Christianity or Islam that he was afraid of, it was Religion, which was another term that always had a capital letter in his mind. It was Religion that would go on trial here in Snow Hill in just three weeks, and Henry Wackford was ready for it, even if no one else was.

Down on Main Street, Annie-Vic pumped on past the Assembly of God, but nobody came out of there, either. She looked neither to the right nor to the left. This was her daily ritual when she was at home, which she was only about half the year. There were people who said she was a force of nature, and Henry tended to agree. She was like a black hole. She sucked in all the light. What reporters had come to town so far, in anticipation of the suit, had all been interested in talking to her, and nobody else. There was even talk of doing a spot on her for *60 Minutes*. Henry sometimes thought he was losing his mind. She didn't understand anything. She really didn't. She might not be religious, she might not even believe in God, but she didn't understand anything. He wasn't even sure she wasn't religious. He only knew he never saw her coming out of any of the churches on Sunday, and that no denomination claimed her as a member and no denomination wanted to throw her out for supporting the legacy of Charles Darwin. What did it mean? What did any of it mean, when you were crushed down under the weight of provincial belligerence? That was how Henry Wackford

12

saw himself, in spite of being the richest lawyer in town, in spite of having been six times chairman of the school board. He was crushed down, hemmed in, stifled—suffocating, under the weight of all this small-town pettiness, without a chance in Hell of getting out.

The door to the office opened behind him, and Henry turned to see Christine Lindsay walk in with a stack of file folders in her arms. Christine was Henry's personal secretary, and she was always careful to wear her gold cross right in the hollow at the bottom of her throat, as if she'd been branded with it. Henry would have preferred to hire somebody who was an ally in the war against Unreason, but there was nobody like that in Snow Hill who had also taken a secretarial course.

"I've got the material you wanted on the Brander Mills development," Christine said. "I ran the schedules and put them on the computer if you want them that way. Do you want me to send in your nine o'clock? It's Mrs. Hennessy about the wills."

"Give me a minute," Henry said. He looked out on Main Street again. Annie-Vic was still walking. She was ninety-one, but she walked more than he did, and she walked faster. He ran his tongue along his lips and wondered why they hurt.

"If you don't need me," Christine said.

"Did you ever meet Annie-Vic?" Henry asked her. "Meet to talk to, I mean."

"Of course I've met Miss Hadley," Christine said. "She's come here, you have to remember. She's come to talk to you about the lawsuit. With those people from Fox Run Estates, and that lawyer from Philadelphia."

"Ah," Henry said.

"I don't like it, " Christine said. "I don't like those people over at the development. They move here from wherever. They don't even have real homes, if you think about it. They don't put down roots. They don't care about their neighbors. They just come in here and all of a sudden we're all supposed to change to suit them."

This was new. Christine didn't usually talk like this. Or maybe she did, at home or at church, but she didn't usually talk like this in the office. They'd taught her better than that at Katie Gibbs. Henry looked at her long and hard. She was young and pretty in that small-town way that wouldn't last, all fair skin and "cute" features. She had a small solitaire diamond on the ring finger of her left hand. The boy she was engaged to had never managed to make it past his second year at community college, but he had a "good" job doing something or the other at one of the technical companies, where all the *really* good jobs went to the people who lived in the development, and who had moved here from somewhere else.

"I don't like it," Christine said again, obviously getting ready to go. "And I don't like Miss Hadley, either. She thinks she's better than the rest of us. She thinks she's smarter. She thinks we're all idiots. But she doesn't know everything. She doesn't know the Lord."

Henry cleared his throat, but Christine ignored him. Surely she knew he "didn't know the Lord" any more than Annie-Vic did, but there was that thing again, that thing Annie-Vic did to people. If she was in the room, nobody noticed anybody else.

Christine turned on her heel and walked out, closing Henry's office door behind her. In another kind of woman, the exit would have said volumes, none of it pleasant. Christine was incapable of making that kind of gesture, or any kind of gesture, with any kind of force.

Henry went back to the window and back to looking at Annie-Vic. It wouldn't work out, in the long run, if things kept on going as they'd been going. Annie-Vic didn't know enough about what was going on to be the sole spokesperson for the lawsuit. She wouldn't know what to say when the time came to say it, or she would say whatever came into her head, whether it helped the cause or not. Besides, it was Henry who filed the lawsuit in the first place. It was Henry who put the coalition together.

"Damn," Henry said, so close to the window that his breath fogged it.

On the street, Annie-Vic looked as strong and vigorous as a forty-year-old. She really was a force of nature. She wasn't likely to be going anywhere anytime soon.

4

Alice McGuffie couldn't remember a time when she had not been angry, and she couldn't remember a time when she had not been laughed at. People in town thought she didn't know what they said about her, but they were wrong. She had always known, all the way back to elementary school, when that prissy Sheila Conoway had called her "a really stupid moron" in the second-floor girls' bathroom right after lunch. Alice was fifty-three now—and she knew she was supposed to be over it, but Alice never got over anything. It didn't matter how "stupid" she was supposed to be, or how many people said she couldn't think her way out of a paper bag—that was Sheila Conoway again, in high school that time, when they'd had that big fight over Alice's asking questions in Miss Marbledale's class. Alice had a memory that wouldn't quit. She remembered every giggle. She remembered every sneer. Most of all she remembered every one of the hundreds of classes she had attended over time, when she had been called on and unable to answer, or just called on and left standing at her place, unable to say anything at all. That was what school had been like for Alice McGuffie, and that was why she hadn't spent a single day in a classroom after she'd finally managed to graduate from high school. She hadn't known it at the time, but she was being prepared for a Great Mission. She was on that mission now, and she didn't intend to quit.

"Vile little bitch," she said out loud to Annie-Vic's retreating back. Alice hated Annie-Vic the way the Lord is supposed to hate sin. She hated everything about the woman, the way she walked, the way she talked, the things she said. It was the one fly in Alice's ointment at the moment that Annie-Vic was a member of the Snow Hill School Board, right at that moment when Alice herself had managed to get elected to it. Not that Alice would have run for school board on her own. It wouldn't have occurred to her. It had occurred to Franklin Hale, though, and Franklin went to Alice's church, and there they all were now, sitting where they could do some good.

Except for Annie-Vic. Except for Miss Ann-Victoria Hadley.

What did it say about a woman that not only had she never married, but that she said she never wanted to be married, that marriage only "got in the way." Got in the way of what? Alice wanted to know. Alice had been married three times, the last time in the church, and she didn't see that it had got in her way at all.

"Vile bitch," Alice said again, but she said it under her breath this time, and there was nobody around to hear her. It was too cold to be standing outside in nothing but her waitress's uniform. The skin on her arms had begun to feel hard and brittle. The roots of her hair stung. Oh, but she did remember it all, every day of it, from beginning to end, without a break. There hadn't even been a break in the vacations, because of course nobody ever went anywhere—this was Snow Hill. People just hung around their houses in the summers or got jobs in town. Sheila Conoway was there, but so was Miss Marbledale, coming into the grocery store to do her shopping, getting a visit from her unmarried sister who lived in Ohio, packing up her small car to go to Ohio herself when August rolled around, but only for a week, because school was about to start. Alice could smell school coming a mile away.

Miss Marbledale was still teaching at Snow Hill High School. Alice still saw her when she came into the diner for a cup of coffee or for her dinner on Thursday nights. Alice had no idea how old the woman was. She had seemed ancient forty years ago. She was even more ancient now. Alice remembered the time when stories had gone all over town about Miss Marbledale. People said that she was a "woman who liked women," because they didn't want to come right out and call her a dyke. People said that the woman who came every summer to visit wasn't really her sister, or that she was, but it didn't matter because they were doing it anyway. Alice couldn't imagine Miss Marbledale doing it. She could imagine Miss Marbledale being a lesbian, because you had to be a lesbian to act the way Miss Marbledale acted and think the things she thought. Miss Catherine Marbledale and Miss Ann-Victoria Hadley. Maybe they were doing it together.

Alice turned away from Main Street and went back into the diner. There wasn't much in the way of business at this time of the morning. Breakfast was always full up, but that was over, and at this time of day people were at their jobs. Alice checked out the booths along the south wall. They were all empty and had all been cleaned. They all had little wire racks for sugar packets and ketchup bottles were all full. Alice had been waiting tables all her life when she met and married Lyman McGuffie, but it was only after that that she had paid any attention to how a business like this was run. There was proof positive, though, of everything she had ever believed in. All that talk about "education" was a crock. You didn't need an "education" to succeed in life. Lyman himself had dropped out of high school in the tenth grade and had built up this diner with his own two hands, and it was one of the most successful businesses in town. Alice had learned nothing by staying to graduate, except that it was all a crock, and the only reason for it was to make it possible for some people to prance around acting like they were better than everybody else.

Alice checked the counter. There were two men, sitting far apart, occupying stools. Both of them had coffee. There was one waitress. The waitress was trying to look busy, because it was Lyman's one inflexible rule that nobody should ever be on the floor without looking busy. Alice went to the back of the room and let herself through the swinging doors to the kitchen. Lyman was back there, checking inventory and keeping an eye on the dishwasher who was not only loading dishes, but trying to clean off the grill.

"Well," Lyman said.

Alice shrugged. "I couldn't help myself," she said. "I can't always be polite, Lyman, you know that. I can't always be Christian. It's a failing. But that woman."

"Which woman?"

"Annie-Vic."

"Ah," Lyman said.

Alice made a face at him, behind his back. "It's all well and good to

17

say 'ah,'" she said. "But that woman does real damage. We wouldn't be in this lawsuit if it wasn't for her."

"It was Henry Wackford's idea to file the lawsuit," Lyman said. "He'd have done it whether she wanted to go along with it or not."

"Still," Alice said. "You know what I mean. She's right in the middle of it. Who does she think she is, anyway? It was a vote. The majority won. The minority is supposed to shut up and like it."

"Well, that's true enough," Lyman said. He started to pull big metal tubs out of the refrigerator: shredded lettuce; shredded cheddar cheese; black California olives; tomato slices; onion slices. It was the setup for lunch. Most of the people who came in for lunch wanted hamburgers of one kind or another.

"I think they make it all up anyway," Alice said, taking two of the tubs from him and carrying them over to the sandwich counter. "I don't think it has anything to do with science. How stupid do they think we are? Nobody could believe that stuff they're saying, and then they throw in all those words—like you're supposed to be scared of their *words*. 'Allele,' that was one of those words. Do you know what that word means? Nobody knows what that word means. They make it up. And then that fussy old maid just came right out and lied. Do you know what she said?"

"No," Lyman said. He had brought out the big stack of American cheese slices for the grilled cheese sandwiches.

"She said that survival of the fittest had nothing to do with the theory of evolution. Can you believe that? Nothing to do with it! What's the theory of evolution anyway, except survival of the fittest? Everybody knows that. Everybody always has known it. They think you're going to be scared of them. They prance around with their noses in the air and they think you're just going to curl up and die because they went to Vassar and they went to Wellesley and they have degrees and you're just an ignorant moron who ought to shut up and stay in your place. Well, we didn't shut up, did we? We're not going to shut up."

"It's a good thing you're doing," Lyman said. "I liked the idea right off, right when Frank came and asked you to run for the school board.

I'd have run myself except I knew it wouldn't look good, because I didn't graduate. But you graduated."

"If it wasn't for Annie-Vic, there wouldn't be any lawsuit," Alice said again. "The whole school board would be united. Henry Wackford wouldn't have dared file a lawsuit then. He wouldn't have dared. I don't know what people in this town were thinking, voting for that old hag. She's an out-and-out atheist. You watch."

"Henry Wackford is an atheist," Lyman said.

"They all think they're so smart," Alice said. "They all think they're smarter than anybody else. Just you watch. Just you wait and see what happens when the television people get here. They'll make us look like a bunch of hicks. But it won't matter." Alice suddenly stopped still. "Lyman?" she said. "It won't matter, will it? We're going to win this one. The judge is going to be just folks."

"Appointed by George W. himself," Lyman said.

"Yes," Alice said, "I know."

She tried to think it through, but it wouldn't come. She didn't trust the judge, even if he had been appointed by George W. George W. was just folks, but you couldn't trust these people who had gone to fancy schools, and it seemed to Alice that everybody who ended up a judge had gone to some fancy school or the other. Oh, Lord. She couldn't stand these people. She couldn't stand the way they thought they were *smarter* than everybody else.

"It would have been better," she said, but Lyman wasn't listening to her. Lyman was getting out the big bag of hamburger rolls they kept in the freezer overnight.

Alice went to the narrow closet and got out the stack of lunch menus. Annie-Vic was probably still out there somewhere on Main Street, walking in that stupid heel-toe way and lording it over everybody else in town, all the people who hadn't gone to fancy schools and didn't buy the crap the liberal media was always trying to sell them. Those people always got everything they wanted. They got it and then they acted like they'd earned something. Alice wanted to wipe every one of them off the face of the earth.

"You got to ask yourself," she said, "what's keeping that woman alive. I mean, she's older than dirt, isn't she? Don't people that age drop dead all the time?"

She turned around to see that Lyman hadn't heard her. He was taking out a small stack of hamburger patties to make ready on the grill. It was edging on up to eleven o'clock. Alice shrugged and headed out to the floor again.

People as old as Annie-Vic died all the time, she thought.

Hell. Most people as old as Annie-Vic were already dead.

5

Judy Cornish was sure there were many wonderful things about living in Snow Hill, Pennsylvania. There was the landscape, for one. Before they'd come out here, Judy had thought that big green spaces like this, full of trees and not much in the way of roads, had become restricted to national parks. It was—interesting—to find out that some people lived their lives in the middle of green, especially on the East Coast. Judy was from the state of Washington, originally. Until two years ago, she'd thought of "the East" as a collection of industrial cities and their high-priced suburbs. Snow Hill was not a suburb. It didn't come close.

The other thing Judy thought was wonderful about living in Snow Hill was the price of housing. They'd never been able to afford the kind of house they had here in any of Dan's other postings. Hell, in Palo Alto, they'd barely been able to afford much more than a matchbox, and in Houston they'd found enough space for the new baby only by saddling Dan with ninety-minute commute. Now they had enough space for all three of their children, and more. They had a six-thousand-square-foot Victorian that had taken only a little time to fix up, including a kitchen the size of their first apartment and a big curving stairway that looked as if it should have debutantes parading down it. Judy loved her house. She loved the stained-glass windows in the ground-floor alcove and the high ceilings in the master bedroom. She loved the walk-up attic, which they had converted to a play room for the children. The attic had a round turret the children could pretend was a medieval castle. Really, the house was perfect. Or it would have been, if it had only been located someplace in civilization.

The parking lot at the Adams IGA was not anywhere near empty enough, Judy could see that right off, and she could tell—from the sudden stiffening of Shelley Niederman's body—that Shelley was thinking the same thing herself. It wasn't a big parking lot, and it wasn't full, but at least half the spaces were occupied, and none of them were occupied by the right kind of car. Judy had learned to read the cars over these last few months, when she and Shelley had gone from being just odd people living in the development to The Enemy. The right kind of car was one like her own, a Volvo Cross Country station wagon, or a Saab, or even a Subaru Forester, although that last one was sometimes iffy. People out here didn't hate Subarus they way they hated Volvos. The wrong kind of car was a Chevy Cavalier, or a Ford Focus, or, the very worst, any kind of pickup truck made by an American car company. God. Judy had told her share of pickup truck jokes in college, and she and Dan had even gone to see Jeff Foxworthy on the Blue Collar Comedy Tour, but for some reason she'd never thought of any of it as real until she'd come here. It really shouldn't have been real. It really shouldn't have been the case that anybody on earth should want to be the kind of person the people here both were and thought was just plain fine.

That last sentence made no sense. Grammar and syntax seemed to be two of the casualties of her stay in Snow Hill. They were getting to her, these people were. They were turning her into some kind of ignorant, stupid, low-rent hick.

Judy pulled the Volvo into a parking place sufficiently far from the store and killed the engine and just sat. Beside her in the front passenger seat, Shelley Niederman rubbed the palm of her right hand rhythmically against her right knee. It was one of the things Shelley did when she was nervous and didn't have room to pace.

"Well," Judy said.

"Maybe we should take the time and go out to the mall," Shelley said.

"We don't have time to go out to the mall," Judy said. "We talked about it. We've got to pick up the food for the meeting and then we've got to get some actual work done on organizing the project materials, or the girls are never going to get this thing in in time for the judging. And Mallory has a piano lesson at two, so I've got that."

Mallory was Judy's fifteen-year-old daughter. She also had an eight year-old daughter named Hannah, and Danny, still small enough to be wearing a diaper in a child-protective seat in the back. Judy looked at him in the rearview mirror. He was asleep.

"Still," Shelley said.

Judy took her keys out of the ignition and put them in the inside pocket of her Coach Basic Bag. She'd always had Coach bags, but she'd had to order this one online, because the nearest Coach store to Snow Hill was in Harrisburg. Actually, it was worse than that. The nearest Starbucks was forty-five minutes away, at that same mall Shelley wanted to drive to, and that was the nearest place with a decent bookstore, too. It was as if they'd been dropped down on an alien planet, stuck not only in the 1950s, but in the 1950s in the hinterlands. Judy kept expecting Jethro Bodine to show up at any minute.

"Shelley," she said.

"I just don't like being yelled at," Shelley said. "Is that so strange? I don't like being followed around and yelled at. Especially not by those people. All they ever want to say to me is that I'm going to rot in Hell."

"They say it to Mallory and Hannah," Judy said. "In school. Mallory came home in tears the other day. But we can't let that matter to us. We can't. What kind of chance do you think you have of being able to get out of here any time soon?"

"Oh, God," Shelley said. "Steve told me that Sun Dynamics is thinking of expanding the campus and moving all their operations out here. Sometimes I think we're going to be stuck in this godforsaken place for decades."

"I heard the same thing from Dan," Judy said. "We can't let it happen this way. We can't. We've got a right to a decent education for our children. We've got a right to our own beliefs. They're not gods, these people here. As far as I'm concerned, some of them are barely human."

"Alice McGuffie," Shelley said, with a little puff of laugher.

"Exactly," Judy said. "We had every right to sue, under the circumstances, and we have every right to win the suit. And we're going to win it. And we're going to be here a long time after that. So we might as well brave it out. I went to Evolvefish and ordered a Darwin fish for the car. You should do it yourself."

"The car will get vandalized," Shelley said.

"Then we'll file a complaint and get the police to find the vandals," Judy said. "We'll just do it and do it and do it. It's time Snow Hill, Pennsylvania, entered the twenty-first century. I mean, for God's sake. 'Intelligent design.' What is *that*? It's just the same old creationism with a fancy new name, and you know what it will mean. You can kiss the Ivy League good-bye. The kids will never get the SAT scores. You can kiss any kind of decent life good-bye. The kids will end up dropping out of school at sixteen and working in convenience stores. Or worse. They'll get religion and start lecturing you about having a glass of wine with dinner. They'll turn in to people like *them*." Judy motioned vaguely in the direction of the parking lot. "They'll turn in to troglodytes."

"I do believe in God," Shelley said, dubious.

"I believe in God, too," Judy said. "I just don't believe in a stupid God. And that's all you get out here. Stupid God. You know why we don't go to church since we've been out here? We tried three churches and they were all the same. Praise Jesus! Get saved! Run and hide from the evil liberals! I never thought of myself as a liberal until I came here, but I sure as Hell do now. And I'm going to run for school board at the end of the year. Henry Wackford asked me to."

"Really?" Shelley said.

"It's not just the creationism," Judy said. "It's everything. These people have a stupid God and they're stupid themselves, if you ask me. Think of the construction on the new school. It's stalled—there's not a thing going on. We're never going to get that school finished if we don't get rid of the people who think anybody who's graduated from the fifth grade is a pointy-headed intellectual. And there are enough of us in town now to swing an election."

"Look," Shelley said. "It's Annie-Vic. That woman is amazing."

Judy looked. Annie-Vic was just passing the entrance to the parking lot, doing her power walk. She looked like she had more energy than most people Judy's age.

"They say Franklin Hale is ready to kill her," Judy said. "He's absolutely livid that she didn't go along with the textbook change, and then of course she joined the lawsuit. Henry Wackford says Franklin really expected to have a unanimous board so that he could say that intelligent design was the will of the people, or some crap like that."

"I just hope she doesn't drop dead in the middle of all this," Shelley said. "It's got to be such a strain."

"She doesn't look like she's about to drop dead," Judy said. Then she popped open her car door and started to climb out. "Let's go," she said. "I don't care who yells at me. If they try to give you pamphlets, don't take them. Maybe we should go further than that. Maybe I should order some material from the Council for Secular Humanism. You know, to hand back to them. When they hand out tracts."

"You're really bad," Shelley said. "You're going to get into trouble. Those people are dangerous."

"Psychochristians," Judy said. "Let's go get the stuff. If they start yelling at us, we can yell back. I'll think of some good things to say."

Actually, Judy couldn't think of anything to say. She hadn't been able to think of anything when Mallory had come home in tears because Barbie McGuffie had backed her into a wall at recess to tell her that she was going to Hell, and her whole family was going to Hell, because they were atheists and worshiped the devil. Mallory hadn't even known what an atheist was.

There had to be a way, Judy thought, there really had to be. There had to be a way to make these people see how ridiculous they were.

Lately, Judy had begun to think that she might really want to be an atheist, if only because it meant she was nothing at all like the long-time population of Snow Hill, Pennsylvania.

6

Gary Albright had been a cop in Snow Hill almost from the day he left the Marine Corps. He had been a legend since one long winter week-end in 2006. The legend part made him nervous, although he understood it, more or less. Mostly, he understood why people seemed to be in awe of his missing leg. He'd been in awe of Marines with missing limbs, once. It had seemed like the worst thing in the world that could happen to anybody. Gary had been an athlete in high school, on the football, basketball, and baseball teams of a small-town school that didn't have the student population to throw up much in the way of competition. He'd understood that from the start. He hadn't been pro-ball material, or even college-team material. He didn't have a chance in Hell of marching off into the sunset after high school grad-uation and showing up in a Dallas Cowboys uniform. Still, he'd been in good shape, active and happy in his own body. The idea of having less of it—less of that body—was what had scared him enough to put off enlisting for three solid months.

This morning Gary was doing what he had been doing since the day they'd found him lying up there in the hills with his leg gone. He was going through the endless paperwork that was now required even of small-town police forces. Not that Snow Hill had much of a force. There was Gary, who had been named chief at the ridiculously young age of thirty-six after the old chief, the one who had been there since Gary was a kid, had been caught dealing marijuana to black kids in Harrisburg. There was Eddie Block, who served as patrolman for the west side of town. There was Tom Fordman, who served as patrolman for the east. It was a simple enough system, and since nothing ever happened in Snow Hill except domestic disputes and teen-agers get-ting stupid, it worked well enough.

Gary was working well enough, this morning. That was a good

thing because he was feeling very tired. Even Humphrey had noticed it, and when Humphrey thought Gary was upset he was likely to get crazy. The town put up with having the dog in the police station—they had to put up with it; after the whole thing with Gary on the hill and the dog and the baby, nobody in town could have refused—but they wouldn't put up with it long if Humphrey started shredding furniture on a regular basis. Fortunately, Humphrey was a very good dog. He only lost it when he thought Gary was losing it, too.

"I'm not losing it," Gary said out loud, still staring down at the papers on his desk.

Across the room, from the desk next to the guard rail that was supposed to keep the public and the officers separated, Tina Clay looked up.

"Did you say something, Gary? Is there something I could get for you?"

Tina was one of those people who seemed to think that because Gary was missing most of his left leg, he couldn't do anything for himself. It was one of those things he found impossible to understand; and there were a lot more things in that category. In truth, Gary found most human beings completely mystifying, and he was sure that this had made him less of a police officer than he should have been.

Gary looked over the papers again. "Thank you," he said. It was always the best policy to be polite. That was one of the things he had not learned from his mother. "I don't need anything you can get me. I'm wondering if we need to hire on some extra men for when the trial opens."

"The trial," Tina said. Then she sniffed. "I don't know how you can be so calm about it. To think of those people. All of them. They're not even from here, most of them."

"Annie-Vic is from here," Gary said calmly. "Henry Wackford is, too. Wackford Squeers has been on Main Street since before I was born."

"Still," Tina said. She was a middle-aged woman with sparse hair that had been tinted too implausible a shade of red, and thick folds of fat that were emphasized because her clothes were always at least a size too small. If Gary had been the kind of man who wondered about how he felt about things, he would have to wonder if he liked Tina Clay.

"And they're suing you, too," Tina said. "They put your name right in the suit. I saw it in the newspaper. The idea of doing such a thing."

"My name comes first alphabetically," Gary said. "They don't bother to list all the names every time they talk about the suit. It would take up too much space. And time."

"They should all move back to wherever they came from," Tina said. "And Annie-Vic and Henry can move on out with them. Whatever happened to democracy? We voted you in for the school board. The people have spoken."

Gary wasn't actually sure the people *had* spoken. In the election that had put not only Gary himself, but Franklin Hale and Alice McGuffie and, yes, even Annie-Vic on the school board, not a single word had been said about the issue that had since become the biggest thing in town since the flood of 1954. There was something about the way this whole thing was set up that made Gary very uneasy.

"It's all about her, anyway," Tina said. "It's all about Annie-Vic Hadley. And you know it. There wouldn't have been a lawsuit if it hadn't been for her."

"I think Henry Wackford could have filed a lawsuit without the help of Annie-Vic."

"He could have, but he wouldn't have. You know it. There she is, and the whole rest of the school board agrees, except her, and so there wasn't a united front. I was talking to Alice about it only yesterday. If the board had a united front, there isn't anything Henry Wackford or those people from the development could have done. We'd have God back in the Snow Hill public schools, and they'd just have to lump it."

"I'm pretty sure they could have sued, united front or not," Gary said. He was still being calm, but talking about the whole thing always made him agitated. He wasn't like Tina. He knew better than to think that all it would have taken to avoid trouble was a school board without a single dissenting voice. Still, he had a problem with Annie-Vic, and he always had had.

27

"She thinks she's so smart," Tina said. "Going away to some fancy college full of rich girls. She thinks she's better than all of us. And now this. This isn't about teaching evolution, Gary, and you know it. This is Annie-Vic making us look like a bunch of rubes and hicks on national television."

Gary almost said that if the town didn't want to look like a bunch of rubes and hicks, it shouldn't act like a bunch of rubes and hicks, but he didn't say it. He didn't say half of what he thought these days. He shuffled the papers around in front of him a few more times and admitted to himself that he wasn't paying attention to them. He had no idea how many extra people they would need with a town full of national reporters—international ones, too. Molly who worked out at the Radisson said there was a booking for some guy from Italy. He didn't know and part of him didn't care.

"I'm going to run on home for a minute," he said. "I left my lunch on the kitchen table."

"Sarah won't bring it out to you?" Tina said. "Sarah's such a Christian woman. I can't imagine her letting you run on home with that leg of yours."

"Sarah's got Lily and Michael to look after," Gary said, and then, to forestall one more question about why the children weren't named after anybody in his own family, he got up and took his jacket off the back of his chair.

"I'll be twenty minutes," he said, heading for the door.

"I think it's a miracle the way you get around on that fake leg," Tina said. "It's like you never lost a leg at all. You've got God's grace in you. There's nothing else to say about it."

There was a lot else to say about it, and Tina would say it, if he didn't get out fast.

The police station was right on Main Street, and when Gary looked left he could see Annie-Vic rounding the intersection at the north end of town, power pumping like a woman half her age. He did have a problem with Annie-Vic, and with all the Annie-Vics of the world, and that was part of what he didn't understand about people. Annie-Vic was a smart woman. He'd talked to her dozens of times over the years. She was smart and well read, but she lived in delusion, and Gary didn't know why. To Gary Albright, the existence of God was as clear and undeniable as the existence of snow. Denying it was like denying the existence of the color green. The scripture said that it was the fool who denied God, but Annie-Vic was not a fool, and Gary didn't think she was that other thing, which his pastor always said explained the vigorous atheist. Gary couldn't imagine Annie-Vic committing one mortal sin after another, even before she had reached this advanced age.

No, Gary thought, moving slowly in the general direction of the Snow Hill Diner—he hadn't really forgotten his lunch on the dining room table; if he had, Sarah would have been down at the station like a shot—whatever motivated the people who had brought this lawsuit, whatever motived people like Annie-Vic, was beyond him. Surely they had to see, not only that God existed, but that teaching evolution as if it were not just *a fact*, but *the only fact*, meant teaching children that there was no such thing as right and wrong, no such thing as morality at all—that it didn't matter what they did, that it didn't matter who they did it to. Gary found this so clear, so obvious, so—well, Gary thought. They had to know it, and yet they brought lawsuits like this one, they railed and screamed about any mention of God to children, they wanted . . . what? Gary didn't know.

He walked past the Snow Hill Diner and kept his fingers crossed that Alice McGuffie wouldn't come out and lecture him. He got past the place safely and headed toward the Baptist Church. He thought about himself up on that mountain with Humphrey and that small infant girl he'd been taking to child services in Harrisburg, and about the blade of the knife as it had glinted in the sun on the day he knew he was going to have to sever the leg. For Gary Albright, there were things that had to be done and it was the job of grown-ups to do them. It was as if all these people—the Annie-Vics of the world, the people from the development—never grew up, and never would.

He went on past the Baptist Church, heading home, because that was where he said he was going. He never liked being caught out in a lie.

Catherine Marbledale was sixty-eight years old, and it was only four years ago, in anticipation of her sixty-fifth birthday, that the Snow Hill Board of Education had changed its retirement policy to allow her to go on teaching. Catherine had been thinking about that event for months now, ever since Franklin Hale had called her in to the board to "grill" her about evolution. "Grill" was Franklin's word. Catherine would never in her life have used it to describe the questioning style of somebody she remembered as nearly belligerently stupid, the kind of student she liked least. Catherine had no problem with real stupidity, with lack of innate intelligence. She knew how to deal with that, and she knew that even ungifted children could learn the basics of modern scientific thought. No, the people Catherine couldn't stand were the people like Franklin, who were bright enough, under there somewhere, but who willed themselves to be as stupid as possible. If intelligence was a sin, Catherine was fairly sure that Franklin Hale had never committed it.

This morning, Catherine was going through the lesson plans for her science teachers for the coming month. April was always a little tricky, because as the weather got better the attention spans got shorter. Of course, Catherine thought attention spans were already too short. It was all the media these children watched these days. Some of them had no idea how to search the library for a book, they were so used to doing their research "online." Even so, Catherine was cautiously optimistic about the media. The fact was that you couldn't ignore it. It was there all the time. And that meant that junk was there, but it also meant that truth was there. So far, she'd sent a dozen students to TalkOrigins, and every single one of them had come away shocked.

The two girls standing in Catherine's doorway were not shocked, and Catherine had been avoiding them for the past ten minutes. She really did have lesson plans to look over. The real reason, though, was that these were two girls who just made her tired. She could remember herself at that age, herself and her sister both, haunting the Snow Hill

Public Library until they could sneak away with "adult" books like *Anna Karenina* and *For Whom the Bell Tolls*. It was her sister, Margaret, who was so very attached to literature, but in those days Catherine read it nonstop, too. It was only later that she had discovered science. Margaret sometimes wondered what would have happened to them if they had been born at a different time and in a different place. Catherine did not wonder. She never really wanted to be a doctor or a scientist. She had always wanted to be a teacher. Teachers were the saviors of the world. They made sure that the students who'd decided to matter got the Hell out of places like this.

Neither Barbie McGuffie nor Susan Clawde was a student who'd decided to matter. Susan was a sniffling pile of fears and resentments who cared only that she might never make the cheerleading team when she finally got to high school, and Barbie had her mother's mulish anger at anything and everything in the universe more intelligent than herself. Catherine remembered Alice McGuffie as a student even better than she remembered Franklin Hale. Unlike Franklin, Alice actually was stupid. Unlike some other stupid students, Alice was—well, Catherine thought, Alice was then just what Barbie was now. And Alice had gotten herself elected to the school board.

Barbie was a big, thick girl with her hair pulled back on her head with a rubber band. Susan was delicate and tiny and dressed like a cross between a fashion doll and a Los Angeles streetwalker. Come to think of it, Barbie was dressed like that, too, but the clothes didn't have the same effect as they did when Susan wore them. Catherine wondered what mothers were coming to. Her own mother would never have allowed her to leave the house—at the age of fifteen!—with enough skin exposed to get a beach tan. But then, Catherine had never imagined that the upshot of Third Wave Feminism, the most wonderful thing that had ever happened in her lifetime, would be this craze on the part of children to look like whores.

Barbie was shifting from one leg to the other. She had started to emit a low-grade hum that was the signal that she was about to get angry, and nobody in her right mind wanted to see Barbie McGuffie angry. Catherine looked down at the lesson plan in front of her and sighed.

"All right," she said.

"You're the one who wanted to see us," Barbie said. "We didn't want to see you."

"I know." Catherine picked up her pen and turned it around in her fingers. Then she put it down again. There was no easy way to do this. There was never any easy way to do it. What gave her a headache was the fact that it kept happening again and again.

Catherine bit her lip. "I had a call from Mrs. Cornish this morning. I talked to Mr. Henderson about it. Apparently, it wasn't the first call."

Mr. Henderson was the vice principal. He was not a tower of strength in difficult times. Catherine suspected him, sometimes, of being on the side of Creationism and Intelligent Design, and if not, of definitely not being on her side.

"So," she said. "Do you want to tell me about it? Mrs. Cornish said that Mallory was very upset."

"Mallory Cornish is always upset," Barbie said. "She thinks she's better than everybody else, living out there in the development with all the rich kids. She's nothing but a secular humanist."

Susan made a strangled sound. Catherine closed her eyes.

"Do you know what a secular humanist is?" Catherine asked Barbie. "I mean, can you define it?"

"Sure I can define it," Barbie said. "It's somebody who worships the devil and hates America."

"I don't think they worship the devil," Susan said tentatively. "I think they just don't believe in God."

"If they don't believe in God they worship the devil," Barbie said. "What else? There's only the two. I bet they have human sacrifices in that basement of theirs. I bet that's why it's got a whole kitchen right there on its own. They have human sacrifices and then they eat them."

Catherine closed her eyes. Her head hurt. Of course, neither Barbie nor Susan had been to any of the houses out in the development. The development children tended to herd together, because most of them did not have a lot in common with the kids who lived in the "real" town. And there was, of course, the money. The people who lived in the development were not rich by absolute standards, but by the standards of Snow Hill they beat anybody but old Annie-Vic.

Catherine opened her eyes again. If this had been forty years ago, she could have required these two young idiots to make a report to the school on what secular humanism was. These days, an assignment like that would only start another lawsuit.

"You cannot," she said, "harass another student just because you don't like that student's beliefs. About anything. You can't corner Mallory Cornish in the girls' room and call her names. You can't follow her to the school bus and throw things at her. You can't do any of that. The first rule of the Snow Hill public schools is civility."

"My mother says she shouldn't even be here," Barbie said. "And my mother is right. She shouldn't be. Why doesn't she go back to where she came from? They're not even from Pennsylvania, most of the people in the development."

"They're northeastern liberal elites," Susan Clawde said earnestly. "My mama said so. And our pastor said so. They're northeastern liberal elites and all they want to do is to send everybody in the country to Hell because that's where they're going and they want company."

Susan Clawde had absolutely no idea what she was talking about. Barbie didn't either. Catherine was willing to bet money that if she asked the two of them to define any of the words they were using, they'd fall flat on their faces. All they really knew was that these words described people who were, by definition, very bad.

"My mama says you don't belong here, either," Barbie said. "My mama says you look down on everybody and God will get you one day and put you into a lake of fire. My mama says you're an atheist."

"Actually, I'm a Methodist," Catherine said. "But the real point here is that you can't call me names, either. If you don't like my ideas, then you have to argue about my ideas. And you have to be logical, and you have to use valid techniques of argumentation. This is a school, and in school you'll behave like human beings."

"I thought we weren't human beings," Barbie said. "I thought we were monkeys."

Catherine looked away, out her window, and the first thing she saw was the new junior high school building, still barely half built. It made some kind of crazy sense that Franklin Hale and his people were opposed not only to the teaching of science but to the construction of new school facilities as well. They would leave that monstrosity sitting out there for decades. In the meantime, big bullies like Barbie McGuffie would chase younger girls around and call them "secular humanists."

Catherine took a deep breath. "Detention," she said. "After school every day for the next week. At the end of that time, I expect you both to apologize to Mallory Cornish in front of her entire home room class. Is that clear?"

"I've got nothing to apologize for," Barbie said. "You're trying to take away my free speech. She's a snotty little snob and she's going to burn in Hell forever."

"If you don't apologize, you'll stay in detention, for as long as it takes. For the rest of the year, if you have to," Catherine said.

"You can't keep me in detention for the rest of the year," Barbie said. "My mama is on the school board. She can fire you any time she wants to."

"She can't fire me at all, Barbie," Catherine said. "I've got tenure. Go find out what that word means. And get out of my office. I never thought I'd live to see the day when my school would be plagued by— well, by what the two of you are. Only God knows who is going to burn in Hell forever. You shouldn't second guess Him."

"Yes, Miss Marbledale," Susan said.

Barbie McGuffie snorted. "I know who's going to burn in Hell forever," she said. "Anybody with any sense knows."

A second later, they were gone. Catherine stared for a moment at the empty doorway. Then she took a deep breath. She never realized how tense she was in these encounters until they were over, and then she felt as if she'd never get her muscles unkinked again.

She got up and went to her window and looked out. Annie-Vic was on her daily walk. Annie-Vic had been Catherine's hero when she was growing up. There she was, a woman who had done it, a woman who had gotten out of Snow Hill and engaged in the life of the mind.

It was too cold to be standing at the window. The cold came through the thin panes of glass and made her joints ache. Catherine wondered if any of the people in this town understood what was going on with the children in the schools, what was happening in the girls' rooms and boys' rooms and lunchrooms and on the playgrounds. That was the very worst of this.

She went back to her desk and sat down. She looked at the lesson plan in front of her. In the space for "Purpose of This Lesson," Marty Loudan had written "to demonstrate beyond doubt that *evolution is a fact.*"

8

Franklin Hale considered himself a sensible man, but he was really a man who believed that everyone on earth was trying to trick him. Well, maybe not *everyone*. Alice McGuffie wasn't capable of it, and most of the old biddies who ran the Outreach Mission at the Baptist Church wouldn't dare to try. No, it was people like Catherine Marbledale who were trying to trick him, and all the people like her, the ones who were about to be piling into town to turn this lawsuit into a freak show. On one level, Franklin didn't blame them. This *was* a freak show. It was a bad joke. Everybody knew that the United States had been founded as a Christian nation, and that the Founding Fathers—with the maybe exception of Jefferson, who seemed to have been some kind of hippie in training all the way back in the days of the Revolutionary War—had wanted this country to stay true to the principles God gave it. That was why American law was based on the Bible, and why Americans took their oaths of office on the Bible, and said "so help me God" when they were through. Except for old Annie-Vic, of course, and Annie-Vic was, was—

Every time Franklin thought about Annie-Vic his head hurt, and then his sinuses started to get infected. If Franklin had believed in witches and devils—but he didn't. Not every Christian went in for that kind of thing. Franklin thought Satan himself was enough evil for anybody—he'd have considered Annie-Vic to be dabbling in the dark arts. When she'd refused to swear on the Bible, and refused to say "so help me God," he hadn't even been surprised. When she'd brought out that copy of the Constitution and pointed to Article 6, and then to that one with the oath for the President, without a single mention of the Bible and without "so help me God," he damned near plotzed. He'd spend the entire next day looking at other copies of the Constitution just to check, because he'd been sure she'd done something to the copy she had.

Of course, Franklin didn't believe for a minute that those things proved what Annie-Vic said they proved—who'd *ever* heard of the Founding Fathers wanting to keep religion out of government? That was Communists and liberals, that's what that was—but he had come to the reluctant realization that even good intellectuals were more intellectual than they were good. He could just imagine what they were thinking, back then. They were thinking that everybody knew what they meant and why they were doing what they were doing. They were thinking they didn't want to keep the Quakers out of government because they wouldn't take oaths, or something like that. What they weren't thinking was what the Enemy would do when He got ahold of the kind of thing they'd actually done.

Annie-Vic was right in front of him, as a matter of fact. She was taking her walk. Franklin could see her pumping around the end of Main Street and saying something to Nick Frapp. Franklin didn't like Nick Frapp much more than he liked Annie-Vic, even though Nick was a Christian. In Franklin's view, Christians should stick together. If they didn't stick together, the secular humanists were going to force that evolution crap right down their children's throats, and then what would happen? The kids would all be out taking drugs and screwing like rabbits. They did that even when they had a good Christian upbringing. Franklin knew, because that was what his life in high school

36

had been like. He'd been captain of the varsity football squad and captain of the varsity baseball squad, and he'd spent every weekend night of his life anesthetized from the neck up and not nearly anesthetized enough from the waist down. God, but that was a long time ago. Franklin had turned fifty-four at his last birthday. He'd have gone back to all that tomorrow if he could have, and he wouldn't have given a damn if his mother complained about the vomit on his shoes.

Annie-Vic didn't actually stop to talk to Nick. She pumped away in place, her knees going up and down like pistons. Most women that age were dead. It wasn't fair that that woman was healthier than Franklin's own wife and likely to last another decade. The real problem was that they had not been entirely clear in their campaign literature when they decided to unseat the old school board. They'd had to base their arguments on incompetence, and God only knew there was incompetence to spare. That damned junior high school building, or middle school building, or whatever it was had been hanging out there on the edge of town for a couple of years, and there was still no sign of it getting done. It was crap that construction was being held up for lack of money. The town taxed the Hell out of everybody. There had to be enough money. Old Henry Wackford was always bitching and moaning about money. He liked to get his hands on it. That was the thing. Henry Wackford and all the members of the old board just liked to control all the money and do everything their own way.

If they'd been able to run the campaign straight, though, Franklin thought, they would never have gotten themselves saddled with Annie-Vic. The voters would have understood. There had been talk around town for years now. Those people from the development were like invading aliens, that's what they were. They came here bringing all their secular humanist crap and then they tried to take over the public schools, and people like Catherine Marbledale helped them. The voters would have understood the need to put a Godly board in place to bring God back into the schools and to keep out the evil rot that was ruining everything, but they hadn't been able to say anything about that. Those lawyers they'd talked to had been adamant. Once they got into court, everything they said would be used to prove that they were trying to inject religion into the public schools, and if it looked as if they were trying to do that, then there would be a lawsuit.

Well, Franklin thought, they hadn't done any of that, they hadn't said a word about God or religion throughout the whole campaign for school board, and now they were in court anyway.

Annie-Vic was laughing at something Nick Frapp had said. Now she was moving on up Main Street on her rebound round. Franklin wanted to just go out there and ring her neck. It was what she deserved. It was what all those people deserved. All of them. Everywhere.

There was a slight cough behind him, and Franklin stepped back from the window, almost instinctively. He didn't want to be where Annie-Vic could see him when she passed. Not that she'd pay any attention to him. She never paid any attention to him except to argue with him, and he hated it when she argued with him. She always got people to laugh at him. Well, she wouldn't be laughing for long. Someday soon, she'd be confined to that great lake of fire and he'd be able to sit up in heaven and look down on every scream she let out— for all eternity. Franklin liked to contemplate eternity. His eternity had nothing at all to do with sitting on clouds and playing harps.

The cough came from behind him again, and this time he turned. It was hard to do, because he was standing right up against the plate-glass window that formed the front wall of the store and was wedged in between two tall stacks of tires. Hale 'n' Hardy, tires, that was the name of the store. He'd started it with his brother–in–law when they'd both been out of high school maybe ten years, and they still had it now, after all this time. In another month or so, they were going to open a branch out on the highway in a new strip mall that was go-ing up with a Wal-Mart as an anchor. Franklin Hale wasn't afraid of Wal-Mart. Wal-Mart was for people who already knew what they were doing. Hale 'n' Hardy was for people who didn't know a lug nut from a banana split.

The cough was coming from Louise Brooker. Louise always

coughed, or "hmmed," or something like that, instead of using actual words when she wanted to get his attention. It drove Franklin crazy. He kept himself from yelling at her by reminding himself that she couldn't live a very happy life. She was plain as ditch water. She had the kind of figure you'd be more likely to see on a mule than a woman. She had nothing to look forward to in her life. The feminists had gotten to her, that was what Franklin thought, back when she was young, before she joined Franklin's church, the feminists must have gotten to her, and now what was going to happen to her? She was going to die old and alone, with nobody to talk to but her cats.

Franklin hired all his help from people he met at church. He would never hire somebody who wasn't a Christian to work in one of his stores. You could never tell with people who weren't Christians. Some of them were all right, but most of them had no morals. How could they have morals? They didn't believe in a God that gave out rules for living.

Louise was hovering. Franklin hated hovering.

"What is it?" he asked her.

Louise cleared her throat again. "It's that man. From the place in Michigan. The law place."

"The Ave Maria School of Law."

"No," Louise said, sounding desperate. "The other place. The one with *institute* in its name."

"The Discovery Institute," Franklin said. "That one's in Oregon."

"Yes, excuse me. I'm sorry. I really am very bad at remembering things. Anyway, he's called here before. He wants to talk to you."

"All right," Franklin said. He didn't move. Annie-Vic was coming closer and closer. She didn't look like she was breathing hard. How could anybody be in that kind of shape at the age of ninety-one? She probably didn't even believe in death. She probably thought she was going to live forever. That was why she was the way she was.

Louise coughed again.

"All *right*," Franklin said, without turning his head.

Annie-Vic was coming right up to the window. She was right on the other side of the plate glass. Her face was flushed, but it was flushed in a good way, a healthy way. Her hair was coming loose of that bun she always put it in. Franklin wanted to shove his hand through the glass and grab her by the neck and shake her and shake her and shake her until the bones broke into pieces and her head came loose. He could almost see the blood on the sidewalk, the deep, thick red spreading out against the white of the pavement. The pavement was very white. It was that kind of chalk white it got when it had been covered with rock salt and then the salt had melted. Annie-Vic was pumping and pumping and pumping and Franklin was thinking about blood, and then she was gone.

"Mr. Hale . . ." Louise said, close to hysterical.

Franklin Hale turned away from the window. His head hurt again. His muscles felt as if they belonged in somebody else's body. He felt the way he did when he and Marcey almost made love but didn't quite, and then she turned away from him and left him hanging.

"I'm coming," he said, to forestall another sigh.

Then he strode right past Louise and to the back, where his office was.

9

Annie-Vic didn't usually power walk all the way home after she'd taken her exercise. It had been at least a decade since she'd been able to do that without feeling that she was about to fall over at the end of it. To-day, though, she was feeling invigorated, and she was fairly sure it wasn't because of the weather. My, but growing up in a town like this developed your antennae, and coming back to it after having been away made those antennae sharp. Or maybe not sharp. Maybe antennae couldn't be sharp. She couldn't remember, and for once she didn't care. If she had been one of those people who thought everything happened for a reason, she would have decided that the reason she had never just bolted from Snow Hill and not looked back was because of this day.

Home was up off Main Street to the north, on Carpenter, and then left up the hill on Jerusalem Cemetery Road. The Cemetary along side the road had belonged to a small church—Congregationalist it was when it was still in operation—that served people who had moved here from New England. Annie-Vic wasn't old enough to remember that, and she didn't think anybody else was either, not the way this world worked. No, the Congregationalists had built their own church right on Main Street around the time of the American Revolution, and that was probably the last time the Calvinists had really had any influence in this part of Pennsylvania.

"Fanatics," Annie-Vic's father used to say, when she was in high school and deemed old enough to hear "serious" discussion. Ah, but Annie-Vic's father had never been able to let go of his need for all kinds of discussion. Annie-Vic had heard it from the cradle, and so had her brothers and sisters, the whole lot of them sitting around that dinner table every night while Papa railed on and on about religion and politics and the moral philosophy of the Greeks. They'd all gone off to "good" colleges, too, in the East, just as Papa wanted them to, and they'd all left Snow Hill forever soon after that. Annie-Vic didn't know why she had never really gone, all the way, since she'd come so close a couple of times.

At Jerusalem Cemetery Road, Annie-Vic stopped power-walking and just walked. The hill was relatively steep, and her own house was at the top of it. The church had never moved their cemetery. She could still see the thin, plain headstones row on row among the weeds and brambles. The weeds and brambles grew up every summer and every winter brought them down, as if something in nature wanted you to notice where the bodies were buried. Maybe they hadn't known how to move a cemetery back then. Annie-Vic wasn't entirely sure how they moved it now. Did they dig up the bodies? If they didn't, what got moved? What would it mean to people if they came out to visit their loved ones and visited only a stone? Did people care?

This was the way she got when she was tired: she asked questions she didn't know the answers to. She reached into her utility belt and came up with her little thing of water—there was a name for the thing, but she couldn't remember it. Her grandniece had given it to her. Her grandnieces and nephews gave a lot of things to her, and one of them had represented her when she'd threatened to sue the AAVC over not being allowed to go to Mongolia.

Up the hill. Into the house. Have some yogurt. Make some tea. Sit down in the living room and listen to the next lecture in the Music History series she'd bought from The Teaching Company. What she really needed was a series on evolution. She hadn't been able to find one of those.

The house was big and dark. It had been her father's house, and her grandfather's. It had eight bedrooms. People in town had called it a mansion when Annie-Vic was growing up, and she supposed that in the middle of the Great Depression it had looked like a mansion. It wasn't one, though. It had only had a single bathroom back then. Every morning was an agony of waiting in line.

Annie-Vic let herself into the pantry door and sat down on the bench there to take off her walking shoes. They were the kind of shoes she would have called "sneakers" when she was younger, but you couldn't call something a "sneaker" when it cost a hundred and fifty dollars at the discount store. There were four bathrooms in this house now, "retrofitted" in the early eighties at the insistence of her plain nieces and nephews, whose parents had all been dying out and who saw old Aunt Annie-Vic as some kind of parental substitute. Annie-Vic didn't understand any of that nurturing stuff. She really didn't. Psychology, like music history, was not something she'd spent a lot of time studying at Vassar.

She'd left a pair of ballet flats under the bench for when she came inside. She was damned if she was going to start wandering around the house in her slippers like an old person. She put on the ballet flats and went through into the kitchen. It had been updated in the eighties, too, but it looked old-fashioned, nevertheless. Annie-Vic wasn't much interested in her kitchen.

One of those things she remembered about being very young was Halloween, and running in among the gravestones of the Jerusalem Cemetery, as if by making enough noise they could raise the dead.

People thought they were crazy, those Hadley children, running around in there among the tombstones as if it didn't matter. But then, people had thought they were crazy anyway, all the time. If Annie-Vic had to put a finger on what it was that made her so angry about this town— and she was angry about it; the place made steam want to come out of her ears—it was the way people had been about the cemetery. It was bad enough to be ignorant. It was something truly evil to be proud of being ignorant, and that was what too many people in this town were.

"Proud of being ignorant and proud of being stupid," Annie-Vic said out loud, because at her age she could talk to herself in her own house without being branded some kind of basket case.

There was something very wrong with people who were proud of what they didn't know and proud of what they couldn't understand, and there was something even more wrong with a place that encouraged it. That was what this whole thing with evolution was all about. It wasn't about religion. Not really. Most of the religious people in town didn't care one way or the other, or they took their problems up with their Sunday school or they sent their children to Nick Frapp's Christian academy.

No, no, what this thing was really about was the temerity of some people to consider themselves smarter than Franklin Hale and Alice McGuffie, a pair of prime idiots at the best of times and now worse off than the Sweeney child at the other end of the road, and the Sweeney child had Down syndrome. It was the resentment, the anger, the endless carping and fury at the mere existence of people who were not only intelligent but willing to work at it, who wouldn't sit down and pretend that being stupid was *just as good*.

"I'm *just as good* as you are," Alice McGuffie had said, coming out of the diner this morning with her voice at full shriek.

"No, you're not," Annie-Vic had told her, and then gone on power-walking up Main Street while Alice went on shrieking, this time something about burning in Hell.

Annie-Vic was old enough to remember when respect was something that had to be earned, and something that could be lost, too.

43

She didn't believe in Hell any more than she believed in heaven, but she knew that Alice McGuffie wasn't even *just as good* as Richard Nixon, who had been a vile man but not a willfully stupid one.

Annie-Vic hated stupidity more than she hated anything else on earth.

She went on through to the dining room. The swinging door with its felt covering rocked a little on its hinges. She would have to ask the proper grandnephew to do something about it before it fell on her foot. The dining room table was covered with papers having to do with the lawsuit, legal papers and informational brochures sent out by the National Center for Science Education explaining evolution in the simplest, clearest, most concise possible way, as if it were possible to get through to people like Franklin Hale, which it wasn't.

Annie-Vic ran her hands over the mess and then proceeded to the living room. The ceilings in this house were so high they disappeared into darkness over her head. The furniture was so dark that it seemed to fade into the shadows. It had been her parents' furniture, all of it. She should have sold it and brought something new in long ago.

She was thinking about the furniture when the attack came—not about evolution, or intelligence and stupidity, or even her lunch—and at the last minute, when her assailant stepped out of the darkness of the niche next to the fireplace and the steel pipe connected with her midsection and knocked the air right out of her, all she could think of was: *That's not who it's supposed to be at all.*

PART I

Nor should the reality of "irreducible complexity" be ignored. While presenting macroevolution as truth, the schools should at least own the fact that "since" it is true, irreducibly complex organisms must have therefore evolved via punctuated equilibrium, and that this phenomenon happened many, many times. All the interconnected parts must have emerged fully developed (or developed enough to provide a beneficial function) in an instant.

—"Ken" of the blog http://walrus.townhall.com, quoted
in *Townhall Magazine* March, 2008

How natural selection can drive the evolution of tightly integrated molecular systems—those in which the function of each part depends on its interactions with the other parts—has been an unsolved issue in evolutionary biology. Advocates of intelligent design argue that such systems are "irreducibly complex" and thus incompatible with gradual evolution by natural selection.

"Our work demonstrates a fundamental error in the current challenges to Darwinism," said Thornton. "New techniques allow us to see how ancient genes and their functions evolved hundreds of millions of years ago. We found complexity evolved piecemeal through a process of Molecular Exploitation—old genes, constrained by selection for entirely different functions, have been recruited by evolution to participate in new interactions and new functions."

—press release from the University of Oregon

ONE

1

Gregor Demarkian had not been part of the staging of his first wedding—and he would never have used "staging" to describe it, because he'd have been set on by dozens of little old Armenian ladies, wanting to know why he had no respect for the Church. He was using "staging" to describe what was happening to his second wedding, though, because it was a word even Father Tibor Kasparian couldn't object to, under the circumstances. And the circumstances were getting more insane by the day. It had reached the point, this morning, that Gregor had been convinced he was hearing things. As it turned out, he wasn't, and the sound of Bennis's voice floating in from the living room was just an aspect of reality he hadn't been smart enough to anticipate.

"You give the swans something to make them constipated," she was saying. "That way, they don't crap all over the buffet."

Gregor was lying in bed, which made him feel more than a little guilty. It had to be seven o'clock. He was usually showered and dressed and on his way to the Ararat by now. Even the gloom of the day outside didn't give him any excuse for slacking off. He lived in

gloomy days. He had chosen to spend his life in Philadelphia instead
of the South, which was where most of his colleagues from the Bureau
eventually retired. He had nothing against the South, as far as he
knew. He had nothing against sunny days and temperatures that never
dipped far below forty. He was just used to Philadelphia, that was all.
He thought of it as home.

Bennis Hannaford also thought of Philadelphia as home, which
made sense, since her people had been here long before Gregor's had.
If America was a nation of immigrants, then people like Bennis relied
on a lot of history to prove their immigrant status. In the case of the
Hannafords, her father's people, that meant an arrival date of 1689.
In the case of the Days, her mother's people, it was even earlier. Gregor could never remember if there had even been a colony of Pennsylvania when Bennis's mother's people arrived, but he didn't dare ask,
because Bennis would tell him. Bennis would be the first to point out
that she had severed herself entirely from the tradition embodied in
her father's great house on the Main Line, but she could reel off the
family history like the secretary-general of the *Social Register*.

Did the *Social Register* have a secretary-general?

Gregor had no idea. In the other room, Bennis was off the phone.
He could hear her moving around, through the swinging doors that
led to the kitchen and then back again. They talked frequently about
connecting their apartments to make a duplex, but they never got
around to it, and now it wouldn't matter. He wondered what else
wouldn't matter, in the change that was coming as surely as the date
of the wedding. He wondered about the wedding, too. It was March.
He was hardly back from Margaret's Harbor. The wedding was the
first week of May. That had seemed like a long time only a couple of
weeks ago, and now it seemed right here, right now, right away.

Gregor was not having doubts about wanting to be married. He
had wanted to marry Bennis for years. He was only having doubts
about the way the world worked, and whether it could ever work in
such a way as to make things come out right.

He sat up and then swung his legs until they were out of the bed and on the floor. The bedroom was not so much a mess—he didn't mind a mess; you could always clean a mess—as a tribute to chaos. There were long lengths of ribbon in a dozen colors over everything. Bennis kept changing the color she wanted for the flowers for the ceremony. There were at least two plaster of paris models of the Forest of Zedalinnia, which was a new locale in the book that would be coming out while they were supposed to be on their honeymoon, which was not going to be so much a honeymoon as a book tour. There were chocolates. Bennis said that the chocolates were to help her figure out which ones she wanted in the favors, but Gregor thought she'd made up her mind about that weeks ago and now only needed an excuse to make order after order from Box Hill. The orders came in purple boxes and the purple boxes were the same shade as at least one of the ribbons that kept getting into everything.

I can't get married in six weeks, Gregor thought, standing up. But that wasn't actually true. He could get married right this minute. He could grab Bennis and take her off to Maryland or one of those places where you were supposed to be able to get married in no time flat, and that would be all right—that would be fine. It was the preparations that made him feel as if he were running out of air. It was that, and the questions they had never answered, the issues they had never resolved. Those were coming, and he knew it.

Gregor got up and went in to the bathroom. His robe was lying across the top of the clothes hamper, looking damp. Bennis was always using his robes when he showered. Gregor shucked off his clothes and tried to make a list in his head of all the things that were making him nervous, but there wasn't a list to be made.

He turned on the water and then made it run hot, so hot he would hear about it from old George Tekemanian downstairs. Old George Tekemanian was convinced that Gregor was using all the hot water in the hot-water heater, which Gregor just might be. Gregor closed the door to the bathroom but didn't lock it, because Bennis liked to come in and talk when he was in the shower. Father Tibor said she did that because she could spring anything on him, and there wasn't much he could do about it when he was a wet as a drowned rat and covered with soap. Gregor got in under the shower spray and pulled the shower door closed behind him. The hot water felt like a massage against his skin.

There were no real issues to be resolved between Bennis and himself. They had been together long enough, and she had been enough of a pain in the ass, so that most of those things had been worked out long ago. No, it was the two of them and their relationship to Cavanaugh Street that needed to be worked out, because up to now they had been winging it. It was odd how that went. There was no such thing as a free lunch, and what you paid for a place like Cavanaugh Street was a certain amount of respect and obedience to the morals and traditions of the place.

And that, of course, they had not done.

Gregor put shampoo in his hair. It was a new shampoo Bennis and Donna had brought him from Antwerp when they were off doing—he didn't know what. That was months ago. The shampoo smelled like peaches, which he didn't think was a very good choice, given Antwerp. Was he really making that kind of cultural connection in his head? Apparently he was.

That was the problem, though. That had been the problem all along, and he had been privileged to pretend it was no problem at all, because mostly nobody had brought it up. But six weeks from now or so, there was going to be a wedding, and there was no way that wedding could take place in Holy Trinity Armenian Apostolic Church.

Gregor put his head against the side of the shower. There. He had said it.

There was an issue, and the issue was about religion.

2

Actually, for most of Gregor Demarkian's life, religion had been not so much an issue as a fact of life. It was a fact of life for every immigrant community, and Cavanaugh Street had been an immigrant community when Gregor was growing up there. In then mostly Catholic Philadelphia, belonging to something called the "Armenian Apostolic Church" was just odd. It didn't engender hostility as much as incomprehension, and once the worst of the incomprehension was gotten through—yes, that was a Christian church, and yes, Armenian families did celebrate things like Christmas—most non-Catholics simply assumed it was a way of being Catholic. By the time Gregor had reached the eighth grade he thought he understood that. Protestant churches were plain and had a lot of singing from the congregation. The minister stood at the front and talked a sermon, wearing either ordinary clothes or the sort of robe people wore to graduate from college in. Catholic churches had priests in robes that were very elaborate and embroidered with thread that shined in the light of the candles flickering at the shrines that lined the sides of the sacristy. Instead of sermons there were rituals, with lots of raising up of things and bowing down to them, all in a foreign language. Even most Catholics in Philadelphia couldn't have told the difference between Armenian and Latin. Gregor himself knew only because he spoke enough Armenian to get by at home.

When had religion become an issue again? he wondered, picking up the bar of black clear soap Bennis liked to use because—well, he had no idea why. She just did. He didn't think it had been an issue when he first came back to Cavanaugh Street after he'd retired from the Federal Bureau of Investigation. That was just after his wife had died, and she had been buried out of Holy Trinity Church with no fuss or bother whatsoever, even though neither she nor Gregor himself had been inside a church of any kind for years, except to go to other people's weddings and funerals. That was when the priest at Holy Trinity had been an old man from Armenia who was inches from retirement. Gregor had wondered why the man hadn't wanted to go straight back to the old country on the nearest boat, since he spoke almost no English at all and made it clear he wasn't interested in learning. Maybe the only reason religion hadn't been an issue when Elizabeth died was that Gregor and Father What's-His-Name had no effective means of communication. Maybe Father What's-His-Name would have objected if he'd realized that Elizabeth hadn't so much as taken communion on Holy Thursday in a decade, and that Gregor thought he might not believe in God at all. It was hard to know what would or would not have been an issue, though, because Gregor had not been in good shape after Elizabeth died. It was possible that Father What's-His-Name had asked all kinds of questions about his and Elizabeth's spiritual life, and he had just answered with whatever had come into his head at the moment. If he hadn't already fallen away from whatever faith he'd been raised in, Elizabeth's dying would have made religion an issue with him. It had taken so long, and it had been so goddamn ugly.

He had, at the moment, no serious excuse for staying in the shower. He was washed clean, and his skin was beginning to wrinkle. The sound of the water hitting the walls of the shower stall drowned out any sound of Bennis's voice that might be coming from the living room. He wondered if she was still worrying about swans crapping on the buffet, and where the swans had come from. He couldn't remember any swans in the plans she had discussed with him up to now. That did not matter a great deal, of course. The plans she discussed with him seemed to change as soon as he left the room, or maybe she felt it was better not to tell him everything. He was a little alarmed at the idea of swans wandering around the reception . . . possibly eating the flowers.

Did swans eat flowers?

There was an old phrase from the Catholic churches that he remembered from when he was a kid: *washed in the blood of the lamb.* People who were cleansed of their sins were said to have been *washed in the blood of the lamb.* He had a distinct memory of trying to explain that reference to Leda Arkmanian—the bit about sins, the bit about sacrificial animals slaughtered on altars—and having her break down in tears at the thought of the poor little lambs with their throats cut and their blood running down, poor little things that should have been kept as pets. They'd both been eight years old at the time, and even then he'd had sense enough not to point out that somebody must have killed a lamb if she was having lamb for dinner.

If he was going to be washed clean of his sins, what sins would he be washed clean of? Sin wasn't a category he had thought of much in his adult life. It seemed to be something beyond crime and yet worse than crime, somehow, something there didn't have to be a law against to be wrong. Most of the things Gregor felt guilty of were things he had failed to do, not things he had done wrong. There had been an old woman on a street corner in D.C. when he was working in the area. She was homeless and she stood every day near the bus stop where he got off to go into the Justice Department and do paperwork that first year he'd been assigned to a desk. It was cold and getting colder, and every time he saw her he thought he should get her a pair of gloves for Christmas. He should just buy a big, heavy men's pair, thick and lined with wool, and drop them off beside her one morning as he passed. He thought about it and thought about it, but he never did it. Then, one morning, she was gone.

That incident must have happened thirty years ago, but Gregor could remember it. There were, in his past, a couple of incidents like that that were still completely clear in his mind. If he *had* believed in God, this was the kind of thing that would have made him believe. All that verbiage about "proofs," and the frantic scrambling about what did and did not constitute science and what did and did not explain the universe, was lost on him. No, it was this kind of thing—that young woman at the grocery store the first week he'd been in Philadelphia, trying to buy a turkey breast and a little package of raw carrots, obviously borderline mentally retarded, obviously hungry, with a food stamp card that wouldn't work. He'd thought of passing over a twenty and taking care of it for her, and then she was gone, and he was left to think about it. That had been at Christmas, too. If he ever decided to believe in God, it would definitely be because of things like this, things that sometimes made him wonder if somebody was trying to tell him something. What would God be like, if He existed?

Gregor got out of the shower and found a towel. Ever since Bennis had started spending more time here than she did in her own apartment, the place was full of towels. She liked good towels, too, thick and soft. He dried himself off and looked at his face in the mirror. He needed to shave. He had the kind of beard that needed to be shaved at least twice a day. He was not a postmodernist, and he was not a moral relativist. He knew there was real evil in the world. He had seen it. He just couldn't put that knowledge together with all the other things people wanted him to believe, and he knew that if he couldn't believe, Father Tibor was not going to officiate a wedding for him in Holy Trinity Church. And the odd thing was, that wasn't actually the problem. Neither Gregor nor Bennis had expected to be married in the local church, and Father Tibor had not expected them to want to be. It was everybody else on Cavanaugh Street who was causing a problem, and they didn't look like they were going to back off any time soon.

The only time people should think about religion is when they're dead, Gregor thought. Then he thought had if anybody heard him say that, even Bennis, they would think he was crazy. Still, he knew what he meant. He also knew it wasn't what it sounded like he meant. He wondered what people were like, inside their heads, when they knew they were going to die. He had been with Elizabeth at the very end, but she had not been up to communicating, and she might not even have wanted to. Surely there had to be some reason, somewhere, that explained all of this.

He got a robe and went into the bedroom. He got a clean pair of boxer shorts out of the drawer and put them on. It was never safe for him to go into his living room without boxer shorts these days. The place was always full of women planning things.

He went out into the hall and listened. There was no sound at all. Either Bennis had left the apartment, or she was off the phone for the first time in six days. He went into the living room and looked around. The swinging door to the kitchen was open, and Bennis was sitting at the kitchen table, drinking a cup of tea the size of a serving bowl, with papers stretched out everywhere in front of her.

She looked up at him, checked out the robe, and wrinkled her nose. "John Jackman called," she said. "He said he had an odd sort of favor to ask you."

3

Later, Gregor would think that everything would have been all right if he had only been *faster*—faster in picking up what Bennis was saying; faster in doing something about it; faster in getting himself out the door. Instead, he stood for a long moment in the doorway to the kitchen watching the light on Bennis's hair. Bennis had truly remarkable hair, as thick as Gregor could ever remember seeing on anybody, and black, and oddly floaty, as if it were a cloud around her head. He'd never paid all that much attention to Bennis's appearance, except when they'd first met, and in that case she'd been a suspect in something, so he had to. But once he had gotten to know her, he had come to think of what she looked like as what she looked like, just that—not particularly attractive or unattractive, not particularly common or unusual. She was Bennis, and the things that were most important about her were on the inside. That included the things he had come to love, and the things he considered sufficient grounds for a plea of justifiable homicide.

This morning, all the things on the inside were being washed away by the way the sunlight backlit her hair from the kitchen window, and the way her green eyes shined. Ridiculously high intelligence, killer education, rich-girl Main Line upbringing, mass of neuroses from all of the above—all of these things were less striking to Gregor Demarkian than those green eyes. It was the sort of thing he wouldn't have said out loud to anybody, even Tibor. He knew better.

Bennis was sitting with her legs folded under her on a kitchen chair. Her head was tilted. She had a very odd look on her face. "Are you all right?" she said. "Didn't you get enough sleep? I deliberately didn't wake you."

"I'm fine," Gregor said.

"Well, I don't know if you heard me, but John called. He sounded very worked up about something. He said he'd left word with what's-her-name that you're to be shown right in any time you show up. It's about the monkey trial."

"What?"

Bennis sighed. "The monkey trial," she said, moving papers around on the table. All the papers had to do with planning the wedding. Gregor knew that. There was a part of him that was deeply and truly frightened of the plans for the wedding. "Even I know about the monkey trial, Gregor. Place a little north of here called Snow Hill got themselves one of those stealth school boards—"

"What?"

"Stealth school boards," Bennis said patiently. "You know, they run on one issue but what they're really interested in is getting creationism into the science curriculum. This place got one of those, and they put a policy in place last summer that—I'm not sure what it did, exactly. Put 'intelligent design' in the curriculum, or something like that. I haven't been following it all that much, except in the last couple of weeks, because of Annie-Vic. I told you about Annie-Vic, Gregor. I told you about her right in this kitchen. Are you sure you're all right?"

There was coffee on the stove. This would be Bennis's coffee, not Tibor's, so it would be drinkable. Bennis always made coffee for him, even if she was drinking tea. Gregor headed for the stove and got a coffee mug out of the cabinet on his way.

"Maybe I'm not awake," he said. "Who's Annie-Vic?"

"Ann-Victoria Hadley, Vassar class of 'thirty-seven. I did tell you about her, Gregor. She's a kind of force of nature. She's over ninety, but she still delivers meals on wheels. Probably to people who are younger than she is. She sued the AAVC about a year and a half ago—"

"The AAVC?"

"The college alumnae association," Bennis said. Now she sounded more than patient. She sounded as if she were talking to a child. "They run trips, you know, for alumnae. They were running one to Mongolia to see a total eclipse of the sun, and they refused to let her sign on to it, because they said she wasn't in good enough physical shape. Anyway, she said her physical shape was fine and they were just indulging in age discrimination, and she sued them. She won, too. Wrote a big picture article about it for the *Vassar Quarterly*. There was one picture with her arms around a couple of yaks."

The coffee was good, and it was having the kind of effect it was supposed to have. Gregor did remember something of a conversation about an old lady with yaks. Bennis's face was still as close to perfect as he had ever seen a woman's face be, and she still didn't have crow's feet. That had to be genetic. She was forty-something.

"Gregor?"

"I'm waking up," Gregor said. "I do remember this a little. Something happened to her. She got mugged, or something. She ended up in a coma. Did she die? What does that have to do with a monkey trial in Snog's Bush—"

"Snow Hill," Bennis said. "And no, she didn't die, not as far as I know. But that's the thing, you see. She was the odd man out on the school board, the one who wasn't a Creationist."

"On that school board?" Gregor asked. Now he did remember. The odd thing that had been going on in his mind about Bennis began to recede. He'd start panicking about getting married later. He topped up his coffee and leaned against the edge of the sink. "I thought that was odd at the time," he said. "I remember that."

"You did think it was odd," Bennis said. "Anyway, I don't really know if Annie-Vic has anything to do with it, but John said he needed a favor and it was about the monkey trial, and this is the only monkey trial I know of, so I figure it all has to fit in. You know, it wouldn't be such a bad idea if you skipped the Ararat today and went down to talk to the newly minted Mayor of Philadelphia. It would save you, me, and Tibor a lot of trouble, and maybe there'll even be a case you can work on to keep you out of my hair."

"I thought you needed me in your hair," Gregor said.

"I did when I was making decisions, but the decisions are made," Bennis said, "and now you're mostly either getting in the way or reminding me that we're a bomb ready to explode. And it is going to explode, Gregor, and you know it. I've been ducking Leda and Hannah for a week. I even offered to send Tibor on a vacation to Jamaica for the duration."

"Is that where we're going, Jamaica?" Gregor said. "I don't understand how you can wait until the last minute to finalize plans for a honeymoon."

"It doesn't matter where we go, Gregor, you'll show up on the beach in a suit, a tie, and wing tips. I really did mean it. It would make a lot of sense for you to get out of here. The closer we get to the actual wedding, the more of this kind of trouble there's going to be."

"I don't understand why there's any trouble at all," Gregor said. "You're okay with it. I'm okay with it. Tibor hasn't said he won't come, he's just said we can't have the ceremony in the church, which makes perfect sense since you don't belong to the church and I don't believe in God. If it's all right for all of us, why isn't it all right with the Cavanaugh Street Ladies Improvement and Meddling Society, or whatever they think they are?"

"If I knew that, I could solve all the problems in the Middle East," Bennis said. "Never mind. Finish your coffee and go down and see John. Snow Hill isn't that far from here. Maybe he has something he wants you to investigate, and you'll have a case, and you'll only be home really late at night and you'll avoid them altogether."

"I wonder if it's even plausible," Gregor said. "Do you think that a bunch of Creationists would mug an old lady because she didn't like Creationism? It doesn't sound sensible, does it?"

"I can't imagine why anybody would want to mug Annie-Vic at all," Bennis said. "Oh, maybe I'm just talking nonsense. Maybe she was walking around with a purse stuffed with money, although that doesn't sound like any of the things I've heard about her. Go and see John. Tibor and I will try to hold the fort."

"We should have just run off to Jamaica in the first place and gotten married on the plane," Gregor said. "Ship's captains can perform weddings. Why can't airplane pilots? An airplane is a ship, isn't it? An airship."

"Go," Bennis said.

Gregor started to go, but he wasn't fast enough. If he'd been paying any attention, he would have known they were about to be invaded. He would have heard the sound of the women on the stairs. They were doing nothing to keep their approach under the radar. And he should have known that his door wouldn't stop them, either. He was not like most of the people on Cavanaugh Street. He had no illusions that this was a special place, hermetically sealed off from the problems of the rest of Philadelphia. He did not leave his door unlocked. It didn't matter. By now, everybody had keys to everything anyway. They might as well all have been living in one big Armenian-American commune, complete with flowers in their hair and substandard plumbing.

There was a knock on the door, and both Gregor and Bennis looked up. There was a rattling of the knob. Hannah Krekorian's voice floated down the foyer toward them.

"For God's sake, Leda, how can you get to your age without knowing how to unlock a door?"

Then they heard the front door pop open, and a moment and a half later the women were there, short but magnificent, both of them carrying armloads of tote bags containing God-only-knew-what.

It was at that moment that Gregor remembered what he'd heard earlier, about the swans and the buffet.

Then Leda planted herself in the middle of the kitchen and said, "We've talked to Tibor, and we aren't going to let him get away with it."

TWO

1

Gregor had taken a cab, and it began to rain as he got out. The day was no longer just cold, it was dismal. The rain felt as if it had hard edges, which didn't bode well. It wasn't unheard of for there to be a snowstorm this late in March, although Philadelphia was less bothered by snow than the rest of the state. Gregor understood the impulse of so many older people to move south, where they never had to worry about snow at all. The last time he had been stuck in the snow it had been in Massachusetts, and there had been nothing like a winter wonderland about it.

He went into the building and the lobby was empty and clear. The floor was so highly polished he could see his face in it. John Jackman liked a clean office, but good old what's-her-name was a cleanliness Nazi. Maybe she came down and followed the janitorial staff around at night. Gregor stopped at the desk and gave his name. Then he admitted to himself that he was not going to remember what's-her-name's name before he was face to face with her.

This was not going to go well.

The guard waved him to the elevators and got on the phone,

probably calling old what's-her-name to tell him Gregor was coming. The elevator doors closed and Gregor felt himself moving upward. He kept pounding at his memory. It wasn't a hard name. It was a simple one. That was the trouble. If it had been a hard name, it would have been easy to remember.

The doors opened at the floor that held John Jackman's office, and Gregor was faced not with old what's-her-name, but with a small, dirty-blond woman in a twin set. She looked very nervous.

"Mr. Demarkian?"

"Ah," Gregor said. "I'm sorry. We haven't met. I was expecting—"

"Ms. Hall," the little woman said.

Hall. Gregor tried to force it into his mind in a way that would make it impossible for him to forget again, but he knew it wasn't going to work. Not only was "Hall" not a difficult name, but there was something about just how angry Ms. Hall could get that made him forget everything about her except the fire in her eyes.

"Ms. Hall is in conference," the little woman said. "I'm Linda Brandowski. I hope you don't mind. The Mayor said you wouldn't mind, but the Mayor is an optimist, isn't he? I do like an optimist. I've always been an optimist myself, but it gets harder and harder the older I get. I don't know what's happening to the world. I really don't."

They were moving down hallways. Every once in a while, they would come to a slightly more open space with desks in it. Gregor didn't know if they were supposed to be reception areas or something else. It suddenly occurred to him that the last time he had seen these offices had been the day after John had been inaugurated, and they'd only been partially up and running then. At least, they hadn't been this full of people.

Ms. Brandowski stopped at a door that said OFFICE OF THE MAYOR and knocked on it. Something muffled came from inside, and she opened it. What she opened on was not John's office per se, but the front room of what appeared to be a large suite. There were half a dozen desks in the front room, all but one staffed by young women at computers. The odd one out was staffed by a young man at a computer, and Gregor thought that he recognized the young man.

"Right through here," Ms. Brandowski said, but as soon as she said it the door at the very back of the suite opened, and John Jackman stuck his head out. It was then that Gregor noticed the glass-paneled door to the side, with the words CYNTHIA HALL stenciled into the mid-level crossbar. Hell, even John didn't get his own name on his door. His door just said OFFICE OF THE MAYOR.

John pushed the door back farther and gestured strenuously for Gregor to come in. "Come on, come on," he said. "I want you to meet this guy. What's the matter with you?"

"I was expecting, uh," Gregor's mind went blank, "you know."

"Cynthia," John said sympathetically. "She's in conference."

"How can she be in conference?"

"Obviously, you don't know Cynthia," John said.

Gregor knew her as well as he wanted to know her. The woman scared the pants off him. He looked over again at the young man at the computer. "Why does he look familiar?" he asked.

"Because," John said, now nearly pushing Gregor into the office, "he's one of Tyrell Moss's boys. Father Tibor introduced me to Tyrell Moss. Tyrell Moss introduced me to this kid, and the next thing we know, we're rehabilitating him."

"He's got a sheet?"

"He's got several. About the size of *War and Peace*. Including one armed robbery and six years in juvie for a gang fight. Don't worry about it. We look good giving troubled kids a second chance, and Cynthia makes sure he doesn't get out of line. She made him get his tattoos removed. And there were a lot of them."

"I always thought it must hurt to get tattoos," Gregor said.

"It hurts worse to get them off," John Jackman said. "Come inside. Sit down. Let us talk to you. Get rid of that awful coat. You're not going to get married in that coat, are you?"

Gregor considered telling John that if he really wanted to run for President one day, it might be a good idea to go a little lighter on the

Armani everything, but it was the kind of comment there was really no point in making.

He allowed himself to be shoved into the middle of John's very large office. The door shut behind him. He looked around and saw that a young man—not so young as the one in the outer office, and white instead of black—had gotten to his feet and was waiting politely. The young man had been sitting on a big wing chair at one side of what was probably called a "conversational grouping." John Jackman had a desk, but it was over on the other side of the large room, near the windows that looked out on the city. The "conversational grouping" was in the middle of the room. It consisted of two wing chairs and two small couches around a glass-topped coffee table. The coffee table had a tray on it, with a cups and saucers and spoons and everything else needed to actually have coffee.

The young man was so still, Gregor didn't notice it until the last minute: a prosthetic leg. The young man did not seem to pay attention to it.

"Ah," John said. "Let's get the introductions done. Gregor Demarkian, this is Gary Albright. He's the chief of police of Snow Hill, Pennsylvania, which is a little town—"

"About an hour's drive north," Gregor said. "I know." He had his attention on the young man. "Army?" he asked, pointing to the leg.

"Marines," Gary Albright said. "But that's not what happened to the leg. The only time I got wounded in the Marines, some idiot got drunk and threw his boots at me. Gave me a black eye that lasted for a week."

"Yes," John Jackman said. "Well. Sit down, won't you? Both of you? Gary here has a problem, and he thought you might be able to help. It's a case of attempted murder."

"It may be murder any time at all," Gary said. "She's an old woman, the woman who was attacked. I can't believe she's lasted this long, under the circumstances. She was pretty badly beaten up."

"If you need help with a homicide investigation, wouldn't you normally just go to the state police?" Gregor asked. "Haven't you had a homicide investigation before in Snow Hill?

"We've had several," Gary Albright said. "There's drugs up where we are just the same as anywhere else. And domestics. We get a lot of those. But these circumstances are different, and I don't like the statie I've got to deal with on this kind of thing."

"What makes the circumstances so different?" Gregor asked.

Gary Albright was sitting down by then. The prosthetic nature of his leg was more obvious when he was sitting, because it settled at an awkward angle. Gary Albright smiled.

"Well," he said, "there the little problem of me. I'm one of the chief suspects."

2

There was something about this man that went farther than the obvious military experience. There was something calm and centered and straightforward about him that was also, in an odd way, innocent. Gregor's mind rebelled at the word. Most people used "innocent" when they meant naive, and he was willing to bet almost anything that Gary Albright was not naive. No, what he had was not a lack of experience or sophistication. What he had was . . .

There was no word for it. Gary Albright was sitting across the glass-topped coffee table, waiting, quiet, still. That waiting stillness was part of the thing that Gregor couldn't put a name to. The man was not fidgety. He was not nervous. He was just waiting.

"So," Gregor said, trying hard not to sound like he was clearing his throat. "That's a little unusual, I'll admit. How do you even know you're a suspect, if you're the one who's investigating the case? Or do I have that wrong?"

"No, you have that right," Gary Albright said. "But I know, and everybody in town does, too, and that's a problem there's no easy way around. I could call in the state police, but I don't want to. I don't like the way they behave, and they don't like me."

"Gary . . ." John Jackman said carefully.

". . . is a Christian," Gary finished for him. "And I mean it. I'd like

64

to have somebody I can trust come in and look at this. Especially because I'm not the only Christian on the suspect list. In fact, everybody on the suspect list is somebody who at least calls himself a Christian. As to whether or not they are really are Christians, I've got a pastor who says that's up to God and not me to judge."

"Ah," Gregor said. "Well, that's unusual too, isn't it? That everybody on the list would call himself a Christian. It would be unusual here in Philadelphia, unless you were including Catholics under the term 'Christian,' which I take it you're not."

"No," Gary said. "And it would be unusual even for Snow Hill these days. We've got a chapter of the American Humanist Association now. Well, we always did have it. Henry Wackford started it years ago, before I was even born, but it's got a lot of members now. Something like thirteen. There are new people. People who've moved in to work at the high tech firms. That's the governor's big idea on how to improve the economy of Pennsylvania."

"All right," Gregor said. "But the chief suspects are all Christians, by which I'll assume you mean evangelical Protestants of some kind. Why?"

Gary Albright made a quick look of distaste. It would be the only time Gregor would see him break his impassivity during this conversation. "There was a deception," he said. "A big one."

"What kind of deception?" Gregor asked.

"End of last summer, we had elections for school board," Gary said. "School board is a big deal in a place as small as Snow Hill. It's where we play out all the drama the town has. School board and town council. There was a school board election. The board that was sitting at the time of the election had been in place for something like a decade, maybe more. Henry Wackford had been chairman for more than that. Some of the other individuals might have gone in and out. Anyway, some people were unhappy with the way the board was conducting business. I was."

"You were unhappy, why?" Gregor asked. "You didn't like the curriculum? You didn't like the teachers they were hiring?"

"I didn't like the confusion," Gary Albright said, "and I wasn't the only person in town to feel that way. Things were sloppy. They didn't get done on time. We're building a new school building, for instance. A junior high school building. The project's been going on for years and it's stalled. Then there was the library at the high school. It was in such poor shape we got put on probation by the accreditation committee. So, when Franklin Hale asked me if I'd run for the board, I said I would."

"And who is Franklin Hale?" Gregor asked.

"A son of a bitch," Gary said, but he was still impassive. It was as if he were imparting a matter of fact. "He owns a tire store, tires, auto parts, whatever. In town. His prices suck lemons, if you ask me, but lots of people from the development don't know enough about cars to get them started in the morning without a manual, so they go to Franklin and he babies them through whatever they need and then he charges them through the nose. He was running for board chairman. He got a few other people to run, including me."

"And I take it you won," Gregor said, "and displaced the old school board?"

"Yeah, we did," Gary said, "except that one of the displacers wasn't one of Franklin's hand-picked slate of candidates. All the old members of the board were forced off, but one of the seats on the board went to a woman named Ann-Victoria Hadley, who was, well, what can I say? Not Franklin Hale's favorite person."

"Not yours, either, I take it," Gregor said.

"No," Gary Albright said. "I have to admit there's something admirable about that woman. I hope I'm in half as good shape at ninety-one. But no, I don't like her much. Her family's been the town's wealthiest since forever. She went off to Vassar College. She thinks she's smarter than everybody else and she's even more than half right. But she's arrogant and she's not a Christian."

"Does she belong to, what did you call it, the American Humanist Association?" Gregor asked.

"I don't know," Gary said. "But I'd be surprised if she agreed to belong to anything Henry Wackford was running. Anyway, Franklin had asked this guy named Holman Carr to run, and Holman didn't make it. Holman goes to our church. The Baptist Church. So does Alice McGuffie. Everybody Franklin asked goes to our church. I should have realized something was up. Especially since Holman—let's just say Holman isn't the kind of guy you'd expect to be on a school board."

"Wouldn't expect, how?" Gregor asked.

"Wouldn't expect because he's barely got a high school education," Gary said, "and he isn't exactly a self-taught genius. Come to think of it now, that's true about Alice, too. But it didn't occur to me. I thought it was a good idea, getting the old board out. I still think it was a good idea. It was just that Franklin had an agenda he didn't apprise me of."

"And that agenda was?" Gregor asked. He noticed that John Jackman had suddenly started to stare at the ceiling. Gary Albright was looking down at his hands.

"He wanted to change the science curriculum to teach Creation Science as well as evolution in biology classes. Starting with what I'd guess you'd call middle-school science."

"Ah," Gregor said.

"You've got to understand," Gary said, "I think the idea of teaching Creation is just fine. More than fine. I don't think Darwin's theory has a leg to stand on, logically or scientifically. And the real problem is the way it's used, used to convince people that there's no such thing as morality. So, you know, if Franklin had broached the idea to me, I wouldn't have been against it. Necessarily."

"Necessarily?" Gregor asked.

"Yes, well," Gary said. "I'm studying nights, you know. I'm thinking I'd like to be a lawyer, so I'm doing courses to get me into law school. It's not very interesting, being on the police force when I can't get around in the field. I had a course in Constitutional law last fall that covered a lot of the cases having to do with evolution and Creation in public schools. I knew as soon as I heard Franklin's proposal that we were going to get sued, and we were going to lose."

"So you opposed it?" Gregor asked.

"I opposed the original proposition," Gary said, "but later Franklin scaled it down some, and we decided that what we'd ask for was a disclaimer in all the biology books, saying that Darwin's theory was just a theory, and not a fact, and that any student who wanted to investigate a different view could go to the school libraries and take out this book, *Of Pandas and People,* that told about Intelligent Design. There hasn't been a case yet about intelligent design."

"I'd never even heard of it," John Jackman said.

"It relies on the fact that some biological structures are irreducibly complex," Gary said. "That means that they work the way they are, but if any part of them is missing they don't work at all. So they couldn't have evolved in little steps, you know, because none of the steps would have made any difference in their ability to reproduce. That's what Darwin's theory says. That traits get passed down because they make the animal more likely to reproduce."

"I think it's a little more complicated than that," Gregor said.

"There hasn't been a case about Intelligent Design, as far as I know," Gary repeated. "I tried looking it up. And I went along with that proposal, because I thought it was the right thing to do. I thought we had a good chance of getting a general agreement, because the whole thing was completely noncoercive. Nobody had to learn about intelligent design unless they wanted to, or their parents wanted them to. The idea was to get the whole board to vote for the policy unanimously. But that didn't work out, because of Annie-Vic."

"She voted against the policy," Gregor said. "All right, from what I've heard about her, that makes sense."

"She didn't just vote against it," Gary said, "she joined the lawsuit against it, which started up less than a month later. Henry Wackford brought it, with a bunch of people—"

"Wait," Gregor said. "Henry Wackford. That's the man who was the old chairman of the school board? The one who was displaced by Franklin Hale."

"That's right," Gary said. "And I do think that there's more than a little revenge going on here. He's a lawyer, anyway. He filed suit with a bunch of different co-plaintiffs, Annie-Vic, some of the parents from the development. That's where most of the new people live. In the development. And Franklin, you know, was furious. But mostly he was furious about Annie-Vic, because she was breaking ranks."

"Did Franklin Hale expect her not to break ranks?" Gregor asked.

"It's hard to know what Franklin expects," Gary said. "There's part of me that sometimes wonders if he doesn't have a drinking problem that he's hiding pretty well. Maybe he did expect her to go along, at least with the second policy, the one we actually voted in, because when she didn't he had a fit. And he kept hounding her. He wanted her to resign from the board."

"And she didn't?"

"No, she didn't," Gary said, "and if you'd known her, you'd have known she wouldn't. She's not the kind of person who backs down under pressure. But that left us going into the lawsuit with a member of our own board on the other side, and the closer we got to the court date the more frantic Franklin got, and the more furious Alice McGuffie got, and there was a lot of bad feeling in town."

"When is the lawsuit due to start?" Gregor asked.

"Next week."

"It won't be delayed because one of the plaintiffs is, I think I heard somebody say, in a coma?"

"No," Gary Albright said. "There are other plaintiffs and she isn't the chief one. But here's the thing. On the day the assault happened, any one of us, any of the members of the board that support the policy, could have hit her. We were all right there on Main Street. We all saw her taking her walk that day, same as always. We all went somewhere or the other in the time just after she left Main Street and went back home. And it's not just us. It's the pastors of the two churches that supported the policy. They were there, too. And it's the congregations. A lot of people resented the Hell out of that lawsuit. They still do."

"And you're sure that was why she was assaulted?" Gregor asked. "There couldn't have been a more mundane reason, like robbery, for instance?"

"She was wearing one of those fanny packs," Gary Albright said, "and it had four hundred dollars in it in tens and twenties. And everybody knew she carried cash when she walked. When she went anywhere, really. But the fanny pack wasn't touched, and her house wasn't broken into. She's got grandnieces and nephews, and living brothers and sisters, I think, but none of them live in town and none of them were anywhere near it at the time of the attack. I checked. So it wasn't robbery, and it wasn't her heirs trying to get rich quick. And if you saw what the town was like over this lawsuit, you'd see why I think—why everybody thinks, really—that that's what's going on here."

3

Gary Albright had somewhere else to go in the city of Philadelphia.

"It's an errand I've got to do for my pastor," he said.

Gregor stayed behind on John Jackman's new wing chair and waited until the coast was clear. John came back from showing Gary Albright all the way to the outer door and sat down in the other wing chair instead of behind the desk. He looked exhausted.

"That man makes me more nervous than my mother used to when I knew I was about to get in trouble," he said. "In about the same way, too."

"Gary Albright makes you feel guilty?

"Something like that," John said. "I don't know. You know anything about him? Anything about his story?"

"No," Gregor said. "I knew he was military as soon as I saw him, of course, and fairly recent military. It's hard to mistake the bearing."

"The story about the leg made all the news shows," John said. "I thought you might have heard about it. It was a couple, three years ago. I don't remember. He was a regular cop in Snow Hill then. He got called out on a domestic in the middle of the night in the middle of a snowstorm at one of those places, you know, up a dirt road, in the mountains, that kind of thing. Found the couple drunk to the gills and too falling-over-incapacitated to do much of anything, and a baby, couldn't have been more than seven or eight months old, left wandering around on its own. So, he took the baby and got out of there. He figured it made more sense to make sure the baby was safe than try to bring the couple in given the weather and conditions and that kind of thing."

"All right," Gregor said. "I can see that."

"Yeah," John said. "So can I. It isn't the kind of trouble we ever had on any police force I was ever on, but I worked in cities. But, here's the thing. He had a dog with him. Did I tell you he had a dog?"

"No."

"He did. Not a police dog, his own dog. Dog he'd had for years. He had the dog in the backseat for company. Most nights he didn't get called on for anything and he was out wandering around on his own. Where was I? Oh, okay. He took the baby with him, worked up an impromptu car seat for the kid in the back, I guess the parents didn't have one. The couple. Whoever they were. He took off and headed back to town thinking he'd turn the baby in at the hospital. They've got social workers. But the weather was really, really, bad, and the road wasn't a real road, it was a dirt rut, and he got lost. He ended up down a ditch and into a snow bank. They were out there for a week."

"A week?" Gregor sat up.

"Car went down a hill, sort of, and they landed at the bottom of it, no communications working, and he'd cracked his leg, that leg, so he couldn't just stand up and march them all out. And it kept snowing. It stopped and then there was another system that came through. They should all have been dead."

"And they weren't? He got the baby out alive?"

"He got the baby *and the dog* out alive," John said, "because when push came to shove, when they had to have something to eat or starve, he used what he'd learned in the Marines and took his leg off. And fed it to the them. The dog and the baby."

"Dear God," Gregor said.

"I know," John said. "You don't know how to respond to it, do you? I don't. Part of me is sickened beyond anything. Part of me thinks

71

there was something almost impossibly heroic about the whole thing. If he needed something for himself and the baby to eat, he could have killed the dog. I'd have killed the dog."

"Dear God," Gregor said again. "That's an interesting person."

"Oh, I agree," John said. "His CO was in my platoon in Vietnam. That's how he happened to end up coming to me. I talked to Derek about him and Derek had the same kind of thing to say. You don't know how to take the kid. He's got an almost superhuman sense of responsibility. He's completely reliable. He's very straight in the military sense of the word straight. Not straight as in not gay, but you know—"

"Dudley Do-Right," Gregor said.

"Yeah, that," John said, "but not exactly. Dudley Do-Right is a mental defective. I don't think Gary Albright is a mental defective."

"No, I don't either," Gregor said. He considered the story again, as far as he was able. It was hard to imagine anybody behaving like that. It was especially hard to imagine anybody behaving like that in order to save a dog. "Do you think Gary Albright was incapable of battering this old woman?" he asked.

John shrugged. "I don't know. It's hard to say what somebody will do when they lose control, and that's what it would have had to be if Gary Albright is guilty of this thing. He'd have had to lose control. But there's a part of me that thinks that if he had done that, he wouldn't have concealed his involvement. He'd have come right forward and confessed."

"Of course," Gregor said, "that's the perfect cover, if you think about it. It's so totally unlike you, nobody would suspect, but just to make sure, bring in a hired gun so you can't be confused of a conflict of interest. What's his problem with the state police?"

John Jackman shrugged. "Religion, as far as I can make out. Gary Albright is very religious, the guy he deals with in the staties doesn't like it. Or Gary Albright doesn't like that the statie isn't. Or something like that."

"Does he know that I'm not very religious?"

"I told him you were an out-and-out atheist," John said. "I was trying to spare you the bother, if I could. Aren't you getting married in a few weeks?"

"It depends on whether Bennis and Donna can ever finish making arrangements. Bennis thinks it would be a good idea if I went up and helped out. It would get me out of her hair, and everybody else out of mine."

"So you're going to go up and do it?"

"I think so," Gregor said. He stared at the door Gary Albright had left through. "It's not my usual kind of thing, of course, but it may be any minute or two. I don't suppose you have any way of finding out what kind of condition this Ann-Victoria Hadley is in."

"I've got phone numbers," John said. "Tell me the truth. It isn't Ann-Victoria Hadley. It's Gary Albright. You can't get your mind off Gary Albright."

Gregor's coat was on the rack next to John's office door. He got up out of the wing chair and went over to get it.

"Is he married?"

"Gary Albright? I don't think so," John said.

"What happened to the baby?"

"I don't know," John said.

"It would be interesting to know, wouldn't it, what went on in that man's head. It would be interesting to know what this case is really about, too."

"Somebody bashed in an old lady's skull."

"Because she opposed putting something calling 'Intelligent Design' in public school science classes?" Gregor said. "Seriously, John, have you ever heard of anything like that happening? We've had monkey trials without measure in this country, and nobody's been killed over one yet. The usual motives are love and money. And Ann-Victoria Hadley has money."

"You just heard Gary Albright said he checked out the relatives and none of them were near the scene. Or even in the same state, I think."

"They could always have hired somebody," Gregor pointed out.

Then he put on his coat and headed out the door.

THREE

1

There were rumors all over town that Gary Albright had gone to Philadelphia to bring in a hired gun to investigate what had happened to Annie-Vic Hadley, and Alice McGuffie just knew that if that was true, Gary had done it because of the television cameras. The television cameras were everywhere these days. There were big mobile production vans all up and down Main Street, right from Nick Frapp's white trash church down to the courthouse itself, and there were people who were saying that the judge had received death threats. Alice McGuffie wasn't surprised about that any more than she was surprised about any of the rest of it, but part of her truly wished that she wasn't making so much money off television people who came to eat in her diner.

"They're atheists, every last one of them," she said to Lyman on Thursday morning. The big, open front room was stacked with people she had never seen before, and the men among them ate like horses. It had to be tiring work, carrying that equipment around all day. The men came in and ate the kind of breakfasts Alice had last seen commonly on farmhouse tables: stacks of pancakes with butter sandwiched between the layers; double orders of sausages and hash browns; coffee by the bucket. If Alice drank that much coffee, she'd be on the ceiling for days.

"Just leave them alone," Lyman said, looking out onto the floor, too. He was exhausted. Alice knew it. If she didn't also know that this surge in business wouldn't last a day beyond the end of the trial, she'd suggest taking on somebody to help Lyman with the cooking.

"It's a shame you can't even hope they'll do the right thing," Alice said. "If they weren't all secular humanists, maybe they'd see something. See how good this town is. Want to come to God. But you know what secular humanists are like."

Lyman made a little snort of assent, and then the phone on the kitchen wall rang. The phone on the kitchen wall almost never rang. It was a different line than the one in the office. People only called it when they wanted Alice to put aside something for them to pick up. They'd had a lot of that kind of business since the television people came. It was as if those cameramen had black holes in the middle of their stomachs. They'd eat like crazy in here, and an hour later they'd be calling up for something to take out. Alice had heard a couple of them complaining about her pizza, but she knew what she thought they could do about that.

The phone was still ringing. Lyman was paying no attention to it. Alice looked him over and sighed. Men were men. There wasn't anything you could do about them. They didn't notice things the way women did. At least Lyman was a good Godly man, and he had this business. Alice was sure that that was better than anything those television women could say about *their* husbands, assuming they even had them.

Alice picked up the phone. One of the television women sat alone at one of the tables in the dining room, but she wasn't eating anything. She was only drinking coffee, black and without sugar. If the men from the television crews ate without ceasing, the women never seemed to eat at all, and they were all so thin they looked ready to snap in half. What Alice really didn't like, though, was the suits. She never thought a woman looked good in a suit, and women looked just stupid in pants suits. Take Hillary Clinton. The woman looked like— well, Alice didn't know what she looked like, but the first question that came to Alice's mind was, who did she think she was? Really. Who did Hillary Clinton think she was? Who did any of those women think they were? What were they trying to prove? They were just women, like any other women.

Alice thought she might have been holding the phone for longer than she should have been. She put it to her ear and said, "Hello?" It wouldn't matter if they missed one take out order, and they probably wouldn't miss it anyway. Whoever it was would probably think there was something wrong with the phone and call right back.

"Hello," somebody said on the other end of the line said. It took Alice a minute to realize she was talking to Catherine Marbledale. *Ms.* Marbledale. Talk about somebody who ought to get the starch taken out of her panties.

"Snow Hill Diner," Alice said. This did not bode well. *Ms.* Marbledale never called up to get something to take out. She never ate at the diner. She bought fruits and vegetables from the fresh produce stands and then did things to them that she found in foreign cookbooks.

"Hello, Alice," *Ms.* Marbledale said. "I recognized your voice. I expect you recognize mine."

Alice made a face. She *expects* I do, does she? God, it was just like that woman.

"It's the middle of the breakfast rush," Alice said. "I've got work to do."

"I'm sure you do have work to do," *Ms.* Marbledale said. "But so do I, and we have a situation on our hands this morning. I have Barbie in my office, and both of the Cornish children."

"Those kids should learn to leave Barbie alone," Alice said. "If you weren't such a secular humanist yourself, you'd see what was going on here. Those kids are *persecuting* my Barbie, and all the other Christian children in school. That's what they're doing. People like you are trying to drive all the Christians right out of school."

There was a long pause on the other end of the line. Then *Ms.* Marbledale said, "You know, Alice, I'm not interested in having this conversation, not now and not in the future. I think I heard you through at least once by now. I'm going to let it go. If you want to find out what's going on, I suggest then you come down here and listen to me. In the meantime, Barbie will spend the day in detention. I suggest you talk this over with Lyman, Alice, because we're getting very close to the point where the Cornishes are going to have grounds to sue."

"Sue me?" Alice said. "I'll sue them, bringing their atheism into the school. Trying to turn my children away from God."

"That's enough, Alice."

The phone was hung up on the other end of the line, and Alice found herself staring at the receiver still in her hand. She put it back into its cradle. It wasn't hard to remember what it had been like to be in school when she was Barbie's age or even older. Alice thought she had never hated anything as much as she'd hated school, and that had not been her fault. There were people who had called her stupid, but she wasn't stupid. She just didn't like being in there among the snots and the snobs, the little crapola people who thought they were just so wonderful because they read stupid books that no sensible person would ever want to read. Alice wasn't even sure she believed they read them. They just liked to make fun of people, those people did. At least, in her day, they didn't make fun of people for believing in God.

"It was better when we were going to school," Alice said out loud.

Lyman turned to look at her. While she had been on the phone with *Ms.* Marbledale, Lyman had gone back to the grill. He was now standing in front of a huge pile of breakfast sausages and a long line of white stoneware plates.

"That was *Ms.* Marbledale who called," Alice said. "I've got to go over to the school."

"Now?" Lyman looked startled. "We're full up. Is Barbie hurt?"

"I don't know." This was true. *Ms.* Marbledale hadn't been clear about what exactly had happened, so Alice had no way of knowing if she'd been hurt or not. If Barbie had been hurt, Alice thought she had grounds for a lawsuit herself. She could sue the school for religious discrimination.

"It was better when we were in school," Alice said, before Lyman had a chance to go back to his sausages. "I don't mean it was good. It was just better. There wasn't all of this stuff around. I never learned about Darwin in school, did you?"

"That might have been later," Lyman said. "Or it might have been in the college course. I wasn't in the college course."

"I don't understand why she thinks she can talk to me that way," Alice said. "I'm her boss, no matter how much she doesn't like it. Me and Franklin Hale are her boss. She ought to have sense enough to be afraid of us."

"Do you have to go over right now?" Lyman asked. "I'm up to my neck. Can't it wait half an hour?"

"No," Alice said. She didn't know if that was true. The way *Ms.* Marbledale had talked, it might have been okay to let it go all day. It was only detention. Alice had spent a lot of time in detention when she was in school, and staying after, too, because teachers thought their work was the only thing that ought to count in your life.

"It isn't fair," Alice said. She had moved through the kitchen to the vestibule in the back. She was standing next to the little rack where she and Lyman and the girls who worked the floor all hung their coats.

As far as Alice McGuffie was concerned, nothing about life was fair. All the good things went to people like *Ms.* Marbledale. No matter how long your walk with God was, you could never catch up to the *Ms.* Marbledales of this world, and the Annie-Vic Hadleys were worse. They all thought they were better than you. They all thought they were smarter than you. They all looked down their noses at you and sneered, and what for? Because you believed in God, that was what for, and they thought only stupid people believed in God.

Alice wound a scarf around her neck. It could have been hers, or it could have been Lyman's. They didn't make distinctions. Out the back door she could see the snow and the icicles that had been hanging around for days. It ought to be spring by now, but it wasn't, at least

78

not as the weather went. Annie-Vic was up at the hospital these days, lying in a bed with tubes coming out of her. One of the women in church worked as a volunteer there, taking the gift cart around and handing out pamphlets. She'd seen Annie-Vic all trussed up like a turkey, and looking bad enough to die.

Bad enough to die, Alice thought, and suddenly her day felt much better.

Annie-Vic was bad enough off to die, and then what would happen to her? She would end up face to face with God, that was what would happen to her, and then she'd spend eternity in a lake of fire. It said so, in the Bible, and it said that believers would have all eternity to watch the suffering of the souls in Hell.

Alice honestly thought she'd like that very much.

2

When Judy Cornish first got the call from Catherine Marbledale, she was panicked. Then Ms. Marbledale let her speak to Mallory directly, and after that, she was all right. She was better than all right, really. Judy had expected what she'd gotten the last time that venomous little Barbie McGuffie had gone after Mallory and Stacey, meaning hysteria and tears, but Mallory had sounded downright calm. *Eerily* calm. It was like listening to a grown woman who had just decided to kill her husband. There was no trace of emotion in that voice at all and quite a lot of rigidly controlled anger.

Judy had been in her kitchen when the call came. It was a spectacular kitchen, better than the one she had had in Somerville when they had been living near Boston. Housing was not a minor consideration for Judy. She liked ten-foot ceilings and two-story great rooms and all those little rooms that made life so much easier. In this house she had a laundry room as large as the dining room had been in their first house, and a mud room with built-in benches and cabinets so that people didn't track in dirt and snow when they came in from school, and a clutter room that was was for messy school projects like posters and dioramas. This was the kind of thing you got when you worked hard and applied yourself—especially when you applied yourself at school. Education was the key to everything, and that meant education at a name college. The Ivy League would be best, but it wasn't strictly necessary. Anything in the first tier would do. If you didn't get that, you might as well curl up and die, as far as Judy was concerned. You might be able to pull your life out of your ass if you managed to get into a first-rate graduate school, but not many people managed to do that, and Judy thought she knew why. Being a slacker was like having a disease. It might even be catching.

The mud room was in the back, in a sort of passage to the garage, although it had a door to the real outside, so that the children could use it coming in from the yard. Judy had loved her own childhood. It had been full of things to do, things she'd found unavailable in Snow Hill to give to her own children. She had had piano lessons, and tennis lessons, and gymnastics lessons. She had had sleepaway camp for two weeks every summer—although that, she'd managed, even from here. She sent Mallory and Hannah to her own camp in New Hampshire, and Danny to Camp Awosting in Connecticut. Stacey Niederman went to camp with Mallory and Hannah. Sometimes Judy thought they were all out here re-creating civilization from scratch, as if there'd been a nuclear holocaust or some kind of supervirus that had wiped out all traces of it across the mid-Atlantic region of the United States. It was scary to think about it, but maybe it was like this over most of the United States. Maybe that was what "red states" were about, and that explained why the country kept voting in Republicans. Judy couldn't understand why anybody ever voted for Republicans, although her mother told her that all the best people used to, the people like the ones they'd grown up with.

"It was in about 1980 that it started to change," Judy's mother had said. "And I don't know what happened, really, but suddenly it was all about those religious people, and so I changed parties. I had to, don't you think?"

Judy didn't know. She couldn't imagine what the Republican Party had been like before "all those religious people." She didn't care. She took her best parka out of her own personal cubicle—it had her name stenciled on it above the hook, at the top—and headed out to the garage and the Volvo. She'd been seven years old when her mother sat her down at the kitchen table with a pile of what looked like books and told her the way the world worked. The pile had not been of books but of college catalogues, which Judy's mother had sent away for even though Judy wasn't out of primary school.

Her mother had stretched out one set of them and said, "Harvard, Yale, Princeton, Brown, Dartmouth, Cornell, Columbia, the University of Pennsylvania. That's the best. That's the Ivy League." Then she had stretched out a second set and said, "Vassar, Smith, Wellesley, Mt. Holyoke, Bryn Mawr, Barnard, Radcliffe. That's the seven sisters. That's almost as good, for a girl, but Radcliffe will be Harvard in a few years. It won't matter. Then there's this." She had flipped over the last book. "That's Stanford, in California. That's the only place worth going to in the West."

Judy had to admit she didn't understand much of any of this at the time. The whole episode scared her, though, because she had understood that there were conditions on her life going as she wanted it to. She would have to have something to do with these places her mother was showing her, and no other places, if she wanted her mother to go on being proud of her. It was a big looming mountain, right in front of her face. Good people, nice people, people like her parents and their friends, went to these places, and after they left they had jobs in companies that everybody had heard of. Other people didn't matter.

Judy climbed into the Volvo and put her seat belt on. She put it on automatically, even if she was just going to sit behind the wheel and not drive anywhere, and so did all of her children. She flicked the button on the garage door opener and watched the garage door pull up behind her. She started the car and put the heat on. It was so cold she was finding it hard to breathe.

By the time she was eleven or so, she had it all figured out. The people who did not go to the kind of colleges her mother had mentioned, the people who went to state schools and then went to work in the small local companies that were everywhere, even in the kinds of towns where Judy grew up, those people did nothing important with their lives. "Most men live lives of quiet desperation," Henry David Thoreau had said, in the book they'd read in Judy's gifted class, and Judy thought she knew what he'd meant. He'd meant *those* people, the ones in remedial everything, or the ones who were just average, who didn't go to lessons, who didn't care about anything. At least, Judy didn't see that they cared about anything. They had all sorts of stuff they did, but none of it was stuff that would help them in the long run.

What we have to do here, Judy thought, is make Snow Hill the kind of place children can grow up in and succeed. We need to tear down that elementary school and build modern schools, a primary school and a middle school and a high school. If there were modern schools, there wouldn't be this problem we're having with Barbie McGuffie.

Judy's cell phone was in her purse. It was a pink Razr. Dan had offered to get her an iPhone, but that hadn't made sense to her. The children all had iPhones. They liked music and looking at the Internet when they got bored with school, which they often were. Honestly, Judy thought. She'd never understood why people were unhappy with the public schools until she'd come to Snow Hill. When public schools were like this, she was unhappy with them, too.

Judy held down the number 6 and waited until the phone started automatically dialing Shelley Niederman's number. She hoped she hadn't waited so long that Shelley had already started driving to the school. She looked at her eye makeup in her rearview mirror. She didn't wear much eye makeup anymore. She used to wear a lot.

"Yes?" Shelley said.

"It's me," Judy said, although she didn't need to. Her cell number was on Shelley's caller ID. "Did you get a call from Catherine Marbledale?"

"I did indeed," Shelley said.

"Are you going in to see what's going on?"

"I don't know. I talked to Stacey. She seemed to be all right."

"I talked to Mallory," Judy said. "She seemed to be more than all right. But I'm going in anyway. I've been thinking. Maybe we've been going about this all wrong."

"You don't think we should be complaining about it when a big thug like Barbie McGuffie beats up on our children."

"Of course I think we should be complaining about it," Judy said, "but I've been thinking and thinking, and it occurs to me that we're doing this backwards. We're being too negative."

"I'm going to be negative about that ape girl hammering on Stacey," Shelley said. "Why shouldn't I be?"

"You should be, you should be," Judy said. "But here's the thing. Every time one of these things happens, what do we do? We try to stop it. Yes, yes, of course we should do that, but is that all we should do? Even the lawsuit. The lawsuit is entirely negative."

"What else can it be?" Shelley asked. "You don't really think we should let them teach a lot of Creationist stupidity in science classes?"

"No, of course I don't." Judy sighed. This was going to be harder than she had thought. When the idea first occurred to her, it had seem to be so obviously the solution that she'd been amazed she hadn't thought of it before. It surprised her Shelley wasn't getting it.

"Look," Judy said, "maybe, instead of just doing the negative stuff, we should do some positive stuff."

"What positive stuff?"

"Maybe, instead of telling people what we're against, we should tell them what we're for. Have you ever heard of the Equal Access Act?"

"No," Shelley said.

"It's a law," Judy said. "It applies to any school district that gets federal money, and Snow Hill gets federal money. Lots of it. So Snow Hill has to abide by the Equal Access Act."

"What a minute," Shelley said. "Is this the thing about Bible clubs? Is this the law about letting kids have Bible clubs in public schools?"

"Sort of," Judy said, "but not exactly. Listen, I'm just on my way to the school. Meet me in the parking lot and I'll explain the whole thing. Mallory made me think of it, really. And it might work. Anyway, we have to do something. We can't let these hillbillies take over our children. It's as if half this town never arrived in the twenty-first century."

3

Nicodemus Frapp had been hearing the same things everybody else in town had been hearing, but Nick had the best intelligence network in the county, and more people he could trust than Christ had had on the day of the Last Supper. Of course, that last one was sort of ironic— and not the sort of thing he could say in front of his congregation. Oral Roberts might not be Vassar, but it was light-years away from spending your life in these hills, and "sophistication" was part of the problem it left you with. Nick didn't believe that everything was relative, but he did believe this was. It was a matter of what you were used to. He was used to two different kinds of things. Only one of them was acceptable as the public face of a Holiness Church.

Still, Nick thought, it was a wonderful thing. The idea of Gregor Demarkian himself, right here in Snow Hill, and there hadn't even been a murder yet. True crime was one of the things Nick loved passionately. Maybe it was the idea that murder happened even among the people who had looked down on him all those years he was growing up, and probably looked down on him still. Maybe it was just that this kind of murder was different than the kind of murder he was used to. People in the hills killed each other all the time. The reality of Appalachia was not the Beverly Hillbillies. Men beat their wives into bloody pulps. Men and women both got so wasted on moonshine that they were damned near brain damaged by the time they picked up the rifle and started shooting holes in the fabric of time. God, Nick knew all about that kind of thing. It wasn't gone yet, although he'd been trying ever since he got back from Oklahoma to make it stop. The problem was, as crime, it wasn't interesting. It was hard to get interested in a couple of sky-high idiots laying waste to the landscape and then coming to on a jailhouse floor, wondering what the Hell had happened to them.

Gregor Demarkian did not deal in that kind of crime. He was too expensive, for one thing. Police departments didn't call him in to "do something" about yet another pair of crackers getting liquored up and violent. Gregor Demarkian was called in when there was a real mystery, when there was a chance that the killer would never be caught by ordinary police work. Or he was called in when the people involved were rich and famous, or "prominent," or one of those things that made treading softly a good idea. Nick didn't think he would ever be the kind of person the police would feel they had to "tread softly" with. Even if he expanded this church into the kind of megachurch that had its own services on big infomercial hunks on cable TV, he would still be a hillbilly. It was bred in his bones, and everybody who met him knew it.

Nick was so excited about the prospect of Gregor Demarkian in town, though, he had almost forgotten his position. This was unprecedented. He had made his life on remembering his position, on knowing precisely what it was and acting accordingly. The problem was that it was hard to remember anything when he was looking up Main Street, waiting to see how Demarkian would arrive. Nick didn't think it would be in a limousine; Demarkian didn't seem like that kind of person. Nick wondered if this meant that old Annie-Vic was dead, or about to die. Everybody thought she would die. Nick wasn't so sure. She was a tough old woman. She might come to yet. Then there would be no need for Gregor Demarkian. She'd just sit right up in bed and tell the world who'd tried to do her in.

Nick was standing at the window in the big pastor's office on the second floor of the church. Below him, the one-level school building that housed their Holiness Gospel School looked active and humming, even from the outside. He saw Alice McGuffie leave the diner and start on out of town in the direction of the public school complex. He was fairly sure he knew what all that was going to be about. Main

Street was clogged through with reporters, and it was going to get worse before it was going to get better, but if somebody killed Barbie McGuffie before it was over, Nick wouldn't be entirely unsympathetic.

There was a tap on the door behind him, and Sister Cleland poked her head in. They had to be careful with the finances of this church. There were a handful of well-off members, but most of them were either poor, or just in the process of climbing out of poverty, so it wouldn't do to spend too much money where it didn't have to be spent. Sister Cleland was a volunteer. There were three church women who volunteered as church secretary every week, and that way all of them could keep jobs at Wal-Mart and the church still got its typing done.

Sister Cleland's name was Susie. If Nick had just met her, he would have remembered it. There was an old Scottish folk song about a girl named Susie Cleland. Susie met a man her fathers and brothers didn't like, and they burned her at the stake when she wouldn't give him up. This Susie Cleland had just been left with the debts from five no-account brothers, and the care and feeding of a father whose brain was lost to alcoholism long before Susie and Nick both had reached the fifth grade.

Susie came all the way into the office and shut the door behind her. She looked better now than she had when Nick had first come back from college. She took care with her clothes and her hair and had something done about her teeth. (Doing something about teeth was something Nick insisted on with all his parishioners. Dental hygiene was a big issue at every grade at their Christian school, and they even brought in a dentist for a free clinic twice a year.)

Susie looked over her shoulder at the door, as if the CIA were out there somewhere behind it. Then she turned back to him. "There's somebody to see you," she whispered. "Not somebody you know." She hesitated a good long while. "It's a reporter."

"Is it," Nick said.

Susie nodded vigorously. "From New York, I think. She seems like she's from New York, anyway. It isn't one of the famous ones, if you know what I mean. I think they want to interview you for the television."

Nick considered this. He had, of course, expected it. Once the national media started pouring in, it couldn't be long before they found out what a "Holiness" church was, or heard about the "holy ghost people." One of the people in town would tell them, even if they didn't ask. Alice McGuffie would tell them, and so would Franklin Hale. Nick supposed there were a dozen more just waiting to swing the spotlight away from the nice people of Snow Hill and onto the crazy stupid hill folk. He wondered if this woman was sitting in his waiting room, looking all around her for poisonous snakes. This was one of those times he wished he had a few.

"I saw Alice go out toward the schools," he said. "Do you know what that's about?"

Susie Cleland shrugged. "Something to do with Barbie, I'd guess. Why Alice McGuffie doesn't know her own daughter is the next best thing to a terrorist, I'll never know. Do you want me to send this woman away? She makes me nervous. She makes me think something is wrong with my hair."

"Does she have a camera with her?" Nick asked. "Does she have somebody with her who's carrying a camera?"

"No, not at all," Susie said. "It's just her. Dressed sloppy, if you know what I mean, so I don't know why she makes me feel so self-conscious about my clothes. It's odd, isn't it, the way people are? She's got a tape recorder."

"All right," Nick said. "We'll ask her to leave the tape recorder with you."

"She's got a tote bag," Susie said. "There might be something in that. It looks full. Maybe she has a camera."

"Maybe." Nick was pretty sure she didn't. Here was something Oral Roberts University was probably much better at than Vassar. They understood what a media onslaught was. Christian preachers were the victims of media onslaughts every day. Oral Roberts himself had been a prime target. In this case, Nick was willing to bet that this woman was just advancing for another, more important reporter. She'd want to check him out and see if he was worthy of airtime.

He went over to his desk and sat down. He was so tall and thin he found it difficult to sit behind a desk like a normal person. He seemed to explode in a profusion of knees. "Send her in, Susie," he said. "She won't bite you."

"I'd like to bite her," Susie said. "You should see the way she's behaving. She keeps looking behind the furniture."

Which meant she was looking for snakes, Nick thought. Susie was out the door. He sat back a little and waited. This room was full of books, and they were not just window dressing. Nick liked to read. He especially liked to read history. He did not restrict himself to what came out of the Christian publishing houses.

The door swung in yet again and Susie came back, followed by a small, very young woman in jeans and a parka. Susie had been right about the sloppiness. The woman looked like she had slept all night in those clothes, then rolled out of bed this morning and pretended she hadn't.

"Ms. Charlene Holder," Susie said. She was very stiff. "Ms. Holder, this is Reverend Frapp."

Then Susie got out, fast, as if shooting were about to start.

Nick had gotten to his feet. This was one of the first acts of politeness he had ever learned and he wasn't interested in giving it up. He held out his hand to the woman and waited until she shook it. Then he waited until she sat down. She was really very, very small. Nick towered over most people. Beside her he was like a tree next to a daisy.

He sat down again and stretched his legs out under his desk. "Well," he said. "You're from CNN. What can I do for you?"

"Ah," Ms. Holder said. She looked at her hands. "Your secretary took my tape recorder. I'd kind of like to get something of our conversation on tape."

"I'm not really ready for tape," Nick said. "What was it you wanted to have a conversation about?"

"Well," Ms. Holder said. She was looking carefully around the room, in all the corners, at the floor. Nick watched her. She did not seem to be aware that she was leaving long stretches of dead air.

"You're not going to see anything," he said mildly. "We don't handle snakes in the church."

"What?"

"We don't handle snakes in the church," he said patiently. There was no point in being rude to these people. They could hurt you. Even so, he wished he could hit her over the head with something right this minute. "There's no point in looking around as if a rattlesnake is going to jump out and bite you. There are no rattlesnakes here. We don't handle snakes in church."

"Ah," Ms. Holder said.

"Most of us don't handle snakes in church at all anymore," Nick said. "It's an old-fashioned practice. We move with the times like everybody else. And nobody's drunk poison around here for a good thirty years."

"Ah," Ms. Holder said again.

"So if that's what you were looking for," Nick said. He tilted his head. "If that's what you were looking for," he said again, "as you can see, I can't help you."

This got Ms. Holder's attention. Nick had no idea why. Maybe she was just paranoid about rejection. She forced herself to look directly at him. Her eyes stayed on his face for a good ten seconds before they began to scan the room again.

"It's not about snakes," she said. "It's about the lawsuit. We're here to cover the lawsuit. We thought we'd get a few, ah, you know, we'd talk to a few people. Creationists. You're a Creationist, aren't you?"

"If you mean do I believe that the world was created as the Bible says it was, then yes, I'm a Creationist."

"Yes. Well. That's it, you see. We want to get a few on camera interviews with Creationists."

"You want me to talk about the biblical account of creation?"

"Um, yeah," Ms. Holder said. "That would be good. Also, you

know, why you think it should be taught in the public schools."

"I don't think it should be taught in the public schools," Nick said.

"What?"

"I don't think it should be taught in the public schools," Nick said. He wondered if he was going to have to repeat everything for this woman. She just wasn't listening. "We have a Christian school here, run by this church. It's enough for me that Creation is taught in the Christian school."

"Oh." Ms. Holder looked stumped.

Nick closed his eyes. He wondered if this woman knew something about the coming of Gregor Demarkian. He wondered if she knew something about anything. Had he sprouted horns and a tail? Did he have an eye growing out of his forehead? For God's sake.

Literally.

He leaned forward on the desk and sighed. "You know," he said, "*nobody* is trying to get Creationism into the Snow Hill public schools."

FOUR

1

Gregor Demarkian had always had a theory that it was not really possible to get away from places like Cavanaugh Street, but it was a theory he tended to forget about in the press of business. He had certainly forgotten about it on the day he was supposed to leave for Snow Hill, and so he went down to the curb with his briefcase without thinking for a moment that he'd have any trouble along the way. He was carrying a briefcase and not a suitcase because, as John Jackman kept reminding him, Snow Hill "wasn't very far," and besides, he wasn't much interested in spending yet another month or so away from Bennis before the wedding. He didn't enjoy the preparations for the wedding. He didn't even like to think about them. Still, he was marrying Bennis because he wanted to spend his time with Bennis. It seemed crazy to him to hole up in motel rooms instead of coming back to his own bed.

The decision would have made more sense if Gregor had been willing to drive, but there it was. He did have a driver's license, but he almost never used it. He wouldn't feel comfortable driving himself to Snow Hill, and none of the other drivers on the road would feel comfortable, either. If it hadn't been for the wedding preparations, Bennis could have driven him, but Bennis was busy, and Donna Moradanyan Donahue had a relatively new small baby to worry about, and the decorations, too. In the end, Gary Albright had decided to do the driving himself.

"Once a day up and back won't kill me," he'd said, when they'd tried to make all these arrangements over the phone. "People go longer to commute. And it's not like I'm doing much work right now."

Gregor wondered if it was really the case that there was so little police work to do in Snow Hill. The town couldn't be entirely removed from reality. There had to be drugs, and Gregor knew from what John and Gary had told him that there were cases of domestic violence. Gregor thought back to the beginning of his career. Surely there had always been cases of domestic violence, although those weren't the kind of cases he would have dealt with when he was at the FBI. He remembered one family on Cavanaugh Street when he was growing up. The husband was an immigrant, just over, and the wife, everybody said, couldn't have done any better. He supposed they meant she was not very good looking. When Gregor had known her, she had been washed out and mousy and plain, but that might have been the result of all those beatings. The police didn't come to do anything about them in those days. They would only have been called in if there had been a chance that he was going to kill her, and all they would have done then would have been to try to calm him down. Surely, the new way of doing these things was better. It made no sense to treat women as natural-born punching bags just because they were married to some idiot; making it easier for abused women to get a divorce was *definitely* an improvement. Still, Gregor couldn't help thinking that there used to be less of it, and not only because it was more seldom reported. It seemed to him that men and women were more brutal to each other now than they had been in decades.

He reached the street with his briefcase and looked up and down it, but there was no sign of Gary Albright. There was no sign of anybody. It was early morning, but not early enough for people to be out and around on their way to work. The day was clear and cold. Even Bennis had disappeared into the mist, running off to Donna's to discuss chocolate sculptures. Gregor had no idea what a chocolate sculpture was. It always made him feel very odd to look at Cavanaugh Street, since what it *had* been was so firmly etched into his memory. When he was growing up, all the buildings had been tenements. People lived in small, cramped apartments with very few windows and only barely adequate heat. The streets were dirty, but the tenement hallways were clean, because the women had come out every morning and scrubbed them down. It was hard to credit the way they had all lived: the clothes that were patched and handed down; the school books that were carefully covered so that the school could not say they had wrecked them and demand to be paid: the old priest from Armenia who smelled of camphor and breath mints and desperately needed a bath. All Gregor had wanted in those days was for his parents to make enough money to move out to the suburbs. It wouldn't have had to have been the Main Line. He'd thought the best thing in the world would be a house and a yard and a car that his father could polish, the way people did on television.

He looked up and down the street again, but the person he saw was not Gary Albright but Leda Kazanjian Arkmanian, crawling down the pavement at a lordly ten miles an hour. Leda always crawled in that car of hers. Gregor thought she only owned it because her children insisted on giving it to her, and he had to admit it was a very impressive car.

"Swedish," she'd said, when she'd first gotten it, and everybody was asking her about it in the Ararat. "They started out saying they were going to give me a Mercedes, but I couldn't have that. It's a German car. I mean, *German.*"

Gregor had wanted to say, at the time, that it could have been worse. It could have been a Turkish car. He said nothing, because he knew better than to interfere when people started fighting World War II all over again. Now he watched while Leda pulled up to the curb just across the street from him, making the vehicle make funny noises as she parked. If Gregor had had someplace to go that wouldn't inconvenience Gary Albright when he finally got here, he would have gone there.

Leda got out of the car and looked up and down the street. There was no traffic. There rarely was at this time of day on Cavanaugh Street. She did something that beeped with her key ring. Gregor thought it was a device that automatically locked or unlocked all the doors of the car. He wasn't up on cars. He didn't understand them. Leda waved to him and began to cross the street. She didn't look happy. Gregor wished he didn't already know what she was going to say.

"Gregor," she said, when he reached him.

Gregor looked up and down the street again. Surely, Gary Albright couldn't be hopelessly lost. If he had been, he would have called. That was what Gregor had a cell phone for. "I'm waiting for the police officer from Snow Hill," he said, as if Leda was going to listen.

Leda was looking impressive as only Leda could look these days. She might be an old lady, but she was a magnificent old lady. She was wearing three-and-a-half-inch stiletto heels and a three-quarter-length chinchilla coat. Here was the great payoff of raising your children to work hard and study and get as much education as they could. Leda's children had done very well.

"Gregor," she said again, as if she hadn't said it the first time, "I came to apologize."

"There's nothing to apologize for," Gregor said. "We've got it all worked out. We really do."

"And you're getting married in the church?"

Gregor sighed. This would be an easier conversation if Leda had been concerned that Gregor and Bennis get married in the Church, with a capital *C*. That would mean she wanted them to have the blessing of the Armenian religion, and Gregor would have had an answer to that that would have been easy for anyone to understand. Unfortunately, Leda was only concerned that the ceremony for Gregor and Bennis's wedding take place inside the physical building of Holy Trinity Church, and she wasn't the only one who was concerned about it.

"I didn't think so," she said. "I do need to apologize. To apologize for Father Tibor. To apologize for the whole neighborhood. I never dreamed that he'd be this stubborn, and about what? About a technicality."

"It's not exactly just a technicality," Gregor said.

"Of course it is," Leda said. "And it's un-American, too. Tibor's always so proud of being an American. My niece Alison got married to a Jewish boy not three months ago, and they had the ceremony right in her Catholic church with a rabbi present to give his side of it. And that's the Catholics. The Armenians were never as unreasonable as the Catholics."

Gregor thought that he could possibly dispute this, but he let it go. "Bennis and I don't want to get married in Holy Trinity Church," he said, thinking that this was closest to the right thing to say. It was out of the question that he could explain to Leda what the issue really was. He knew that because he had tried, on several occasions. "We really aren't looking to have a religious ceremony."

"It's not a matter of a religious ceremony," Leda said. "It has nothing to do with religion. It's a matter of community. You're one of the family here on Cavanaugh Street, and he's treating you as if you were an outsider."

"No," Gregor said. "Really. He's not. He's even agreed to perform the actual ceremony, the civil version, you know, just not in the church."

"Hannah and Sheila and I have come up with a plan," Leda said. "We're going to make him change his mind. Don't you worry. We know how to make Father Tibor see reason. And if not, well, what of it? I don't want to belong to a church that wants to keep people out more than it wants to bring them in. That isn't what Christ came to teach us. Why should I go to a church that's more snobbish than one of those Main Line country clubs?"

"Really," Gregor said desperately, "you have this all wrong. You're not thinking about it clearly. If freedom of religion is going to mean anything—"

He cringed as soon as he said it. That was the tack he had tried before, the one that had not worked. Then, at the same moment, he saw it: a big white pickup truck, the kind almost nobody had in the city. It looked oddly outsized next to all the regular cars. Gregor was sure it was the salvation he was looking for.

"I think that's my ride," he said, waving at the truck even though he didn't know for sure who was inside it.

Leda wasn't listening. "I think the old ways of religion were bad for everybody," she was saying. "They were all about keeping people out, and what happened? We all hated each other. We all treated each other as if we were aliens. It can't be like that anymore, Gregor, and I won't put up with it in my own neighborhood."

The white pickup truck stopped in the street. It didn't bother to even try for a place at the curb. There wasn't enough room, anyway. The driver's-side door popped open and Gary Albright popped out.

"Mr. Demarkian?" he said.

"I've got to go," Gregor said, grabbing for his briefcase. For a split second he thought he'd lost it. He couldn't remember putting it on the ground. He got a firm grip on it and mouthed a kiss in Leda's direction. He hated that whole custom, whether the kiss actually landed on a cheek or not. "I've got to go," he said again.

Then he rushed off to the passenger side of Gary Albright's truck. He didn't like climbing into trucks any more than he liked kissing cheeks, but at least this promised relief from the endless machinations of the women of Cavanaugh Street.

"I'll be home tonight," he said, because he felt he had to say something. "Tell Bennis I got off all right."

Leda Arkmanian made a face. "Don't you worry," she said. "We'll fix this. Hannah and Sheila and I have a plan."

2

As it turned out, riding in a pickup truck was almost more uncomfortable than getting into one. Gregor didn't understand the fascination the damned things had for so many people. It wasn't that he was from the wrong generation. It was men his age who bought these things when they didn't have to—doctors and lawyers who wanted to seem like—what?—in their spare time. Maybe he just had the wrong history. He'd grown up poor. His experience with rural life had been almost entirely negative until he was well into his twenties, and even then it was more negative than not. God only knew that special agents of the FBI hated the very idea of being assigned to some country backwater, and not because it was bad for the career. There were nuts in them thar hills, and the nuts were armed.

Gary Albright was armed, but that was only to be expected. Gary Albright was a police officer. He had taken himself off this particular case, but Gregor had no reason to believe that he'd stepped down in total. There would be other cases to handle while the problem of Ann-Victoria Hadley went on.

The scenery going past their windows was still unmistakably, uncompromisingly Philadelphia. Gregor took a little comfort in that.

Gary Albright was staring straight ahead. "Mr. Jackman said you were getting married," he said finally. "Sometime soon. Congratulations."

"Thank you." Gregor couldn't think of anything else to say.

There was a long silence. Gregor had the uneasy feeling that there would be many long silences with Gary Albright. He didn't seem like a man who would talk just to talk.

"Mr. Jackman said you were widowed," Gary Albright said finally. "I was sorry to hear it. That's a hard thing."

"Yes," Gregor said. The statement was true enough. "It was a hard thing. But it's been many years now."

"Miss Hadley isn't widowed," Gary Albright said. "She isn't divorced, either. She's never been married."

"And you think that had something to do with her being attacked?"

"No," Gary Albright said. He was still staring straight ahead. He was the calmest man Gregor had ever seen who wasn't a serial killer, and Gregor had to remind himself that he had no way of knowing for sure that Gary Albright wasn't a serial killer.

"It's just that I don't understand it," Gary said finally. "Not being married, I mean. Life is a lonely place. I'd think everybody would get married, if they could. Even homosexual people want to get married. But Miss Hadley could have. From what I've heard, she could have a couple of times over. She was in the Navy, did you know that?"

"No," Gregor said.

"She was a WAVE, in World War II," Gary said. "She was a prisoner of war for a while, with the Japanese. Not for long. There's people who say that she was proposed to by an admiral."

"They could have gotten that wrong." In Gregor's opinion, small towns got most things wrong. They also got most things in their worst possible light.

"Maybe," Gary admitted. "But there was a guy in town, a guy I knew, died a couple of years ago. He was a judge before he retired. He asked her to marry him, and she turned him down. She said she didn't want to give up her independence. Do you understand that?"

"I don't know that I do. I do know there are a lot of women who say they feel that way."

"In her case it wasn't as bad as it could have been," Gary Albright said. "She had a lot of brothers, so she's got a lot of nieces and nephews and grandnieces and nephews. They come up to visit a couple of times a year. She has them all up to that place of hers, dozens of them, so many there're people sleeping on her floors. I still don't understand it."

"Maybe she was hard to get along with."

"Miss Hadley?" Gary considered it. "I don't think so. I mean, she wasn't exactly easy. She wanted her own way and she tended to get it. It's kind of funny. There's somebody else like that, right in town, and she isn't married either. Miss Marbledale."

"Who's Miss Marbledale?"

"She runs the school, pretty much," Gary said. "You'll meet her. She's on the suspect list for the case. Not that I think she killed anybody, mind you, or even tried, as it is, and really if she killed anyone, it'd be Franklin Hale. Or maybe Alice McGuffie. But, here's the thing. She's a lot like Miss Hadley. Only—I'm not sure I know how to put this—only with less of a spirit of adventure, I guess."

"No stint in the Waves," Gregor suggested.

"And no running around on foreign trips," Gary said. "Miss Hadley went to Mongolia and lived in a tent for a couple of weeks. That was only last year. Miss Marbledale's only been foreign maybe two or three times that I remember, and it's always been to regular places like, you know, Rome or England. With a tour with other schoolteachers. And then she brings back slides. You know how that goes?"

"Yes," Gregor said. He did, too. He knew exactly. He had had teachers like that when he had been in school.

"I was out of the country when I was in the Marines," Gary said. "But I haven't been except for that. I don't see the point. I belong here. I can't see they have anything that we don't have. Art, you know, but I'm not that big on art. I like Beethoven."

"That's good," Gregor said.

"It was Miss Marbledale who turned me on to Beethoven," Gary said. "Now I've got the beginning of the Fifth Symphony as my ring tone. But she doesn't teach much anymore, if you know what I mean. She's an administrator."

"Why is she on the suspect list?" Gregor asked. "You said you didn't think she'd kill Ann-Victoria Hadley. There must be a reason."

"Oh, there is," Gary said. "And maybe you'll change the suspect list when you get your hands on it, but I put everybody involved in the suit on it if they were in the position to have done the battery. If they were in the vicinity, you know. Miss Marbledale used to be a science teacher. She presented the science teachers' case when the policy was being debated before the school board. As if the science teachers' side was the official side of the school."

"Not in favor of Intelligent Design, I take it."

"No," Gary said. He looked suddenly unsure of himself. The moment passed and was gone. He looked impassive again. "Here's the thing," he said. "It was the first thing that made me think there might be something to it. To Darwin's theory, I mean. Miss Marbledale is the smartest person I've ever known. And she's not like Miss Hadley in one way that's important. She doesn't create a fuss just to create a fuss.

I could see Miss Hadley being all insistent on evolution because she thought it would make people upset, but I can't see Miss Marbledale doing that. If Miss Marbledale says she thinks evolution is true, then she really thinks evolution is true. And I'd bet anything she's really looked into it."

"And you don't think evolution is true?" Gregor asked.

Gary Albright made a face. "I'm not a scientist," he said, "but I wasn't bad at science in school, and I've tried to read this stuff. And it makes no sense to me. The people who want Intelligent Design say things that do make sense to me. Think of all the things there are. Your spleen, you know, and that kind of thing. All that stuff works together, and if one of the parts is gone it doesn't work. I mean, everybody knows that. They can't just take your pancreas out and have the rest of the parts go on working. That's why you die of pancreatic cancer in the first place. I think I'm making a mess of this explanation."

"No," Gregor said. "I understand what you're saying. I also understand that there's an answer to that particular objection."

"That's what she said," Gary Albright said. "Miss Marbledale, I mean. At the first board meeting we had on the subject, she said that the problem was that we were thinking as if the thing a thing did now was what it always did. But she said that wasn't the case. Sometimes a thing evolved to do one thing, and then as more evolution happened, the body started using it for something else. So it could have been important to the animal in its first use and that's why it evolved at all, but then it became important later in its second use when its first use wasn't needed anymore. I'm not an idiot. I can understand that. I just—"

"What?"

Gary Albright shrugged. "I just don't buy it, I guess. Not entirely. Because I don't think this is an argument about animals and how they got their parts. It might be that for Miss Marbledale, but it really wasn't that for Miss Hadley and it really, really, really isn't that for the people who are bringing this lawsuit. Henry Wackford, I mean. And the people from the development."

"Who's Henry Wackford?"

"He's the village atheist," Gary Albright said, making a face. "He's somebody who likes to make a fuss just to make a fuss. Started a chapter of the American Humanist Association in town a few years ago. Now he's got half a dozen people or so who meet at his house every month and talk about I don't know what. And the people from the development, Mrs. Cornish and those people, they come from out of town, they move in to take jobs and then move out again. I don't think any of them really know anything about Darwin's theory. I mean, they can't explain it when you ask them. Miss Marbledale can explain it."

"If they don't believe in the theory, why do they want it?" Gregor asked.

"Well, that's the thing, isn't it?" Gary said. "It's not about biology, it's about religion. It's about taking people away from religion, taking children away from it. Making religion look stupid. And it's about morality. If religion is true, it isn't all right for people to go off doing whatever they feel like—drugs, sex, you name it. But if religion isn't true there's no reason why people shouldn't be doing those things."

"I know a man," Gregor said carefully, "a priest in the Armenian church, who would say you were wrong."

"Wrong about what?" Gary said. He didn't wait for an answer. "It's all about how they think we're all hicks and hillbillies. I mean that's what it's all about for the people in the development. And for Henry Wackford, it's all about how he's smart and nobody else is. But I know this isn't an argument about biology, even if Miss Marbledale thinks it is."

"So you've put all these people on the suspect list? Henry Wackford? Mrs. Cornish? I thought you said all the suspects called themselves Christians."

"All of them except Henry Wackford," Gary said. "And I don't really think of him as a suspect. Most people don't try to kill off their allies. But he was there that morning. They were all there that morning. They were all in and around Main Street. Any one of them could have gone up the hill and got to Miss Hadley. So I've tried to be inclusive. But mostly it's just a mess, and there are reporters. Dozens of them. The trial is due to start at the beginning of the week."

Gregor looked around. The landscape was getting less and less urban. He thought they might be out by Hardscrabble Road, where the nuns were. He wondered what Sister Beata Maria would think of Intelligent Design, and lawsuits about Darwin. He knew what Tibor thought about it. He wondered again, as he had in John Jackman's office, if there had ever been a case in which somebody was killed for not being a Creationist, and then he reminded himself, for the thousandth time, that nobody was dead yet.

Gary Albright was looking much happier. "This is better," he said. "We're almost out in the country. I hate feeling all cooped up in between the buildings."

3

In the end, Snow Hill was almost exactly what Gregor had expected it to be. It was not so far north as Holman, the last small town in Pennsylvania that Gregor had spent any time in, and not so high into the mountains. It didn't feel quite as claustrophobic. It was probably smaller. When Gary parked the truck in front of the modest little storefront that offered a sign saying Snow Hill Police Department, Gregor wondered where all the people were. It was odd to see a town this deserted in the middle of a good weather day.

He opened his door and got down to the ground as best he could. He felt as if he was climbing out of a child's jungle gym, something he hadn't liked to do even as a child. It really was much colder here than it had been in Philadelphia, but he was prepared. He was wearing a heavy winter coat. It was a city coat. Gregor felt it was wrong for the pickup truck, and possibly wrong for Main Street altogether.

On his feet and solid ground, Gregor took a moment to look around. There were churches everywhere. The most impressive one was all the way down at the end of the street, a big white and stone modern thing that seemed to have several smaller buildings behind it or maybe attached to it. It was hard to tell. There was a diner, called the Snow Hill Diner—not much to go on there. There was a tire dealership. There was what would have been the most impressive church in town fifty years ago, the Episcopalian one, all stone and arches. He checked one side of the street and then the other. There were a few news vans parked at the curb on the other side, but there was no more sign of the people who belonged in them than there was of the people who belonged to the town.

Gary Albright had come around to see what Gregor was doing. Gregor pointed vaguely up and down the street.

"Where's the public library?" he asked.

Gary Albright looked embarrassed. "We don't have one," he said.

"You don't?" That went against the grain of everything Gregor knew about American small towns, at least in the Northeast. Small towns always had libraries. In Gregor's childhood, they had been staffed by women who had desperately wanted an education and been unable to afford one.

"Did you never have one?" he asked. "That's unusual for Pennsylvania, isn't it?"

"We used to have one." Gary looked up one side of the street and down the other. "It wasn't exactly public public. I mean, it was a public library. The town paid for it. But the town didn't set it up. Miss Hadley's grandfather did. It was known as the Hadley public library."

"And then what?"

Gary shrugged. "I don't know. Maybe ten years or so ago, the town council decided it was too much money to go on spending. Not all that many people used it, you know. And there were always, well, you know, problems."

"Problems?"

"With books," Gary said. "And with the Internet. What you could do with them and what you couldn't. What you could give to children. And then there was some lawsuit somewhere about the Internet, and about libraries not being able to use filters for the porn, or something, and so the town council decided it didn't make sense to go on with it.

Except I think the thing about the Internet was an excuse, really. Nobody could see the point."

"Nobody could see the point of books?"

"People don't read much anymore," Gary Albright said. "It's a fact. It might not be a good thing, but it's a fact."

"What became of the library building?" Gregor asked. "You didn't just abandon it, did you?"

"Oh, no," Gary said. "The thing was, it turned out the town didn't own it. The way the original agreement was set up, when Miss Hadley's grandfather turned the running of the library over to the town, it turned out he hadn't deeded the building to the town. So it reverted to Miss Hadley and her brothers and all that."

"What did they do to it?"

"They rented it to Nick Frapp," Gary said. He turned around and pointed down the street to the big modern church Gregor had been so impressed with. "They only charge him a dollar a year. It's part of that big complex of buildings now that the church has got. Anyway, Nick and his people took it lock, stock, and barrel, except they took out the computers. They've got computers in the school. They took all the books, though. Even the, uh, objectionable ones."

Gregor didn't want to ask what the objectionable ones were. "Is that your church?" he asked. "Is that the one where you and the other members of the board—"

"Oh, no," Gary said quickly. "That's a *Holiness* Church. The Holy Ghost people. You know. Hill people."

Gregor drew a long blank, and then it hit him. "The people who handle rattlesnakes," he said. "And drink poison, and that kind of thing? But I thought that was an Appalachian thing. I thought that was—"

"Hillbillies," Gary said. "Exactly right. That's what they are. Hillbillies. You're in Appalachia, almost, in Snow Hill. We're right on the edge of it. Except that Nick Frapp has this thing going. He got them to build that church. And most of them don't live in the hills anymore, or at least not that far from town."

"Do they still handle snakes?" Gregor asked.

"Not on my watch," Gary said. "It isn't legal. And it causes a lot of trouble. I wasn't on the force when they were still doing that. I didn't get into police work until I left the Marines, and by then Nick was back from that college in Oklahoma and he'd started this. But I remember it growing up, the sirens, the ambulances out of wherever. We don't have a full service hospital in Snow Hill. People would die, and the police and the fire department and the ambulances would be tied up for hours, trying to treat these idiots and all the time they'd be shooting at you. But it isn't a problem anymore. Nick doesn't put up with it and they all listen to Nick. I think they think he's God."

"And is he part of this lawsuit?"

"No," Gary said. There was a strange note in his voice, one that sounded half-strangled, so that Gregor turned to look him straight in the face. He couldn't read anything there.

"Nick," Gary said, "I don't know how to put this. Nick says he thinks public schools should teach whatever the teachers want, or something like that. It didn't make any sense to me at the time, and it doesn't make any sense to me now. You've got to pay attention to the things your children learn. If they learn the wrong things, they could—bad things could happen to them. Drugs. Sexual diseases. It's a nasty world out there."

"But Nick Frapp doesn't mind his children learning about it?"

"Nick's children don't go to the public schools," Gary Albright said. "The church has a Christian school. All the kids from there go to that. It costs money, but if you're a member of the church, there's a fund to make sure your kids can go there even if you can't afford it. They take other kids, too, you know, from families that don't belong to their church. Not that many other kids go."

"Is that because of religious differences?" Gregor asked.

"It's because they are what they are," Gary said. "Hillbillies. The last thing people in Snow Hill want is to be looked at as a bunch of hillbillies. Ignorant, low-rent white trash. At least, that's what we all thought, when Nick and I was growing up. What I thought. Nick was a hillbilly."

"I take it you think he isn't one now," Gregor said.

Gary Albright shrugged. "Nick is Nick. You're going to want to talk to him. He was here that day that Annie-Vic got attacked. I think he may have been the last person to talk to her while she was still on Main Street."

"Really. Did they get along?"

"Nick gets along with everybody," Gary said. "He's one of those people. You've got to wonder what he would have been like, if things had been different. If he'd have been born to different people."

Gregor had a thought. "Do *you* get along with Nick Frapp?" he asked.

Gary Albright stared up the street at the Holiness Church. There it was again, that Marine Corps face, the face you couldn't read.

"I think Nick Frapp is some kind of genius," he said finally. "I just wonder sometimes what it is he thinks he's doing."

FIVE

1

Franklin Hale saw Gary Albright drive up, and when he did he stood stock still next to the big plate-glass window that served as the front wall of his shop until Gregor Demarkian got out, too. Everything about Demarkian made Franklin Hale's skin crawl. There was just something *about* those people—secular humanists, whatever you wanted to call them. They exuded their snobbery the way skunks exuded smell. Or something. Franklin sometimes found it hard to put together, and he never found anything hard to put together. It was as if they were looking down their noses at you, but it was worse than that. It was as if they expected you to do something. Franklin wasn't sure what. It all got mixed up in his mind. But he knew the signs, he really did. Gregor Demarkian had all the signs. Franklin was willing to bet that Demarkian listened to "classical music" when he thought people could hear him. Franklin was fairly convinced that nobody listened to "classical music" for any other reason.

Of course, there were other people who had all the signs, who weren't secular humanists. There was Nick Frapp. Just what was going on there, Franklin didn't know. What was Nick Frapp, anyway, but a trumped up hillbilly without the sense God gave a good dog? Franklin remembered Nick's parents, and Nick, too, back in high school. He'd been able to beat the crap out of any of those kids. They hardly got decent food, and all their mothers drank, and their fathers, too, and then there was the religious stuff, which was just plain weird. The world was not the way it ought to be. Franklin was convinced of this. If the world was the way it ought to be, he wouldn't be standing here worrying about being arrested for pounding the living shit out of Annie-Vic.

"If I'd pounded the shit out of her, she'd have stayed pounded," he said out loud.

"What?"

It was Marcey's voice, coming from behind him. Franklin's back stiffened. Marcey never came down to the store during working hours. In fact, it was part of their agreement, unstated but adhered to religiously for years. Marcey never came down to the store and she was never sick for church. Those were the only two rules that mattered. Franklin didn't care about anything else. And yet here Marcey was, hanging on to a stack of tires in a display and on the verge of tears. Marcey was always on the verge of tears.

"I thought we agreed that you didn't like to come down here," Franklin said. He was still looking out the window. Gregor Demarkian and Gary Albright seemed to be talking about something. Gregor Demarkian was looking up and down Main Street as if it were an exhibit in a zoo. Well, that was what those people thought, wasn't it? They thought that all decent people were exhibits in a zoo.

"Franklin," Marcey said.

"You're not supposed to be here," Franklin said. "It causes trouble. It upsets the staff. You know that."

"But Miss Marbledale called me."

"So what?" Franklin said. "Miss Marbledale called me, too. About that damned new school building. Somebody whacked Annie-Vic and now everything is going to Hell."

"Well, this isn't about the new school building, is it?" Marcey said.

"It's about Janey. And it's not the first time. We're going to have to do something, Franklin. I don't think Barbie McGuffie is a good influence."

"Of course Barbie McGuffie is a good influence," Franklin said. "She belongs to our church. Barbie and Janey have been going to Vacation Bible School together for years."

Marcey took a deep breath. It was loud. Franklin could hear it. He nearly cringed. There she was, and her voiced sounded as if somebody had fuzzed it up around the edges. Marcey always sounded as if she were talking through velvet. Franklin bit his lip. Gregor Demarkian had gone into the police department building with Gary Albright.

"I don't think it's right," Franklin said. "Bringing somebody in from outside like that. If you're going to bring in somebody from the outside, you bring in the state police. That's what they're for."

"Franklin, please. Janey's in detention. And it's all because of Barbie McGuffie. Barbie McGuffie—"

"Barbie McGuffie is a nice kid who's being persecuted," Franklin said. He turned away from the window and looked at Marcey straight on. There was nothing left to look at in the street. He couldn't avoid it.

"Franklin," she said, and she wasn't near tears anymore. She was crying. "Please. They did something, they wrote something on the back of that girl, that Cornish girl—"

"We should have a Christian school here," Franklin said. "A real Christian school. Not that hillbilly version Nick Frapp put up. We should have a place to send Janey so she doesn't get harassed by people like that."

"By Barbie?" Marcey said. "You think Janey is being harassed by Barbie? Maybe—"

"Of course Janey isn't being harassed by Barbie," Franklin said. Marcey's expression fell, but he ignored it. He ignored the tears that were streaming down her face. He ignored the mess that was happening to her mascara. "It's that Cornish girl, and all the rest of them. The people from the development. The secular humanists. What right do they have to come in here and tell us how to run our school? They don't know anything about this town. And they never will know, because they never stay, and you know it."

"Oh," Marcey said. She put a hand up and wiped at her cheek. The gesture smeared black mascara across her face in a wide arching sheet.

"For God's sake," Franklin said.

He grabbed her arm and headed for the employees' bathroom. That was the only kind of bathroom he had in the store. He didn't believe in executive bathrooms, putting himself ahead of his people. It only caused resentment, and people didn't work as hard. He didn't believe in customer bathrooms, either, because when you put those in, people came in from off the street just to use them, and they never bought tires.

There were people in the store and they were looking at Marcey. Franklin got her behind the counter then into the corridor in the back.

"For God's sake," he said again. "You're making a scene. There are customers out there."

"I'm just worried," Marcey said. "I'm worried about Janey. I'm worried about you. You tell me it's all the fault of the secular humanists, but it doesn't matter if it is, does it? I mean, Janey is in just as much trouble, and you say you're the chief suspect in a mugging, or whatever that was, you say they think you—"

"Henry Wackford thinks I did," Franklin said. He pushed Marcey down on the closed toilet seat and got the door shut and locked behind him. "Sensible people don't think that. How much of that stuff did you take, for God's sake? You're a mess."

"I don't know what you're talking about," Marcey said. "I'm just worried. And Miss Marbledale called to say Janey was in detention, and I tried to call you, but you didn't answer. All I ever got was people from the store and they kept saying you couldn't come to the phone, so I came down here, I had to. You have to see that."

"Catherine Marbledale is a secular humanist, too," Franklin said. "I don't care what it is she pretends to be. Where did you get them? I thought I had them all locked up."

"I don't know what you're talking about," Marcey said again, and this time she sounded mulish. That was a very bad sign. That was the worst sign there was. "I had a good reason to talk to you. I did. You shouldn't tell the people here not to put me through to you. I'm your wife. You're supposed to talk to your wife."

"I didn't tell them not to put you through to me. I was probably busy."

"You're just lying," Marcey said, and now her voice had gone from velvet to acid. It never took more than a moment. "You lie to me all the time, Franklin. You shouldn't do that, and you know it. I had a right to talk to you. I had a real problem. You never want to deal with the real problems. You just want to yell and scream about secular humanists, and in the meantime that poisonous girl is turning your daughter into a—into a something. I don't know what. But you won't listen."

"You have to go home," Franklin said, trying to be calm. He was not calm. Marcey could panic him, sometimes. She always panicked him when she got like this.

"I'm not going to go *home*," Marcey said, her voice rising up into the stratosphere. "I'm not going to go home and hide away like I'm ashamed of something. I'm not ashamed of anything. I'm not your crazy old aunt you can hide away in the attic. I'm your wife. And I want something done. I want something done about Barbie McGuffie and I want something done about Janey and I want something done now. I'm not going to have Janey suspended from school just because you won't listen to me."

"Marcey," Franklin said.

"If you don't do something, I'll scream," Marcey said.

And then she did. Franklin had known, from the moment he had realized she was in the store, that it was going to come to this. And she knew exactly what effect it would have, too. He could see it in her eyes. They weren't teary anymore. They were hard and bright with malice. They sparkled.

"Marcey," he said again.

She just put back her head and let it rip, a long, high-pitched wail that could be heard all the way out to Main Street, the sound of an animal in pain and dying, a sound that could break eardrums.

It only took a second before people were pounding on the bathroom door.

2

Henry Wackford was with a client when he heard the screaming start, and he knew what it was as soon as it pierced the glass of his closed front window. Edna Milton knew what it was, too, and Henry was willing to bet pretty much anything that everybody else on Main Street knew, too. After all, Main Street was a small street, Snow Hill was a small town, and Marcey Hale was very, very loud. She was loud even when she was screaming through the walls of her builder's colonial out on the Cashman Road, and her neighbors there were a lot farther apart than Franklin's neighbors were here.

When Henry stopped looking at the window and turned around to look at Edna, she had her head tilted and a smile on her face. Edna Milton was one of Henry's closest allies in what he thought of as the War Against Idiocy, but told everybody else, in public, was the War Against Mediocrity. That had always seemed to him to be the best way to put it when he was running for school board. There wasn't a parent alive who wanted his child to grow up to be a mediocrity. At least, there wasn't one alive who would admit it out loud. Henry had the feeling that there were definitely people in Snow Hill who would be satisfied with nothing else but mediocrity in their children. Anything better than that would mean that their children were getting to be "stuck up."

Edna was clucking. She was a short, compact middle-aged woman who didn't like to fuss with herself, as she put it. She wore very little makeup, she had let her hair go grey long ago, and she cut it off short so that it wouldn't be much of a bother. Even so, she'd been married twice, and she could have been married again if she'd wanted to be. That was partly force of personality, and partly the fact that she had a very good head for business.

The paperwork for Edna's latest real estate deal lay sprawled across Henry's desk. Henry did all Edna's legal work up here; she had some expensive lawyers in Harrisburg for the deals she did there. Sometimes Henry wondered why she bothered to stay in Snow Hill. She couldn't lack the money to leave.

"Honestly," she said. "It takes the kind of mind that populates this town to think that that man would be better at managing anything than you. He can't even manage his own wife. He can't even cope with her."

"I hear rumors that she drinks," Henry said carefully. "But I've never seen her drink."

"It's not drinking," Edna said. "It's Oxycontin and probably half a dozen other prescription medications. That's why she stopped going to Dr. Dumont here in town. He wouldn't go on writing prescriptions for her. She got some guy up in Harrisburg, and as far as I can tell he just gives her what she wants. If I were Franklin, I'd shove her straight into rehab."

"I don't think it's that easy to shove somebody into rehab if they don't want to go," Henry said.

"Well, it should be," Edna said. "Honestly. There are some people who just can't take care of themselves, and it's time we recognized it. We're strangling in a mythology of equality, the wrong kind of equality. We don't give a damn what kind of money people have, and what is that? It's like letting them have loaded weapons at their disposal when they can't think their way out of paper bags. And we let them vote for school boards, which is worse."

Henry stiffened. "I thought I did a pretty good job on the school board."

"You did," Edna said. "But it wasn't going to last, was it? Of course it wasn't. The board was going to go straight on over to the yahoos sooner rather than later—"

"I was chairman of that school board for over ten years."

"Yes, and then what happened? Franklin Hale happened, that's what," Edna said. "There couldn't have been anybody in town who didn't know what he was up to even if he didn't say it right out loud.

Oh, except maybe the people from the development, of course. They don't know him. But the rest of us did, and if most of the rest of us hadn't voted for him, he wouldn't be where he is. And what do we get? We get what he wanted us to get all along. People living alongside the dinosaurs and God creating the world in six days."

Henry cleared his throat. Edna was one of those people. Once she got going, it was hard to get a word in. "I don't think they're actually asking for God creating the world in six days," he said. "This is a new kind of Creationism. They call it Intelligent Design."

"I know what they call it," Edna said. "But I know Franklin Hale, and so do you. He thinks the world was created in six days and he thinks it's less than ten thousand years old and the only reason he isn't saying so is that he wouldn't get help from that fancy think tank to go to court with if he did. He a small-town, small-minded idiot loon. You've got to wonder what goes on in that church of his, except you don't have to wonder, do you? We all know. So why do we think it makes sense to let people like that be on a school board? Or people who agree with him run for school boards? Education should not be amateur night. It should be left to the people who know something about it."

"Teachers," Henry said solemnly.

"Oh, teachers," Edna said. "Half the teachers are just as bad as Franklin is. It should be left to people with good doctorates, that's what. We should have a national curriculum, that all schools have to follow, and home schools, too. All schools. Even the private ones. That's what they do in Europe. That's why they're so much better educated over there."

"*Pierce v. Society of Sisters,* 1925," Henry said.

Edna waved it away. "We make a fetish of the Constitution. We do. We act like it's scripture. It's not. That sort of thing was all right when the world was a different place, before we knew anything about science, but it's a disaster now. You can't leave that sort of thing in place. Think of the children. Think of the future. And when we do have democracy, which we do here, not only do we not get a decent education for our children, we don't even get all that competence Franklin was blithering about. I ran into Catherine Marbledale this morning. She's climbing the walls. She's had another call from the teachers' union."

"Has she," Henry said. He was feeling a little distracted. It wasn't that he didn't appreciate Edna. He did. In a town like this you had to really treasure the people who understood what was what and were willing to stand by you. Henry thought it was too bad that all Edna's children were grown, so she was unable to join the lawsuit. He could have used her in the courtroom.

"Henry," Edna said. "You ought to at least listen when I talk to you. Catherine's had a call from the teachers' union, and they're hopping mad. The schedule on the new contracts was supposed to be out weeks ago—and has Franklin done a single thing about it? No, he hasn't. Of course he hasn't. He's a piss-poor businessman, if you ask me. The only reason that shop of his stays in business is that too many of the new people don't know a lug nut from a cherry tree. And it's not only the teachers' contracts. It's that damned school building, too. He was going to fix that up and get the building back on schedule, you remember that? Well, there it sits, and not a brick has been moved for six months. Honestly, what do people think they're doing when they vote for a man like that? I always said I thought it would make sense to give intelligence tests to people before we let them vote, but whenever I say that you all look at me like I've gone over to Hitler."

"Catherine can handle the teachers' union," Henry said. "And she's lucky enough not to have anything to do with the building. We'll muddle through until we get them out of here."

"Are you sure we're going to get them out of here?" Edna said.

"Every other town that's gone through this has done it," Henry said. "Hell, the entire state of Kansas did it. People don't actually want Creationism in the schools, no matter what they say. When they know that that's what's on offer, they vote for somebody else. I think we have to live with this until the spring, and then there will be another vote and we'll take back over. Don't you want to do something about this stuff you brought me? You look to me as if you're buying huge piles of rocks nobody is going to be able to move."

"I'll move them," Edna said. "Don't you mind about it. What about that man Gary Albright brought in? Have you met him?"

Henry blinked. "He got here about a minute and a half after you did. I saw him get out of Gary's truck when you were using the ladies'."

Edna nodded. "Now, there's something I approve of. I looked him up on the Internet, and I asked some people I know in Harrisburg. He's not just a big noise, he's very good. And he's not about money. I don't know if that's a character trait or a matter of circumstances. He's about to marry a ton of it. Still, you've got to wonder what Gary Albright is up to. You have to wonder what any of those people are up to. I don't trust anybody who says he gets down on his knees and talks to an imaginary friend every night. It's bad enough if he's lying, but it's worse if he's telling the truth. Marcey's still screaming. Can you hear it?"

Henry could hear it. He was sure everybody could hear it. Down the street from the shop the noise ended up being something in the background after a while, but you never lost the understanding that it was there. If you were actually in the building where it was happening, though, that was something else. Then it was like a form of torture. Marcey was not only loud, she was extremely high pitched and could hold a note damned near forever.

"Listen," Edna leaned over Henry's desk. Her eyes were lit up. They glittered. "I heard something. And not only from one place, and it wasn't just idle gossip. I heard the federal judge they've got coming down here for the trial is getting death threats. Lots of them. I heard the FBI has been called in. They think there's going to be an assassination attempt."

"Really," Henry said.

Edna sat back in her chair. She was smiling. "Well," she said, "what can you expect? Religion is a form of insanity, isn't it? And you never do know what crazy people will do."

Miss Marbledale had heard the rumors about the death threats to the judge for the same reason everybody else had: because Edna Milton had been spreading them. She was not particularly upset about them, and she didn't expect she would ever have to be, because she was fairly sure that they were nothing but Edna getting some attention again, just like the time Edna claimed that the Bush administration was spying on her peace group. Catherine Marbledale had almost as little use for Edna Milton and her peace group as she had for Franklin Hale and anything he was involved in. It was all part and parcel of the same thing. It was all another manifestation of a descent into irrationality. Miss Marbledale had pinned it the first time she realized that conspiracy theories were no longer the exclusive province of village cranks and village drunks. Now half her students thought that the Republicans had blown up the Twin Towers themselves, or that the Democrats were in secret negotiations to get the UN to invade Washington and suspend the Constitution in favor of European law. It all depended on who their parents were. None of their parents made any sense at all.

It wasn't the rumors about the judge that made Miss Marbledale decide she had to get out of the building for lunch. It wasn't even her run-ins with Alice McGuffie and Judy Cornish. Those women might be on opposite sides of the political divide, but they had identical tendencies to shriek. And their children, Miss Marbledale thought, were identically warped by their enthusiasms. Granted, she'd rather have a student like Mallory Cornish than one like Barbie McGuffie any day of the week. Mallory was going to get stellar SATs and go off to a name college one of these days, and she would always know how to respond to Shakespeare and have her history homework outlined in the meantime. Still, Mallory was in her own way just as much of a bully as Barbie, and in this time and place that was going to cause a lot of trouble. People like Judy Cornish didn't understand what the issues were. They thought they did, but they didn't. Catherine Marbledale was ready to bet lots of money that Judy Cornish had been a popular girl in a high school where popular girls had damned well better have the grades to go off to some-place first rate, or they wouldn't be popular at all.

Catherine was just thinking of calling her sister, Margaret, for moral support when one of the secretaries in the outer office buzzed her, and she found herself face to face with little Mrs. Morton. Try as she might, she couldn't remember the woman's first name. What did that say about the state of her memory? The Mortons were town, not development. Catherine had had *Ted* Morton in class when she was still teaching. For all she knew, she'd had this woman too, although she couldn't remember it. It was hard to tell. It was hard to bring her into focus. She was a mousy thing, and she was in tears.

"I'm very sorry, I really am, about the way Elaine behaved," Mrs. Morton said, sniffling, "and I do know there's no excuse. But I can't help but thinking, well—you know. I mean, it isn't really her fault, is it? I mean, it's her fault that she made fun of those other girls, yes, I understand that, and it was wrong to write things on them, you can't trust Barbie McGuffie, really, she's too forward. But still."

The day looked cold and hard outside the office window, and Catherine was tired. "But still what?" she asked. "I should think it's a fairly simple issue."

"But it isn't, is it?" Mrs. Morton said. "I mean, I heard you speak at the school board, you know, and I know how you feel about this, but it's a controversial issue, isn't it? It's controversial. People say all kinds of things about it. You don't know who to believe."

"People say all kinds of things about bullying?"

"No, no," Mrs. Morton said. "About evolution. They say all sorts of things about that. It's a matter of opinion, isn't it? And everybody has the right to their opinion."

"Mrs. Morton," Catherine said, dredging up the energy from she didn't know where, "evolution is not a matter of opinion. Evolution is a fact."

"Well, I know you think so," Mrs. Morton said, "but that's just your opinion, isn't it? Other people don't agree with it. And every-body has the right to express his opinion. That's free speech, isn't it?"

"It has nothing to do with free speech. Would you want our science classes to teach that the earth is flat, or that water flows up?"

"Well, no, of course not," Mrs. Morton said, "but that's the thing, you see. That's the difference. Those are things everybody knows. There's nothing controversial about those. But this is something else. It's not like water flowing up."

"It's *exactly* like water flowing up," Catherine said.

"If it was, there wouldn't be so much disagreement about it," Mrs. Morton said.

She really was a mousy thing, Catherine thought, staring at the top of her head. Her hair frizzed. It was some light color, or maybe an absence of color. And she looked mulish, the way children do when they refuse to be persuaded that they are not going to get their own way.

"I think it's wrong to tell people they can't express their opinions," Mrs. Morton said. "I do. It's un-American. It's against free speech. Everybody should be able to express their opinion. And everybody should have their opinion heard. That's all that Franklin Hale and the school board want, and I don't think it's right that you won't let them have it. I think that's what causes these—these situations."

"You think your daughter is writing nasty words on the backs of other students because she can't get her opinion heard on evolution? What's stopping her? She can express her opinion about anything she wants."

"But then you say it's wrong," Mrs. Morton said triumphantly. "You say she's wrong and those other children are right, and how is that supposed to make her feel? You take sides with those other children and then they make fun of her, they make fun of all of us. Then they call her stupid and things happen. I don't see why you should be surprised. I don't see why my Elaine should be the only one punished. You should punish those other children for calling her stupid. And you should let other opinions be heard and not, you know, make them seem like they're wrong, because it's all a matter of opinion."

Catherine Marbledale's head hurt. She didn't want to call Margaret anymore. She'd only yell at her if she did, and Margaret had done nothing to deserve that. She stood up from behind her desk and tried to make it clear that this interview was over.

"It's an in-school detention," she said firmly, "and I really am not preventing Elaine from expressing her opinions, only from physically attacking other students."

Mrs. Morton had stood up, too. She looked even more mulish. "It's a matter of opinion," she said. "You're not God. You don't know everything. Everybody has a right to their opinion, and nobody has a right to tell them their opinion is wrong."

The long-range implications of this sort of policy were staggering. Catherine thought about pointing them out to Mrs. Morton, but she had the horrible realization that even if she tried, it just wouldn't work. Mrs. Morton wasn't interested in listening to reason; she wasn't interested in reason at all. Catherine wondered which of the various conspiracy theories Mrs. Morton adhered to. It would have something to do with UN troops massing in Canada, or liberals plotting to fix the next election, take over the White House, and declare martial law. Catherine was sure of it.

They were both on their feet. It was only a matter of getting the woman out of her office but the exact protocol for this was eluding her. She headed for the door; Mrs. Morton followed her, still talking. She was still talking about how everybody had the right to his opinion, except she wouldn't say "his," or even "his or hers," she would say *their*, because for the Mrs. Mortons of the world grammar was a matter of opinion, too. Catherine got the office door open and stood next to it, and Mrs. Morton went scurrying out.

"It isn't fair," she was saying, "it's all a matter of opinion."

When the door was shut and Catherine was alone again, she suddenly realized she couldn't stay that way. She couldn't just sit here and stare at the four walls of her office. She couldn't eat the salad and the thermos of soup she'd brought with her from home this morning. Sometimes she thought she was going to go crazy.

Her coat was hanging on a coat tree in a corner near the door. She'd bought it the last time she and Margaret had spent a long weekend in Philadelphia. It was a good coat, with some percentage of cashmere—a city coat—not a parka or snow jacket, which was what most people wore in Snow Hill. Catherine got it down and put it on. Then she went into the outer office. Everything was quiet in the outer office. The girls were typing at their stations. No students were at the counter, looking for help or excuses. Mrs. Morton was gone.

"I'm going to run home," Catherine said. "I think I can be away for an hour without everything getting completely messed up, but if there's an emergency I'll have my cell phone on."

"Go eat something decent," one of the women said. "I saw that salad. It looks dead."

It probably did look dead, Catherine thought. She didn't notice what she ate, at least during the school terms. When she and Margaret traveled, they went to good restaurants, and she noticed then. Now she just nodded at the women and went on through to the big front foyer of the school. She'd have to be fast, because she had a meeting with the rep from the teachers' union at one thirty. For God's sake, the teachers' union. She wasn't supposed to be negotiating with the teachers' union. She wasn't supposed to be talking to the contractors for the new school. She wasn't supposed to be having meetings with the suppliers' salespeople, either. Nothing was getting done. Not a thing. That's what happened when you got somebody on the board like Franklin Hale, who didn't care that the board's major purpose wasn't to set school curricular policy but to run the goddamn district.

I must not swear, Catherine told herself as she reached her car. She didn't actually approve of swearing, because it was the kind of thing you did if your vocabulary was inadequate to the situation—and Catherine's vocabulary was usually adequate to any situation. Her car was a shiny silver Prius she had waited six months to get her hands on. She unlocked it and got in behind the wheel. She shut the door against the cold and started up.

Really, she thought. If she didn't know what kind of a disaster would happen here if she ever left, she'd quit right this minute and let Franklin Hale take care of the blowback.

SIX

1

Gregor Demarkian worked, most of the time, as a consultant to police departments. Police departments, being government entities, didn't like to spend money when they didn't have to, mostly because they could be sure there would be editorials in the papers about how many of the taxpayers' dollars they were wasting even if they did have to. But because of this, and because he was expensive to hire, Gregor was used to having the media's attention on the case he was working on. After all, it took something special to justify calling him in; and if he got involved otherwise, it was usually because he'd volunteered. What he was supposed to do about a situation like the present one, where the press was coming out of everybody's ears, but why none of the reporters seemed the least bit interested in an attempted murder, he didn't know.

Main Street had gotten far less deserted in the few minutes Gregor had spent on it. By the time he and Gary Albright went into the police station, there were several people from the town popping out onto the sidewalks to see what there were doing, and men and women burdened by camera and sound equipment were everywhere. Gregor took a quick look at them and then let Gary lead him into the building. It was the kind of place that might have served as a sheriff's office in Mayberry, except that it was a separate building instead of part of the courthouse. Gregor found himself wondering where the courthouse was. It had to be close, but he didn't think he'd seen it right on Main.

Most of the first floor of the police station was open. There was a counter for the public to stand at when they wanted something. Gregor guessed that most of the people here had known Gary Albright since childhood, which meant they weren't likely to be all that patient about standing at a counter to talk to him, or to his officers, either, who were likely to have been in town forever, too. There were three desks on the other side of the counter, only one of which was occupied. That one was serving as a computer station to a woman with wispy hair and too many metal things holding it back. She looked up when Gregor and Gary came in and Gary nodded to her.

"Tina," he said. "Mr. Demarkian. This is Tina Clay."

Tina Clay waved. She was the kind of woman who would wave indoors. The longer he looked at her, the longer Gregor was sure she was almost excruciatingly self-conscious.

"Tom and Eddie out?" Gary asked her.

Tina nodded and then tried a smile. It didn't quite come off.

"Tom and Eddie are our officers," Gary said, heading toward the back where there were two more doors leading, Gregor supposed, to regular offices. "We don't usually need more than that in Snow Hill. We wouldn't need that if it wasn't for the drugs. People don't spend a lot of time killing each other here."

"There are robberies," Tina said helpfully. "Breaking and entering, you know."

"Mostly, there are domestics," Gary said. "I can't say I'm all that fond of the new approach to policing domestics. I don't have anything against arresting a guy even if the wife doesn't want to press charges. That's sensible enough. It's all this treatment that gets me."

"Gary isn't very fond of treatment," Tina said. The delivery was completely deadpan. Gregor had no idea if she had meant to be funny or not.

"I'd be fond of it if I thought it worked," Gary said. "But it doesn't work, does it? These guys go in and they take anger management classes and get signed up for AA, and it's all fine as long as they're locked up because as long as they're locked up there are guys who can make them do all that. Then they get out and what happens? They head straight for the liquor store, if we're lucky. If we're not, they head for some of Nick Frapp's less respectable church members and the next thing you know it they're pounding the Hell out of somebody and there's blood on the walls. There we are again." Gary gave Gregor a look. "Are you one of those guys who are really impressed with treatment?"

"No," Gregor said. "In my opinion, the common house cat knows more about human nature than most of the psychologists I've met."

"Exactly." Gary looked very satisfied. He was also standing next to the door to Gregor's left. The door to Gregor's right contained an office of the usual configuration. There was a desk, covered with work, but not messily covered with work. Gregor got the impression, once again, that Gary Albright was more organized than any human being had a right to be.

Gary opened the other door and stepped back. "We fixed this up as an office for you," he said. "It's not completely adequate. It isn't supposed to be an office."

"It's supposed to be a closet," Tina said. "But it's got a window, and it's got heat, so we thought it might do."

It also had a desk, a chair, and a computer and had been thoroughly cleaned out. Gregor stepped inside and immediately felt more than a little claustrophobic. It was very small. He would have to keep the door open. There was a thick manila folder on the desk. He picked it up and looked at it.

"That's everything we know so far," Gary Albright said. "We thought we'd put it on a hard copy and you could take it home with you if you wanted to. But it's on the computer, too, and you can send the files to yourself, or Tina can send them. That way you can look at them off site, too. We weren't sure what you would need."

Gregor wasn't sure what he needed either. "I take it Miss Hadley is still alive?"

"Alive and in a coma," Tina said. "The hospital has orders to call here if there's any change. I went up to see her myself the other day. It's very sad. She just lies there. She doesn't have the, I don't know, whatever it is she had when I used to see her."

"General cussedness," Gary suggested.

"Oh, really," Tina said. "She wasn't like that at all, Mr. Demarkian. Not like some of them, if you know what I mean. Some of the Darwinists, I guess. She wasn't like Henry Wackford, or those awful people in that organization he started. Mad at us, mad at themselves, mad at the world. She wasn't like that at all."

Darwinists, Gregor thought. He let it go. "Was she on the old school board, too?" he asked. "The one that mostly got thrown out by this new bunch?"

"No," Gary said. "The old board had been in place for years, but they had a gap—Edna Milton had to resign last year because she had some medical thing—"

"Drying out, if you ask me," Tina said.

"Some medical thing," Gary said firmly. "Anyway, for some reason she had to drop out, so Henry asked Annie-Vic to run in her place. We were all a little surprised that she said yes. She doesn't have a lot of use for Henry."

"She doesn't have a lot of use for anybody who speechifies all the time," Tina said, "which I think is entirely to her credit. Anyway, I have to admit, it was a good thing she got on, even if it did mean we ended up in this lawsuit—"

"Annie-Vic isn't the reason we ended up in this lawsuit," Gary said, "no matter what anybody says. Even if the board had been unanimous, somebody would have sued. That was inevitable."

"Well, the people in the development," Tina started.

Gary shook his head. "It's not the people in the development, not entirely, and you know it. You and I both know people who've been in town forever who are on that side of things. And not just Henry

Wackford and his people. If you ask me, I don't think they should teach anything at all about evolution *or* creation in the public schools. There's no consensus. It doesn't matter which side a school board takes. There's always trouble. I don't understand why they can't leave all that to the colleges and let the school districts alone."

"The way I understand it," Gregor said, "evolution is the foundation of modern biology, so if you don't teach evolution, you don't teach modern biology."

Gary waved this away. "We didn't learn about evolution in high school here when I was a student, and we still learned lots about biology. Cells. Animals. Plants. Personally, I don't see why evolution is necessary to any of that, but even if it is, my point stands. There's no consensus. You can't even discuss the subject without everything going to pieces. We've got people in this town who've known each other since they were in diapers, whose grandparents knew each other since *they* were in diapers, who aren't talking to each other over this thing, and it's not going to get better when the judge hands down the ruling. People have said things they're not going to be able to take back. They've said things they won't forget. And that's a damn shame."

"And it also means that nothing's getting done, again," Tina said. "In case you were wondering, Mr. Demarkian, the town didn't elect the new school board to do something about evolution. They elected it because nothing was getting done. And I do mean nothing. I talked to Catherine Marbledale just this morning and she was tearing her hair out because some guy from the teachers' union was coming in today. The school board is supposed to deal with the teachers' union, but it isn't. It's doing this, so still nothing is getting done, and the union is threatening to take the teachers' out on strike if there isn't some kind of movement on contract terms this week."

"That was what Franklin was supposed to fix," Gary Albright said. "Then it turned out that he is as much a lunatic about Creationism as Henry Wackford is about the holistic curriculum—"

"What?" Gregor said.

"The holistic curriculum," Gary Albright said. "Don't ask me to explain it. I can't. It had something to do with integrating something or the other into something or the other, and bringing in speakers from the outside to 'broaden' people's minds. Student minds. That and sex ed, which is supposed to be abstinence-only here, but Henry didn't like it. It was a mess."

"Did Miss Hadley have positions on any of these issues?" Gregor asked.

"Not really," Gary said.

"Well," Tina said, "she did say once that teaching abstinence-only was like leaving a loaded gun in the middle of a room full of toddlers and telling them not to touch it."

"It wasn't a major issue," Gary said. "But at least she got down to work on the practical stuff, and now it seems as if nobody is going to do that until the trial is over. It's good of Miss Marbledale to meet with the union rep, but she can't actually do anything. It's the board that has to approve contract terms. We're just going to sit and burn money while a bunch of people fly in from New York and call us all a bunch of hick-town idiots."

"Unless somebody shoots the judge," Tina said. "There's rumors everywhere that there's been a death threat on the judge, and the judge called in the FBI to protect him. Wouldn't that be something? All we'd have to do is kill a judge over this thing, and this town will go down in history as no better than—well, no better than anything."

"Maybe I'll sit down and read through the file for a while," Gregor said. "When I've done that, I may know where I need to start."

"Go right ahead," Gary said. "Tina will get you anything you need. There's a diner up the street if you want something to eat. You can take stuff out and eat it here if you don't want to hassle the place at lunchtime."

It was a long time before lunch, Gregor was pretty sure. He just shook his head and took himself around the desk to the chair. It really was a very small room.

But it wouldn't do him any good not to get started.

2

The first thing Gregor did was open the file the department had put together for him, and as soon as he did so he could see it was going to take some weeding out. There were all kinds of things in it. Some of those things were part of standard operating procedure. There were reports from the hospital and from two local doctors. There was a forensics summary that seemed to include not only the scene itself but most of Miss Hadley's house. There were background notes on a good two dozen people. Gregor hadn't heard of most of them, and he wasn't sure what he was supposed to make of them. The longest set of notes concerned the pastor of the big church at the end of Main Street, Nicodemus Frapp. Nicodemus, Gregor thought. That must have been some way to go through high school.

In the end, he put the file away on the other side of the desk and tried to think his way through what he'd heard. He did have a telephone. Somebody had plugged one in to a jack somewhere out in the big room. Gregor could see the thin clear cord snaking away from his phone and through his door. He got out his cell phone anyway, because ever since he'd had it he'd developed complete amnesia about phone numbers. There had been a time when he'd been able to remember a dozen or more. Now, he didn't even know Bennis's number, and he probably called Bennis two or three times a day.

He wasn't going to call Bennis now. He really was not up for another round of wedding preparations. He thought that if the wedding preparations went on much longer, they'd rival the plans for celebrating the year 2000. Hell, they'd rival the conspiracy theories about a worldwide computer meltdown.

He punched around on his keypad for a while—it bothered him how quickly he'd gotten used to that; he'd never used his thumb for so much before Bennis had given him this phone, and now he could practically touch-type phone functions. He got to the address book and scrolled through it a little, trying to make up his mind whether it made more sense to stay local or go straight to Washington. He decided that he'd hated it when people had gone over his head to Washington when he'd been a field agent. Besides, how could the citizens of the United States of America expect the Bureau to operate efficiently with its own field offices if they treated the field offices like—

Gregor didn't know like what. Lackeys? Nobody used the word "lackeys" any more. He found his number and pressed the little green circle. You didn't have to dial anything anymore. The phone dialed for you.

This was not the time to indulge in morbid nostalgia for a technology-free universe. The phone had been picked up on the other end, and a woman's voice was saying, "Federal Bureau of Investigation, Harrisburg Office. Office of the Director."

"Yes," Gregor said. "Hello. My name is Gregor Demarkian. I was wondering if I could talk to Kevin O'Connor for a moment."

"I'll see if Mr. O'Connor is available," the woman said. "Could I ask what you're calling in regards to?"

Well, there was something that hadn't changed since Gregor's retirement. He'd sometimes thought that the Bureau had to hire these women and then train them to be as ungrammatical as they got on the phone.

"I was Mr. O'Connor's field training officer back in—well, it was a long time ago."

There was a pause on the other end of the line. "If you could spell your name," the woman said.

Gregor didn't blame her for being wary. He spelled his name and waited. The FBI probably got more crank calls than any other agency in the United States government, or in the state governments, either. When Gregor was with the Behavioral Sciences Unit, they got four or five people a month who called in to confess to serial murders they couldn't have been anywhere near, and they were sane next to the people who called to say they thought the Bureau had implanted microchips in their brains.

There was a click on the other end of the line. Kevin's voice came bouncing down the wire, sounding happy. "Gregor! What are you doing? I read about you in the papers all the time! It gives me hope, you know what I mean? It's possible to do this job for twenty years without becoming a basket case."

Gregor liked Kevin O'Connor. He just wished the man wasn't so enthusiastic about everything.

"You got a promotion," he said. "I thought you said you'd never take a desk job."

"Yeah, well. Five years sitting on my ass in freezing weather staking out kidnap suspects and I got tired of it. But what about you? Are you just in town or do you have something I need? It's really incredible to hear from you."

Gregor was sure Kevin found it incredible to hear from him. Kevin found it incredible to hear from anybody.

"At the moment," Gregor said, "I'm sitting in the police department of a place called Snow Hill, Pennsylvania."

"Oh, the monkey trial place," Kevin said. "Yeah. We've got a couple of people out there, just as a precaution, you know. What are you doing out there? Has somebody been killed?"

"Not yet," Gregor said. "Somebody's been attacked. A woman named Ann-Victoria Hadley."

"Annie-Vic! Yeah, I did hear about that. Wasn't that some kind of mugging. It's a damned shame, really, she's an incredible old bat. Did you know she was on Nixon's enemies list?"

"Was she? For what?"

"Oh, I don't remember. She ran some organization for a while, I think, some anti–Vietnam War organization. Like I said, she's an incredible old bat. Isn't it kind of overkill bringing you in on a mugging?"

"The chief of police here seems to think it may be more than a mugging. He's of the opinion that somebody tried to kill her because she was the only member of the school board that wouldn't sign on to the new policy of Intelligent Design."

There was a long pause. "That's not too likely, is it?" Kevin said. "I mean, there are certainly lots of nut cases out there. You can't deny that. But I don't remember there ever being any violence over teaching evolution. Just a lot of, you know, hot air and screaming."

"That's what I thought," Gregor said. "The chief of police seems to think otherwise, though, and he's the friend of a friend. So here I am. I take it that you've got nothing on the order of militia activity or that kind of thing going on around this."

"The militias are pretty much over," Kevin said. "Not that they ever amounted to much, anyway. What's that line from the *Blues Brothers* movie? A bunch of sad, sorry sons of bitches who're just jerking off, or something like that."

"And no chatter saying that there's somebody out there looking to pick off the opposition, piece by piece?"

"Gregor, please. Do you know what these things are like? They're a bunch of middle-class, middle-aged people striking attitudes. On both sides, if you ask me. They're not looking for bloodshed. They're looking for time on the evening news. I think the only people who care about the science is the scientists they bring in. Everybody else is starring in their own movie."

"I've just been told that there's been a death threat against the judge who's supposed to sit on this case."

"A death threat on Hamilton Folger?" Kevin said. "No. If there had been, I'd have heard about it."

"Everybody here has heard about it."

"No, Gregor. Everybody there has heard somebody say they heard about it. If there had been a real death threat, if somebody had actually threatened Folger—I mean, for God's sake, Gregor, you remember Hamilton Folger. He's got a stick so far up his ass it comes up out of his head and he uses it for a flagpole. He was appointed by W. He takes himself more seriously than God."

Gregor thought about it. He did remember Hamilton Folger. "Prosecutor in Chicago?" he said finally. "That weird case of the woman who'd—I don't remember—something about she got caught with co-caine—"

"She got caught with a lot of cocaine," Kevin said, "but she'd just lost both her daughters in some kind of freak accident. So she went down to the nearest slum neighborhood she could find and bought enough of the stuff to kill herself with and everybody knew that was what she was trying to do, but he went after her for dealing, anyway. I mean, seriously, Gregor, the man makes conservatives look like bleeding hearts. If he'd had a death threat, I'd know about it, the national office would know about it, CBS News would know about it, and so would you."

"All right," Gregor said. "But the rumors are here, and rumors like that are dangerous. You say you have some agents in place?"

"Molly Trask and Evan Zwicker, yeah. They're both about twelve years old. I'll give them a call and ask them to accommodate you if you want. They're competent enough."

"That would be excellent," Gregor said. "I'm just trying to be cautious here. You're sure you've never heard of one of these trials where there's been any violence?"

"Absolutely sure," Kevin said. "The violence tends to be limited to what the school kids do to each other, and they're nasty. Nasty, but not Columbine. They call each other names. They bully each other. Some kid goes home in tears because somebody told her on the playground that she's going to burn in Hell. That sort of thing. I've got the numbers. You have a pen to write these down?"

Gregor had a pen. He took the numbers down as Kevin reeled them off—both were cell phone numbers. He put his pen down on the desk and stretched a little.

"I wish I understood these things," he said. "Everybody seems to get angry for no reason. Or no reason that makes sense to me."

"That's the trouble with the world, Gregor. Everybody *is* angry with no reason, or at least they're not angry for the reasons they say they are. Never mind. You're getting married in a few weeks, aren't you? Congratulations!"

3

In the world Gregor came from, protocol mattered almost more than anything. Who did what when, who had jurisdiction over which or whom was the first question any sane man asked about any action he was about to take. In the universe of Snow Hill law enforcement, there seemed to be no protocol, and not many personnel, either. He left his closet office for the larger room and looked around. Only the woman named Tina was there. There was no sign of any other person. Even Gary Albright had disappeared.

"I'm going to take a walk," Gregor said.

Tina looked up at him and blinked. "All right," she said. "Diner's down the block to your right, if you're looking for coffee."

Gregor made a noncommittal noise, then went out through the front door to Main Street. There were more people there now. The mobile news vans had visible staff. People were walking along the street. Gregor stopped and listened for a while, but that odd high-pitched wail he'd heard for a few moments earlier had ceased. He wondered what it was. He'd thought a car was about to explode.

He looked to his right, in the direction of the diner. People were going in and out of it, quite a few of them carrying Styrofoam cups of what he presumed to be coffee. He looked to his left. There at the end of the street was that big, white modern church and the little cluster of buildings behind it. Now that he had a chance to study it, he didn't think the building was modern by nature. It had been remodeled, somehow. The skeleton of it was venerable, but all the ornamentation was new.

He turned in that direction and walked slowly down past the storefronts. He had no idea what he was expecting to see. The stores and other buildings were what you would expect in a small town like this. A lot of them were churches of one kind or the other, the very biggest was the Baptist one, but it seemed to Gregor to be much less impressive than Nick Frapp's semi-modern. There was a tire store—could something be called Hale 'n' Hardy?—and a place for greeting cards and gifts. That one had a Hallmark sign, which meant somebody must have gotten lucky. The nearest mall must not be so near after all. There was a feed store, proof that people around here raised cattle or horses. There was a "package store," which was how liquor stores liked to disguise themselves when they had opened up in nice neighborhoods.

He got to the big semi-modern church and stopped. There was a lot of activity here, if you looked for it, although not in the church itself. The buildings behind the church seemed to house some kind of school. There were a couple of dozen children shivering on a playground, not quite motivated by the adult who was trying to spur them into action. Gregor smiled. He remembered that. Why was it so many adults were so convinced that fresh air was good for children, no matter what the temperature of the air.

He heard somebody cough low in the throat and looked up to see that tallest, thinnest man he had ever encountered standing just outside the church's front doors. He was more than tall and thin, though, this man. He was straight out of central casting. He could have starred in a remake of *Elmer Gantry* tomorrow, and been more convincing than Burt Lancaster ever was.

The tall, thin man had his hands in the pockets of the pants to a very good, but not spectacular, wool suit. He held out his hand.

"It's Gregor Demarkian," he said. "I've seen you on television. I'm Nick Frapp."

It wasn't just the look. It was the voice. Okies had that kind of voice. Hillbillies had that kind of voice. Gregor reached out and took the man's hand.

"How do you do," he said.

"You ought to come inside," Nick Frapp said. "It's freezing out here, and there's going to be another one of those reporters any minute."

"Another one?"

"They hear about us and all they want to talk about is snakes," Nick Frapp said.

Gregor followed him through the open door of the church. It was not particularly unusual for a church: it had a big wide open vestibule with racks for pamphlets and a big box with a sign that designated it a collection for the poor. Nick Frapp saw him look at the sign and shrugged.

"We get maybe a couple of dollars every week in that," he said. "It's not a bad idea. I don't find it as useful as organizing something concrete, though."

"Do you organize a lot that's concrete?"

"Sure," Nick said. "In a way, this whole place is an organization of something concrete. We've got half a dozen outreach programs running. We go up to the prison in Allentown. We have a halfway house for those of our people who get out on parole, or anybody else who wants to use it. We've got a mothers and children drive, which is important, because the social workers won't go up into the hills anymore. And of course, we've got the school."

They had been moving as they spoke, and now they were in a long hall lined with photographs of people who were posing too self-consciously to look natural. Gregor tried to catch the nature of those poses but couldn't. Nick was up ahead, holding a door for him.

"Susie Cleland is around here somewhere, but I don't know where she's got to," he said.

"Susie Cleland?"

"Our volunteer secretary for today," Nick said. "We can't really afford to hire too much in the way of full-time staff, and I'd rather spend money hiring teachers for the school than getting myself a fancy church secretary, so some of the women volunteer. They're very good. Can I get you a cup of coffee? We've got coffee all over the place. Susie really likes to make coffee."

"Thanks," Gregor said. "I'd like that."

He was standing in Nick Frapp's office now, and the first thing that hit him was the books. There were literally hundreds of books. Every single available space on all four walls of the room was a bookshelf. Nick Frapp didn't restrict himself to whatever the Christian presses were publishing, either. He had Aristotle and Kant. He even had Spinoza. Gregor looked from shelf to shelf. Thomas Aquinas. Hobbes and Lock. John Stuart Mill. Saint Irenaeus.

"I know somebody else who reads like this," Gregor said. "I don't suppose you sneak Judith Krantz novels on the side."

"True crime." Nick was coming back with coffee. He handed Gregor a cup and gestured across the room. "Cream and sugar and that over there," he said.

"But you've obviously read these," Gregor said. "Or somebody has. They're not here for show. Where did you go to college?"

"Oral Roberts University."

"Are they this good with the Western Canon? I didn't think anybody was this good with the Western Canon anymore, except that place in Maryland, you know, that does the great books."

"They're all right," Nick said. "I was reading this stuff before I went there, though. And I still read it. I'm looking for something I know I'll find, eventually, except probably not until after I'm dead."

"What?"

"The face of God," Nick said. "That's what all these people were looking for, really, even the ones who didn't think they believed in God. It's what we're all looking for. Man cannot rest until he rests in Him."

"If you're quoting, it's going to be wasted on me," Gregor said. "Maybe what I'm trying to say is that I don't understand it. What are you doing here? If you do this sort of thing, if this is the way you think, you could have gone off to graduate school and ended up at a university. Instead of—"

"Instead of ending up in a backwater small town where most of my neighbors can't pronounce Liebniz, never mind read him?"

"Something like that."

Nick sat down behind his desk. It was a big desk, which was good, because he needed big furniture to accommodate him.

"How come you came to me first?" he asked. "Did Gary Albright point me out as a prime suspect?"

"No, not at all. He did say a few things. None of which I understood."

"Gary and I went to high school together," Nick said. "Hell, we went all through school together. And I've got to admit it up front that Gary's a remarkable man. He had a record of courage in the Marine Corps. And there was that thing with the leg. Not many men could do what he did, and even fewer would do it to save a dog."

"But," Gregor said.

"But," Nick agreed. "In the end, Gary can't help being who and what he is. He was the football hero. I was the trash. We were all trash to the people in town, all of us who came from up in the hills. We'd come down here to town for school and we might as well not have bothered, because the teachers all assumed we were mentally retarded and they treated us that way. You don't know how many of the boys I grew up with ended up in prison before they were twenty. Real prison, not juvenile hall. And dead of drugs and alcohol. And all the rest of it. Year after year, decade after decade, going back generations. Because there's no point in trying to educate the retards."

"You got educated," Gregor said.

"I did indeed," Nick said. "But that was Miss Marbledale, combined with the fact that I have an unusual amount of drive. When I finished college and came back here, I looked around and I saw that it was still going on. They were still treating the hill kids like retards. So I went back up into the hills and I started preaching, and after a while we managed to buy this place. And after that we managed to start the school. We don't have it all done yet. I mean to have a full high school by the time we're finished. But we do the first eight grades now. And, lo and behold, our hill kids do better on every standardized test than anybody from town."

"It makes me wonder," Gregor said. "I'd think they'd like you for that. Gary Albright seems mad at you."

"Yes, I suppose he is. We didn't join the lawsuit. Although, you know, I'm not sure just what old Franklin Hale wanted us to do. Our kids don't go to the public school. We aren't interested parties. But he wanted us to do something. Stand up in solidarity, or something. I'd say he wanted us to file an amicus brief, but I don't think Franklin knows what that is."

"Why didn't you file an amicus brief?" Gregor asked. "Are you teaching Darwin here on top of everything else?"

"Our eighth graders are asked to read parts of *The Origin of Species* in their world history class. But no, since that's what you're asking, our biology classes don't teach evolution here. Or rather, they do, but they concentrate on the problems with the theory. Yes, and I do know that there aren't any problems the scientists think they can't answer, but then we're not worried about the science when it comes to evolution. Nobody is. Did you know that?"

"Gary Albright said as much," Gregor said. "It's a little beyond me. Evolution is a scientific theory. If you aren't worried about the science, what are you worried about?"

"The culture," Nick said firmly. "There's a lawsuit going on in this town and it has nothing to do with the science. Franklin Hale wouldn't know science if it bit him in the ass and left a note. It's the culture that matters, the culture that says that people who believe in God are ignorant idiots, that there is no grounded morality of any kind, that it doesn't matter what you do with yourself or your life, it's all just—choices, I suppose. You have no idea how I hate that entire ideology of choice."

"Choice as in abortion?"

"I'm not in favor of abortion, either," Nick said, "but it's not abortion I'm talking about here. Not directly. It's the idea that there is no right and wrong, no good and evil, no *solidity*. Everything is just a choice. And our choices are not very important, because men and women are just animals, like cats. You don't get angry at cats for killing mice or getting pregnant by five different fathers. Why should you care if people do the same thing? It's their nature. Christianity says we were all born children of God and we're all called to perfection, even if we can't reach it on this earth. And let me tell you, starting with that as your basic assumption, you'll lead a much better life than you would living it their way."

"But you didn't join the lawsuit," Gregor said.

"No," Nick said. "We don't have anything to say about the public schools. And I'm not sure that this approach somebody has sold Franklin on would really work, anyway. Intelligent Design. Do you know what this suit is actually about?"

"Teaching Intelligent Design instead of evolution?" Gregor hazarded.

"No," Nick said. "If it was, this lawsuit would make a lot more sense. They don't want to teach it instead of evolution. They don't even want to teach it alongside evolution. They want to put a sticker in all the biology books that says that some people don't accept Darwin's theory, but accept Intelligent Design instead, and that if you want to know about Intelligent Design, there will be a book in the library called *Of Pandas and People* that you can take out to read about it. That's it. That's all they want. They just want to *suggest* that people might want to take in another view. And that got Henry Wackford and those people in the development to start a federal case—literally a federal case—to stop it. You've got to wonder about that, don't you think? You've got to wonder why it's not supposed even to be mentioned. And what harm they think is going to come to their children if it is mentioned?"

"I don't know," Gregor said.

"I don't either," Nick said. "But you didn't come here for that, did you? You came because of Miss Hadley. I think I was probably the last person to talk to her before she went on back to her house and got beaten up."

"What did you talk about?"

Nick shrugged. "The usual. What an idiot Franklin Hale is. How much trouble there was going to be if the school board didn't do something about the teachers' contracts and the school construction and the textbook orders. She was all worried about the textbook orders, because if you don't have them in on time, the books don't get here when they need to be in September. She just did her little rant thing and then she went on up Main Street and then up the hill to her house.

Except I shouldn't say that. I didn't really see that. After she left I went back into the church and got some work done."

"She didn't seem unusually upset by anything? Or fearful?"

"Annie-Vic was never fearful," Nick said. "She was just not a fearful woman. But she was always 'upset,' sort of. She always had a head full of steam about something. And that day, like I said, it was all the nuts and bolts stuff the board was supposed to do, but mostly the textbooks."

SEVEN

1

Gary Albright had been very careful to stay away from ordinary policing for most of the long stretch since he had been stuck behind his
desk, but today he was restless, and he couldn't help himself. It was
not that he resented having Gregor Demarkian in Snow Hill, or on the
case, or any of the rest of it. It had been his idea to ask the man in.
He'd had to do something, under the circumstances, and he had a bad
feeling that the circumstances were only going to get worse as time
went on. It wasn't that Gregor Demarkian was probably a "secular humanist," either. Gary wasn't entirely sure he knew what that meant,
anyway. Obviously, a secular humanist was an atheist, but if that was
all it was, why not just say they were "atheists"? He had asked his pastor about it once. Pastors were supposed to know that kind of thing.
What he'd got as a reply was something along the lines of "Well, they
call themselves secular humanists because people don't like atheists."

Gary Albright was pretty good at surfing the Internet, although he
had to surf it at work, since there were so many parental controls on
the machines he had at home that he couldn't find anything useful on
them. He'd toyed with the idea of getting a single machine just for his

own use and installing it in the master bedroom, but there was just no way to lock that door. Sarah went in and out of there all day, and Lily and Michael were used to being able to use the room at will as long as nobody was asleep in it. Gary had a half-formed but very stubborn idea that children were natural-born computer hackers. If there was something you didn't want them to find, and there was any way to get to it, they'd find it.

Gary had ended up staying late one night. He called up Google and typed in "secular humanist." That was when he'd discovered that his pastor was not entirely correct. For one thing, atheists didn't always worry that nobody would like them if they were atheists. Some of them came right out and said what they were. They had organizations, like American Atheists and the Freedom from Religion Foundation, and pins and badges, too. He'd even found a Web site where you could order bumper stickers and other stuff for your car, like Darwin fish decals and a little plaque that said GOD IS JUST PRETEND. So there was that. Then there was something called the Council for Secular Humanism, which was mostly just confusing, and the American Humanist Association, which looked like it belonged back in 1968. The American Humanist Association was the one Henry Wackford belonged to, and the one that was the national to Henry's little local group, so Gary tried to pay attention most closely to that, but he just didn't get it. Mostly, everything on the site seemed to be very, very angry about something, but he was never entirely sure what. He went through four or five articles without being able to figure out the point. It had made him realize, yet again, that he was not very good at figuring out people.

Now he realized that he was halfway out to the hospital, and that he had intended to go all along. Sometimes, he understood that he was not very good at figuring himself out. He pulled in to the large visitor's lot across the asphalt drive from the main doors and turned off his engine. He came out here two or three times a week to double-check on Annie-Vic. He thought he could put this visit down to that and nobody would question it. But that wasn't why he was here. It didn't even begin to explain why he was here. He wished there was somebody or something that could explain the world to him. It was the kind of thing you could ask God after you were dead, but he wanted an answer a lot sooner than that.

The hospital was not in Snow Hill. There had been a hospital in Snow Hill once, back in the Depression, but there had been more people in town then, and not so much in the way of expensive technology too dear for tiny hospitals to afford. This hospital was big and sprawling and very modern, and Gary was glad it was here. It was a symbol, though, of all these other things—of what had brought this lawsuit, Snow Hill, and Gregor Demarkian, too.

He pocketed his keys and got out of the car. It was his own car, not a town police vehicle, so he didn't bother to lock it up. Nobody locked up much of anything around here, but you did have to worry if you had a police cruiser, because some people took it as a challenge. Gary thought a good half of the minor-league misdemeanor crime in Snow Hill was motivated by a desire to create personal legends, to be able to say to sons and grandsons, "Well, there was the time Bobby and I stole that police cruiser and parked it in the Dairy Queen." Somebody had parked a police cruiser in the Dairy Queen once and done a lot of damage, too, but Gary had never been able to pin it on the two idiots he'd known all along had done it. If they didn't wait long enough to tell their story, he might be able to get them that way.

He walked across the parking lot and then across the drive. There were lots of parked cars, but no people around. The ambulance entrance was around the corner, so he couldn't see that, but he couldn't hear any sirens, either. It was remarkable how often he came by here when nothing much was going on. He'd gone by a hospital in Philadelphia when he'd been down talking to people, on the trip that led to his securing Gregor Demarkian's help. The emergency room he looked into there had been totally crazy and it had been the middle of the morning, too. It hadn't been a time when you'd have thought there'd be a lot in the way of emergencies.

He went in through the front door and signed the visitor's book.

He told the girl at the desk who he was—she probably already knew—and asked her if she could page Dr. Willard for him. Then he went up in the elevator to the second floor. It was just that he didn't understand it, he really didn't. He supposed that some people might not believe in God just because they didn't, for the same reason some people didn't like the color red. He could see where there might be people like that. What he didn't understand were the people who did it deliberately, who *decided* not to believe in God, and who then always seemed so proud of themselves for doing it. To Gary, a life without God seemed like a lonely thing.

The elevator stopped at the second floor. He got out, made himself known to the nurses at the nursing station, and went on to Annie-Vic's room. Sometimes when he came to see her, there were people in the room visiting. Her grandnieces and nephews kept cycling through. They had jobs and busy lives, but they came anyway and looked in on her. So did her surviving brothers, most of whom were younger than she was. That didn't mean much. They were all in their eighties. From what Gary had heard, Annie-Vic's entire family had been atheists, all the way back to her grandfather. They'd been the Henry Wackfords of their day. Still, you couldn't say that they didn't value family, or that they were dishonest or cruel or given to running wild. If you could say that, Gary was sure he'd have heard about it. Annie-Vic herself was one of the most upright, morally straight women he'd ever known. It never made sense, no matter how much he thought of it. And yet there had to be an answer out there that would bring it all together.

He let himself into Annie-Vic's room. The shades were open, letting in the sun. The plate glass of the windows looked as if it would be cold to the touch. He walked over to the bed and looked down at her. He was glad the family wasn't here this time. He always felt that they didn't trust them. Annie-Vic in her bed looked tiny, so fine-boned she would break if she so much as turned over. Somebody had washed her hair and brushed it back away from her face. Gary wondered yet again if she had seen the person who had attacked her. He supposed she had, but even if she woke up out of this coma, there was no guarantee that she'd remember. Gary had talked to the doctor about that, and he'd been very firm.

There was a cough from behind him, and Gary turned. Dr. Willard was standing in the doorway, wearing his white coat, a stethoscope around his neck. Gary wondered why doctors were always dressed like that, even in their own offices. It was like a costume that they all felt required to wear, so that if they ever wanted to stop being real doctors they could at least play doctors on TV.

Dr. Willard came into the room. He wasn't local, and he was very young. Gary could never remember his first name.

"She's comfortable," he said. "And I look in on her at least twice a day. But there hasn't been any change. I'd call you if there had been."

"I know. I just like to check."

"I think it's a very good thing that you check," Dr. Willard said. "I think she knows when people visit. I think she knows when people talk to her. I don't think she knows it the way you or I would know something, but I do think she knows."

"Does she have brain damage?" Gary asked. "I understand that she's in a coma, so that means she doesn't wake up or respond to people in the normal way. I just don't understand why she's in a coma."

"Nobody understands why anybody is in a coma," Dr. Willard said. "We do know that comas tend to happen when there's been trauma to the brain, but that's not saying very much. Lots of people have trauma to the brain without ending up in comas, and lots of people in comas don't seem to have sustained that much trauma to the brain. And trauma is not the same thing as damage. So—"

"So you still can't answer my question about whether she's going to remember anything if she comes round."

"Sorry," Dr. Willard said. "I really would like to help you. It's not much fun, thinking that there's somebody out there who was willing to bash in the head of an old woman just for kicks. I do hope you find him."

"I do, too. We've brought in a consultant—"

145

"Gregor Demarkian," Dr. Willard said. "I heard about it. Somebody who's been on *American Justice*. We've all been impressed."

"Yeah," Gary said. He looked down at Annie-Vic again. She hadn't moved. There was no change of expression on her face. He turned away. "Well," he said. "I'd better be getting back. Call me if there's any change."

"Oh, I will," Dr. Willard said. "But it's like I told that Miss Marbledale this morning. There are always changes in coma patients, they just don't mean much."

2

Coming back down from the schools complex, Alice McGuffie thought she was going to explode. Who did any of those people think they were, anyway? She wasn't some tenth grader with missing homework. She wasn't a fool, either. Schools complex, for God's sake. She'd liked it better when the schools had been the way they were when she attended them, right there in the middle of town, and made out of red brick with big windows. They were built in the thirties, those schools, and they were good enough. It was a crock, all this talk about education and how important it was. It was important for people to be able to read and write, yes, and to speak English, which a lot of them couldn't do, at least down in places like Philadelphia, but all the rest of it was just stupid. History, for instance. Who the Hell cared about what happened in history? There was the American Revolution and the Pilgrims and all that, and it made sense to teach it especially to immigrant children who weren't real Americans, but what difference did it make in the end? She hadn't been alive when any of that happened. She didn't know why anybody should expect her to know about it, and she didn't see why anybody should expect Barbie to know about it, either. Barbie had a right to a real American high school experience, with cheerleading and football and proms and all the rest of it, and pretending that people like that Mallory Cornish were important in any way was, well, just stupid.

Stupid, stupid, stupid, Alice thought. Then she thought of Judy Cornish's smug little face—Judy Cornish and that other woman, Niederman. God, Alice hated all those people, all the people from the development, making fistfuls of cash for doing what? Not for working, that was for sure. Not for getting their hands dirty and their legs tired. Most of them had never done a day's work in their lives. They went to offices, or they were like Judy Cornish and didn't go anywhere at all. They just drove SUVs no decent person could afford the gas for and stuck their noses in the air because they were *educated people*.

"Educated people," Judy Cornish had said, sitting in Miss Marbledale's big outer office, "haven't taken Creationism seriously for eighty years. You may not care whether or not your daughter can get into a good college, but I do care about mine."

Good college. Oh, that was something. Of course, as far as Judy Cornish was concerned, the University of Pittsburgh was not a "good college." Nothing was a "good college" except those fancy Ivy League places. Alice wasn't sure which schools were in the Ivy League, although she knew about Yale and Harvard, because everybody had heard of them. She thought they were all in New England or someplace. She wasn't sure. It didn't matter. God, these people were all so, they were all—they had been just like that even back in high school, the one or two who were going to go away to "good colleges," but it hadn't mattered then, because nobody had to take them seriously then. They didn't play sports, those people, or if they did they played fag sports like tennis, and nobody liked them.

"I think a club devoted to expanding investigations into serious academic topics would be a good thing for a school like this," Judy Cornish had said. "There isn't enough civic education in our schools, not even at the best of times. That's why we end up with silly lawsuits like the one we have."

God, Alice thought again, and then. Who would join a club like that? They'd be laughed at, and rightly. It wasn't natural. Sitting in that room, she had been so angry she had had a hard time getting herself to speak, and it hadn't helped that Miss Marbledale had been off somewhere when she got there. Nobody had any idea where Miss Marbledale had gone, and by the time she got back Judy Cornish was in full swing, with that Niederman woman standing right behind her, outlining the whole "agenda" for the vice principal.

"Agenda." Alice hated big words. Alice hated people who used big words.

"I'm fairly sure that if enough parents chip in, we could bring some fairly important speakers to town to address the club," Judy Cornish was saying. "We could get somebody from the National Center for Science Education, for instance, to clear up some of these misunderstandings about evolution. We could get somebody from Americans United for Separation of Church and State, and maybe at least someone from one of the local chapters of the ACLU. The club could sponsor the talks and we could hold them in the evening and open them up to the entire town—"

That was when Alice had first noticed that Miss Marbledale was back. She must have come in while Judy Cornish was talking. Judy Cornish went on talking. She was talking and talking.

"Nobody would go to see those people," Alice had said. "Nobody would. We don't want Communists here. Communists and, you know, liberals. Secular humanists. I don't care what you call them. We don't want them here, and we don't need them to confuse the Hell out of everybody when any fool knows what's true and it isn't what they say."

"I want them here," Judy Cornish had said. "Shelley wants them here. I'll make some phone calls this afternoon. I'd bet anything I could get a good dozen parents who want them here."

"Shelley" must be the Niederman woman, Alice thought. They all looked alike, these people. They all carried around the same big pocketbooks. Alice looked at Dick Henderson. He looked uncomfortable as Hell. He ought to look uncomfortable as Hell.

"You can't start any club like that," Alice said. "It's against the rules."

"It's not against any rule," Judy Cornish said.

"It will be against the rules," Alice said. "We'll pass a rule. Wait and see. You're not in charge here. I'm on the school board. I'm the boss.

We'll make sure you can't bring that kind of thing in here to contaminate our kids—"

"You *can't* pass a rule," Judy Cornish said triumphantly. "There's a law called the Equal Access Act. It says that any school that gets federal funds has to allow any school club that any student wants to form without engaging in viewpoint discrimination. It says—"

"Oh, shut up," Alice said. "You can go on like that all day and I won't listen to it."

"If you try to stop our club, we'll complain to the federal government," Judy said, "and then they'll make you let us or they'll take away the federal money we get around here and we get a lot of it. I've looked it up. We can start any kind of club we want to and you can't stop us. We could start a Wicca club if we felt like it—"

"It isn't legal to have Satan worship in schools," Alice said. "And don't you try to tell me it is."

"Wicca isn't Satan worship," Judy said. "We can start any kind of club—"

And on and on. On and on. Alice stopped in her forward march and looked around. She had left the schools complex on foot, without her car. She had no idea why she had done that. She had just been so damned steamed up, so damned furious, at Judy Cornish and all the rest of them, and at Catherine Marbledale. Who did any of them think they were? She was Catherine Marbledale's boss. She kept pointing that out. Catherine Marbledale didn't seem to care.

"It's that tenure," Alice said, to the air, to the birds, to the cold, to nothing. She'd only learned about tenure since she'd been on the school board. Apparently, it meant that if a teacher had been around long enough, you couldn't fire her, no matter what.

Alice stopped and tried to catch her breath, and that was when she realized she was almost all the way back to town—so maybe she wouldn't walk all the way back to the schools complex. Maybe she'd have Lyman come out and fetch the car later. But she wasn't just almost back to town. She was right there where the worst thing had happened, right in front of Annie-Vic Hadley's house. It sat back from the road behind a high hedge, looking like something out of a horror story.

"Damn," Alice said.

She was suddenly very cold, and she didn't like being here. She really didn't. She had never liked this house, even before all this trouble started. It was dark in a way she couldn't define. It was made of dark wood, for one thing, and its bricks were brown instead of red, and the windows had slats what went sideways, as if they belonged in a monastery somewhere. Alice had never seen a monastery except in horror movies, and she was pretty sure she didn't want to see one. This house always made her feel as if it were haunted. Maybe that's what old Annie-Vic did in her spare time. Maybe she hung around and talked to ghosts.

There was a big gate in the hedge, but it didn't have an *actual* gate. There was nothing to bar anybody's way. Alice went up to posts that defined the entry and looked in. Some of Annie-Vic's family had been staying in the house for a while, but they must have gone. Alice couldn't see any sign of them. She edged right up to the opening. She'd never been so much as up the walk here. She wasn't the kind of person Annie-Vic deigned to notice, except when she came into the diner, and then she treated everybody like they were fools and peons. Alice wondered what it was like in there. Maybe Annie-Vic was like those old women you heard about, the ones who collected things, bits of paper, lengths of string, cats. They piled everything on top of everything else and died in the garbage one night when it got too much for them to handle.

Alice looked behind her. There was nobody there. She looked to one side and then to the other. There was nobody anywhere. She was out here all by herself.

Alice looked back at the house. It was blank, the way empty houses were. It was much too big. She took a step on the flagstone entry path. She was standing right between two lines of hedges. She took another step. She was in the front yard. There was nothing much in the front yard. There were no lawn ornaments, and no flowerbeds. There was no lawn furniture for people to sit on when the weather got warm. People like Annie-Vic didn't sit in their front yards when the weather got warm. If they did, they might have to talk to people who came walking by.

There really was nobody around to see her, and she didn't mean to do damage or cause harm. It wouldn't hurt to see what it was like, just this one time. Alice had always wanted to get herself into that house.

She took a deep breath. Then she looked behind her again, and from side to side. There was still nobody in sight.

It really *wouldn't* hurt just to go up on that front porch and look in through the front door.

3

Ann-Victoria Hadley knew that time was passing, out there, somewhere, where she was not. She knew it because people came and went from her room. The problem was, too many people came and went from her room. There was Tom Willard, who seemed to be her doctor. He wasn't local, but she knew him from hospital benefits and that kind of thing. There was Gary Albright, who kept coming back and coming back. At least, Annie-Vic thought he did. It turned out that when "time stood still," that didn't mean it just stopped, so that you were alive in an eternal present. No, that wasn't it at all. Instead, time *meshed*, all the times in your life. There were so many people coming in and out who had nothing to do with her life in Snow Hill, or had something to do with it, but something that was long over. There was her father, looking as if he'd never passed the age of forty, pacing up and down in front of the window that looked out on the cemetery, smoking a pipe. They didn't let you smoke pipes in hospitals any more. There was Miss Gardham, who had been her professor in Russian literature at Vassar, still looking twenty-two, or whatever she had been. She had been new Annie-Vic's senior year, and the girls had all teased her. It was because of Miss Gardham that Annie-Vic kept thinking of that line from Chekov, from one of the short stories.

It was a tiny town, worse than a village, inhabited chiefly by old people who so seldom died, it was really vexatious.

What a thing to remember. Annie-Vic was sure that Miss Gardham was not a ghost, and that her father was not one either. She also did not think that they were properly hallucinations. It was as if they had been locked up in her head in some alternative form nobody yet knew anything about, and now that she couldn't control anything about herself, they had come out.

She really *couldn't* control anything about herself. She wanted to toss and turn in bed. She wanted at least to turn over on her side, because she slept on her side. She much preferred it to sleeping on her back. She just couldn't make her body move, to her side or anywhere else. She couldn't make her eyelids open, either, even when she could feel the light on them, and even see it, more or less. She couldn't reach out her hand to any of the people who came and sat beside this bed.

For a little while—there was really no way to judge how long; the human person is not provided with a biological mechanism for telling ordinary daylight time—she was so frightened she thought she might have trouble breathing. She couldn't count the number of times she had told various members of her family that she would never want to be left in a "persistent vegetative state." She had railed on and on about it during the Terry Schiavo thing, when her grandnephew Cameron, who was a doctor, had been *adamant* that it was never permissible to remove a feeding tube.

"Artificial life supports, yes," he had said. "If you've got her heart pumping by machine or her lungs breathing that way, of course you can remove those. But a feeding tube. Food and water. You have no right to remove food and water."

Annie-Vic had made some remark at the time that Cam's view was a result of his newly minted Catholicism. Cam had converted to the Catholic Church during his residency in oncology. She felt bad about that now, about what she'd said. She'd been so annoyed at Cam for converting. There hadn't been a religious person in the Hadley family for generations, and they'd been proud of the fact, but there was

Cam, reading Walker Percy and going to Mass. She should have had more respect for his opinion.

"I don't think you should never starve someone to death because I converted to Catholicism," he had told her at the time. "I converted to Catholicism because I don't think you should starve people to death. Sorry, Annie-Vic, but on questions of life and death, it looks to me like the Catholic Church is the only sane institution on the planet."

Catholic Church. Sane. Who would have thought it, in her own family? What about birth control? What about censorship? They'd had a fight, that evening, but Annie-Vic didn't think of it as having ruined her family dinner. The Hadleys always fought about things like that at family dinners. It didn't stop any of them from staying at the table for the key lime pie.

Annie-Vic wanted to turn her head from side to side, but she couldn't do that any more than she could do anything else. She wanted to scratch the side of her nose with the tip of her finger. It was as if some vital link between her body and her mind had been severed. Sensations came to her, but her ability to react did not. At one point, Tom Willard had pricked her with a needle. It had hurt like Hell, and under any other circumstances Annie-Vic would have jumped half a foot and cursed him, but she could make no response at all.

"She's not responsive," Tom Willard had said, at the time, to somebody in the room who might have been Cam, or Cam and Lisa both. Lisa down from Vassar. Annie-Vic was pretty sure she hadn't imagined that.

"Of course, she's not deteriorating," Tom Willard said.

Annie-Vic had felt a great relief at that. She wasn't deteriorating, which meant that this problem might work itself out in time. It might not, but at the moment, that didn't seem to be all that bad. Being dead would be worse, Annie-Vic was sure. She didn't know why she was sure. She was glad Cam was here. He would refuse if the rest of them tried to talk him into allowing the hospital to let her die. Or to kill her. It wouldn't be just letting her die, under the circumstances, would it? They'd have to take the tubes and things out. They'd have to take the feeding tube out. They'd have to actually *do* something.

The door to the room opened and a nurse came in. She came over to the bed and fussed with things. She checked the tube and then went to work changing the bag at the top of it. Annie-Vic knew nothing about hospitals. In spite of her age, she'd never spent much time in them. She had always been a healthy person. The nurse leaned over the bed and put her hand flat on Annie-Vic's face. Then she yanked up Annie-Vic's left eyelid with her thumb. It hurt like Hell, and the light hurt even more. The nurse let the eyelid drop. Annie-Vic wondered why she could see people in her room, the real ones as well as the memory ones, when her eyelids were always closed.

The nurse made a notation on the chart at the foot of Annie-Vic's bed. Then she went away. There was nothing in this room to keep a mind working. There was no music. The television was never on. Annie-Vic didn't like television much. There was Poirot and Miss Marple. She liked those. She'd taken a mystery tour once, gone on a cruise where the guests were given parts in a murder mystery and then were supposed to solve it. She'd liked that cruise, even if it had only gone to the Bahamas, which she did not like. She needed something to keep her mind moving, so that it wouldn't atrophy. She imagined her mind as a big balloon with the air slowly leaking out of it. She wished they would play some Bach harpsichord piece, or even one of Beethoven's more triumphal symphonies, anything. She wished she could hear her memory people talking.

Every once in a while, time did a loop, and she was back there— not in this hospital room—but there, with that thick aluminum thing coming at her face. She always saw it in motion. She always concentrated on the metal. She always remembered herself thinking that it was all wrong. You thought you knew people. You thought you understood how the town worked, how the people in it thought and felt and acted, and it turned out that you had it all backwards, you didn't know what really mattered at all.

Years ago, Annie-Vic had been a prisoner of war in the "Asian theater," as they'd put it then. She'd been a prisoner of the Japanese. It was more than sixty years ago now. It was so far in the past that she should never feel it was more real to her than the last five minutes, but she did. She hadn't understood anything then, either, and it had taken her years after her release to come to terms with how wrong she had been.

If she could only get back the ability to sit up and talk and make herself understood, she could explain it all to them. She could tell them not only what had happened, but why.

Annie-Vic had the distinct feeling that they didn't know what had happened yet. If they did, Gary Albright wouldn't be parking himself in her room every day like a cold that refused to go entirely away.

EIGHT

1

The first impression Gregor Demarkian had when he walked into the Snow Hill Diner and found Molly Trask and Evan Zwicker waiting for him was that the Bureau had begun advancing twelve-year-olds to the rank of agent. The next impression he got was that Evan Zwicker didn't even really look young. He had one of those faces that used to be called "boyish" and that went to seed early and without remorse. At the moment, he looked like an evil and alcoholic college boy. In ten years time, he would look like a troll.

Molly Trask, on the other hand, was definitely young, although not as young as she looked. She had her hair pulled back in a bun, but it didn't really help. It was blond and she was so fair that her eyebrows looked bleached.

Evan Zwicker rose when Gregor came into the diner, which was how Gregor knew for sure who he was. The diner was full of booths with plastic seats, all lined up against the walls. The best ones were against the wall to the street, because those had windows, and Evan and Molly had managed to get one of them. The place was packed with people, yet none of them looked like they belonged here.

"The locals are at the counter," Even offered, when Gregor came over to sit down. "I don't think that's the usual thing, in fact I know it's not, but with the television crews here they don't have much choice. Our friends in the press always seem to have somebody staked out here to save a seat for the crew."

"Oh, honestly," Molly said. "He's always bitching about the press, but I can't see why. It isn't as if they're bothering us."

"They bother everybody," Evan said. "I've been around long enough to remember when we could run a case without having the whole thing filmed for 'Live at Five.' Or whatever. Not that there's much here to investigate."

"They're here because of the trial," Molly said, meaning the press. "You can't blame them. Monkey trials are a big thing these days."

"And does that make any sense?" Evan asked. "I mean, for God's sake. What a thing to sue about. It's totally nuts."

A waitress came over, and Gregor asked her for a mineral water and a club sandwich. He hadn't looked at the menu, but he'd eaten in dozens of diners like this across the United States, and club sandwiches were always a sure thing. They were a sure thing here, too, because the waitress didn't even blink. She took the order down on the pad and walked away. Gregor watched her go. She was wearing a white polyester-knit dress and big, white, clunky rubber-soled shoes of the kind nurses used to wear when Gregor was much younger. Now nurses wore colored baggy cotton things. Gregor had no idea when that had started. He looked back to Molly and Evan.

"Well," he said. "I hope I'm not blowing some kind of cover here."

"We're not working undercover," Molly said. "We're hardly working, if you want to know the truth. Kevin wants somebody to keep an eye on things, so we're keeping it, but there's not much going on. The most these people seem to want to do to each other is yell."

"But something was done, wasn't it?" Gregor asked. "This woman, this Ann-Victoria Hadley, was assaulted."

The waitress came back with Gregor's coffee. Gregor thanked her and pulled it close to him. Under Bennis's influence, he had stopped loading it up with cream and sugar. Under Bennis's influence, he had also started eating a lot of vegetables. It was a terrible thing what a man would do to get a woman to marry him.

Molly was looking into the depths of her own coffee cup. "Your Miss Hadley was certainly assaulted," she said, "and we've heard all the talk that it was all about the trial, but Evan and I don't exactly buy it. Not that it's impossible, I suppose."

"There's this guy," Evan said. "Local lawyer. Heads the biggest firm in town."

"He used to be the chairman of the school board before these guys were voted in," Molly said. "Henry Wackford."

"The firm is called Wackford Squeers," Evan said. "Can you imagine that? If I had a firm with a name like that, I'd change it. To anything."

"Ignore him," Molly said. "Henry Wackford has been going around telling everybody who will listen that it was Franklin Hale, that's the *new* chairman of the school board, anyway, that he was the one who went after Miss Hadley. According to Henry Wackford, the fundamentalists are evil, violent fascists and they've taken to going after scientists with their guns."

"Ann-Victoria Hadley was a scientist?" Gregor was surprised.

"No," Evan said. "That's just how these people talk. There's another one. Edna something or the other."

"Edna Milton," Molly said.

"That's the one," Evan said. "She's going around saying there have been death threats against the judge sitting on this case—did Kevin tell you about the judge? Old Ham Folger, for God's sake. A man so self-important he takes himself more seriously than God."

"Kevin did tell me about that," Gregor said. "He also said it was a no-go."

"It is," Molly said. "There have been no threats against Hamilton Folger. And I mean none. Not even nonviable ones. But according to this woman—"

"Edna Milton," Gregor said.

"Yes, according to her, the fundamentalists are going to murder Judge Folger unless he flies right and decides the case their way. It's driving us crazy. We can't not check out the rumors when they come. They've got us running ourselves ragged checking out sheer nonsense."

"And is the nonsense all from one side?" Gregor asked. "It's all the evolution side talking about the Creationism side?"

"Hardly," Evan said. "There's Franklin Hale. He says Henry Wackford whacked the old lady because he can't get over being voted out. Although why he'd do that, I don't know. You'd think if Wackford was angry about being voted out, he'd go after Franklin Hale. He's the new chairman."

"And there's a woman named Alice McGuffie; she and her husband own this diner, as a matter of fact," Molly said. "She says that Henry Wackford did it because he wants to make 'good Christian people' look bad. She always says it that way. 'Good Christian People.' As if it were in capitals."

"Both those claims seem pretty lame," Gregor said. "They're certainly as lame as the ones the evolution people are making."

"In general," Evan said, "you'll find that the evolution side seems, at least on the surface, to have more rational arguments than the Creation side. About who assaulted Ann-Victoria Hadley, I mean. But it's only on the surface. Once you start talking to them, they're all equally crazy. And I, for one, just don't get it."

"No," Molly agreed. "I don't get it, either. You'd be amazed at what's going on in this town. Even the children are beating each other up, both figuratively and literally. And over what? It isn't as if the new board actually wanted to stop the teaching of evolution, or even to start the teaching of Creationism—"

"Intelligent Design," Evan said. "It's not the same thing."

"It doesn't matter what it is," Molly said. "All the new board wants is to put a little thing in books saying that some people don't accept Darwin's theory and if you have questions you can go to the library and take out this book. That's it. How many times did you go to the school library when you were growing up? I honestly don't understand what all the fuss is about."

"I don't either," Evan said. "And if you explained all this on the evening news, I'd bet you anything most of the American people wouldn't understand it. It would be a different thing, you know, if they wanted to hold classes talking about God passing over the face of the waters or something, but they don't."

"Although Franklin Hale probably would like to," Molly said. "But Evan is right. The way things stand, it really doesn't make any sense. And of course this Miss Hadley was against the idea, and she joined the lawsuit. The whole thing is just ridiculous."

Gregor's club sandwich came. He looked at the remains of the food on Evan's and Molly's plates. They'd eaten lunch before he got there, which made sense, since he wasn't meeting them for lunch. They'd both eaten club sandwiches, though. Gregor picked up one quarter of his own—like all club sandwiches, the thing was cut into four little triangles—and then put it down again. The bacon looked hard as a rock. The lettuce looked like it had been frozen and was still full of ice crystals.

"*Could* any of these people have committed the assault?" he asked. "Or didn't you check that out?"

"We definitely checked it out," Evan said. "And the answer is yes. Anybody on either side of the lawsuit *could* have gone up there and whacked the old lady. You'd have to ask the doctors about it to get the specifics, but as far as I can tell, she was found nearly right away."

"If she hadn't been, she'd have been dead," Molly said.

"That was mostly a fluke," Evan said. "But all the people involved were out and about at the time. They were all wandering around Main Street or back and forth to the schools complex or something. So any of them could have done it."

"Who found Miss Hadley? Does she have servants in that house? Were there people around?"

"No servants," Molly said, "except for a woman who comes in to clean twice a week. No, it was a woman named Catherine Marbledale

160

who found her. She's the principal of the high school. She'd gone up there to deliver some papers about something or the other—not the lawsuit, some stuff to do with the school. And it was a good thing. If Miss Hadley had been there for another hour or so—" Molly shrugged.

Gregor looked into his coffee and suddenly realized. He hadn't ordered coffee. He'd ordered a mineral water.

"Huh," he said.

"He just got it," Molly said.

"They do that to everybody," Evan said. "Couple of days ago, this woman who works for Fox had a complete fit in here because she kept ordering mineral water and they kept giving her coffee. We don't think they even have mineral water. At least, we haven't seen it."

"It isn't on the menu," Molly said.

Gregor sighed. "I suppose the next thing is to talk to the doctors," he said. "Is there a guard at the hospital, looking after this woman?"

"Not that we know of," Evan said.

"She is a living witness," Gregor said. "If she comes to, she might be able to finger her attacker."

"True," Evan said, "but if her attacker is who we think it is—"

"Meaning some local asshole just out for a grab," Molly said.

"—he's not going to go back after her anyway," Evan said. "And seriously, Mr. Demarkian, we can't see that it would be anyone else. No matter what kind of trash is being talked around here, there's really no reason to beat the woman up just because she won't resign and the school board wants to put some stickers in some textbooks. And that's about all it comes down to."

"But I was told that she had money on her." Gregor asked. "If it was smash and grab, shouldn't whoever smashed've done some grabbing?"

"Maybe this Marbledale woman came by right as the guy was going for that," Molly said. "Maybe she scared him off. Anyway, you should try to talk to the doctors. They can give you more information than we can. With any luck the old lady will come to, and then you won't have to do anything accept take her statement."

2

There was no such thing as a taxi in Snow Hill, Pennsylvania. Gregor should have guessed, but he was so used to living in cities the question never occurred to him. Instead, back in his "office" after "lunch" with Molly and Evan—was *everything* connected to this place going to need to be put into scare quotes?—he went futilely through the yellow pages, trying one car service or another, until he got to the point where he thought it might make sense to pretend he was a funeral.

In the middle of all this, with Gary Albright still missing somewhere in town, both of Snow Hill's regular officers came in to check on what was happening. Very little was happening, as a matter of fact, in spite of the upcoming trial and the news people with their mobile production units everywhere, and the fights that were breaking out between teenagers over one thing or another. Gregor came out and introduced himself to them. They were not friendly, but they weren't hostile, either. Gregor supposed that was to be expected.

"It's not that we don't want you here," the one called Eddie Block said. "It's just that we both have a lot of respect for Gary, and we don't like the idea that anybody would think he'd beat up an old woman."

"I'm not sure anybody does think that," Gregor said. It was only half true, but there was no point in going through all the ambiguities he saw in Gary Albright's personality with these two men. "I thought it was his idea to bring me in."

"Oh, it was," the one called Tom Fordman said. "But that's the thing. He wouldn't have had to think of calling you in if it wasn't for the fact that some people might suspect he—you know. We don't like it."

"If Gary was going to go after someone," Eddie Block said, "he'd do it straight. He wouldn't sneak up behind them with an aluminum bat. He'd face them straight on and shoot them."

"And he wouldn't do that," Tom Fordman said. "He's never shot anybody in his life except, you know, maybe in the military."

"He'd've had to shoot somebody in the military," Eddie Block said. "He was in combat."

Gregor's head hurt. They were all out in the big room, which was a good thing. If they'd been having this conversation in his office, they would have sucked all the oxygen from the air by now. Gregor looked around, found a chair, and sat down. It was one of those computer chairs on wheels. He hated chairs on wheels. He was convinced they were going to shoot out from under him.

"All right," he said. "Let me ask you two a few things. You said hit from behind. That isn't something I'd heard before. How do you know she was hit from behind?"

The two men looked at each other. They were, Gregor thought, chronologically older than Gary Albright, but they'd had less real world experience, and it showed. Gregor got out of his chair, went back into his office, and got the big thick file Tina had left for him. Then he came back out and sat down again.

"Just a minute," he said. He flipped through page after page. The file was much too thick. "Here it is. 'Bruising consistent with a frontal assault,'" he read. "Who did this examination?"

"Somebody out at the hospital, I'd guess," Tom Fordman said. "That guy Willard, maybe. He's not from around here."

"We say it's the Snow Hill Hospital, but it isn't, not really," Eddie Block said. "It's three towns together. We're not big enough to have one for ourselves."

"It's a private thing," Tom Fordman said. "You know, not government. It's got some kind of foundation and they hold fund-raisers and like that, and that's how we got a hospital you can get to from here. Which is a good thing, because I think the next real hospital is in Harrisburg."

"Does it have a morgue?" Gregor asked.

"Oh, yeah," Eddie Block said. "It's got one of those."

"How about a medical examiner?"

The two men looked uneasy. "We usually use the state police for that," Eddie Block said. "There isn't call for that kind of thing out here, not very much. We get the usual domestics, you know, and there's always one or two kids a year who kill themselves on drugs or driving drunk."

"It's mostly driving drunk," Tom Fordman said. "Not that we don't have drug problems, because we do, but drugs are expensive and it's easier to get liquor. Except last year when we had a couple of meth labs."

"Out in the trailers," Eddie Block said. "They rig up these labs and then they blow themselves sky high. Don't know what else you would expect of a bunch of people would've flunked chemistry in high school if they'd stayed long enough to take it."

"But there it is," Tom Fordman said. "We're mostly quiet around here. Which makes the thing with Annie-Vic so weird. And you said, what? Frontal assault. So somebody came right at her. Must have been somebody she knew."

"Of course it was somebody she knew," Eddie Block said. "This is Snow Hill. She knew just about everybody, except the people from the development, and she knew a lot of those. And the people from the development don't go wandering around town much. What would one of them have been doing out at the Hadley house?"

Gregor flipped through the file again. Small towns always made him nervous. They made him even more nervous when they seemed to be full of people too naive to be real.

He closed the file again. He hadn't really been looking for anything in it. He'd sit down and read it through tonight, but for the moment it was just a matter of hearing and seeing what he could hear and see.

"Let me ask you a few things," he said, "if you've got a minute. Would you say that Ann-Victoria Hadley was well liked by people here? I mean, I suppose somebody must have liked her, they voted her on to the school board."

"Well, her election to the school board was practical," Eddie Block said. "Annie-Vic may be old, but she knows how to do business. She always has. Father left her that house up there and the money had to be divided between all the brothers and sisters, and Annie-Vic put it in the stock market and made a pile. Or so everybody thinks. So people just figure, if she could do that, she could fix some of the financial problems the school district was having, because Henry Wackford didn't want to do crap when it came to the practical stuff."

"We've got a problem with teachers' unions you wouldn't believe," Tom Fordman said. "I wish I was in a union like the one the teachers have. I could've retired when I was forty."

Tom Fordman didn't look thirty. Gregor bit his lip. "So what does that mean?" he asked. "That people didn't like Ann-Victoria Hadley?"

"Well, people liked her and people didn't," Eddie Block said. "I guess the general take was that she was a snob, because she was that. Is that. Hard to talk about her lying up there the way she is. But she always was a snob. Came from the richest family in town. Went away to some fancy college in the East."

"Vassar," Tom Fordman said. "Jacqueline Kennedy went there. And Jane Fonda. And that blond girl from *Friends*."

"Yeah, well," Eddie Block said. "She went away to this fancy college and she came back and thought she was smarter than everybody. Or maybe she always thought that. That was before I was born. But you see how it is, people resented it, a little. That's not surprising. That's not the same thing as saying they hated her."

"Alice McGuffie hated her," Tom Fordman said, "but Alice hates everybody, and she's never done anything about it before. Except bitch, you know. She does that day and night."

Gregor thought about it for a second. "Alice McGuffie," he said. "She owns the diner?"

"Alice and her husband, Lyman, yeah," Eddie Block said. "Own it and run it. That's Lyman, though, not Alice. Alice couldn't run a business if her life depended on it."

"I was just over at the diner," Gregor said. "She wasn't there."

"She takes off a lot during the day," Tom Fordman said, "unless she's waiting tables, or the counter or something. Most people around here figure she's more of a liability to Lyman than an asset. She really does bitch. To everybody. And she isn't above being rude as Hell, either."

"Better not let Gary hear you swearing in the office," Eddie Block said.

"Well, how else would you put it?" Tom Fordman said. "If she doesn't like you, she'll tell you so right to your face, even if you're having lunch in her own place. You should hear her talking to Catherine Marbledale. Except it doesn't work with Miss Marbledale, because Miss Marbledale does it right back, and she uses really big words. Alice ends up like to pop."

"Was she ever rude to Ann-Victoria Hadley?" Gregor asked.

"Alice is rude to everybody," Eddie Block said.

"Could she have killed Ann-Victoria Hadley?" Gregor asked.

"I don't know what you mean by could she have," Tom Fordman said. "Do you mean did she have the time? I'd guess so, sure. It's not that far from Main Street to the Hadley house. And I'd guess she'd have the psychology, too. I'd bet anything there are dozens of people Alice would like to kill."

"Starting with Miss Marbledale," Eddie Block said. "Alice had Miss Marbledale as a teacher in school."

"But here's the thing," Tom Fordman said. "You wouldn't think she'd have the strength to do it, if you know what I mean. She's a small woman, Alice is, short, I mean, not skinny. And she's middle-aged. And she's not exactly what you'd call physically fit. I keep thinking it must have taken a lot of strength to do what was done to Annie-Vic."

"It might have," Gregor agreed. He looked down at the folder. At some point while he was unaware of it, he had put it down on the desk nearest his chair. He tapped the top of it. "Is there any way I can find somebody to drive me around a little? I want to go out to the hospital and talk to the doctors who treated Miss Hadley when she was brought in. And I want to go out to the house where the attack happened. And then I'm going to want to talk to some people."

Somewhere on the other side of the room, the phone rang and Tina picked it up. Eddie and Tom looked at each other and then at Gregor Demarkian. Gregor thought they must have known that he didn't drive. That was why Gary Albright had come all the way into Philadelphia to get him. It was possible that they hadn't really believed it until right that minute.

"Well," Eddie Block said. "It's a police case, so we could probably get you where you want to go, if nothing else came up."

"Nothing much else ever comes up," Tom Fordman said.

"We could take you around in the patrol car," Eddie Block said.

"As long as Gary doesn't mind," Tom Fordman said.

They looked back and forth at each other. Gregor thought about hiring a car and a driver for the next week, but it occurred to him that doing that would make him look like an even bigger snob than Annie-Vic.

Gregor was just about to suggest some kind of compromise, he wasn't sure what, when Tina Clay came over to them.

"Listen," she said. "I think there may be some kind of emergency."

3

The "some kind of emergency" was happening at the Hadley house, and if Tina Clay hadn't been as confused and concerned as she was, they could all have walked. People had been saying that—that the house was close to Main Street—since Gregor had first been asked to look into the incident, but for some reason he hadn't really visualized what that meant. The house was not just "close to" Main Street, it was not far off it, up a steepish hill on a tiny side street lined with the kind of two-story frame houses that comprised the heart of every small town in the Northeast. The houses were single family, too, or at most two-family conversions with a second door stuck hastily on the side. Gregor could imagine a time during the Great Depression when the families in those houses had been the luckiest ones. The poor people would have lived off and away from things, in the country, in the hills. It was only after World War II that the bias against living in town had begun.

They started out from the police station. The town was quiet, there were a few cars on the street, and those mobile news vans were parked along the curbs, but there were few people out anywhere and nothing like traffic. Eddie Block was careful not to put on the siren when they started for the Hadley place. There wasn't that far to go, and he didn't want to attract the attention of the news crews. Then, in a blink, they were there, so fast that Gregor hadn't really had a chance to assimilate the fact that there was "something" happening that might connect to his case. They were parked at the hedge outside an older house with half timbering accented by brick and stone, set well back from the road. Another car was parked there, too. It was a dark Volvo station-wagon of the kind Gregor associated with certain towns on the Main Line, and there was a very young woman with blond hair leaning against the side of it and sobbing.

Eddie and Tom were in the front seat. They got out first. Gregor waited a moment while they walked over to the young woman and then got out himself. He could see how this had been the house of the richest family in town, even though they wouldn't have been rich by city standards. He suspected that people in Snow Hill still thought of the Hadleys as "rich." They would have just enough to be enviable.

Eddie and Tom had reached the small blond woman. Gregor sped up to be sure he heard everything that was said.

"She was taking too long," the woman was saying. "She said she'd be just a minute and it was minute after minute, I was just sitting here, and you know there are things to do, I have my children to pick up at school and she has, she had hers, she was supposed to, we were both supposed to, because we can't just leave them there now, can we. I mean, there are all the problems they're having, those horrid children, yelling at them, calling them names, playing tricks. They used to ride the school bus but we can't do that anymore. We really can't. We have to pick them up and she said she'd only be a minute and then it was all so long so I thought I'd just go to the door and tell her we had to go and then the door was wide open so I walked right inside and it felt wrong to do that it wasn't my house but there it was, you see what I mean, and there she, there she—"

"Take a deep breath," Eddie Block said, not unkindly. "Take a deep breath, hold it in for a second, then let it out. Then I'd appreciate it if you told me your name."

The woman took a deep breath and held it. She looked like she was about to turn blue. She let the breath out again. "Shelley Niederman," she said. "My name is Shelley Niederman."

"Good," Eddie Block said. "Very good. Now, I take it you live in town."

Shelley Niederman blinked. "Yes," she said, sounding faintly annoyed. "Of course I live in town. I live in Fox Run. So did she. So did Judy."

"Who's Judy?" Eddie Block said.

Now Shelley Niederman looked very annoyed. "You don't have to do this, you know? You don't have to pretend you don't know who we are. I mean, for God's sake, what's wrong with you people here? You're all a pack of savages, that's what you are. I don't know why Steve wanted to take this job, I really don't. The money is good, I know that, but there are other things beside money, and we're stuck out here with a bunch of hillbillies who still think the earth is flat and then this happens—something like this happens and—"

"I still don't know who Judy is," Eddie Block said calmly. "It's not that uncommon a name."

"Judy Cornish," Shelley Niederman said. "And you know who she is and you know who I am. Everybody in this godforsaken town knows, because we had to file a lawsuit to make sure our kids got a decent education, because if we'd left it up to you people you'd have been presenting Noah's Ark in history class. God, I hate this place. I really hate it."

Eddie Block was taking deep breaths himself. So was Tom Fordman. Gregor stepped forward a little.

"Excuse me," he said.

Shelley Niederman looked him up and down. "I know you. I know who you are. We saw your picture on the Internet. You're Gregor Demarkian. Well, it's a good thing you're here. Now there's a murder for you to solve. That's probably why they brought you in in the first place. They probably knew there was going to be a murder to solve. I don't understand what's wrong with these people. I don't understand what's wrong."

Gregor took a deep breath of his own and shot a look at Eddie Block. He would have shot one at Tom Fordman, too, but he was looking at the ground. Both of these men were ready to strangle this woman, and Gregor didn't entirely blame them.

"What you're saying," he said, "is that this woman, this Judy Cornish, has been murdered?"

"Of course she's been murdered," Shelley Niederman said. "How else could that—Could that—" The tears welled up again and threatened to spill over. Then they did spill over. Shelley put a hand to her face and wiped them away. "She's in there, don't you understand? She's right in there and she was only going in for a minute, just to check something, it didn't make any sense to me but then nothing ever makes any sense to me around here. She was only going to be a minute and then she was gone too long and I called out to her and she didn't answer and then I went inside and then there she was and then I came out here and called on the cell phone because I've got a cell phone, of course I do, I'm not a Neanderthal like some people around here—honest to God, you'd think technology was the devil. You'd think everything was the devil. They see the devil under their beds and they probably hunt witches, really, they probably burn them right on that green thing with the war memorial—"

"Wait," Gregor said. It was like standing under a waterfall. "Judy Cornish has been murdered, and her body is—where?"

Shelley Niederman blinked again. "I told you where the body is," she said. "I told you first thing."

"Maybe you told Officer Block or Officer Fordman, and I didn't hear."

"All right," Shelley said. "It's up there."

"In the house?"

"Yes, of course in the house."

"Where in the house?"

"In the dining room," Shelley said. She put her head in her hands. "It's right there, in the dining room, in the doorway to another room, I don't know which, I wasn't paying attention. Because she was just there, wasn't she? She was dead and then I ran out here and I called on the cell phone and how far are we from the police station, anyway? It doesn't take a minute but you people took forever and I was just standing out here and she was lying in there dead and—"

"How do you know she was dead?" Gregor asked patiently.

"What do I mean, how did I know? I'm not an idiot, am I? Anybody could see she was dead. There was blood everywhere—"

"Did you try to take a pulse? Or check for breathing?" Gregor asked.

"Oh, Hell," Eddie Block said.

Then both he and Tom Fordman took off running.

Gregor and Shelley Niederman watched them go.

"Of course she's dead," Shelley Niederman said. "She couldn't be alive with so much blood everywhere. Nobody could be alive like that."

PART II

It is tempting to quarrel over Harris's use of the term "unintelligent design." But there is a more important problem with his statement, namely, that it ignores the true reason why so many people reject the position that life on earth has evolved entirely through a natural process. That reason, of course, is a lack of fossil evidence supporting the notion that evolution explains variations between, not just within, species.

Mike S. Adams, Associate Professor of Criminal Justice,
University of North Carolina at Wilmington,
"Second Letter to a Secular Nation," Townhall.com 4 April 2007

6. There are no intermediate fossil forms.

This is a claim for which there is a monosyllabic definition: lie. Not error, which implies honest ignorance, but lie, because the people who make this claim are generally fully aware of the fossil record and simply choose to misrepresent it. Archaeopteryx, the earliest known fossil bird for a long time (some recent finds may be earlier) has a thoroughly reptilian skeleton with a bony tail, teeth, and four paws with jointed fingers (not merely the horny skin growths at the middle joint that a few modern birds have). And it has feathers. If that's not an intermediate, what is? More recently, evidence is accumulating that some dinosaurs had hair and feathers. If we'd lived 100 million years ago, we might have put birds, mammals and reptiles in the same class or at least put the divisions very differently from today. Therapsids are the intermediates between reptiles and mammals, crossopterygians and ichthyostegids are the intermediates between fish and amphibians, and so on.

Steve Dutch, Professor of Natural and Applied Sciences,
University of Wisconsin at Green Bay, "Ten Myths About Evolution,"
The Steve Dutch Home Page, 21 January 2003

ONE

1

It was never possible to tell if the victim of a battery was really dead, not by just looking at him, but Gregor Demarkian was willing to bet that this was as close to certainty as he was ever going to get. The two officers had raced to the house and gotten there well before him. When he came in through the dark central hall, he could see Tom Fordman kneeling next to the body, bent over the head as if he were about to administer mouth-to-mouth resuscitation. A moment later he leaned back and then stood up, shaking his head. Gregor saw Eddie Block turn his away from the body and look at the walls, the ceiling, everywhere. There was a lot to look at. Even in the gloom—and gloom seemed to be practically the theme of this house—it was obvious there was blood everywhere.

"It's like something out of a horror novel," Eddie Block was saying as Gregor came in. "You ever been in this house before? You ever know it was this dark?"

"I've been in the parlor," Tom Fordman said.

Gregor was just then passing the entry to the "parlor," which he would have called a living room. It was dark, too, but the effect was less oppressive than it was in the hall, because the room had a big line of cross-hatch windows looking out on the front lawn. Still, the effect was heavy and funereal, and not just because there was a lack of natural light. Everything about the place was dark. The furniture was upholstered in dark colors where it was upholstered at all. Otherwise, it was made of dark woods. The woods were highly polished, but that only made them look darker. The walls were painted white where they were painted at all, but in other places there was dark wood paneling or ancient wallpaper in dark colors and closely figured. It was a house meant to express the sober thoughtfulness, the gravity of the person who owned it. Gregor was willing to bet it hadn't been changed in fifty years.

He reached the officers and the body, which was lying half in and half out of the dining room. Here the darkness was absolute, in spite of the two great windows in one wall. There were curtains on those windows, and the curtains had been pulled shut. The dining room table was piled high with books and papers. They looked a mess. The body was so bloody it looked as if its head had been ground into hamburger and left to rot.

Gregor did not bend down to check it out. He had seen enough dead bodies in his day. They had never added a single clue to his investigation. Medical examiners knew about bodies. He knew about crime scenes. He looked at the walls and then at the ceiling. Yes, there was blood on the ceiling. Not a lot of it, but blood. There was blood on some of the papers on the table. There was blood on the single pair of shoes someone had left next to the door that led to the kitchen.

Coming back around to the two officers, Gregor was astonished to see they were still just standing there.

"Isn't there something we ought to do?" he said gently. "There's the obvious to consider here."

"We need to call Gary," Tom Fordman said. "Gary will know what the procedure is."

"Gary can't work on this," Eddie Block said. "That's why we have

Mr. Demarkian here. Mr. Demarkian is supposed to lead the investigation. That's what Gary said."

"We don't know that he's supposed to lead this investigation," Tom Fordman said. "We don't know if the two things are connected. Annie-Vic and this. Just because this woman is in Annie-Vic's house doesn't mean—"

"Of course it means," Eddie Block said. "She's in the house and she's one of the plaintiffs in the lawsuit, isn't she? She's that woman from the development—"

"Wait," Gregor said.

They turned to look at him as if they were surprised to find him there. This was not a good sign. It was obvious that these two men were not used to dealing with murder, and whatever training they had received hadn't mentally prepared them to take on something of this kind. Gregor didn't know where to start. He wondered what had happened when Annie-Vic was attacked. Gary probably got the call and he at least would have been mentally prepared, if only because he had served in combat zones.

Gregor tried to go slowly. "Didn't you tell me, didn't somebody tell me, that Annie-Vic has family here, visiting from out of town?"

"That's right," Eddie Block said. "A grandniece and a grandnephew. Or a grandnephew and a great grandniece. Or something like that."

"Do they come from far out of town?" Gregor asked.

"Oh, yeah," Eddie Block said. "I think one of them is from Chicago."

"Fine," Gregor said. "Where are they staying now?"

Eddie Block and Tom Fordman looked at each other. Gregor had no idea if he was getting through to them. They looked confused.

"I don't know," Eddie said. "I just assumed they were staying, ah, staying—"

"Here?" Gregor suggested.

"They would stay here, wouldn't they?" Tom Fordman said. "That would be the normal thing."

"I think so too," Gregor said. "And that brings us to the question, where are they?"

The two officers looked at each other again. Gregor didn't really think they were stupid, just inexperienced. Maybe that was a hopeful sign, that there were still small towns in America where people weren't killing each other often. Still, this was an emergency and he needed to get that across to them.

"Do you mean you think one of the relatives did it?" Tom Fordman said. "But the relatives couldn't have attacked Annie-Vic. They weren't anywhere near Snow Hill."

"Maybe it was one of the relatives who attacked this woman and somebody else who attacked Annie-Vic?" Eddie Block tried.

"Listen," Gregor said. "This woman has been murdered. She's in the house of someone she knew—what? Well? Slightly?"

"They'd have to know each other at least a little," Eddie Block said. "Because they were both plaintiffs in the lawsuit, you know."

"All right," Gregor said. "Would you say she knew Ann-Victoria Hadley well enough to be in a position to just walk into her house whenever she wanted to, without an invitation, without being let in?"

"Oh," Eddie Block.

"*Nobody* was like that with Annie-Vic," Tom Fordman said. "You didn't know her, but you can trust me. She wouldn't have put up with that kind of thing from anybody. Even the relatives knocked."

"Fine," Gregor said. "Then what the Hell is this woman doing here? How did she get in? Did someone let her in? If someone did, where is the someone? *Could* she have just walked in? Did Annie-Vic usually leave her doors unlocked? What about the relatives? Would they have left them unlocked if they went out?"

"Ah," Eddie Block said.

"I don't think the relatives would have left the doors unlocked," Tom Fordman said. "I mean, they're from out of town. They live in big cities and people don't do that kind of thing there."

"Do they do that kind of thing here?" Gregor asked. "Do people leave their doors unlocked in Snow Hill?"

"Oh, yeah," Eddie Block said. "I can't remember the last time I locked mine. Maybe when we went away on vacation last summer, but maybe not. But I'm with Tom. The relatives would have."

"Fine," Gregor felt as if he were swimming through molasses. "Then here's what we've got. We've got a woman dead on the floor who has no reason to be in this house and, as far as we know, no way to get into it. We've got a woman outside who was with her but who didn't come in, and if the murderer had run out the front door and down the front path, that woman would have seen him. Or her. Never mind. Do you see what I'm getting at?"

"The murderer might have gone out the back way," Eddie Block said.

"Is there a back way?" Gregor asked, although he supposed that there would have to be. "Never mind," he said. "Yes, the murderer might have gone out the back way, or he might not have. He could still be in the house. The times are close enough that that's not impossible. And there's another thing to worry about. Something else might be in the house."

"What?" Eddie Block said.

"More bodies," Gregor told him. "Think about this for a minute. Annie-Vic was assaulted. This woman was murdered. We have no reason why any of it has happened, but we do know that it's all in some way connected to Annie-Vic. Which means that there might be something here, something in the house, that's triggering all this. And the relatives are staying in the house. And we don't know where they are. For all we do know, they could be upstairs at this minute lying in pools of their own blood, because whatever is important enough to somebody to kill for is something they've been stumbling over since they arrived in town—"

Eddie Block and Tom Fordman looked at each other. Their expressions were still both blank.

That was when Gregor made up his mind. It didn't matter that Gary Albright was a suspect in his own case, he could not be dispensed with. In Snow Hill, at just this moment, there was no other person who could make this case work at all. If they weren't going to have Gary Albright, then they were going to have to call in the state police. Gregor was with Gary Albright on that one. You didn't do that except as a last resort.

Gregor got out his cell phone. "Give me half a second to make a phone call," he said, "and then we'll go upstairs and search."

2

Years ago, so many now that he couldn't imagine what he had looked like then, as a newly minted special agent of the FBI, Gregor had been sent on a kidnaping detail with a veteran agent and a tech crew. The case was being worked out of a small town in eastern Massachusetts, close enough to Boston and the Cape to be the location of serious money, but far enough away to look rural and "unspoiled." In those days, Gregor had not understood the concept of "unspoiled," or why so many of the people he worked with seemed to worship it. Unlike most of the people he worked with, and most of the people he'd gone to college and graduate school with, he had not grown up middle class in a suburb. He'd been raised in what would now be called the inner city, except that instead of a racial enclave he'd come from an ethnic one. Tenements full of apartments that never had enough windows, schools that had been built in the 1920s and not updated since—the only thing that broke the routine of work and grind and hope was the trip, once a year, to visit relatives who lived in "the country." The country was a farm somebody had bought after coming over from Armenia with a little extra cash, or after working a few decades in a factory somewhere. Farming was the big thing, because in Armenia a man who owned his own farm was a man of stature. The farms Gregor had visited in his childhood, however, had *really* been unspoiled, untouched by human progress. The bathrooms were out the kitchen door to the back, in little wooden sheds that had no heat. Gregor could only imagine what they would be like in the middle of the night in the middle of winter. They were bad enough in the middle of the night in the summer heat. Water came into the kitchen sink by a hand pump. The roads were dirt. The nearest approximation of civilization was a small town thirty miles away that consisted of a feed store and a dry goods store and a gas station with a single pump. Why anybody would want to live like that, Gregor didn't know—but of course the people he worked with didn't want to live like that. They wanted to build big modern houses in the emptiness of the countryside and then travel an hour to get to what they'd consider a "real" job, where they could complain about the hardships of having to drive on the dirt roads and the glories of buying only locally grown vegetables.

That kidnap detail had been centered on a house like that, fairly new, with a kitchen that looked like it could have served a small restaurant but that Gregor was willing to swear had never been cooked in. There were pots and pans hanging from the ceiling over a large center island, and one wall consisting of nothing but big banks of windows. One end of the island was constructed like a diner's counter, with stools, and the mother of the victim sat at it while they talked to her.

"It was his idea, this house," she said, talking about the husband she was in the middle of divorcing, the one they thought had taken the child and run. "I never wanted a house like this. I wanted an antique house. I wanted dark wood and mullioned windows."

Going upstairs, Gregor thought that this was the kind of house that woman had meant, that this was what she had wanted instead of what she had. He also remembered how the case had worked out: it was his first real case, the one that was supposed to stay with you. There was the kidnap note left next to the phone on the built-in desk in the kitchen. There were the police cars and Bureau cars that came in and out of the driveway. There were the bodies, father and daughter both, lying on the floor of the third-floor playroom as if they'd been there for eternity. The man must have come back after the police first searched the house. He must have been watching and waiting and biding his time.

Gregor and Tom Fordman were going up the stairs to the second floor of this house, where nobody was supposed to be home. There was a cold blast of air of, cold enough to make Gregor want a coat. Windows were open somewhere, in the rooms at the end of the hall. Somebody must have been airing the place out. Gregor knew how the houses of old people got when the old people lived alone.

"Did you come up here and search the house when Annie-Vic was attacked?" he asked.

"Gary did," Tom Fordman said. "I didn't see any point to it. The guy wasn't going to be hiding out in the house."

"The guy?"

"The guy who attacked her."

Gregor wanted to say that there was nothing he knew at this point that would rule out a woman, but he let it pass and opened the first closed door on his left. It was a walk-in linen closet, with built-in shelves lining the walls. There were sheets and pillowcases and towels, all neatly folded and segregated into categories. He went on to the next door, which was open. That led to a bedroom that had obviously been slept in, and recently. The bed was unmade. There was an oversize T-shirt lying on the end of it, the kind of thing college girls wore to bed instead of regulation nightgowns. Gregor walked in and looked around. He opened the door to the big wardrobe that stood against one wall and then closed it again. There was no closet. He wondered, idly, when it was that houses had started to have closets in every bedroom. It was so standard now that zoning boards didn't count a room as a bedroom unless it had a closet.

Gregor went back into the hall. "We should really get a team," he said, "and go all the way through here thoroughly."

"Looking for what?" Tom Fordman said. "You never say. Do you really think the murderer is up here somewhere, hiding out?"

"It's possible," Gregor said. "There are other possibilities."

"Like what?"

Gregor thought of those two bodies on the third floor. Then he went into the next room, and that one he was sure was Annie-Vic's own. It was scrupulously clean and mostly empty. There were two big wardrobes instead of just one. The furniture was old but not shabby. It had been well made and kept up over the years. Still, the wood was as dark here as it was downstairs. Everything was dark.

"I think if you think the murderer is here, we ought to do this the way we were trained to," Tom Fordman said. "We ought to have our guns out."

"I don't have a gun."

"Really? You mean on you, or at all?"

"At all. I don't like guns. I carried one when I was required to, of course, but I was never happy with it. I'm not really interested in shooting at anybody. I'm not really interested in getting shot at."

"You were in the FBI, weren't you? Gary said something about that. And you can't count on not getting shot at."

"No, I know you can't," Gregor said. He was out in the hall again, and then into another room. The rooms seemed to go on forever. How did anyone live alone in a house of this size? If it had been him living alone here, he would have rigged up a place to sleep on the ground floor and restricted himself to that and the living room and the kitchen. He would have left the upstairs alone to gather ghosts. It felt to him as if the ghosts had gathered anyway.

He went in and out of another room, and another, and another. There was one more that had been slept in. Gregor assumed that that was where the grandnephew was staying. The rest of the rooms were all perfectly made up and perfectly clean—museum pieces, really, exhibits on How We Lived Then. When he had seen the last of them, he went out into the hall and looked around.

"What about upstairs?" he asked. "Are there servants' quarters?"

"You must be joking," Tom Fordman said. "Nobody in Snow Hill has servants' quarters. It's not that kind of place."

"But this house is clean," Gregor said, "and Annie-Vic can't have been cleaning it herself. And I can't imagine her mother cleaning it herself, either. Not a family with enough money to send a daughter to Vassar. They'd have had somebody in to clean."

"Had somebody in, sure," Tom Fordman said. "There's a woman from out at the trailer park, you know, one of those, came in to do stuff for Annie-Vic. But she didn't live here. You couldn't get somebody to live here."

"All right. What about an attic? A house this old would almost certainly have one."

"Yeah," Tom Fordman said. "I think it's got an attic."

"Has anybody looked into it?"

"I don't get what all this is supposed to be about," Tom Fordman said. "Nobody was killed in the attic, and nobody could hide out around here for long without somebody noticing. What is it you expect us to find?"

"I don't know," Gregor said, and that was true. He had no idea. He just wished that things were being done more thoroughly, because in the long run thoroughness mattered.

There were sounds outside. Gregor could hear them through that partially opened window at the end of the hall. He went to look and saw the ambulance pulling in. It hadn't had its siren going. There was another police car, too, which Gregor assumed meant the arrival of Gary Albright. The Volvo that had been there when Gregor first arrived had not moved.

"We'd better go down," he said, gesturing to the driveway below them. "There are going to be some questions to be asked. Who is that woman who called us, the one we talked to? Who is she exactly?"

"I don't know about exactly," Tom Fordman said, "but she's from the development. I think she was that Cornish woman's friend."

Gregor sighed. He was sure that the woman in the driveway was Mrs. Cornish's friend, too, it was just common sense, but that wasn't what he was asking. He stayed at the window for a moment and watched as men got out of cars and milled around.

"We'd better go down," he said. "We'll find someone to do a better search here later."

3

Gary Albright was leaning up against the driver's-side door of Snow Hill's other police cruiser while a tangle of EMT people went back and forth into the house, without getting anywhere. Someone had reminded Eddie Block of the rules of procedure for a crime scene, or Eddie had known them already and suddenly remembered them under the pressure of events. Yellow crime scene tape now surrounded the body. Shelley Niederman was still sitting in the Volvo, crying. Nobody looked as if he knew what he was doing.

Gregor went up to Gary and looked around, one more time. "You do realize that you've got no choice but to call in the state police," he said. "I know you're reluctant to do it, but you don't have the equipment for a proper crime scene investigation, and your people aren't behaving as if they've got the training. If you don't get some experts in here, you run the very real risk of going to trial against a murderer and losing. And once you've lost, you've lost. It doesn't matter if somebody shows up with a photograph of the guy caught in the act."

"What did we do before we had all these forensics?" Gary Albright said. "I watch old television, *Perry Mason,* old cop shows from the fifties, old movies. No forensics, yet we still caught murderers."

"Now that the forensics exist," Gregor said, "defense counsel can and will use your lack of them as reasonable doubt."

"You know how to run a crime scene investigation," Gary said. "You've run dozens of them. I looked you up."

"I knew how twenty-five years ago," Gregor said. "We didn't have 'all these forensics,' as you put it, even then. And it might be longer than that, because my last ten years at the Bureau I had a desk job. You've got a dead woman in there. I don't know if you've been in to look, but she's bloody as Hell, and so is the scene. Assuming we're looking for the same person in both cases, our guy decided he wasn't going to miss the second time, and he didn't. There's somebody walking around who doesn't mind doing a lot of brutal physical damage, and somebody like that is very dangerous. Call the state police."

Gary Albright was staring off into the distance. "I know how to run a crime scene investigation," he said finally. "It might not be up to the standards of a place like Philadelphia, but we do have the equipment and I do know how to use it. That was the plan, all along. That I'd learn how to use it and then use it when the time came, and then all we'd have to do is send the samples to the state police lab. We wouldn't have to actually call them in here."

"Well, that's up to you," Gregor said. "I thought from the beginning that you might be being a little over scrupulous in removing yourself from the case. If you can place yourself somewhere for sure for the relevant time—"

"You mean if I have an alibi?"

"I mean if you have an alibi," Gregor agreed. "And we're lucky in a way, at the moment. We can pinpoint the time within maybe half an hour or so, because that woman over there," Gregor cocked his head in the direction of the Volvo, "saw the dead woman go into the house and sat there waiting for her every minute until she called the police department. Then she sat some more. This time, we know when the murder occurred almost as surely as if she'd witnessed it herself."

Gary Albright was still staring off into the distance. There was something about him that was very, very still, so quiet he might almost have been an inanimate object. Even dead bodies exhibit more of an air of movement than Gary did now. He had that open, steady, straightforward look of certain kinds of military people, the ones, Gregor admitted, that he had always liked. Gregor just wished he could figure out what the man was thinking.

Gary Albright moved. It wasn't really a sudden move, but it felt that way to Gregor, because he wasn't expecting it.

"The guy they're going to send from the staties is named Dale Vardan," he said. "They'll send him with a partner, but they'll definitely send Dale. The partner won't matter. Dale will try to take over the case. You're supposed to be running it. That's what I hired you for. Is that clear?"

"It's perfectly clear," Gregor said. "I don't usually run investigations these days. I usually consult for the people who do."

"I want you running this one," Gary Albright said. "That really is why I hired you. I want you running it, because I don't want Dale Vardan running it. If the choice comes down to me or Dale, it's going to be me, even if I ruin this case completely and get myself fired."

"I take it you don't have an alibi for the time in question," Gregor said.

"I don't know what the time in question is, yet," Gary said, "but I don't have an alibi for most of the morning, so my guess would be no. I've been driving around town, trying to think. Annie-Vic. The lawsuit. Even Nick Frapp. They all made me want to think. The world was not what I expected it to be, when I was growing up here."

"The world is never what we expect it to be when we're children," Gregor said. "That's the nature of childhood."

"Maybe. But it seems to me that things ought to be arranged better than they are. It seems to me that it should be easier to tell the good guys from the bad guys."

"I think that's a very dangerous opinion for anybody in law enforcement to have."

"Yeah," Gary Albright said. He looked down at what Gregor knew was his prosthetic leg. "Maybe Dale won't try to do to you what he's always trying to do to the rest of us. You're from Philadelphia. You're famous. I don't think you're a believer. On the other hand, maybe Dale just pulls that stuff on whoever happens to be in the room at the time. Excuse me. I'm going to sit down and make that phone call."

Gregor watched as Gary pulled away from the car, got the door open, then got in behind the wheel almost as if he had two good legs. It was cold out here in the open, and the milling had reduced itself to men standing in place and stamping their feet. Shelley Niederman was still in the Volvo, waiting, probably, for somebody to tell her she could go, or not. Gregor wondered what this was going to entail. The dead woman had had children, which meant she'd probably had a husband. There would be people to notify. There would be questions to ask. Gary had left the car door open and Gregor could hear his voice on the radio, calling something in to Tina Clay.

A moment later, a man in a paramedic's uniform came up and introduced himself, sort of. "I'm with the ambulance," he said. "I was just wondering. That guy over there said you were in charge."

"That guy over there" turned out to be Eddie Block. "I suppose I am," Gregor said. "What can I do for you?"

"It's about the body," the paramedic said. "There's nothing for us to do here, you know, but usually when the patient is dead we take him in to the hospital anyway, you know, to be checked out, or sometimes to go to the morgue. We take him, anyway. Her. Can we take the body now?"

"Not yet," Gregor said. "There should be some people here from the state police in a little while. They'll have some things to do. When they're done, they'll let you take the body. The procedure is a little different in a murder investigation."

"Yeah," the paramedic said. "Who'd've thought? I mean, we get murders up here, you know, but not like this. We get the ordinary stuff. Guy gets drunk as Hell and kills his girlfriend. Couple of guys get too happy in a bar and take out the knives. But this. This is brutal."

"Yes," Gregor agreed, "it certainly is that."

"If you ask me, it's because we've taken God out of the schools," the paramedic said. "Just wait till this investigation is over. It will turn out to be some high school kid looking for a thrill. They don't have morals anymore, these kids, because they don't know anything about God. They go to school and their teachers tell them there isn't any right or wrong, everything is relative, it doesn't matter what they do. What do you expect? We didn't used to have murders like this in places like this."

Gregor thought about Charles Starkweather and Caril Ann Fugate, with eleven people dead in Nebraska and Wyoming in the early fifties, and Dick Hickock and Perry Smith, leaving the entire Clutter family dead in Kansas in 1959, all years before the U.S. public schools had ended their practice of praying at the start of the school day.

He thought about them, but he didn't mention them, because there didn't seem to be any point.

TWO

1

It was the only serious mistake Catherine Marbledale ever made in her career—but it was a *very* serious mistake, and she should have seen it coming. It wasn't that she had spent her entire teaching life in this particular small town, or even that she'd grown up in another one just like it. She knew these places, strung out along the rim of Appalachia, scattered across the Midwest, set down in tangles of kudzu and moss throughout the South. It wasn't true that "news travels fast" in such places. Most news never even got in. Catherine was willing to bet her life that she could stop the first fifteen people she met on Main Street and not one of them would be able to name the prime minister of Great Britain or the president of France. Genocide raged in Darfur, and most of these people never had never heard of it. War broke out in Central Europe, and the only time it made a dent was when some-body's son, away in the Marines, was deployed. Other kinds of news, though, not only traveled fast, it traveled instantaneously—even be-fore the advent of cell phones.

She knew something was wrong as soon as she pulled into the park-ing lot in front of the school. She had her special assigned place, marked PRINCIPAL, closer to the building than any others except the handicapped spaces right next to the main doors. Of course, she already knew there was "something wrong," a lot wrong. She had a cell phone of her own. The office had called her as soon as they had gotten word that Judy Cornish was dead. The Cornish children would need to be told, but their father would do that. He was already on his way out. There were arrangements to be made: Catherine would have to talk to the teachers to make sure the children were not loaded down with homework at a time like this; she had to make sure they knew they could go home or stay at school, whatever made them feel best. There was so much that needed to be figured out.

She got out of her car, thinking that she would have to call a meeting this afternoon. She would have to talk to that Mr. Demarkian who Gary Albright had brought in, and have her teachers talk to him, too. This had something to do with the school, even if she didn't believe it had anything to do with "Intelligent Design." They'd all known Judy Cornish. They might have information the police would find valuable. She went in through the big glass double doors. Most of the front wall of the school was glass. The glass had replaced tight but crumbling bricks in a remodeling a few years ago. The remodeling had taken forever, just like everything else the school board was asked to handle.

The foyer at the front of the building was large and open. The left wall was lined with display cases, full of trophies for one thing or another. Every once in a while, Snow Hill fielded decent sports teams. The boys who played on them almost never got athletic scholarships, though, or they only got them for small schools that wouldn't matter much. Catherine Marbledale could remember a time when every college mattered. Just going to college mattered. The world as it had come to be made no sense to her at all.

She headed to the right, to the row of doors to the offices, and it was then that she saw Mallory Cornish standing alone against the cheap polished paneling. A class period was just letting out. There were people coming into the foyer, students with books in their arms, because there was a policy that backpacks had to be left in lockers during the school day. She felt as if she were trapped in gelatin. Everything was moving impossibly slowly, except, all of a sudden, it wasn't.

Mallory Cornish stepped away from the wall. She was a pretty girl, small and compact, and with that obvious air of intelligence girls had when they were destined to be valedictorians. Catherine watched as Mallory advanced into the foyer, and then, a second too late, realized why it was happening. Barbie McGuffie and those two idiot friends of hers were marching their way from the east to the west wings.

Mallory got out into the middle of the open space, put her arm out, and stopped Barbie in her tracks. Barbie was furious.

"What do you think you're *doing*?" she demanded.

Barbie was supposed to be in detention, Catherine remembered that; that was decided right before she left school and went driving around. And Dan Cornish couldn't possibly have gotten here already. Mallory shouldn't even have known what was going on. But it wasn't like that, was it? This was the kind of news that traveled instantaneously. And there were cell phones.

"Your mother is a murderer," Mallory Cornish said. She said it so loudly, it literally bounced off the walls. It sounded as if it had come over the intercom. Everybody in the hall stopped dead.

"Your mother is a murderer," Mallory said again, "and she's going to die for it. There's the death penalty in this state. They're going to stick a needle in her arm and she's going to die for it, and then do you know what's going to happen to her? She's going to be a rotting corpse, just a lot of dead meat with maggots all over her, rotting in the ground."

"Get the Hell away from me," Barbie McGuffie shrieked. "You're going to Hell, that's what's going to happen to you. You're going to Hell and so is your mother. You're both going to burn for all eternity."

"There is no Hell," Mallory said, and Catherine could see the gleam in her eye, the triumph, as if this had been bottled up for so long it was an achievement to let it out. "There is no Hell. There is no life after death. There is no God. Only stupid people think there is.

Stupid people who want to make the rest of us all stupid, too, and it isn't going to work. Because you know the truth, Barbie McGuffie. There is no God. There is no life after death. Your mother is going to die from that lethal injection and then she's going to rot."

Barbie McGuffie threw her books on the floor and advanced on Mallory Cornish, but Mallory wasn't moving. "You listen to me," Barbie said, "there is a God and there is a Hell and your mother is in it right this minute, your mother—"

"Angels floating in the sky, Barbie? Women having babies when they haven't had sex? Noah and his *ark,* for God's sake. Tell me this, Barbie, what happened to all the shit? You know. There were all those animals there. They must have shit. They must have shit a lot. Where did all the shit go? Noah must have been up to his eyeballs in shit by the second day."

"You shut up," Barbie shrieked again. She had her hand on Mallory's shoulder. She shoved. Mallory still didn't move. She shoved again. "You're going to Hell! You're going to Hell!"

"You're going nowhere," Mallory said. "Twenty years from now you'll still be sitting in Snow Hill, working at the diner and getting fat, when I'm out doing something with my life and then that will be it. Only stupid people believe in God and you're the stupidest of the bunch, except for your mother, and she's going to die. She's going to die right there in the death chamber. It's going to be on *American Justice.* And then she's going to rot in the ground. And that's what's going to happen to you."

This time, when Barbie shoved, it was with the full weight of her body behind it. Mallory stumbled back, and as she did Barbie stumbled forward, and teetered, and then fell, right down onto the hard linoleum of the foyer floor, onto her knees. Catherine could hear the crack of a bone all the way from where she stood at the doors.

Mallory caught her balance and walked back to where Barbie was, kneeling and howling at the top of her lungs.

"Your mother murdered my mother," Mallory said, "and I know it and so do you. She said she was going to do it, and now she's done it.

I heard her say she was going to do it. I'm going to tell the police all about it, and when I do they'll arrest her, and she'll go on trial, and she'll be found guilty, and that's when they'll put her to death. To rot. As a corpse in the ground. With maggots coming out of her eye sockets. To rot with nothing to show for her life, just like the rest of you idiots."

"My leg is broken," Barbie screamed. "My leg is broken."

"Well," Mallory said, "why don't you pray to God and have Him heal it? Just pray to God, and I'm sure, if He's listening, He'll just go *zap* and put it back togther. Because, you know, it says in the Bible that if you pray you'll be healed, so that's going to happen."

2

There were lawyers involved in this case, lawyers besides himself, Henry Wackford knew that, but he didn't think this issue was ever going to be resolved in a courtroom. No, it wasn't. This issue wasn't about courtrooms, and it didn't matter how many judges told these people that they were being stupid, that they were breaking the law—no, that didn't matter either. Henry was having a hard time breathing. It was all so obvious to him. All of it. You had to make people see the truth, and it was a truth they didn't want to see. No, Henry thought, most people didn't want to see the truth even for a minute, and that was why you had things like this, that was why this country had descended into a medieval cesspit complete with torture chambers and grand inquisitors.

All right, Henry admitted. Not torture chambers. Not literally. But that was the problem, too. People took things far too literally. People thought that if somebody said that religion was good for them, that it made people happy and pleasant and industrious and kind, then that must be true, just because somebody said it. Or maybe because a lot of people said it over the course of a lot of years. Hundreds of years. He wasn't thinking straight. Even so, he knew what he meant to think, and that was enough, at least until he got in front of a camera

193

and made somebody listen to him. Religion was not good for people. It made them believe in delusions. It made them stupid. It made them *vile*. That was the message that had to get out, somehow, someday, if the good people were ever going to get this country back from the bumpkins and the idiots and the yahoos, if this country was ever going to be great and honorable—well, he wouldn't say again. Henry Wackford didn't think the country had ever been great and honorable before now, except maybe for a few years during the administration of Franklin Delano Roosevelt. And even then, there was the racism to consider.

He really was spinning his wheels here, he thought. He made himself stop and take a deep breath. He was in his office, but he'd been outside just a little while ago, listening to the talk on Main Street. By now everybody in town had to know that Judy Cornish was dead, and that she'd been battered to death just the way Annie-Vic had been battered almost to death. It was a pattern, that's what it was. It was obviously the same person, or persons, and they were following a pattern. He just had to make people see the obvious. They were all of them, *out there*—just like his ex-wife had been.

"What the Hell makes you get out of bed in the morning?" she would yell at him. "What do you bother to go on living? If it's all going to end up in nothing, what's the point?"

Yes, Henry thought, he understood, he really did. These people were afraid to face their own mortality. They were afraid to live every day knowing that it would all come to an end some day and that end would be the end, the absolute end, with nothing to make up for their disappointments or their failures or any of the rest of it. God wouldn't reward them for being "good" and really pushing ahead to get that promotion, or not chucking their "obligations" to go off to school. God wasn't there to make up for all the things they'd missed. God just wasn't there. No wonder they got murderously violent, the whole pack of them. They couldn't stand the thought that they weren't important, that they didn't mean anything, that if they failed they failed and there was nothing and nobody who could make it up to them. Here was the thing, though, Henry was sure. Down deep somewhere, they knew. They knew there was no God. They knew evolution was true. They knew the Bible was nothing but a pack of lies and fantasies. They knew it. That was why they had to kill anybody who threatened to prove it.

Henry took another deep breath. It didn't do for him to think about his ex-wife, or the girls he'd dated in college, or even the decision, so long ago now, to come back home to practice law. He didn't believe in dwelling on the past, for one thing, and for another it got him too worked up to think. He had to think now, it was important: first Annie-Vic, then Judy Cornish. There was no telling how many more attacks there would be before this thing was over. The FBI had two agents in place. Henry knew that. They weren't even bothering to maintain a cover. They also weren't taking any of this seriously. It was just like with the militias a few years ago. Those were the same kinds of people, too. Small-town backwoods Christians. And what came out of that? Timothy McVeigh, that's what. Timothy McVeigh and that big gutted federal building in Oklahoma City. The woods were full of these people, and nobody ever paid attention to them.

He took yet another deep breath. Christine was in the outer office, talking on the phone and crying. He could hear her. She was definitely on the other side, but he hadn't had a choice about hiring her. She was the best he could get in Snow Hill. He hated the idea of her in the outer office all day, saying little prayers over her lunch and sending up little "messages to God" in the hopes he would have a change of heart. He knew she was doing both, and that she always asked the Baptists to pray for him when there was a call for intentions on Sunday.

He went to his office window and looked out on Main Street. The cable news vans were still standing where they had been all morning. Henry thought they would have moved if anybody had told them about the murder. Nobody would have told them, though, because they were outsiders, and because the yahoos here were intimidated by them. That was something else that came of being stuck in wretched small towns like this day after day and year after year. The big world out there started to intimidate you. It made you feel every one of your inadequacies.

Christine was probably praying for the soul of Judy Cornish. She probably also thought Judy had gone straight to Hell. Henry's ex-wife had prayed for him a lot, and her family had prayed for him too, because they'd all been convinced that she would "bring him to the Lord" one of these days. The marriage had started to go sour as soon as she realized that that was never going to happen. She would have been happy to live forever in Snow Hill. She'd come from a nearly identical small town in Michigan, and when the marriage was over she'd gone back there.

"I'm not going to be in Snow Hill much longer," Henry said, to the air. His breath fogged the window in front of him. There were people in the mobile news vans. CNN and Fox. It wouldn't be hard to pick one over the other.

Henry had never taken off his coat. He'd unbuttoned it, and now he left it unbuttoned. He went through to the outer office. Christine was still on the phone. Tears were running down her face, and her mascara was running as well, making dark rivulets down both her cheeks. She looked like a gargoyle, or one of those whores with the hearts of gold from the old noir detective films. She'd go to seed in another ten years and look like all the other women around here. She'd gain weight and her hair would frowse. He didn't even know if "frowse" was a word.

"Oh, Mr. Wackford," Christine said as he walked past. "Isn't it terrible? Isn't it the most terrible thing you've ever heard? I've been praying and praying, but I just don't understand it."

Henry was tempted to tell her she would never understand anything by prayer, but he didn't see the point of it.

"I'm going out," he said, and then he was out, all the way into the cold air again. Main Street was not deserted now. People seemed to come out of the cracks in the sidewalk when something really awful happened. It was as if they lay in wait, their lives on hold, until there was gossip that was really going somewhere.

Henry crossed Main Street and went up a block and a half, toward the CNN van. The familiar logo calmed him down a little. There it was, the emissary from the outside world, the ambassador from sanity. Of course, nothing in the United States was entirely sane, if it was they wouldn't have elected the Shrub for a second term—Henry refused to say that the man had been elected for his first—but there were degrees of insanity, and CNN was considerably more sane than Snow Hill.

He went up to the van's cab and looked inside. It was empty. He went around to the back. It was closed up. He looked up and down the street. They had to be somewhere, these people.

Half a block further, the door to the diner swung open and a young woman came out with a young man. The young woman was dressed in a skirt and sweater and the young man looked like he'd just walked out of a Greenwich Village beat joint from the fifties. Henry took notice.

The young man and the young woman were talking. They were also carrying Styrofoam cups of coffee. As they got closer, Henry could hear the man saying: "Something's going on. I grew up in a place like this. People don't get this way unless something's going on."

Nobody had told them. Very good. They were practically at the van.

Henry waited. It was still very cold. He wanted to button his coat, but he was afraid he would look like a hick if he did it.

He approached the man and woman as they got to the van. The man said, "Can we help you with something?"

"I thought you might like to know what's going on," Henry Wackford said.

The man looked him up and down again. Then he held out his hand. "Mitchell Frasier," he said, "and this is Charlene Holder."

"I'm Henry Wackford," Henry said. "I'm the Wackford in Wackford Squeers, the law firm, up there."

"And you're one of the plaintiffs," Charlene said. "I remember that name."

"Do you remember the name Judy Cornish?" Henry said.

Charlene Holder paused. "I remember a Cornish. Mr. and Mrs. Daniel Cornish?"

"Judy would be the Mrs. Cornish," Henry said.

"So what happened?" Charlene asked. "Did she do something about the case, did she withdraw, or something like that?"

Henry blinked. Did these people honestly believe you could get an entire small town buzzing just because one plaintiff, out of God only knew how many, had decided to drop out of a suit? Besides, Judy hadn't decided to drop out, she'd never have done that.

"She's dead," Henry said, although that wasn't the way he'd intended to tell them. "She was battered to death out at the old Hadley house just a couple of hours ago. Somebody left her dead and bloody on Annie-Vic Hadley's dining room floor."

Maybe it was a lot for these two people to take in. Henry didn't know. They weren't reacting the way he was expecting them to. What had happened to the old crusading spirit and the scoop reporter? Shouldn't they be leaping into the van and taking off to report on what was going on?

"For God's sake," Henry said, and then there was something in the back of his mind that said he ought to stop saying that. Too many of the yahoos thought that if you said that you secretly believed in God, or why else would you call on his name, even in vain?

"Up there," he said, pointing in the direction of Annie-Vic's house. "It isn't far. If you go in that direction, you'll find the whole pack of them. Everything but the ambulance. That already went. You must have heard it. Don't you realize what's happening?"

The two of them still seemed to be hesitating. The young woman rocked back and forth on her legs, obviously freezing and obviously completely unwilling to dress for the weather. Henry thought the "stupid" in "stupid American" was applying to more and more of his countrymen by the day.

"They're killing us off," Henry said patiently. "The Creationists. They're killing us off one by one, because they don't care what they have to do to get their religion imposed on everybody in the country; they don't care if they have to commit murder. They're going to make this a Christian nation no matter what any of the rest of us wants. And I'm going to tell the world about it. I'm going to call a press conference, with all the remaining plaintiffs on this case, and we're going to *tell* the American people what these Creationists are really like."

3

Alice McGuffie got home late, so late that the whole town was full of it, full of the murder, and full of that idiot Henry Wackford, mouthing off for the TV cameras on every television set in town. On every television set in the country, as far as Alice could tell. She wasn't thinking straight. It was so hard to know what to do. It was harder because there had been so much in between. Barbie was hurt, hurt by that little bitch of a secular humanist, or whatever these people liked to call themselves. It was atheism, pure and simple, as far as Alice was concerned, and she knew what came along with atheism. Atheists had no morals. How could they have? They didn't believe in God, and they didn't believe in Hell, so they had no reason at all not just to do whatever they wanted. If you asked Alice, and nobody every did, they thought she was stupid, or, worse, a hick, or something worse than that, a hillbilly, but if you asked her, it was a crock, all this stuff about atheism and secular humanism. There wasn't a person on earth who didn't believe in God. These people were just looking for an excuse, that was all. They wanted a reason to go on doing what they wanted to do instead of what they were supposed to do, throwing over their families and run off to jobs on the other side of the country, dumping their kids on nannies so that they could pose around like big executives, calling themselves "vice president" this and "doctor" that. Oh, the women were the worst. Alice knew. She'd been living with these people all of her life.

Her hand hurt. Barbie needed her painkiller prescription picked up at the pharmacy. She could call Holman Carr and have him send it home with Lyman. Except that she'd have to get the prescription in somehow. It didn't used to be that way. It used to be that if you called Holman and read him the thing over the phone, he'd make it up for you and bring it over and then check the slip on your doorstep. He couldn't do that now because *they* had come. *They* wanted all the rules followed. *They* were always talking about "unacceptable risks" and "inappropriate behavior." If there was a word Alice had come to truly hate in the last three or four years, it was definitely "inappropriate." None of those people came out and said they thought something was wrong. None of them even called you a name to your face. They just said that whatever you wanted to do was "inappropriate," as if that was supposed to mean something, as if that was supposed to be a reason for stopping.

Barbie was in the living room, on the couch, whimpering. They'd given her painkillers at the hospital, but those were going to wear off in another hour or two. She'd need something more, and something stronger than Advil. Alice hated the very idea of going into town. She didn't even want to go into the diner, and she would have to do that. Lyman couldn't run the place by himself. It would be full of people now, too, just the way they had expected it to be when the trial started next week. Those newspeople would come in and swarm this murder. They'd interview everybody. They'd want to interview her. She was a member of the school board. She was on the side of Right and Good. Of course they'd want to interview her. They'd want to make her look like a fool.

"Mama?" Barbie said from the other room.

Alice looked around. She was standing in her own kitchen. She was never in her kitchen in the middle of the day, except on Sundays, because they didn't open the diner on Sundays. Let them go to the mall and eat at one of those places that were run by corporations that didn't care about the Sabbath, or about honoring the Lord, or about anything. Let them do whatever they wanted to do. She just wished that Holman had been elected to the school board instead of that stuck-up snobby Annie-Vic Hadley. If Holman had been on the board, none of this would have happened.

"*Mama*," Barbie said again.

Alice made herself move. Her house looked nice in the sunlight. They painted the inside every other year, because Alice didn't like dirt, and she didn't like dinge, and she didn't like coming home to the smell of futility, either. She just wished sometimes that they could do something with the living room like those houses in the development, the ones with the high ceilings that went up and up and ended in skylights. This house had been in Lyman's family for as long as anybody could remember, at least as long as Annie-Vic's house had been in hers. It was a family heirloom, or something. But it wasn't like Annie-Vic's house, either.

"Mama, please," Barbie said.

Alice made herself move. To get to the kitchen you had to go through the dining room. The house was only fifteen hundred square feet. In the dining room there was a long table and six chairs, all passed down to her by Lyman's mother, and all made in Grand Rapids, too. Alice remembered when that used to mean something, and when Lyman's family had been so much better off than hers. The time when she was growing up had been better. There was no development then, and there was Annie-Vic only some of the time. She was always off doing something somewhere. Showing us up, Alice thought, and then she pushed that firmly out of her mind. There was no way that somebody like Annie-Vic could show her up. There was nothing on earth that was better or more valuable than good ordinary folks living their lives and minding their own business while those people, people like Annie-Vic, went running around trying to ruin everything.

The living room was long and narrow, but it had a fireplace with a fancy white mantel where they could hang stockings every Christmas. Alice believed in doing Christmas big. She liked to have the house decorated and she liked to have lights on the trees outside. What would happen to this country when the secular humanists had abolished Christmas and everybody had to live through the entire long month of December, in the dark and the cold and the awful weather, with nothing to look forward to?

The couch Barbie was lying on had been bought new at Sears five years ago. It needed to be reupholstered. Alice hadn't noticed that before. Barbie had a cast up to her knee, a big thick one. The leg with the cast was up on the arm of the couch, because she was supposed to keep it elevated.

"Mama," she said, when Alice came in.

"I was just going to call your father and have him come out and get this prescription," Alice said. "He can run out and get it and then run back into town and give it in at the pharmacy, and then Mr. Carr can send it over. I don't like the idea of leaving you here alone."

"I didn't bother her," Barbie said. "I really didn't bother her, Mama. I knew her mother was murdered. Everybody knew it. I was just walking along minding my own business and going to class and then she was just there. And she slapped me."

"Well," Alice said, trying very hard to be fair. "Her mother had just died. She probably wasn't thinking straight."

"She said some things," Barbie said. "She said there wasn't any God. She said that all that happened after you died was that your body went into the ground and worms came out of it."

"She's afraid her mother is going to go to Hell, that's all that was," Alice said. "Having your body rot in the ground is a lot better than going to Hell. If you rot in the ground you can't really feel anything. If you go to Hell, all you feel is pain and it's the worst pain in the world and it goes on for eternity. It never stops for even one instant."

"Do you think Mrs. Cornish went to Hell?" Barbie asked.

"We can never tell who goes to Hell and who doesn't," Alice said, because that was the right thing to say. She'd heard about it in church. No matter how bad you thought a person was, no matter what awful things she'd done, you couldn't read her heart. Only God could read her heart. Only God could know for sure.

"I think Mrs. Cornish is in Hell," Barbie said. "I think she's there right now, screaming for somebody to help her, and nobody will. I think Mallory Cornish is going to Hell one of these days, too. I hate them, did you know that, Mama? I hate all those people from the development. I even hate the way they talk."

"You shouldn't hate," Alice said, still being conscientious. She could sympathize with Barbie. You shouldn't hate, the Bible said so, but then it said you were supposed to hate the sin and not the sinner. But that didn't make much sense, either. How could you do that?

"I know I shouldn't hate," Barbie said, looking as if she were about to drift off to sleep. "I know that. But she said you were a murderer. She said you killed her mother."

"What?"

"She said you were a murderer," Barbie repeated. "Right there in front of the office at school. She said you'd killed her mother and you were going to go to the death chamber and have a lethal injection and then your body was going to rot in the ground and worms were going to come out of it. She said it over and over again."

"She probably wasn't thinking straight," Alice said. It was something she'd said already, but she couldn't think of any new words.

"I knew she was talking trash," Barbie said. "I knew it. But there's that man here, the one not from here, helping the police, and I thought he might not know she was talking trash, and she might get you in trouble. Are you going to get in trouble, Mama?"

"No, no, of course not," Alice said. "You should try taking a nap now. I should go call your father and get something done about this prescription."

"She's probably in Hell right this minute," Barbie said. "She's probably burning up in the flames and wailing for mercy, but you don't get any mercy in Hell, do you, Mama?"

"No," Alice said.

"Well," Barbie said. "That's good then. That makes me feel better."

THREE

1

Gregor Demarkian didn't spend much time at crime scenes anymore. One of the better aspects of being a consultant, instead of part of a regular force, was that he didn't have to. The crime scenes were often ancient history by the time he showed up. On the other hand, one of the better aspects of being a consultant instead of a private detective was that he was allowed onto crime scenes when they happened in front of his face, and he only wished he could learn to stand the boredom and the confusion they inevitably entailed. This crime scene was mostly confusion, with nobody really in charge. Gary Albright had not left, but he was leaning back against his police car, being careful not to contaminate anything. Tom Fordman and Eddie Block were trying, but it was obvious that they had little experience. Gregor had no idea what the procedures were in this department, except in a sort of vague and general way. It gave him a great sense of relief when the crime scene technicians from the state police arrived, although it seemed to make everybody else nervous.

"He'll be along in a bit," Gary told Gregor, meaning, Gregor presumed, this man named Dale Vardan, but there was no sign of him yet, and Gary Albright wasn't talking.

Gregor looked over at the Volvo sitting in the drive. There were police cars all around it now, but the woman inside it didn't seem to have moved for hours. She had her head against the steering wheel and her arms wrapped around it. Gregor looked back at the big, old house, thinking how odd it really was that there was a time when houses like this had been in vogue, and then walked out to the Volvo and the woman there. Niederman, he remembered, feeling a little relieved. It was Mrs. Niederman.

Gregor knocked against the driver's-side window. Mrs. Niederman put her head up and looked out. It was colder than she was expecting it to be. She pulled her coat more closely around her chest.

"Hello," she said.

"I'm Gregor Demarkian," he said. "We did meet, a little while ago—"

"I know who you are," she said. She looked up and around. "It's cold. I want to put the window up."

"Could I come around and sit in the car with you?" Gregor asked. "I just wanted to ask you a few questions."

Mrs. Niederman looked out across the driveway, at the police and the ambulance and the state evidence van and shuddered. "Come right in. Come in. I want to go home. I want to get out of here. Somebody else is going to get killed. Just you wait."

Gregor left that alone. Until he knew what was going on here, he had no idea if it was likely or not that somebody else would be killed. He wished he could pinpoint what it was about this case that kept reminding him of that other one, the one where the man had killed himself and his child in the attic playroom of the house he had once shared with his wife. The case had been on his mind all day, and there didn't seem to be any point of connection to this one. He came around the back of the car, opened the door, slipped into the deep bucket seat, and closed the door behind him.

"I'm going to run the engine for a while," Mrs. Niederman said. "It's cold."

It was, indeed, very cold. Gregor waited while she got the car started and the heater pumping out hot air at the highest possible rate. He thought she would have been a mousy little woman if she hadn't had an air of self-confidence that made you forget about her looks. The air was there even though tears were streaming down out of her eyes and she was doing nothing to stop them.

"Judy always said somebody was going to get killed," she said. "And that was before. Before the lawsuit. Judy always said that these people didn't want us here, and they were going to do something about it. We even had to watch when we went to the grocery store."

"Excuse me?"

Shelley Niederman wiped tears off one cheek with the palm of her hand. "There are tissues here somewhere. Judy always had tissues. This is Judy's car, did you know that? I don't know why I got in behind the wheel after I found her. I just did. I just did. What are Dan and the children going to do without her?"

"You were saying something about the grocery store," Gregor said gently.

"Oh," Shelley Niederman said. "Yes. They don't like us here, you know. The people in town. They never did like us, even before there was all this trouble with evolution. It's like a movie out here, it's like *Deliverance*. Except I never saw *Deliverance*. You know what I mean. It's like. Oh, God, I don't know, they're hillbillies, even the ones that live in town. They're just not—I don't know—they're just not. And we'd go shopping in this grocery store in town and they'd *say* things to us. All of them. Even the checkout girls."

"Say what to you?" Gregor asked.

Shelley Niederman shrugged. "Some of the younger people would call us bitches, but the older ones never use language like that. And maybe it wasn't that they said things to us, it was that they said things about us. 'Ooh, look, a Coach bag. Doesn't she think she's the Queen of Sheba.' That's one I remember. Somebody said it about me. Oh, that woman, Alice McGuffie, she said it about me."

"I see," Gregor said.

"And then, later, when the lawsuit was on, they did say things directly to us. We used to go to the supermarket and look around the parking lot to see who was there before we went in. And it was a pain, you know, because the nearest other supermarket is a good half-hour drive away, although it's a better one, you know, and we went there sometimes, but other times you just want to pick up a few things and you don't have the time. But we had to be careful, because they'd come up to us, and not just in the supermarket, on Main Street, too, sometimes, they'd come up and say things. 'I'm going to pray for you,' one of them said. 'Because you're an atheist, and atheists rot in Hell.' Oh, no, that wasn't just somebody. That was that McGuffie woman again. But I'm not an atheist. Judy wasn't either. I don't know where they get this stuff. And then they said it to the children in school."

"The women did? Alice McGuffie did?"

"The other children did," Shelley Niederman said. "The first few times it happened, Mallory was nearly hysterical. Mallory is, was, Judy's daughter. I don't know what tense I'm supposed to use. It's impossible to know what tense I'm supposed to use."

"Don't worry about it," Gregor said. "Would you mind if I asked you a little about today? I'm not really clear about today."

"She's dead," Shelley Niederman said. "What else do you want to know about today."

"Well, for one thing, I'd like to understand why the two of you came here. From what I've been able to figure out, two of Miss Hadley's relatives are staying here for a short while while she's in the hospital. Were you looking for them?"

"I don't know," Shelley said.

"You don't know?"

"Judy didn't say," Shelley said. "She just—we were talking about the children. At school. You know, the trouble they'd been having, and Judy said—this was before—she said that we were going about it the wrong way. We were always playing defense, and that instead we should learn to play offense. Because they were playing offense. And then she said there was something called the Equal Access Act, and we could use that to make the school allow Mallory and Stacey—Stacey is my daughter, she and Mallory have been best friends since we moved here—Judy said that we could make the school allow Mallory and Stacey and their friends form a Biblical Criticism Club, or something like that, that would talk about the stories in the Bible that weren't really true and how we knew they weren't true. It sounded, I don't know. . . . It was the kind of thing Judy would think up and Mallory would go along with. It was just to cause trouble, you know, and I understood the point and all that but it sounded so serious, if you see what I mean. And then we were driving along and we were passing this place and all of a sudden Judy said there was something she wanted to see about. And then we pulled into the driveway."

"She didn't tell you what it was she wanted to see about?"

Shelley Niederman shook her head. "I think, the way she was behaving, I think she might have seen something. Or somebody. Anyway, I said, you know, whatever, and she said she was just going to go up and knock on the door and she went. But you can't see from here to the front door, not really. There's that hedge thing in the way and the porch, and it's so dark. So she just sort of disappeared and I thought somebody must have been home because she was gone so long, and then I got nervous and went up there and the door was open—"

"The front door was open?"

"Wide open. Almost all the way back. And I went in and I called out and nobody answered."

"Did it feel to you as if somebody were in the house?"

Shelley Niederman shrugged again. "I didn't think about it. It was very quiet, you know. There wasn't a television on or anybody talking or anything like that. So I just kept walking forward along this hall, but then there wasn't anywhere to go except what looked like a private area in the back, you know, a back door, that kind of thing. There wasn't anywhere in that direction so I backed up a little and went into the living room, and when I got into the living room I saw her legs on the floor. Right there next to the dining room table. Under it. Next to it. I can't remember. She was just there and there was blood everywhere, blood on the walls, and her head looked like, her head looked like—like sponge. Like sponge."

Shelley Niederman's head went up. Then she turned away from Gregor, opened the door next to her, leaned out, and began to vomit onto the ground.

Gregor waited until it was over, and it was not over for a very long time. Beyond the car's windshield he could see the crime scene investigation still going on, a little more organized now, at least on the surface, men and women with crime scene kits going in and out of the front door. Judy Cornish's head had looked like a sponge. He had seen it himself. He had seen other heads that looked like sponges.

Shelley Niederman sat up. She closed the door next to her and then twisted around to rummage in the back. She came up with some bottled water and a box of tissues.

"Judy always had everything on hand," she said. "She was always very organized. I'm not so organized. But I hate these people, do you know that? I've never hated anybody else before in my life, but I hate these people. They're just so petty and crabby and pinched—somehow, I don't know the words. They're so small. And they hate you for things, because you went to a good college, or you read books instead of watching *American Idol*, or whatever and they just . . . they just . . . I don't know. If this is what religion is like, it's not surprising that people become atheists. I mean, it isn't. I can't imagine not believing in God, but the God I believe in isn't like this. He isn't hateful and small. He isn't—"

Shelley put her forehead down against the steering wheel and closed her eyes.

"It's all right," Gregor said, thinking as he said it that he had no idea what he meant. Of course it wasn't all right. "Just tell me one thing, if you don't mind. Just tell me if you touched anything, anything at all, when you went into the house."

Shelley sat up and blinked at him. "Touched anything? Like what? What am I supposed to have touched?"

"I don't know. The walls. The door. A piece of furniture."

"Oh, wonderful," Shelley Niederman said. "Now they're going to think I did it. I was here, and she was supposed to be my friend, so they're all going to think I did it. Because none of them could be guilty, could they? I'm a secular humanist. They're all good Christian people."

2

Back in the middle of the chaotic yard, Gary Albright was still standing against his police car, as if he had been carved out of wood and left to rot there. Gregor skirted another little clutch of technical people—the state police had always had a lot of technical people, and a few years ago they'd received an enormous grant from the Department of Homeland Security, so that they now had too many technical people—and stopped next to Gary. His face was blank. There was no way to tell what he was thinking.

Gregor looked up at the house, and said, "The relatives should be back soon. They should talk to them. When I was with the FBI, the thing I hated most about investigations was how clueless we were about real conditions on the ground. It's impossible to come into a small town, or even a large city, to come in cold and know what you need to know to do an effective investigation. That was why I was never the kind of special agent who liked to take over from the local police forces. The local police forces usually knew better than I did what I needed to pay attention to."

For a moment, Gary Albright didn't seem to have heard. Gregor watched his face. They taught you to do that in the military, that look of blank openness, as if you were so completely honest and honorable that you had nothing to hide. Most men lost it after they left the service. A few months, sometimes a few years, and dealing with ordinary human beings on an everyday basis made that whole pretense of calm impartiality a liability, and it was more of a liability if it wasn't a pretense. You learned, Gregor thought. He had learned. He wondered why Gary Albright had not.

Gary finally looked away, and then up, straight into the atmosphere, as if he were trying to see a comet pass by. "I don't know what I'm supposed to know that you need to know," he said. "If I did I might not have had to call you in here. I don't even know what I need to know."

Gregor gestured toward the Volvo with his head. "I was just talking to that woman, Shelley Niederman. She is, I take it, from 'the development,' as everybody here calls it."

"She surely is that," Gary Albright said. "They're all like that, you know. Like Shelley Niederman and Judy Cornish."

"Everybody out at the development?"

"All the women," Gary Albright said. "I got around a little, you know. I saw women like that once or twice. But there were never women like that in Snow Hill before the development."

"Women like what?"

Gary shrugged. "I don't know how to put it. As if they were channeling some women's magazine all the time. The words they use. 'Proactive,' that was a big one. And they say things like, 'I had a meeting with Johnny's teacher so that we could work out strategies to help him succeed.' I mean, what kind of talk is that? What kind of a way is that to think of school? School is school. If you've got a brain in your head and you do your work, your grades are good. If not on either account, they're not. And that's not all."

"I didn't think it was," Gregor said.

"It's like they think they can control everything," Gary said. "I don't mean they run around trying to boss people. I mean they *define* everything as a problem to be solved."

"They didn't do that in the Marines?"

"We didn't do it like that," Gary said. "We didn't define *people* as problems to be solved. No, that's not what I mean. It's the way they do it." Gary looked into the sky again. Then he shook his head. "There was this woman, Miss Marbledale was telling me about it a few weeks ago. She's got a son, he's fourteen, and he just won't do his homework. So she, the woman, not Miss Marbledale, she took this kid to a psychiatrist. They did all this testing to find out if he had attention deficit disorder. They got him a shrink and put him into therapy for his 'problem,' but for God's sake, Mr. Demarkian, what problem? He's a fourteen-year-old boy who doesn't want to do his homework. That isn't a psychiatric disorder, it's puberty. And they're like that about *everything*. It's never the case that the kid isn't very bright, he must need medication. It's never the case that the kid is undisciplined and not much interested in changing that; if he thinks that way he must have psychological problems. They define *being human* as a psychological problem. Am I making any sense?"

"Yes," Gregor said. "Quite a lot of it."

"A fourteen-year-old must need a therapist because he doesn't want to do his homework. Or, you know, God forbid, he doesn't do it and then he lies about it to stay out of trouble. It must be a pathology. Mark Twain was wrong."

Gregor smiled. "They seem to think you've got a lot of pathologies," Gregor said. "At least, according to Shelley Niederman."

"Well, yeah," Gary said. "They think believing in God is a pathology. And voting Republican. We can't really know what we're doing and mean to do it. We must be sick."

"She said that she and the woman who died, Judy Cornish, were harassed at the supermarket, among other places. That they were called names, mostly, I think. And that their children were called names. She mentioned somebody named Alice McGuffie. I'm pretty sure that's one of the names on the school board list you gave me in that folder you left for me this morning."

"It is," Gary said. "And if Mrs. Niederman said Alice was following her around in the supermarket calling her names and, say, telling her she was about to go to Hell, I wouldn't be surprised. Some guy said once that the best argument against Christianity was Christians, and when he said that, Alice was the kind of Christian he was talking about."

"I take it she's someone you know well."

"Alice is what we call 'deep local,'" Gary said. "She's from here. Her parents were from here. Her great-grandparents were from here. Her family's been here at least as long as the Hadleys have been. Everybody knows her. Which is too bad, if you ask me. She's a nasty piece of work, and she is not getting better with age. In either direction."

"Excuse me?"

"She's got a daughter," Gary said. "Just the one. Which, considering the fact that Alice is opposed to birth control and willing to tell you why you're going to Hell for using it, is an interesting fact. Her daughter's name is Barbie and Barbie is, if anything, worse than she is. Barbie McGuffie is a world-class bully, and like most bullies, she's got less self-respect than pond scum."

Gregor considered this. "Would you say that this Alice McGuffie was violent? Would you say her daughter was violent?"

"If you mean physically violent, no," Gary said. "If you're thinking of that in there," he looked up at the house, "I'd sincerely doubt it. Hell, Mr. Demarkian. Alice doesn't want people dead. What fun would that be? She wants them where she can torture them."

"What about other people who share her point of view?" Gregor asked. "Are there a lot of these people in town? People who resent the people from the development? Who would have resented Ann-Victoria Hadley because she was like the people in the development in some way?"

"I'm sure half the town resents the development," Gary said. "I don't find that surprising. They've got a town here, and a way of life, and these people come in, and they don't even try to fit in. And it's not just that the people in the development think they're better than us, it's that we think they're better than us. More education. More money. More sophistication. So, yeah, there's a lot of resentment. But I don't think anybody would have committed murder over it."

"No," Gregor said. "I know what you mean. It doesn't seem very plausible to me, either."

"Besides," Gary said. "It isn't just resentment that people in town are feeling. Some people in town actually think the people from the development might be a good thing. In some ways. You know."

"No, I don't. Who thinks that, and in what ways?"

"Well," Gary said, "I do, a little. I mean, these people, they don't just expect their kids to go to college, they expect them to go to *Yale*. There's nothing wrong with ambition. And it matters what the people you're with are like. If they're all ambitious, you're more likely to be ambitious, too. I don't have my heart set on my kids growing up and growing old in Snow Hill."

"All right," Gregor said.

"And then there's Nick Frapp and his people," Gary said. "The people from the development don't have any preconceived ideas about who people are and who they come from, so since they've been voting, Nick's had less trouble getting his easements and things. People around here just tend to think he's a hillbilly and his people are hillbillies and they don't want them hanging around bringing down the town, but the development people just listen to his plans for a new school building, read the plans, and decide it sounds like a good idea. And I suppose it has been. A good idea, I mean. That church. That school. The hill people mostly down here instead of holing up in the hills the way they used to do."

"You don't sound convinced."

"Hill people are not pacifists," Gary Albright said. "You're looking at a very old and very insular culture there. Up to the point where Nick got all that up and running, the ATF used to lose two or three guys a year up there. They'd disappear and never be found again. There's probably something like an elephants' graveyard in those hills somewhere, bones stacked on bones over the course of decades."

"Do you think one of them would be willing to murder one woman and almost murder another to stop the teaching of evolution in Snow Hill public schools?"

"They don't go to Snow Hill public schools," Gary pointed out, "and I can't imagine anybody committing a murder over that. Not even Alice McGuffie or Franklin Hale, and Alice is mean and Franklin is a nutcase. But I can't imagine any of the development people committing a murder to keep evolution in the schools, either. It's not the kind of thing people commit murders about. No matter what they're saying this week on MSNBC."

"Funny," Gregor said. "I was thinking the same thing myself."

"There's Dale Vardan," Gary said. "He's brought an entourage."

3

Dale Vardan had not brought an entourage so much as he'd brought a small army, in uniform, that seemed to have nothing to do but wait for his instructions. Gregor Demarkian watched him walk across the now muddy expanse of the driveway with some curiosity. Gary Albright did not seem the kind of man who took a visceral dislike to anybody. Even with people he did not like, Gary tended toward patient forbearance. But it wasn't only Gary Albright who didn't like Dale Vardan. The entire Snow Hill Police Department recoiled automatically at the mere mention of "calling in the state police." Gregor thought it was a lot of energy to expend on a small, thin man who looked too small for his suit.

A moment later, with Dale Vardan literally in his face, Gregor changed his mind. Dale Vardan might be too small for his suit, but he was too big for his britches—which was one of those things rural people were supposed to say, but that Gregor had never heard it from them. Vardan was the kind of man who liked to come right up to your chest and stick his nose into your own, except this time it didn't quite work, because Vardan was no taller than five four, and Gregor was six four the last time anybody had measured him. Gary Albright was well over six feet, too. Gregor couldn't imagine that a man like Dale Vardan could intimidate him.

"You're Gregor Demarkian," Vardan said. "That's right, isn't it?"

The trick was not to back up, even instinctively. This was dominance behavior. This was like cats. What Vardan wanted was to take control of the space. Gregor needed not to give it to him.

"I'm Gregor Demarkian," he said. "Gary tells me your name is Dale Vardan and you're with the state police."

"We can take over here now," Vardan said. "I knew we were going to have to, soon as I heard the first reports on that Hadley woman. These small town police departments, they don't know what they're dealing with. They're not—*equipped*—to handle the pressure."

"I don't think we're having trouble with pressure," Gregor said. "And from what I've understood so far, the Snow Hill Police Department isn't interested in having you take over the investigation of anything. What they did was ask for assistance."

"Uh-huh. Well," Vardan said, "I've been asked for assistance before. They're out of their depth, that's what it is. They've got some guy running around smashing up people with an aluminum baseball bat, and they don't know what to do about it."

"How do you know it was an aluminum baseball bat?"

"It was a figure of speech," Vardan said. "It could have been anything, just a blunt instrument. I'll find out what it is, exactly, once I get this investigation organized."

"And how do you know it was one person," Gregor said. "And how do you know it was a he? You're making a lot of assumptions here."

"You think there are two people running around smashing in women's faces with blunt instruments?" Dale Vardan demanded. "That's what you got, you bring it in here from the FBI and the city of Philadelphia? How many times you think that's going to happen, two people, fifty people, all running around bashing faces in, and all the faces belong to people who are suing the school board?"

"It only has to happen once," Gregor said mildly.

"Yeah, sure, it only has to happen once. Let me tell you what's happening here, Mr. Demarkian from the FBI."

"It's been close to a decade since I was with the FBI."

"You just listen to me," Dale Vardan said. "This is hillbilly country, up here. That's what you've got, a bunch of hillbillies. You think you don't, 'cause this is Pennsylvania and not West Virginia, but this is Appalachia and we all know it. And these people here, they like to

216

think they're a cut above that, living in town the way they do, and not up in some shack somewhere with a still in the back shed, but they're nothing but hillbillies, either, and it shows."

"Ann-Victoria Hadley doesn't seem to me to be a hillbilly."

"No, she isn't," Dale Vardan said, "but Gary Albright surely is, and so are his boys, and as far as I'm concerned they could all kill each other off one fine spring morning and the entire state of Pennsylvania would be better for it. The entire country would be better for it. And then there's that other one. He'll be involved in this somewhere."

"What other one?" Gregor asked.

"Dale is talking about Nick Frapp," Gary Albright said. "Dale has big problems with Nick Frapp."

Gregor was going to point out that Gary himself had big problems with Nick Frapp, but he didn't. "I don't see what the Reverend Frapp has to do with any of this," he said instead.

"The Reverend Frapp." Dale Vardan spit on the ground. "Reverend, my ass. Went out to Oklahoma where they have an entire college for hillbillies, that idiot Oral Roberts, saw a nine-foot-tall Jesus in his backyard. That's what hillbillies do when they're not drunk on their asses. They see Jesus in the backyard. Jesus in a ham sandwich. You name it, they've got Jesus in it."

Gregor looked at the small, round bald spot directly on top of Dale Vardan's head. It was difficult for him to look at anything except the top of Dale Vardan's head, because Vardan had not backed up.

"If you're assuming, as I take it, that the assaults are the work of someone angry with the people who filed the lawsuit against the school board," Gregor said, "then I don't see what the Reverend Frapp has to do with it. He doesn't have anything to do with the public schools. His church runs a private school. Why would he care, one way or the other, what happened with the lawsuit?"

Dale Vardan raised his eyes to heaven. "It's *Jaysus!*" he said. "That's the reason for everything. It's *Jaysus!*"

"Ah," Gregor said.

"They'd kill their own mothers for Jesus," Dale Vardan said. "Then they'd speak in tongues and roll around in the mud and writhe like they're having a fit. That's the power of the Holy Ghost for you. That's the power of the Lord. Then they get bit and they end up in the emergency room half dead. Stupid assholes."

"Ah," Gregor said again.

"Sit back and watch me work," Vardan said. "I've been waiting for this a long time. I've been waiting for one of them to pull something they couldn't get out of by shutting all their people up. If you don't know what you're doing, I do."

"I think I know what I'm doing," Gregor said. "And I will repeat, I've been hired by the Snow Hill Police Department to run this investigation. They have the right to do that, and I have the right, as head of this investigation, to decide both what help I want from the state police and what help I'll do without. So, if you don't mind, I'll make some use of your crime lab and your tech personal, both of which you have to put at my disposal. It's the law, and don't think I don't know it. Beyond that, I doubt if your services will be necessary."

Vardan backed up this time. He really was a small man, Gregor thought, tiny, and it was as if he was refusing to admit it to himself. He wore clothes that were too big for him the way some women always wore clothes that were too small, because they didn't want to admit to their real size. Vardan was looking him up and down, back and forth, side to side.

"Well," he said. "I can always start my own investigation. I can always declare this a state police matter."

"Not without a plausible excuse," Gregor said pleasantly, "or a way to claim jurisdiction, neither of which you have. I've got some people I need to talk to now. I suppose I'll run into you later."

"You're just like all of them," Dale Vardan said. "You come in here from the city, you think you know what's going on. You don't. You don't understand these people. You don't know them. You don't even begin to get the picture."

Gregor thought he got the picture perfectly well, but what bothered him was that Dale Vardan was a distraction, and would probably stick around to be a distraction.

"I'm sorry," Gregor said to Gary Albright, almost whispering in his ear. "I should have listened."

Gary Albright shrugged. "It's going to be late by the time we finish up here. You might want to think about staying over instead of going back to Philadelphia tonight. Unless it's impossible, you know, what with the wedding coming up, and that kind of thing."

"It's not impossible," Gregor said. "I was thinking myself that it might make sense, if I'm going to wait around to hear some of the tech people give preliminaries. Where's the nearest motel?"

"Fifty miles away out on Route 10," Gary Albright said. "The best thing would be for me and Sarah to put you up. She won't mind, the food is half decent, and we've got a perfectly good spare room."

"Ah," Gregor said.

"Oh, don't start," Gary Albright said. "I'm about ready to explode. Come home with me and eat meatloaf and you don't have to talk about the case if you don't want to. Lord only knows I don't want to."

FOUR

1

Sometimes, Franklin Hale thought the world was full of women who thought they knew everything. Annie-Vic Hadley was that kind of woman, and this one who had just died, this Judy Cornish, she was one, too. Right now there was another one on the television set, and it wasn't even Hillary Clinton. As far as Franklin was concerned, Hillary Clinton was the ultimate in women who thought they knew everything. She was your mother and your bossy fourth-grade teacher and that nurse in that movie all rolled into one. The woman on the television was not that bad, exactly, but Franklin knew the type. They'd all gone to fancy-ass colleges in New England and talked like they were in the middle of writing a textbook. Franklin hated New England. It was as if the place existed only to breed more of these women, and the women it couldn't breed it transformed, like people being turned into zombies in an old black-and-white horror movie. Franklin *did* like black-and-white horror movies. He could remember going to them on Saturday afternoons at the Palace Theater in town, before that closed because of the competition from the multiplex out in Dunweedin. Sometimes he could almost understand these evolution people. All life is change. All life is competition. Eat or be eaten. Kill or be killed. He remembered the guy who had owned the Palace Theater, too. He was one of those guys always whining about how they were getting killed by the "big fellas." Franklin hated assholes who talked about the "big fellas." It was like juvenile delinquents who talked about how they only did what they did because their daddies weren't around.

The woman on the television was named Eugenie Scott, and she was head of something called the National Center for Science Education. Franklin watched her head bob up and down and she explained something or the other to Larry King. National Center for Science Education, my foot, Franklin thought. None of these people cared a damn for science education. If they did, they'd actually listen to the science. By now it was no secret. Even the scientists didn't believe in evolution anymore. They just thought they could go on fooling the American public forever. Pastor Jack down at the Baptist Church said that they did that because they wanted to win souls away from God and for the devil, but Franklin thought that was a crock, too. What they wanted was to prance around preening themselves on how smart they all were, smarter than anybody else, so smart they didn't even have to talk to all those ordinary stupid people. It was what that kind of person always wanted, and there were lots of that kind of person out there running around. There was Larry King, for one. There was any news anchor on MSNBC. Franklin had to thank God for Bill O'Reilly, because as far as Franklin was concerned, Bill O'Reilly was the only honest news reporter in the history of television.

Somewhere, off on the other side of the house, he could hear somebody knocking at their front door. He looked down into his coffee cup and frowned. The cup was only half full of coffee. As soon as he'd come in tonight, he'd taken out his private stash of Johnny Walker to stiffen it up with something serious. It had been one Hell of a day, what with Marcey acting up the way she had, and right down at the store, too. Not that anybody in town didn't know about Marcey by now, but even so. You had to keep your work life and your home life separate. That was the way it had been for Franklin's parents, and he was sure that that was the way it should be for him. But Marcey had come down, and then there was the problem of getting her back here, and then there was the problem of getting himself back to the store. And in the middle of all that, somebody had killed this Cornish woman.

Franklin got up out of the Barcalounger he had been sitting in and went to the bookshelf built right into the paneling of the wall. He'd never liked bookshelves much, but on this one he kept the prizes he'd won for football and track in high school, and there was a loose board on the bottom shelf that could be pried open to reveal an empty space underneath. The empty space was just big enough to fit his bottle of Johnny Walker. That was a good thing. Marcey didn't drink—it would be easier on all of them if she did; at least they could explain it to their friends—but Franklin thought it was just taking precautions to make sure she *couldn't* drink, at least when she was at home. That stuff she took did not work well with alcohol.

Franklin put another slug, a good long one, into his coffee cup. Then he put the bottle back and fixed the shelf again. He could hear Janey's footsteps coming down the carpet in the hall that led to the foyer. Marcey was quiet now, knocked out not so much by another round of pills as by the sheer exhaustion of a day spent creating one scene after another. She had taken another round of pills, though. Franklin was sure of it. Sometimes he went around the house trying to find her stashes and eliminate them, but it was a losing battle. Marcey knew more places to hide pills than a Jew knew where to hide money. And what good did it do, in the long run? She was going to kill herself one of these days. Franklin understood that. He thought even the children understood that. Marcey was going to end up in the emergency room with an overdose of that Oxycontin and then he wouldn't have to think about this any more. This was not the way he had expected his life to work out, back when he was at high school. This was not the way he thought it should be working out, now. The world was supposed to be a simple place. You did what you had to do. You met your responsibilities. You followed the rules. There shouldn't ever be a case where bad things happened to good people, because God was watching over the earth.

Janey came to the door of the rec room and stuck in her head. "It's Mr. Carr," she said. "He's out in the hall and he says he wants to see you."

Holman Carr. Franklin hadn't thought much about Holman Carr lately. He was a good man. You could count on him to help out at the church. You could count on him to help out. It was too bad he'd lost the election for school board, and to Annie-Vic, of all people. But Holman was like that. He was so mousy and so quiet, nobody ever noticed him.

"It's Uncle Mike, too," Janey said helpfully.

"Well, send them on back," Franklin said. "I'm not doing anything."

He looked back at the television. That woman was still on. She was nodding and explaining, still. Franklin shuddered and took a long drink out of his coffee cup. There had still been enough coffee in it when he'd added this latest shot of Scotch that the whole thing tasted funny, but he really didn't care.

The door opened again, and it was Mike who came in first. Holman would never come in first, not anywhere, and not for any reason. Franklin wondered what he did when there was nobody else with him.

Mike looked at the television set. "What are you doing?" he asked. "What're you watching Larry King for?"

Franklin waved his cup at the set. "That's Eugenie Scott," he said. "That's a name, isn't it? *Her* mother must have thought she was just too perfect. Now she runs something called the National Center for Science Education."

"Oh," Holman Carr said. He sounded surprised. Then he blushed. "It's just—well, she's on the list. I mean, that organization is on the list. To testify in the trial."

"On the atheist side, I take it," Franklin said.

"Let's not worry about sides," Mike said. "How can you be watching that now? We've got a situation, if you haven't noticed. We've got a problem."

"And I can solve it?" Franklin said. "I didn't kill that Cornish woman. It doesn't have anything to do with me."

"If you'd been watching the local news," Mike said, "you'd have seen old Henry Wackford, telling anybody who'd listen that it's us that did it. He says we're killing off the people who filed the lawsuit, like we think if they're all gone the suit will go away."

"That's cracked," Franklin said. He took another long drag at his coffee cup. Mike and Holman wouldn't care if they found out he was drinking. He could just go over to the bookshelves and get himself some more when he was done.

Mike grabbed a chair from next to the coffee table and turned it slightly, so that he could sit down and look Franklin in the face at the same time. "Henry isn't just making noise this time," he said. "He's making accusations. That didn't make the news. The television stations aren't crazy. They don't want to get sued. But he's talked to a dozen people by now and he's come right out and said he thinks he knows who did it. Who did them both. Annie-Vic and this one."

"Who?" Franklin asked.

"Me," Holman Carr said.

Franklin started to laugh. "Oh, God," he said.

"It isn't funny," Mike said. "That is what Henry's saying, and you know Henry. Once he starts saying it, he's going to go on saying it. And it isn't as if we can shut him up by threatening a lawsuit."

"Especially not now," Holman said. "Especially not when nobody knows who did do it."

"And what is supposed to be Holman's motive for killing one woman and practically killing another?" Franklin demanded. "Oh, I know. It's Henry, so it must be evolution. Holman's running around killing people because it's the only way to keep evolution out of the Snow Hill public schools. Do you know what a crock that is? Evolution is already in the Snow Hill public schools. Miss Catherine my-shit-don't-stink Marbledale put it there, and she doesn't give a crap what the rest of us think. Excuse me. I think I'm going to start drinking for serious. It's been a very long day."

"It would help if we had a little more public support," Mike said. "Part of the problem here is that you didn't get elected to get evolution out of the public schools, you got elected to fix the mess Henry Wackford and his people left the school district in, and nothing's been getting done about it. You've been so busy worrying about Intelligent Design that there's still a problem with the new school construction and there's still a problem with the teachers' unions and the contracts and the pension funds and I don't know what else. So people aren't disposed, if you see what I mean, to come running to our side to help."

"You can't just come out and tell people things," Franklin said. "You know that. You've got the courts to worry about, they're all in the hands of the secular humanists. Think of that mess a few years ago in Dover. You've got to come at it sideways."

"You've also got to do something about the day-to-day," Mike said.

"Well, Annie-Vic was doing something about the day-to-day," Franklin said. "She seemed to like it. It's not my fault that somebody smashed her head in. Which isn't to say I'm surprised. Somebody should've done it long ago."

"Franklin, for God's sake," Mike said.

Franklin got up and went back to the bookshelf. They really would not care. Or they would, but they'd put up with it.

"I can't help it if somebody is killing off these women," he said. "I'm sick to death of women, if you want to know the truth. I'm sick of the nagging and I'm sick of the, the thing, whatever you want to call it. I'm going to drink until I don't give a shit anymore, and then I'm going to get up tomorrow morning and blame my hangover for the mood I'm in. Far as I can see, there isn't a damn thing else I can do about things."

"Well," Mike said. "You could think a little more seriously about what it means that that Gregor Demarkian person is in town, and what it means that Gary Albright brought him here."

2

Nick Frapp didn't watch CNN. He didn't watch MSNBC. He didn't even watch Fox, which he thought of as the news's version of professional wrestling, with everybody shouting apocalypse at each other for no apparent reason. When he watched the news at all, instead of getting it from newspapers or the Internet, he watched the "local" channels, which were only local in the sense that they originated somewhere in Pennsylvania. There was no news service that was truly local to Snow Hill, or to any of the even smaller towns south and east of it, and Nick didn't expect there ever would be. If there was one thing that was eternally true of the fallen and temporal world, it was that the people who inhabited it were only interested in other people who were richer and more privileged than they were.

The "local" news was actually semi-local tonight, though. There was footage from the crime scene up at Annie-Vic's house, pictures of yellow police tape strung out between trees and cars parked every which way in that long, curved, gravel and rut drive. If Nick had gotten himself up out of his chair and gone to the window, he could probably have seen something of what was happening, if anything still was. The parsonage was attached to the church. It was right there on Main Street, or a little off, in the compound they had built on the land behind.

Nick could remember walking past the Hadley house when he was a boy. It was the great secret of his late childhood and early adolescence. Maybe there was something to Gary Albright's constant refrain all the years they had gone to school together. Maybe he was a freak. No, Nick thought, he *was* a freak. He'd known it growing up, and he knew it now. A freak was not necessarily a bad thing to be.

When Nick was growing up, he'd stay behind until all the other kids around him were already on their way to school, or stay behind after when they had already scattered at the end of the day, and work his way around so that he could pass that house. At the time, he'd thought he was looking at the rich people, that it was Annie-Vic's money that had intrigued him. Whatever it was had certainly seemed to have something to do with money. There was the house itself, large and imposing and almost like a fortress, way back there, with its gate. There were the people who worked inside and on the grounds. Nobody in Snow Hill had full-time servants, of course. That would have been considered putting on airs, and if there was one thing the people of Snow Hill would not tolerate, it was putting on airs. Annie-Vic had women who came in to "do" for her, and she had men who worked in the yard a couple of times a week. But then, Annie-Vic was definitely somebody who put on airs, and Nick was fairly sure, even then, that not having enough money to hire a cleaning woman to come in and do the dusting was not the problem.

The picture on the screen now was of the woman who had died, Judy Cornish. The news anchor called her "Judith Leighton Cornish," the way he would have done if she'd been a writer or a Supreme Court justice. The details were a little sketchy. The woman had gone up to the house and parked in the drive. She'd left her friend in the car and gone into the house itself. Her friend had waited and waited and waited, and then gone in herself to see if there was something wrong. That was when she found the body. It was simple and straightforward enough, except of course that it made no sense at all. Why had that woman gone to Annie-Vic's house in the first place, and then why had she gone in when there was nobody home? No, Nick thought, that wouldn't do. There might have been somebody in the house, and that somebody might have asked her to come inside. That could be the murderer. It still left the question of why Mrs. Cornish had gone up there to begin with, and it was fairly obvious by now that the news reporter didn't have a clue. There were always people who lamented that the American public wasn't really interested in news. Television news divisions were being cut back, budgets were being slashed. All of that might be true, but as far as Nick could see, television news had too much time on its hands. There wasn't really all that much news out there. The reporters went in front of the cameras and said the same things over and over again for hours on end. And this with the murder wasn't even a particularly bad case. At least there had been a murder. At least there was actually something to worry about. The very worst was in the hour or two before the polls closed on an election day. Then there was no news at all, and the reporters and the anchors just stood there blithering about nothing in particular for minutes on end.

Nick got up and went to the window. He had always liked the fact that he could get a glimpse of Annie-Vic's house from here. At night, when he was here alone and Annie-Vic was alone herself, he could sometimes see her lights coming through the darkness and the trees. He didn't know how long it had taken him before he understood what it was she represented for him, or how long after that it had been before he realized that she was not a particularly good specimen. Still, she had been there, it had been there, the faint promise of something else besides the life he'd grown up with, and something else besides the life he saw all around him. It wasn't true that poor people thought about nothing but the material things they lacked. He'd almost never thought about those. What he'd thought about were books, and the way the librarians sometimes looked at him when he came in to read in the library.

There was a light on in the church's main floor annex, the place where the offices were. He rubbed the side of his head with his long, thin fingers and wondered what was going on now. He had his Rosetta Stone program open on the computer. The computer was against the wall opposite the television set. It had originally been in the study, but he hadn't liked it in there. Living alone the way he did, there was too much silence. He'd dragged the computer in here so that he would at least have a little background noise to keep him company. The Rosetta Stone program was for Italian, which he had been working on learning to read for about six months. He really ought to get a dog. Either that, or he ought to bite the bullet and get married. The problem was that he'd never met a dog or a woman that seemed to fit him for more than a week or two.

Unmarried pastors are disasters waiting to happen, he thought. Then he took another look at the light in the annex. There were definitely people down there. That was all right: The annex was used for all kinds of things, and members of the church had the right to be there. But usually if there was going to be something going on, somebody told him about it. If for some reason the police had wanted to search the place, they would have had to come to him with a warrant. He was sure of that. He wasn't sure why he half-expected the police to want to search the place. But that was how it was in a place like Snow Hill. In the end, the most expedient course of action was to blame the hillbillies.

Nick went out his front door and looked around. It was dark, and Main Street was crammed solid with news trucks. This was going to be bigger than the trial on its own ever could have been. He wondered what Gregor Demarkian was doing right this minute. He wondered how Gregor Demarkian was getting along with the state police. That was what they'd said on the news, that the state police had been called in. Nick had met that idiot from the state police. The man had to be a joy to work with.

It was cold, but the annex was only a few steps away. Nick didn't see any point in going off to find a coat. He crossed the small courtyard on the cement path and let himself in the annex's back door. He could hear voices coming from the big room at the front where they sometimes held meetings of the church board. The voices were anxious, and they all had that twanging drawl that meant they belonged to hill people. Nick wondered if there would ever come a time when that particular accent would no longer signify stupidity, and brutishness, and ignorance. These people weren't stupid or brutish or ignorant at all, but anyone who heard them would assume them to be all three. It was a terrible thing, stereotyping. Or maybe it was just human nature.

The door to the meeting room was open. Nick could see through it as he came up the hall. Harve Griegson was there, and Pete DeMensh, and Susie Cleland's brother Martin. A few more steps, and Nick could see Susie, too. They none of them seemed to be doing anything. They were just standing around and looking unhappy.

He got to the door and knocked. Pete jumped. Susie cried out. You would have thought they were all in a horror movie.

"It's just me," Nick said. "I saw the light."

"We didn't mean to bother you," Harve said. "We were just talking."

"About what?" Nick asked him.

The four of them looked at one another. Susie looked away first, and then looked at the floor. "I know it's not a good thing to gossip," she said, "but this isn't gossip really. I don't think it is. And it might be important."

"What might be important?" Nick asked.

The four of them looked at one another again. By now, Susie was blushing brick red.

"Well, here's the thing," she said. "You can't help but notice it, can you? It isn't as if she's quiet about it. She was screaming her head off for nearly an hour this afternoon. Everybody on Main Street must have heard it."

"She, who?" Nick asked, although he knew. That was the kind of incident where everybody knew.

"Marcey Hale," Susie said. "She came down to Franklin's shop and I don't know what she wanted, but she ended up screaming her head off. And then he had to get her home—it must have been terrible for business—so he took her out the back. And yes, I looked. I couldn't help myself. I was worried about her. He was throwing her around as if she were a sack of potatoes, he really was. I thought he was going to end up throwing her on the ground. He looked so angry. And he had the truck back there and he shoved her into it and then he slammed the door. He could have taken off her hand."

Nick looked from one of them to the other. None of them was willing to meet his eyes, and Susie had taken on that defiant attitude people got when they were forced to admit to they thought something was discreditable. Nick cleared his throat.

"I can see how you'd feel better if Franklin were kinder to Marcey, and more careful about the way he handled her, physically," he said.

"And if it were one of you, I'd definitely be counseling more gentleness and delicacy than Franklin tends to show to anybody. But Marcey's hard to handle when she gets like that. And it can be hard on a man who has to try to deal with it over an extended period. I take it he didn't break any bones that you could see."

"It's not what he did with Marcey that's got us worried," Harve said.

"Really?" Nick said. "Then what does?"

"I know I shouldn't have been looking," Susie said. "I mean, I should have come on back here to work and let him get on with what he was getting on with. But I was worried, you see what I mean. He shoved her in the car, and he shut the door on her, and then he used that thing he has, the gizmo that lets you lock the doors from the outside."

"I'm getting one of those the next time I get a car," Pete said.

"Anyway," Susie said. "He did that. And then after he did that he left. He walked on around back of us here, right through the Serenity Corner—"

"He came onto our property here?" Nick asked.

"Exactly," Susie said, sounding suddenly satisfied. "And you can't blame me for watching him then, can you? I mean, it's not like we've got barbed wire and security around the place. We don't mind people coming in most of the time. But what was he doing there? I mean, really. If he wanted to go up to Annie-Vic's place, why didn't he do it on the sidewalk like a normal person?"

Nick leaned back. "He went up to Annie-Vic's place," he said.

"Well, I assumed so at the time," Susie said. "Where else would he be going, going up that hill? There's nothing much out there except Annie-Vic's and some other houses here and around, and he wouldn't be going to any of them, would he? And Annie-Vic's is right at the top of that hill, isn't it? And then he was gone a long time. It must have been fifteen or twenty minutes. And now there's this woman, murdered, and murdered right up there. So I don't see what it was I was supposed to think, or what it was I was supposed to do about it."

3

Gary Albright never wondered, even for a moment, if Sarah would be ready to receive an overnight guest on less than an hour's notice. That was not one of the things anybody had to worry about with Sarah, unless she was truly and significantly ill, and she was almost never that. Gary had had his ideas about what marriage should be like before he ever considered getting himself into it, but he was honest enough about himself to understand that it would be the person who mattered most to him in the end. If Sarah had wanted to go to law school, or to work full-time as soon as the children were in kindergarten, he would have been willing to adjust himself and his life to make her happy. It was his luck that she had wanted for her life what he had wanted for his: a home, and children, and the ease that came with having one person dedicated to taking care of both.

His house was a new one, not in the development—nobody could afford a house in the development on what the town paid its chief of police—but in a row of raised ranches along a leafy and otherwise undeveloped stretch of Route 107. There were five houses on that row, all on the same side of the road, and all of them built to be identical. It was their colors that distinguished them, and now, five years or so since they'd been built, so did some of the additions and oddities their owners had tacked onto them for the duration. Gary's house now had a large, octagonal deck off the back of it. He and his brother-in-law had built it together. It was big enough to serve for an outdoor party with just about everyone he knew. He was hoping it would one day serve as a graduation party for Michael or an after-prom for Lily. He pulled up into the driveway and didn't worry at all about what Gregor Demarkian would think of it. It didn't even occur to him to worry. It was an achievement, buying a house like this, supporting a family like this. Gary expected people to recognize it.

The light was on over the front door as they came in. It was already dark, and what had been a cold day was now a frigid evening. Gary turned the ignition off and got out, waiting for Gregor to get out too before locking up. The front door opened and Sarah stuck her head out. Seeing them, she came forward all the way onto the front steps and waved.

"Eddie Block called," she said. "He says don't bother to call him back, but you should know Henry Wackford called and demanded police protection. Honestly, I'd like to protect that man myself."

"This is Gregor Demarkian," Gary said.

"How do you do, Mr. Demarkian," Sarah said, holding out her hand for him. "I've got your room all set up for you. It's right downstairs, and it's at the front, so you've got windows on two sides. It is off the playroom, I'm afraid, but the children go to bed early and they're not allowed down there with the television on on school mornings, so you should be all right. Oh, and there's a bathroom just off, and I've set up some towels for you. Oh, and I've left you some pajamas, and some boxer shorts, brand-new ones, still in their package. Gary said you were about the same size, and you are. It's really amazing. When I was growing up, all the men I knew were short, and now the world is full of tall people. You should go down and freshen up a little. Dinner will be ready in half an hour."

They were in the front hall now. Stairs led up half a flight to the main level and down half a flight to the lower level. Sarah was leading the way down, to make sure Gregor Demarkian got where he needed to go without getting lost. Gary saw that the playroom down there was empty, which was unusual. The children were usually down there watching videos after they'd done their homework. The playroom had the only television in the house. Sarah didn't approve of televisions in the living room. Sarah caught his eye.

"I've got them up reading that Bible stories book my aunt Evelyn gave them," she said. "I'll let them come down and watch a video while we're all having supper. They've been fed already. I know you like us to eat together as a family, Gary, but it was getting late and I didn't know when you'd be home."

"I didn't know when I'd be home either," Gary said. He looked at Gregor Demarkian, who was looking around the playroom and the door that led off of it to the spare bedroom. "Why don't you relax for a minute or two and Sarah can call you for supper? Or you can just come up whenever you've settled in."

"I'll send Michael down with some coffee if you like," Sarah said. "We do have some beer in the house if you'd like that, but I don't let Michael carry it, so—"

"I'm fine," Gregor Demarkian said. "I really am. I just need to make a couple of phone calls."

"Of course," Sarah said.

"Of course," Gary said.

Then both moved off, a little awkwardly, leaving The Great Detective on his own. That was how Gary thought of Gregor Demarkian, as The Great Detective, but he hadn't until that moment realized it. He must have been thinking that way about Gregor all along.

They made their way to the upper level in silence. Then Sarah turned and looked down the stairs again.

"Well," she said. "He doesn't look all that frightening. In fact, he seems very nice."

"He is very nice," Gary said, going over to the dining table and pulling out a chair. Michael and Lily were sitting together on the couch, pouring over a book that had ten times as many pictures as words, which was about right for their age. "We ended up having to call in the cavalry," he said.

"Oh, Gary," Sarah said. "But why? I thought that was the reason for calling Gregor Demarkian in. So that we wouldn't have to deal with Dale Vardan just this once."

"We only half-have to deal with him," Gary said. "Demarkian doesn't seem to like him any more than we do. But we had to do something. This was the second attack—even if it wasn't the second murder—and you know as well as I do that whoever went at Annie-Vic meant to kill her. I get up every morning wishing she'd open her eyes and just tell us who whacked her, and I don't even know if she knows. I don't know if she saw him."

"Do you think it's true, the kind of things Henry Wackford keeps saying?" Sarah asked. "Do you think it's really some religious maniac running around killing people just because they believe in evolution? I mean, things happen, don't they? Those people who killed the abortion doctors. That kind of thing."

"Those people who killed the abortion doctors," Gary said, "were members of a nutcase organization called the Army of God, and there were about six of them. Can you imagine any of our people here doing that kind of thing? Who? Franklin Hale? Alice McGuffie? How about Holman Carr?"

Sarah smiled. "Okay. Holman probably couldn't kill a spider without that wife of his telling him to. And she wouldn't tell him to, because she'd be afraid he'd get caught, and then who'd pay her bills? But you know, Gary, it's not impossible that one of our own people here—well, it has to be one of us, doesn't it? Somebody is doing these things. And I could see Franklin killing somebody, under the right circumstances."

"Because that person didn't want Intelligent Design in the public schools?"

"All right," Sarah said. "What about Alice?"

Gary took a deep breath, and shrugged. "I can see Alice killing somebody. I can even see her saying she did it for religion. I just can't see her actually doing it for religion. We were standing out there at the crime scene and I was thinking about Alice. Alice's Barbie is in the same grade as Mrs. Cornish's daughter Mallory. Apparently, they don't like each other much."

"I'll bet," Sarah said.

"Here's the thing," Gary said. "Things are changing. Ten years ago, Barbie McGuffie could have been a small-town popular girl with everything that entailed and never had a second thought about it until she was forty-five and fat as a pig and suddenly realized she hadn't done squat with her life."

"*Gary.*"

"But it isn't ten years ago," Gary said, ignoring the protest. He was pretty sure the children had not heard him say "squat." "The kids from the development have a lot more money than our kids do. They have fancier clothes. They've got their sights fixed on going to fancy colleges on the coasts. And they don't care what the Barbie McGuffies of this world think about anything. It changes the dynamic."

"And you can see Alice McGuffie killing a woman because that woman's daughter is, I don't know, responsible for the fact that it isn't such a big deal around here to be a majorette?"

"I can see Alice killing out of spite," Gary said. "I can see her doing just about anything about of spite, because spite is what that woman runs on."

"And she would have tried to kill Annie-Vic out of spite? But why? At least, why now? She's known Annie-Vic all her life. We all have."

"I know," Gary said. "I go around and around and around it, and I just don't get it. The only thing Annie-Vic and this Judy Cornish had in common that I can see is that they were both involved in the lawsuit and they were both on the evolutionist side. And it just doesn't make any sense. Because I just don't believe that anybody would kill over something like this, and yet we've got a dead woman, who was in the house of another woman who is nearly dead, and I don't know why that is, either. I don't know the why of anything at all."

"Does Gregor Demarkian know why?" Sarah asked.

"I hope so," Gary said. "Because if he doesn't, we're going to have Dale Vardan around our necks for months, and if he doesn't know, he'll just make it up."

FIVE

1

At first, waking up, Gregor Demarkian had no idea where he was. Then he did, and he found himself suddenly depressed. If there was one thing he had thought would be an advantage when he took up consulting, being able to go home at night to his own bed and his own refrigerator was it. It just never seemed to work out that way. Even with cases that were close enough to Philadelphia so that only a snail would need to commute, he found himself sleeping in strange houses, in hotels that obsessed about towels and Pay-Per-View, and even in cars. He'd thought he'd given up sleeping in cars a lot longer ago than he had given up the rest of it. He remembered being promoted off kidnap detail and into a desk job more vividly than he remembered his wedding.

His last wedding. He turned a little in the bed he was lying in and looked at the cell phone lying on the nightstand. There was nothing wrong with this room. It was small, as bedrooms go, but it was clean and well furnished and comfortable. Gregor remembered the first time he had ever seen a "raised ranch." They called them "high ranches" back then, and they were absolutely the newest thing, out in those minor suburbs—not in the Main Line, nothing expensive like that—where some of the Armenian-American families who had started out on Cavanaugh Street had moved. His own family had not be able to afford anything that . . . well, wondrous. Wondrous was how he had thought of it back then, when he'd been ten years old.

And it had all seemed perfectly normal, he thought. It had all seemed to be just the way things were, with no point in thinking about it, and that was the way it had felt ever since then. The more things changed, the less Gregor had noticed the changing.

He reached over to the nightstand and got the cell phone. It was something called a Razr that Bennis had bought it for him. He didn't understand why none of these companies could spell anything properly. He flipped it open and checked the time. It was just six o'clock. He had no idea if Bennis would be up by now or not. She was up by this time when he was home, but he'd spoken to her late last night. She might have been up doing wedding things. This would be his last wedding, this one. There was a bit of changing he *had* noticed: Elizabeth and Bennis, the two women in the world he would least have expected to find himself married to, and the world as it was when he had nobody like either of them in it.

He pressed down on the number one, which was the only speed dial he had set up. He waited while the phone rang at the other end. He was always sorry about the fact that the person calling couldn't hear the ring tone the person receiving heard. Bennis's ring tone for him was the theme music for Perry Mason.

The ringing stopped and Bennis's voice said, "If you've found another body already, I'm going to come and get you and we can elope."

"If we elope, we can never go back to Cavanaugh Street," Gregor said. "They'd kill us, and you know it. I was thinking about raised ranches."

"What?"

"When I was ten, some people from the street, the Brabanians, moved out to some little suburb somewhere. It wasn't on the Main Line. It was one of those places, you know, a lot of houses pretty

238

much alike on a quarter of an acre, one after the other. They bought a raised ranch, except I think we called them 'high' ranches then. I'd never seen one before. I thought it was the most wonderful thing that existed in the universe. You have no idea how I wanted one."

"You want a raised ranch? Gregor, you know, if you really do, we could get one. They're not expensive particularly. But I don't think they'll live up to your memory."

"I don't want a raised ranch. The town house will do, once we get it set up. But I'm in a raised ranch, you see. The place where I'm staying."

"Gary Albright's house."

"Right. And it's pretty much the same deal, except this is a lot farther out in the country, so there are houses only on one side of the street, and the yards are bigger. And you know what? I never was comfortable when people made fun of people who wanted houses like this, of people who were happy to have houses like this. I feel like I'm going around in circles here."

"I understand. You don't like snobs," Bennis said. "That's admirable. I don't like snobs, either."

"I know," Gregor said. "What I'm trying to say, I think, is that I think Gary Albright has built a good and admirable life here. He's got a lovely wife. He's got two beautiful children, and the boy is smart as Hell. He lives comfortably. He does his job. What is there to laugh at, exactly?"

"Gregor, if I knew the answers to those kinds of questions, I'd be writing something more serious than fantasy novels."

"You'd also be making a lot less money," Gregor said. "Never mind. It's the kind of thing I think of when I come to places like this. Because our friend Liz is right. She always says that small towns are the cesspit of humanity, and I can see it. I've run into people here who would fit, and I've heard about others who would really fit. But then there's this, and this is good, and there's something wrong about laughing at it."

Bennis sighed. "Gregor, are you all right? Did something happen?"

"Between ten last night and now? No. I actually called for a reason, it's just that I've been thinking. About a lot of things. About the wedding. Have you managed to get all those women to talk to Tibor again?"

"I think he'd be happier if they stopped talking to him," Bennis said. "It's only been a day, Gregor. It will work out. They just think Tibor is being, I don't know, mean, I suppose, not to let us get married in Holy Trinity."

"He isn't refusing to let us get married there," Gregor pointed out. "We don't want to get married there. We never asked him. And we won't. Because I don't want—"

"Yes, I know," Bennis said. "It's all right, really. I'll do my best, Gregor. I've ordered a bunch more chocolate from Box Hill to give to Mrs. Varamanian so she'll take the evil eye off Tibor. It will work out."

"The evil eye," Gregor said.

"They're just trying to be good to you," Bennis said.

"Listen," Gregor said, "do me a favor. Stop planning the wedding and achieving social peace for a minute and call Sister Beata for me. I'd do it myself but I don't have her number on this phone and I never seem to get ten minutes to myself where I can talk. I want you to ask her about the Catholic Church's position on evolution and Intelligent Design. If she's got something on paper, a pamphlet, or she knows of a book, something I could get my hands on and read, that would be even better."

"This is almost as odd as raised ranches," Bennis said. "Don't you already know what you think about evolution? Have you got Catholics there who don't accept it? I thought what this was about was Protestants, fundamentalists, that kind of thing."

"It's not who it is," Gregor said, "it's this odd thing. I've been here for a day, I must have talked to half a dozen people, they all talk about the lawsuit. But do you know what none of them talks about? Science."

"I don't understand what you mean."

"I mean," Gregor said, "that if an alien dropped down from his spaceship into this town right this minute and listened to what people are saying, he'd never in a million years guess that this is a scientific question. Everybody is talking, and from what I see they're doing a fair amount of yelling at each other, but none of them is talking about science. Even the head of the group that's bringing the lawsuit, this local lawyer named Henry Wackford, even he doesn't talk about the science. He was on CNN last night, handing out hot and cold running anathemas, and the issues were persecution of atheists, radical fundamentalist nutcases trying to run the country, the rising tide of superstition in the nation, all the fault of eight years of George W. Bush, but not a word about the science. And I find that very odd."

"I don't," Bennis said.

"You don't find anything odd anymore," Gregor said. "You spend too much time with Donna and Tibor. But I want to know. Does the Catholic Church have anything to say about the science, or are they worried about declining moral values and the rise in drug abuse and the attempts of radical secularists to make it a crime to be a practicing Christian in America."

"What?"

"That's the kind of thing I'm getting," Gregor said. "I don't know what I thought I was going to find when I got here, but it's nothing at all like what I've got. So if you could get in touch with Sister Beata and explain my problem and get some information for me, I'd appreciate it. I'd really like to have a better handle on what it is I'm supposed to be dealing with here."

"Are you staying up there for the duration?" Bennis asked. "You're going to need some clothes if you are."

"I'm hoping to be home tonight," Gregor said. "And I mean it. But, yes. Just in case, it had occurred to me to ask one of the people who are showing me around if we could run out to a store somewhere. I'm pretty sure I saw a Wal-Mart on the way in."

"Gregor Demarkian shopping at Wal-Mart. There's something I'd like to see."

"Call Sister Beata," Gregor said. "I've got to get ready in time for Gary Albright to give me a ride down to Main Street."

Gregor closed up the phone and looked at it in his hand. It was a black phone, and he had not told her he loved her when he said good-bye. He almost never told her he loved her. He hadn't told Elizabeth, either, except at the very end.

Maybe that meant something, but he didn't know what.

2

Gary Albright was dressed and waiting by the door by the time that Gregor made it upstairs. He didn't look impatient, but then he never looked impatient. That was something else Gregor had noticed about people who had spent a certain amount of time in the military. Sarah was waiting by the door, too, and she seemed not so much impatient as exasperated.

"Let the man eat breakfast, Gary," she said. "Not everybody can be you and function on nothing but coffee for three days running."

Gregor glanced involuntarily at Gary's legs—he didn't actually know which one the man had lost; he thought John Jackman might have told him, but it had slipped his mind, and he hadn't been paying attention in the time since—and then looked away again.

"I don't need breakfast," he said. "It's very kind of you to ask, but I almost never eat breakfast. Coffee will be more than fine."

This was not true. Gregor ate almost every morning of his life at the Ararat, and, if anything, he ate too much breakfast. He wasn't hungry now, though, and although he'd found nothing particularly awful about Sarah's cooking, he'd found nothing particularly wonderful about it, either. The great White Anglo-Saxon Protestant culinary ethic. There was something wrong with food if it tasted like anything at all.

"He still shouldn't be stuffing you in the car when you're practically still in bed," Sarah said.

"Do you drink coffee?" Gary asked. "Or do you drink that caramel chocolate crappu–"

"Gary."

"Sorry," Gary said.

"I drink coffee," Gregor said. "I've never been able to figure out how to order one of those, you know, whatevers."

"You'd think a man would be ashamed," Gary said. "But I don't know. You're from the city. Maybe that's what everybody does up there."

"It's Philadelphia, not Fire Island," Gregor said. "We're pretty normal, most of the time."

"Of course you are," Sarah said. "Don't listen to him, Mr. Demarkian. He's convinced the entire country is going to Hades in a handbasket. I keep telling him, if he's so sure, then we should send Michael and Lily to the Christian school, but he won't listen to me."

"It's not a Christian school," Gary said. "It's Nick Frapp's school."

"He means a school for hillbillies," Sarah said. "But we've got friends from church who send their children to that school, and they're very happy with it. And it isn't like it used to be. There aren't so many hillbillies anymore, not the way Gary is remembering them."

"You only think that because you don't see them," Gary said. He got his hands out of his pockets. His keys came with them. "We'd better go. I've got to at least pretend I'm running the department. And Mr. Demarkian has to deal with Dale Vardan."

"First thing in the morning?" Gregor asked faintly.

"Oh, Dale's an early bird," Gary said.

They went out to the truck, still sitting in the driveway from the night before. Gregor climbed in and settled himself as well as he could. The cab was already warm. Gary Albright must have come out and started up a good fifteen minutes ago. Gary got in and slammed the driver's-side door behind him.

"If you were only being polite about breakfast, you can get a decent one at the diner up the street from the department," he said. "That's one of the places you're probably going to want to go at some point anyway. Alice McGuffie and her husband run it."

Gary started to back the truck out of the driveway. Gregor looked up the road in both directions: It was an ordinary two-lane blacktop, one of dozens throughout the state. In spite of the houses, the landscape looked entirely devoid of people.

"It's the emptiness I find it hard to adjust to," Gregor said. "The lack of people. I've lived most of my life in cities. I'm used to either seeing people around or being sure I was in some kind of danger."

"You mean there's danger when the people aren't around, in cities? I've never lived in one, myself. I've been in them, but I've never lived in one. It's always been either here, you know, or the Marines."

"And they didn't station you in a city overseas?"

"Nope. In combat zones once or twice. I think one of those places used to be a city. I don't know. I would have reupped if it hadn't been for Sarah and the kids. After 9/11—" Gary shrugged.

"In cities," Gregor said, as they began bumping along the blacktop on what he presumed was the way back to town, "any area that seems to have no people in it only seems to have no people in it. There are always people, but they're sometimes out of sight. And it's never good news when all the people are out of sight."

"You mean, like, they're lying in ambush?"

"Sometimes," Gregor said. "That's the worst case scenario. But the more likely thing is that what you've got around you is drug addicts. Depending on the drug, that can be various kinds of bad news."

"I never understood drugs," Gary said. Then he paused, seeming to consider something. "A couple of times, when I was first in the Marines, I tried smoking some marijuana. A lot of the guys did it. But I couldn't see the point. It was like having about three beers, and I don't see the point in that, either. You get fuzzed out. You can't think. I was bored as Hell."

"Yes, well," Gregor said. "The kind of drug addicts I was thinking of tend to take one of three things. They take heroin, they take cocaine, or they take methamphetamine. A heroin junkie on a full high is no trouble to anybody unless he overdoses, because heroin pretty much acts like a sedative. When a junkie is flying, he's pretty much passed out at the same time. He just lies there and feels completely calm. Mind you, he could be freezing to death in the middle of an ice storm. He won't notice. We've got people who go into abandoned buildings looking for these guys when things get bad—"

"You mean the police do that?"

"No," Gregor said. "We've got organizations in the city, mostly volunteer. Quite a few of them run by churches. The hard core of homeless people in Philadelphia, the hard core of homeless people anywhere are either addicted to something or mentally ill, and there's nothing anything can do except for involuntarily committing them to get them off the streets permanently. And we can't involuntarily commit them just because they're living on the street—"

"False imprisonment," Gary said, nodding.

"And they're not going to be willing to go into a shelter for the long term, because shelters have rules, the first one always being that they have to give up any substance they're using, which they don't want to do."

"Really don't want to?" Gary asked.

"Some of them, yes," Gregor said. "I think we underestimate how much of a role choice plays in addiction. Which doesn't mean that most of these guys aren't out of control, or that they could quit any time without help if they wanted to, but the fact is that they can't quit at all if they *don't* want to, and quite a few of them don't. They're engaged in a form of slow suicide, really. They think they've made a complete waste of their lives, which may be true, and that there's no point in cleaning up because there's no way to atone for the things they've done, no way to build a life no matter how clean they are, and getting clean would mean nothing but having to face all that and living in pain. So, yes, there are some of them who don't want to."

They had turned onto another two-lane blacktop. The houses here were on both sides of the road, set way back and often on a downslope, so that the front lawns made for fairly decent sledding hills. Gary Albright was thinking. Gregor was surprised how easy it was to tell that that was the case. Most of the time, it was impossible to read anything in Gary's face.

245

"Here's the thing," Gary said, finally. "That thing that you described, these people who don't want to get clean because they've got nothing to live for, they've got no way to build a life. It isn't true. If you're right with God, that's never true. It would always be possible for you to get clean and to build a life in Christ. Do you see what I mean?"

"I've got no idea how many of these people believe in God," Gregor said. "And I don't think you can assume that, just because they're addicts, they don't."

"I'm not assuming that," Gary said. "I'm just trying to say—I mean, think about it. When you give your life over to Christ, there's always something to live for. There's always something He can do with you. Christ works in all of us. He uses us for His own purposes. I mean, yes, He wants you to live without sin, but we don't all manage to do that. Most of us fall. Adam and Eve fell. But even if we fall, even if we spend forty years in a mess of drugs, living on the street, being out of it most of the time, even then, our lives our not a waste if we give them over to Christ and let him use us as He wants to use us. Even if we only have a couple of weeks left between the time we accept Him and the time we go to Him, even then, our lives haven't been a waste. Even if we only have a couple of minutes. Do you see what I mean?"

"I understand what you're saying, if that's what you're asking," Gregor said.

"Not exactly," Gary said. They had made yet another turn, and now they were entering Main Street from its least populated end. "If I know that Christ has a plan for me," Gary said carefully, "if I know that He wants me, that He can use me, then I've got an incentive to get clean no matter how long I've been addicted. But if I don't know that, if there's nothing but just this life right here, nothing more anywhere, nothing else anywhere, then the behavior of the addicts you're talking about makes perfect sense. What would be the point of any of them getting clean when they're not going to live very long and they have nothing to look forward to?"

They were coming right up to the police station. There was a parking lot in the back. Gary was pulling into it.

"And?" Gregor asked.

Gary pulled into a parking space. "I went over to the high school the other day, and Miss Marbledale has a big exhibit up. All about evolution. She's got posters up, I don't know. 'Evolution is change over time.' DNA. Fossils. And you know what? It's all beside the point. I don't care if animals evolved or not. I don't care if humans evolved or not. Not a single one of us who wanted the ID book in the library—and that's all it was, we wanted the book in the library, and we wanted a little sticker in the textbooks telling people it was there—none of us cares if evolution happened or not. That's not the point. And it's not the point for Henry Wackford, either."

"I would have thought it was the whole point," Gregor said.

"Do you ever read that guy, Richard Dawkins?" Gary asked. "He doesn't think it's the point, either. He thinks evolution proves that God doesn't exist, and we have to teach children evolution because that's the only way to raise a generation that will believe that God doesn't exist. Henry Wackford will tell you the same thing—just listen to him on television. Well, I'm not interested in raising a generation that believes that God doesn't exist. I don't think it's good for them. I think it leads to depression, and addiction, and hopelessness, and all your addicts who want to stay addicts because they have nothing to live for. I think I've known a lot of decent people who aren't believers and a lot of nasty people who are believers, but at the end of the day, all the hopeful people I know believe. And that's my bottom line. The science doesn't matter a damn one way or the other."

3

Every once in a while, Gregor thought about actually learning to drive. He had a driver's license and renewed it religiously every time the paperwork came in the mail, but he didn't think he had been behind the wheel in years. The last time he remembered was in a small

Pennsylvania town called Holman, and then he'd only been trying to divert a horde of paparazzi. He had been only nominally successful.

Still, there were times when he wished he could drive instead of be driven, because there were times when being driven meant losing all sense of where things were and how far they were from each other. When Gary Albright went into the police station, Gregor stayed in the small back parking lot and looked around. Then he went out to Main Street and looked at that. Then he took his notebook out of the inside pocket of his suit jacket and looked at that. The problem with small towns was that they were, very often, not really small. When people said "small," what they really meant was "only lightly populated." It was the lack of people they noticed, not the physical size of the place. Gregor had been in "small towns" in Kansas and Nebraska whose square footage would overwhelm places like Los Angeles and New York, at least if you stuck strictly to the city limits. That was because of the farms. People had farms out there that felt as large as some small countries, but there were very few people on them.

Gregor didn't think there were farms of that kind anywhere near Snow Hill. The landscape was wrong, for one thing. For farming on the scale of the American Midwest, you needed a lot of flat, and not much about Snow Hill was flat. Still, he had no idea what the physical size of the town was, or what people thought of as "walking distance." People seemed to come and go, back and forth, up and down, and Gregor had no sense of what that meant in terms of time, or of effort. It was one thing to go up to Annie-Vic's house on foot when it was a distance you would walk on any stray day. It was something else to go up there if it took an extra expenditure of effort to make the trip. There was that, and there was the question of cars. It seemed to Gregor, given what people had told him about the things they'd done over the last few weeks, that at least some of the people from "the development" went everywhere in cars. He thought that the people who were really local, deep local, probably did not. It was very hard to work out.

He looked to his left. Nick Frapp's church was down there, on the end and a little tilted, so that that end of Main Street was almost like a cul de sac. On his right, up about a block and a half, there was the Snow Hill Diner, where the infamous Alice McGuffie held sway on most days. Another block and a half or farther in that direction, the road began to make its way out of town. But Gregor thought, from what he remembered about the drive to Gary's the night before, there were more houses before "town" ended.

He was thoroughly exasperated with himself. He went to his right, looking back and forth, at the store fronts, at the very few street signs, at the churches. There were churches everywhere, and they were by far the biggest buildings on the street. He checked out the Baptists from across the street. Then he looked through the windows of the Snow Hill Diner. The diner was doing a very good business, probably half full of the people who belonged to the news vans parked up and down the street, still. Gregor was beginning to think of them as fixtures. The diner had those little gingham cafe curtains, on rods that were placed only midway up the glass. Gregor had never understood the attraction of that particular look. He did understand it was supposed to represent something "homey." Gregor thought of suggesting something to Bennis that took in the idea of homey, and her imagined reaction was so immediate, he almost winced.

He got to the end of Main Street proper, to the end of the stretch where the street was lined with stores on either side. Like the other end, where Nick Frapp's church was, there was a little slant that made it almost seem as if the street was closed off. It wasn't, though. It just angled off to the right, and there was a steepish hill. Gregor wondered if it made people claustrophobic to live in a town where the Main Street looked like a closed loop. He imagined that some people found it comforting, as if they were being protected from something.

He stopped where the street angled and looked around. The hill really was steep, but the road beside it had been well plowed and sanded. The only snow was on the bare ground behind the Main Street buildings, and there wasn't much of it left. He turned around and around and around, trying to place everything in reference to everything else.

Then he went back to looking up the hill. The branches on the trees were bare and black, except toward the top of the hill, where there were evergreens. He went a little ways up the angled road and looked to the left. There wasn't much there, but it wasn't entirely barren, either. There were houses, older houses mostly. They looked like they might have been built in the twenties, in that last big building boom before the Great Depression. He looked to the right and saw only one house, and that set back from the road.

It wasn't until he saw the police tape that he realized what he was looking at. Then he walked back a little, looked up and down Main Street again, and returned to where he had first understood what he was seeing. The house was right here. Anybody who was on Main Street could have walked to it, right on the road. It was likely that he could have been seen, too, without anybody thinking anything of it.

Gregor started to climb. He didn't get all that much physical exercise, but he was large and powerfully built. There was a time in his life when people had tried to talk him into playing football. Football was not his kind of thing, then or now. Walking was, but he went slowly, so that he could look around.

There wasn't much to see. The houses looked empty, but that didn't mean anything. Houses of that era often looked empty, because they were dark and hulking things. He wondered who these particular houses belonged to. He had been given an excellent rundown on the Main Street locations, or non–Main Street locations, of most of those on the suspect list during the day, but he knew nothing at all about where they went at night.

He got to the top of the hill, and he was right there. There was a state policeman sitting in a car at the end of the driveway, and another, in another car, on the far side of the front walk. Gregor wondered if they had somebody in back, guarding the back door. He supposed they did. He stopped and looked the house over again, up and down, the hedges, the entry with its overhang, the blank windows on the second floor. That was when the policeman at the front entrance got out of his car and came over.

"Can I help you?" he said. He was polite, but he sounded faintly disgusted. Maybe he'd had enough rubberneckers for this lifetime.

"I don't think I need any help," Gregor said, looking up to the second floor again. "I was just trying to get myself oriented. I'm Gregor Demarkian."

The policeman hesitated, then looked closer, then stepped back. "Well," he said. "You are."

"I didn't mean to bother you," Gregor said.

"No bother. You don't know the kinds of crap we're getting, though. People from everywhere coming by, just to see where the body was. And not just people from here, either. They've come all the way from New York, some of them. I've seen the plates."

"But some of the people have been local?" Gregor asked.

The state policeman shrugged. "Sure, I suppose so. And there's the grandniece, or whatever she is. She came by and complained about the mess in the dining room. There was a woman bludgeoned to death in the dining room, and she was worried about papers being all over the floor. Can you believe that?"

"It does seem like the wrong priority," Gregor said.

"I think it's bats, myself. Papers on the floor. According to this woman, the grandniece, whoever, according to her, the woman who usually lives here, the first one who was attacked, always kept her stuff very neat, kept paperweights on it to make sure it wasn't blown away, that kind of thing. And then when she, the grandniece—when she got here today to pick up her things the papers were blown all over the place and they didn't have their paperweights, and they had them when the grandniece left the house on the morning of the murder, and blah blah blah. I couldn't believe the whining."

"Yes," Gregor said.

"Some people," the state policeman said. "I've been doing this job for twenty years, and I still can't get over some people. I don't know. Maybe it isn't a good thing, being in police work for the long haul. You get peculiar. You get so you don't trust anybody anywhere. You want to go in and have a look around? The crime scene boys have been here and gone. Well, girls maybe—the ME is a woman—but you know what I mean. We're authorized to let you in any time you want to go."

Gregor looked at the house again. It could have served as the setting for a fifties horror movie. He couldn't imagine an old woman living there alone. He turned and looked down the hill again.

"All right," he said, finally. "I would like to have a look around, if it wouldn't be putting the two of you out."

"Not at all," the state policeman said. "It's like I said, we're supposed to allow you in if you want to go. And, to tell you the truth, I'll be glad to have somebody in there that's alive and well and sane. This place creeps the Hell out of me."

SIX

1

Henry Wackford saw Gregor Demarkian go in to the Snow Hill Diner at one of those odd times between breakfast and lunch that could not be explained by any normal-sounding reason. There was a coffee machine in the police station, for God's sake. Henry had been on the town council that had authorized the payment for it. It wouldn't be the greatest coffee ever made, but if Demarkian thought he was going to do better at the Snow Hill Diner, he was in for a rude shock. Alice wasn't just one of the stupidest women in Snow Hill, she was also one of its worst cooks. If that diner had had any competition close enough to matter, it would have gone out of business long ago.

Henry reminded himself that he was in favor of small, independent outfits of any kind and against their corporate behemoth competitors—at least in principle—and tried to concentrate on what Christine was saying. She had been on at him all morning, and he still couldn't figure it out. Part of that was the fact that he was more than a little distracted. This murder—this murder. He had a hard time putting it into words in his head. There were events that changed the world. This wasn't anything so momentous, but it might be. It might be. It might change his world, and for the moment he thought that was enough.

Christine was hovering around his doorway. She looked reluctant to come in, at the same time that she had that mulish expression on her face that said she refused to go out. You work with people for years and you don't really know them, Henry thought, but he was convinced he knew Christine. The gold cross around the neck. The little gold stud earrings. The Sunday mornings helping out in the Sunday School over at the Baptist Church. The fiancé stashed in the background somewhere, who would learn to keep his hands to himself except on one or two occasions when neither of them could help it, because sexual repression brought sexual explosion, and then she'd end up pregnant five months before the wedding.

At the moment, she wasn't pregnant. She was just standing there. She had a file in her hand, Henry had no idea what it was for. He was still standing at the window. Maybe Gregor Demarkian had gone in to the diner to grill Alice McGuffie. He wished to Hell he had that one on videotape.

"Mr. Wackford," Christine said.

"Gregor Demarkian just went into the diner," Henry Wackford said. "Has he talked to you yet? He'll be talking to everybody in town. That's how these people work. Maybe I'll go over there and see if I can talk to him myself."

"Mr. *Wack*ford," Christine said.

Henry forced himself away from the window. God, it was impossible, living in this place. People had no sense of occasion. They had no sense of the immensity of the world outside their little plastic prison. He wished he'd never come back to town to practice. He wished he'd never seen Snow Hill in the first place.

He made himself sit down behind his desk. He put his hands flat against the felt blotter. He looked up. This was the way bosses and secretaries were supposed to interact. Maybe it would allow her to say whatever she needed to and get it over with.

"Well," he said. "Do I have an appointment, is that it?"

Christine took a deep breath. "You do not have an appointment," she said. "There are some people who want to see you, from Fox News, I think—"

"Fox?" Henry was interested. "I always said if I ever got the chance, I'd refuse to talk to Fox, but that could be counterproductive. They've got the best ratings of all the cable news organizations, and they reach the enemy. And I think I may have talked to them the other day, I don't remember. But that was off-the-cuff stuff, not a real interview. We could be making history here, Christine. Do you realize that?"

"I don't want to make history," Christine said. "I want to do my job every day and go home at night and have nothing on my conscience. And I can't do that here. I can't do that when you're trying to get God out of the United States government and out of the schools and take away the right to free speech from every Christian."

Henry's chair was one of those tilting, swivelled ones—not the new kind made for computers—the old kind. It had been made for his father, out of good mahogany wood, and it had arms like the arms of a captain's chair on a particularly expensive cruise ship.

"God has nothing to do with the United States government," he said. "If you'd ever believed He did, you should have been disabused of the notion by the administration of George W. Bush."

"And there's that," Christine said. "Why do you have to insult the President of the United States. He's the President. We're supposed to respect the President."

"It would take a tree sloth to respect George W. Bush," Henry said, "and he's not the President any more. He's been out of office for months. Did you really come in here to talk to me about George W. Bush?"

"I came in here to quit," Christine said. "I've been trying to do it for days, but you never let me get a word in edgeways."

"You mean you're giving me notice?" Henry was flabbergasted. "How can you do that? There's a pile of work out there. Somebody has to do it. If you think you're going to be able to bring a new girl up to speed in two weeks, or even find somebody who can replace you in two weeks—"

"It's nothing to do with two weeks," Christine said. "I'm not giving you notice. I'm quitting. I'm quitting now. Right this minute. I'm leaving my book on my desk and then I'm going home. I'm not going to be a party to this anymore, Mr. Wackford, I really am not. I gave my life to Jesus Christ when I was eleven years old and I've never regretted it. Not for a single minute. I can't go on helping you persecute Christians the way you do."

"I don't persecute Christians," Henry said. "What are you talking about? It's the Christians who are persecuting me. Shoving their prayers down my throat. Hell, going to a school board meeting these days is like listening to an official town pronouncement that I'm not even an American citizen. One nation under God, for God's sake."

"It is one nation under God," Christine said, "and I like it that way, and I'm not going to help people like you ruin it and turn this into—I don't know what you want to turn this into. It doesn't matter. I'm going to put this folder on your desk and then I'm going to leave and I'm not going to come back. I don't care what you say. Get that Edna Milton woman to help you if you need help. She's just like you. She hates God, too."

Henry watched her back out of the room. Why was she backing out of the room? You'd think she thought he was King of England, or something equally ridiculous? She was ridiculous. He'd never seen anybody so ridiculous. He jumped out of his chair and ran over to her.

"You're the one who's ruining the country," he barked at her. "You and all the people like you—superstitious, petty, stupid, racist—oh, yes, you're all racist as Hell. You hide behind religion but what you really care about is keeping the black people out of here and out of everywhere. And don't I know it. Religion, my eye. None of you cares any more about God than I care about butter pecan ice cream, and I'm allergic to ice cream."

"I'm going," Christine said.

She had left her coat lying across the top of her desk. The outer office was deserted except for one young man in a black blazer and a black T-shirt. Henry was vaguely aware that this was some kind of media look. He thought it might have been out of date.

"You're the one who's ruining the country," Henry said. "Doesn't that religion of yours teach you any responsibility? Doesn't it teach you to abide by your obligations? You have an obligation here. You can't just leave me in the lurch. There's work to do."

"It's evil work that you're doing," Christine said, "and you can get somebody else to do it for you. There isn't anything in the world that could make me stay here."

She was out the door a second later. Henry stood watching her go, watching the door swing open and shut, listening to the sound of the street door open and shut. The man in the black blazer had put down his magazine and was looking up expectantly. Henry thought he was far too interested in what he was seeing.

"Mr. Wackford?" the young man said.

Henry gave another long look at the door. "Welcome to Snow Hill," he said. "That's what happens when you run your life on superstition instead of reason. The whole world goes to Hell. If we let these people win, we'll all be back in the Dark Ages. The Dark Ages. That's what we call the time when religion ruled the world. Come in and tell me what I can help you with."

2

The note was waiting on the shelf of her cubby when Alice came in to work, and that was impossible, because the diner had been closed all night, and she was just opening up. She was so tired, what with staying up with Barbie half the night, and taking phone calls from everybody she knew, she almost didn't see it. She was just putting her coat onto the hook when a breeze coming in from the back door made the note flutter, and she put her hand up to touch it. It was an ordinary note. It wasn't anything like she'd seen in movies. There were no words cut out of magazines. It was just a plain piece of lined white notebook paper, cut in half and then folded, and the words on it said:

I saw what you did up at Annie-Vic's.

Lyman was over on the other side of the room, fussing with the grill. He always fussed with the grill first thing in the morning. Alice put the note in her pocket and told herself there was nothing to worry about. She had been up at Annie Vic's, yes, but she'd been alone. Somebody must have seen her go in or come out. That was a problem, a bigger one than her brain could really get around, but it was not a catastrophe. It was not the kind of thing that deserved an anonymous note. It was nothing to worry about. And the note might not even be for her. It didn't have her name on it. She could drop it on the floor in the dining room and nobody would know who it belonged to. Maybe that was what she would do, later. Maybe she'd just let it fall next to one of Their chairs, if one of Them ever came in for a cup of coffee. They almost never did. They preferred the Starbucks out at the mall. They didn't want coffee so much as they wanted coffee-flavored milk shakes.

She felt a small rivulet of sweat go down the back of her neck, in spite of the fact that the kitchen wasn't really warm yet. Barbie was staying home from school today. Alice thought that the Cornish children probably were, too. She couldn't imagine what it was like being the Cornish children. She didn't believe it when people said they just didn't believe in God, or the afterlife, or judgment. She was sure they knew, deep down there somewhere, that God was real and that the way they were living meant they would spend eternity in horror. What must it be like to be the Cornish children, knowing all the time that your mother had been condemned to Hell, that she was down there somewhere burning, and that the best you could hope for is that you would never see her again?

By the time Gregor Demarkian came into the diner, Alice had passed through the phase of thinking about Judy Cornish in Hell, and was thinking about the writer of the anonymous letter burning in Hell. It was a wicked thing to write anonymous notes, and it was dangerous, too. She was a good Christian woman. She was just going to sweat about it for a while. Send a note like that to somebody who really was a criminal, though, and you had no idea what you'd get: a knife in the back? An ambush on the way home from work or school? A little drop of poison in your coffee?

Gregor Demarkian was taller than Alice had expected him to be. He had one of those names that usually belonged to small dark people, not black but *dark,* square little men with hair that looked oiled. Gregor Demarkian's hair didn't look oiled, and he was taller than anybody Alice had ever seen except Nick Frapp. She wiped the palms of her hands on her apron. She ought to go home today and rest and look after Barbie. She wasn't feeling well. If it wasn't for the fact that that Connie Sutpen hadn't shown up again, she would just tell Lyman and leave.

Gregor Demarkian sat down at the counter. Alice took a deep breath. Of course he would sit down at the counter. He belonged in a booth, that man did. He wasn't a trucker, and he wasn't trying to pretend to be a trucker like these television people. It was the truckers who sat at the counter, or the regulars. Or at least it had been, until all this fuss had started.

Gregor Demarkian was talking to the man next to him. This was one of the television people, not anybody Alice knew, although she'd seen him in here half a dozen times in the past week. She put her hand in her apron pocket and fiddled with the anonymous note. It was odd how things went. You'd think you know everything, absolutely everything, about everyone in town, you'd think you know what their handwriting is like, but she couldn't make this out at all. Maybe it was one of the television people who had sent it. Maybe it was one of the people from the development. The trouble with that was that they would have no way of knowing that she had a cubby back there, with her name on it. People from outside would have put it in an envelope in her mailbox or something like that.

Alice got the coffee pot and headed over to where Demarkian was sitting.

"My reporter would wet her pants if you let her have an interview," the television man was saying. "Especially now. Even with a murder, we've just been hanging out around here spinning our wheels."

"No signs of violence by the forces of the religious right?" Gregor Demarkian asked.

"If you ask me, the forces of the religious right mostly want to get on camera and fulminate," the television man said. "But nobody listens to me. The network wants coverage of the trial; it thinks we have to be here before anything happens, so here we are. We interviewed that Reverend Frapp the other day. It fell absolutely flat. No snake handling, no drinking poison, and a guy who can quote Seneca in Latin."

The coffee pot was full. All the coffee pots were kept as full as possible at this time of the morning. Alice put her free hand around the side of it. It was hot, but not so hot she was in danger of being burned. She walked over to the two men and reached for Gregor Demarkian's still-overturned coffee cup. The counter was set with coffee cups turned upside down on saucers, and paper placemats with a picture of the American flag on them, and paper napkins with forks and spoons and knives holding them down.

"Can I get you anything?" Alice said.

Gregor Demarkian looked up at her. She hated his eyes. He had eyes like black marbles.

"Are you Mrs. McGuffie?" he asked.

"Yes, of course I'm Mrs. McGuffie," she said. She knew she sounded rude, but she really didn't care. She really didn't. Who were these people, anyway? They didn't belong here. They'd be gone as soon as this trial was over. The only difference between Gregor Demarkian and the television people was that he'd probably try to pin that murder on a good Christian just to make the Christians in town look bad.

"Can I get you anything?" she asked again.

"Some scrambled eggs and toast," Gregor Demarkian said.

Alice made a show of taking out her pad and writing it down. In those fancy restaurants out at the mall, nobody wrote anything down. It was just another way of telling people how much smarter you were than they were. Not writing anything down, as if you had a perfect memory. She bet they made plenty of mistakes, and then pretended they hadn't, so they could all go on pretending together. That was what it was all about with those people. Pretending. They pretended to understand things you didn't, and they pretended that the silly things they said meant something real, and then they pretended that they were nothing like you at all.

She put her book into her pocket and brushed her fingers against the note again. Then she blushed.

"Are you all right?" Gregor Demarkian said.

Alice started. Gregor Demarkian looked like he was *peering* at her. The television man looked like he was doing the same thing. She tried to straighten her back and succeeded only in creating a little spasm.

"I don't have to talk to you," she said, the words coming out when she had only meant to think them. "I don't care what Gary Albright says. You're not the police, and you're not on our side. I don't have to talk to you, and nobody else does, either. Your eggs will be out in a minute. Good-*bye*."

She turned her back to both the men and walked away, to the little window that led to the kitchen, to hand in her slip. The note was still in there, in her pocket. It made her cold, just to think about it.

I saw what you did up at Annie Vic's.

Well, Alice thought. What of it? What had she done up at Annie Vic's that should be anybody's business but her own?

3

It was cold in the room now. Sometimes it got that way. Annie-Vic thought about the window, and about how easy it ought to be to close it, but she couldn't close it, and she knew she couldn't. It was odd to be here like this—to float, to be able to hear everything anybody said without their knowing you could hear it. It was a revelation, really. If she came out of this—and she thought she would, if only because she wasn't panicking—she would recommend a stint of it to everybody. It was amazing, the kind of things people said when they thought you couldn't hear them.

This man, this person called Gregor Demarkian, didn't say much of anything. Annie-Vic had been interested as soon as she'd heard Dr. Willard use his name. She'd heard of him, of course. She could barely help it. When she was home and on her own, she was practically addicted to Court TV, or Tru TV, as it had started calling itself. It was a silly change, and the mangled spelling of "true" offended her. She hated to sound like an old person, but she thought the standards of everything had declined badly since World War II. Even in the early days of television, when there was practically nothing on the box but the criminally stupid, nobody would have put up with a spelling like "tru." Ed Sullivan had classical musicians on his variety show: pianists and violinists playing Beethoven, Mozart, Brahms. People were ashamed to admit that they were ignorant of the important monuments of the Great Tradition, never mind grammar, punctuation, and spelling. And tattoos—nobody had tattoos except the members of motorcycle gangs, and women never had them at all. The whole world seemed to have devolved into ugliness and squalor. It was as if one day she had gotten out of bed, and the hillbillies had won.

At the moment, she wasn't getting out of bed, or even turning over. Annie-Vic wanted to turn over, because her back hurt. She couldn't lift her arms. She couldn't open her eyes, not on purpose. They sometimes opened on their own, she didn't know why. They were open now, so that she could see something of what was happening in the room. Being flat on her back, she couldn't see much. The Demarkian person was very tall, and broad, like somebody who played professional football. He was probably too old. Annie-Vic had no idea how old you had to be to play professional football. That nice black man, that Michael Jordan, had gone in and out of being retired for years, and she didn't think he was much more than forty. But that was professional basketball, so maybe that was different.

There were things that Annie-Vic believed to be necessary. One of those things was a commitment to curing your own ignorance. There was something intrinsically wrong about being proud of what you didn't know. So many of these people these days were proud of just that. They took it as a badge of honor that they never listened to Bach

262

and couldn't tell a Renoir from a Picasso. Franklin Hale, for instance, seemed to be making a career out of boasting about his own ignorance, and Alice McGuffie—

Annie-Vic made her mind stop. Alice McGuffie. There was something about Alice McGuffie. On the day that this had happened, she had been thinking about it. Now it was gone, lost because of the condition she was in or lost for no other reason than old age. It didn't matter why. Alice McGuffie was not just proud of being ignorant, she was also furious at people who weren't. She wasn't stupid, that wasn't the point. She was willfully stupid. Annie-Vic wouldn't have believed, back all those years ago when she had set off for Poughkeepsie and college, that anybody on earth could be willfully stupid.

The other thing Annie-Vic believed was that too much money wasn't good for people. She knew that these things were cyclical. There was a short, intense period of wealth-building followed by a longer, less intense period of wealth consolidation. She had learned that in economics in 1936, and she'd brushed up on it since. Periods of wealth building were all about money. New people replaced the old families and all the new people had to distinguish themselves was money, so they spent it. They threw it around. They wore the labels on the outside of their clothes. It was only natural. But it wasn't good for people, Annie-Vic thought. It really wasn't. Money was like a drug, if you had to much of it. You couldn't really say it was a religion. Religions provided explanations, and consolation, and hope. When the world got into those times when money was the only thing that mattered, that was ugly, too, almost as ugly as ignorance.

Gregor Demarkian was walking around the room, looking at her things, looking at the equipment the hospital staff had left. There seemed to be a lot of equipment in the room. Annie-Vic had no idea what it was for, or who had put it here. She had an IV in her arm, which was giving her food and water, in a clear stream of glucose or something. She knew what that was for. As for the rest of it, she didn't seem to need it. She wasn't on a breathing machine. She wasn't on a machine to make her heart beat.

Somebody else came into the room. It took Annie-Vic awhile to realize who it was. It was Lisa. This made her feel immediately better. Annie Vic always liked it best when Lisa was in to visit, although it had to be a mortal bore for the poor girl. Annie-Vic tried to remember what Lisa did with her life, but the information wouldn't come. She was in college, maybe. That sounded about right. The last thing Annie-Vic wanted was to wake up from this thing and go immediately senile.

Mr. Demarkian and Lisa were talking. There was something about papers and something about the dining room.

"I didn't look through any of it to begin with," Lisa was saying. "I'm sorry, Mr. Demarkian. I really do want to help. You have no idea how much I want to help. I don't understand people like the people who did this. I really don't."

Mr. Demarkian said something Annie-Vic couldn't catch. It was so damned frustrating. Her hearing had been going for years, of course, but she could do well enough if she could just look people in the face.

"I went through every piece of paper that was there," Lisa said. "I looked at all of them. There was a lot of stuff about a new contract for the teachers. Stuff about the teachers' union, and about teacher pensions. There was a lot about textbook requisitions. Not just this new one about Intelligent Design—"

Intelligent Design, Annie Vic thought indignantly. More like moronic idiocy.

"But I don't know what was there to begin with, if you see what I mean." Lisa sounded close to tears. "It was all such a mess when I got home after that, after that thing. And I can't stay there now, of course. Cameron can't, either. It was never just because it was a crime scene, you know, we just can't stand the idea of it. But it never occurred to me to look through those papers when I first got there, and I never did. So I just don't know what's missing."

More vague, fuzzy noises from Gregor Demarkian. Annie-Vic wanted to hit something. Here she had a Great Detective right in the room with her, right in Snow Hill, and she'd bet the only person in town getting any use out of him was Nick Frapp.

Here was something else Annie-Vic believed. You had to treat human beings like human beings. You couldn't rope off one whole segment of humanity and declare that they were too addled to know their own minds or too malevolent to be let loose with a printing press. That was what Franklin Hale did to people, and it was what Henry Wackford did to people, too. They were practically Siamese twins, those two. They just had different vocabularies to describe what they were doing. Annie-Vic had lived through the age of totalitarianism. She knew what a totalitarian looked like when she saw one.

Something in her head stopped, again, and she tried to focus. She found it impossible. She did focus sometimes, but it was always involuntary. Since she'd been like this, she hadn't been able to make herself sit still and zero in on any particular thing, on purpose. And yet there was something. Something about the dining room table. Something about Gregor Demarkian in this room.

"I suppose you're right," Lisa was saying. "All the papers I looked at were financial. I don't think there was much of anything about evolution and Intelligent Design. Or maybe I'm wrong. I'm sorry, Mr. Demarkian. I'm being fairly useless here. Maybe you can ask Cameron. He might have noticed more."

The dining room table, Annie-Vic thought, but it was useless.

She was drifting off to sleep.

SEVEN

1

Gregor Demarkian did not like to think he was avoiding Dale Vardan, but he was avoiding Dale Vardan, and as he stepped out of Eddie Block's police car in front of the Snow Hill Public School Complex. He looked around for a moment, not knowing what in particular he expected to see. It was a school complex like hundreds of others across the United States. There hadn't been one like it in Philadelphia when Gregor was growing up, and there wasn't one there now, but that was only because Philadelphia was a city and its students rode public transportation. In suburbs and small towns there was the question of what to do about school busses, and also how to make sure there was enough land for athletic fields. The athletic fields here seemed to be off to the back, covered with snow, marked only by their goal posts and score boards. Beyond even those, all the way at the back, the semi-stalled construction of the new school building rose up out of the hills, a skeleton of ice and steel.

Eddie Block didn't bother to lock up, which Gregor thought was a very bold move. If Gregor had been a seventeen-year-old boy, bored to Hell in trigonometry, the chance to take a police car on a joy ride with the sirens wailing would have been far too tempting to give up.

Of course, if Gregor had done something like that, when he was seventeen, the worst that would have happened to him was a fine and a lecture from a judge, or—if this was his third or fourth offense—maybe a night in jail, just to "scare some sense into him." These days, any kid who tried it would probably actually be sent to jail, and kept there for a year or two.

"It doesn't make sense, what we do about incarceration these days," Gregor said.

Eddie Block looked surprised. "Excuse me?" he said. "It's not a jail, it's the school. I mean, it felt like jail when I was here, you know, but it isn't really. I know that now. I've seen real jails."

"Right," Gregor said. He made a gesture toward the door, and Eddie started to lead him inside.

It really didn't make sense, what they did about incarceration these days. It was as if the whole country was in a rut. There was never any more than one answer to any question, and often only one answer to several questions. He suddenly wondered what would happen to Mallory Cornish, Judy Cornish's oldest daughter. Somebody had told him this morning that she had pushed another girl yesterday and the other girl had injured her knee and been forced to take a few days off school.

"But her mother had just been murdered," Gregor said. Then, realizing he had said it out loud, he looked to see if Eddie Block had heard him.

Eddie was standing in the big front doorway with a tall, thin, no-nonsense-looking woman in late middle age.

"Mr. Demarkian," he said, waving Gregor over. "This is Miss Marbledale."

Gregor was impressed. Most school administrators these days would have put several layers of people between them and any kind of visitor. There would at least have been a secretary to come out and lead them to the office. Gregor walked over to the door and noticed that Miss Marbledale wasn't wearing a coat. He looked inside and saw one of those vast open foyers that had been one of the defining characteristics of school architecture for several years in the early 1980s.

"Mr. Demarkian," Miss Marbledale said, holding out her hand. "I'm so glad to see you here. Come inside and we'll get you a cup of coffee. The wind is awful here."

The wind was awful. Gregor had been so distracted, he hadn't noticed it. Miss Marbledale held open the door and waited for him to walk through. He went into the foyer and looked at the big display case that lined one wall. There was some kind of exhibit up at the moment, but he couldn't puzzle out what it was supposed to be about.

"We turn the display case over to student groups every now and again," Miss Marbledale said. "They do all sorts of things. This is where I'm supposed to be enthusiastic about their learning, but mostly I'm just grateful none of them have done anything drastic as of yet. We used to have the sports trophies in there, but eventually, I just couldn't stand it. So I had them moved to the gym. Will you come with me, please?"

The office was on the right side of the corridor as they stood looking into the school. Gregor went in through the office door and found, again, what he would have expected to find. There was a counter separating the public—or, in this case, the students—from the secretaries at the desks in the open area beyond, and then a small row of doors to the private offices. The offices were labeled generically: principal; vice principal; guidance counselor. Miss Marbledale lifted the movable part of the counter and waved him through.

"Didn't somebody tell me you have been here for many years?" Gregor asked.

"I've been here my entire career," Miss Marbledale said. "It's been decades. Four, at least, and then some. I could work it out if I tried."

"Have you been principal long?"

"For the last fifteen."

Miss Marbledale had her office open. Gregor could see through the door and across the desk through the windows, to the big oval front lawn ringed by the asphalt driveway that would let busses come in and out without getting in each other's way.

"You can't see the construction from here," Gregor said.

"Ah, the construction," Miss Marbledale said. "You have no idea how long I waited for this town to approve this project, and I've been waiting ever since. I don't understand people sometimes. There's work to be done here, real work, not arguing about whether teaching evolution gets students thinking that there is no God. I'll admit I wasn't happy when Franklin and the new board were elected, but I had some hopes for Annie-Vic. She's got her priorities straight. And then, of course, now this."

"Yes," Gregor said. "This. Did Annie-Vic have her priorities straight, as you put it? I thought she was involved in this lawsuit."

"Only pro forma," Miss Marbledale said. "Henry Wackford went to the ACLU, and to the local chapter of Americans United for Separation of Church and State. The ACLU, I think, found him a lawyer, and the lawyer gave him some advice on how to put together a set of plaintiffs."

"Henry Wackford is the old chairman of the school board?" Gregor said. "I thought he was a lawyer himself."

"Oh, he is," Miss Marbledale said. "And for all I know, he may be a good one. But this is a federal case, literally. A federal court and a Constitutional question. And the stakes are high. Nobody wants to take any chances."

Gregor looked around the office. Miss Marbledale's degrees hung on the wall, including a doctorate. There was a picture in a frame on the desk, of Miss Marbledale with a woman who could have been her clone. Gregor supposed that was a sister.

"Try to help me understand something," he said. "From Gary Albright, I've gotten the impression that no matter what I've heard on the news, this is not a case where the school board wants teachers to teach Creationism, or Intelligent Design, I suppose I should say, anyway, they don't actually want teachers to teach it in school."

"That's right," Miss Marbledale said. "The courts have been fairly clear about that. There would be no point in trying that here or any-where else, given the relevant case law."

"What they want," Gregor said, "is for there to be some kind of no-tice in the biology textbooks, saying something about how evolution is one way some people try to explain the great variety of living things on earth, and Intelligent Design is another way, and if students are in-terested in Intelligent Design, there's a book in the library they can go to see."

"Yes," Miss Marbledale said. "To be specific, the book is called *Of Pandas and People*. It's a famous book in its way. It started out as a straightforwardly Creationist text, and then with the outcome of the case in Arkansas, when it was clear the courts wouldn't allow it in the schools, the book was retooled for Intelligent Design. There's a woman named Barbara Forrest who's done excellent work tracking the history of that book."

"Well," Gregor said, "what occurs to me, and what I think would occur to a lot of other people, is that this lawsuit seems a little like overkill. It's a disclaimer, and a book in the library. It's not teaching Genesis in science class, or even mentioning Intelligent Design in sci-ence class. So why file a suit against the school board over something that innocuous."

Catherine Marbledale looked Gregor Demarkian up and down and back and forth. Then she took her seat behind her desk.

"Are you a supporter of Intelligent Design?" she asked.

"To tell you the truth, I know nothing at all about it, except what I've heard since I came here," Gregor said.

"That woman I mentioned, Barbara Forrest," Miss Marbledale said. "She'd be a good place to start to understand why the fuss, as you put it. But let's start with me. The problem, for me, is just this: that disclaimer is *functionally* a lie, even though it may technically be true."

"Which means what?"

"Which means," Miss Marbledale said, "that it's true enough that 'some people' accept evolution and 'some people' reject it for Intelli-gent Design, or outright Creationism, for that matter, but putting a disclaimer like that in a science textbook implies that the 'some people' who reject evolution for Intelligent Design are scientists who have scientific reasons for rejecting evolution."

"And that's not true?" Gregor said. "I thought I'd seen scientists who support Intelligent Design."

"Oh, you have," Miss Marbledale said. "There aren't many of them, and the only biologist of any standing is Michael Behe, who's from Lehigh, not that far up the road here. But he doesn't prefer Intelligent Design for scientific reasons. He prefers it for religious ones. And the one 'scientific' idea he's come up with to 'challenge' evolution is a recycled chestnut that's been around for a hundred and fifty years."

"And that is?"

"He calls it irreducible complexity," Miss Marbledale said. "To put it simply, it says that some organs are so complex, that if you take away even a single one of their parts, they'd cease to function. So natural selection can't account for those, because in order for those organs to evolve, they would have to come into existence, *poof*, all at once, with all their parts intact exactly as they are. And that is—and everybody agrees on this—impossible."

"But you said it is an old chestnut," Gregor said, "so I assume it's not impossible."

"Oh, it's impossible, all right," Miss Marbledale said, "but the fact is that nobody is claiming any of that. Certainly evolutionary biologists aren't. Behe assumes, like the people who have proposed the same idea before him, that each one of those parts has never had any other purpose but the one it has now in the organ in question. But that's not true. There are plenty of examples of parts of organs that serve purposes now that they didn't originally—Behe's big example, for instance, of the flagellum, has been exposed time and again. There's a good article by Kenneth Miller, if you want it. I have it around here somewhere."

"Later, maybe," Gregor said.

"And there's the eye and the inner ear," Miss Marbledale said. "We've been able to trace prior uses for parts of those organs. The whole concept of 'irreducible complexity' depends on the entirely false idea that whatever function an organ or a part of an organ has now is the one it must always have had."

"And that's it?" Gregor said. "The entire case for Intelligent Design rests on the work of one man?"

"It rests on nobody's work," Miss Marbledale said. "At least, it rests on nobody's scientific work. There is no scientific work in Intelligent Design. There are no peer-reviewed papers. There are no reproducible experiments. There are no falsifiable predictions. None. The entire movement consists of people sitting around saying, 'I don't see how evolution could have made that happen, so God must have done it.' And that, you see, is the point. They don't want to advance the cause of science. They don't want to expand human knowledge. All they want is to make it seem, to the general public, that there's something wrong with the theory of evolution, that it's just a guess, that it's probably not true."

"And you think it's true?"

"Of course I think it's true," Miss Marbledale said. "If you're actually willing to look at the evidence, there's nothing else to think. Evolution is a fact. Virtually everything that book says about it is false. Everything. Evidence in the fossil record? There's a ton of it, a huge, overwhelming mountain of it. Macroevolution? We can prove it. We have transitional fossils out the wazoo, full transitional sequences between reptiles and birds, for instance, and many more. The only point of that book is to lie and lie and lie again until it gets children so confused they don't know what's true, and the purpose of that, in the long run, is to discredit science. It's science that those people are afraid of."

"Because science disproves religion?" Gregor asked.

"Because science disproves *their* religion," Miss Marbledale said. "I've been a practicing Methodist for over sixty years, and evolution presents no challenge to my religion at all. But science is important and the scientific method is important. It doesn't solve everything, and it isn't the only thing people need in their lives, but it's important.

Antibiotics, heart transplants, even central heating and safe refrigeration for foods, we can't do without it. And science is the project of trying to find natural explanations for natural phenomenon. That's what distinguishes it from everything that came before. And if we don't teach that, if we teach children that it's all right to go back to the fifteenth century and look for supernatural causes instead of natural ones, we might as well fold up our tents and go back to the desert to eat locusts and honey. *Of Pandas and People* should not be in our school library because the things it says are lies. And evolution should be taught in our biology classes because evolution is true. And that ought to be enough of a reason for anybody."

2

Back out at the front of the school, Gregor Demarkian looked around again and again at the skeleton of the new school building. He was carrying a little stack of books Miss Marbledale had given him, all hardbacks. She seemed to have dozens of copies of each one in boxes all around her office. There was Mark Isaak's *The Counter-Creationism Handbook.* There was Tim Berra's *Evolution and the Myth of Creationism.* There was Donald R. Prothero's *Evolution: What the Fossils Say and Why It Matters,* sitting on top.

"That's the best book out there for a popular audience that not only lays out the evidence from the fossil record, but directly counters Creationism and Intelligent Design," Miss Marbledale said. "I just wish it would come out in paperback. You have no idea how much it cost me to get all these in hardcover. And I give them to everybody. I even tried to give them to Franklin Hale and Alice McGuffie, but they ran, true to form. They wouldn't even take copies for the sake of being polite. And that's the enemy, Mr. Demarkian, and it really is an enemy. That small-minded, smug pride in being ignorant. I have no idea what Creationists are like outside of Snow Hill, or what the Intelligent Design people are like when they're attached to those big national think tanks, but the simple fact of the matter is that here, on the ground, what you have are two kinds of people who want Intelligent Design. First are the people who just don't know much about evolution. Second are the people who don't want to know, because they've made up their minds, and they won't let you confuse them with facts. And those second kind of people are the ones who run for school board."

Gregor looked up at the new school building yet again, and then got into the car next to Eddie Block. Eddie started up the engine and turned up the heat right away. Gregor was grateful. He never understood why March had to be so cold, when it was supposed to be the start of spring.

Gregor had put the books on the floor at his feet. He caught Eddie Block eying them.

"Well," he said. "Have you read any of these? Miss Marbledale was your teacher, wasn't she?"

"Miss Marbledale was everybody's teacher," Eddie Block said. "No, I haven't read those books."

"Did you listen to what she said?"

"Sure I listened to what she said. Everybody listens to Miss Marbledale. She's the kind of person people listen to."

Gregor was going to point out that, technically, she was Dr. Marbledale, but he didn't. She hadn't used the title, for whatever reason. He waited while Eddie backed up and got them turned around, pointing to the way out. Then he said, "So, what about it? Are you like Gary Albright? Do you think the Intelligent Design people ought to get to put their book in the library?"

"Maybe," Eddie said.

"Maybe?"

Eddie looked uncomfortable. "Here's the thing," he said. "It's a book in a library. I mean, I know it's the school library, but still. A couple of years ago, Henry threatened us with a lawsuit—"

"Another one?"

"Yeah," Eddie said. "Henry likes to sue the town. Anyway, there was this book by this guy, Sam Something. *The End of Faith*. We got it in to the library and then Alice complained, because Alice complains.

Henry likes to file lawsuits and Alice likes to complain. Anyway, she complained and the librarians put it behind the desk so that people could only get it if they asked for it, and Henry tried to sue the town because he said putting it back there like that where people had to ask for it would discourage people from reading it, because they might be embarrassed to ask for it and have everybody know they were taking it out when this is such a fundamentalist town. You got that?"

"Sort of."

"Yeah, my point exactly," Eddie said. "I mean, for God's sake, Mr. Demarkian. Henry's an atheist and he's been shouting it from the rooftops since he was in high school. People roll their eyes, but they don't bother him about it. He's even got a secretary straight out of some Christian television program. And it's not that I agree with Alice on this, either, because I don't. But that's the thing, see? If it was censorship or whatever it was to keep that book behind the librarian's desk when the Christians complained about it, then why isn't it censorship to keep that *Pandas* book out of the library when the atheists complain about it? It always seems like there are two different sets of rules for different people. One rule for the Christians and another rule for the atheists."

"Miss Marbledale says she isn't an atheist."

"Yeah," Eddie said. "Well, you know."

"What?"

"Well, that's the thing, isn't it?" Eddie said. "The Bible lays it all out. In the beginning, and then it says how God did it, right?"

"Maybe," Gregor said.

"I don't see that there's any maybe about it," Eddie said. "I've read that part of the Bible. I read it in my Bible study group at church. And it seems to me, you know, that it's clear. If that evolution stuff is true, then the Bible can't be true. And if the Bible isn't true in that place, it might not be true in any place. And then what happens? There's no Jesus Christ, and no salvation, and no life after death. There's no anything."

"A lot of Christian denominations see Genesis as a metaphor," Gregor said. "They think it's poetic, a kind of allegory—"

"Meaning a lie," Eddie said. "That's all all that stuff means, Mr. Demarkian. A lie."

"I don't think fiction is a lie," Gregor said carefully. "Bennis—Bennis is the woman I'm about to marry—Bennis says that a writer named Ken Kesey said that literature is something that's 'the truth, even though it didn't happen.' That you can tell the truth about something through scenes and images that get to the core of what you're trying to say, but are still imaginative and dramatic renderings."

Eddie was staring straight ahead. "I still think that comes down to a lie," he said. "But I'm not going to argue about it. There's no point in arguing about it. I accepted Jesus Christ as my Lord and Savior, and I'm going to trust in him, and not in a bunch of science books. And I think evolution is just a theory, not a fact, no matter what Miss Marbledale says. And I think the least we could do is say so, so the kids don't get the idea that there is no God and the Bible is all a lie. You know what kids are going to do with that. They're going to think that if there isn't any God, there isn't any reason to behave themselves, and then it's all going to go to Hell in no time flat. You can't get around it, Mr. Demarkian. No matter what Miss Marbledale says, or what the Pope says either, you can't have evolution and God at the same time, and anyone who says you can isn't a real Christian."

Gregor would have given some thought to this restrictive definition of what made a Christian—a definition that wiped out not only all liberal Protestants, but all Roman Catholics and most of the Eastern Orthodox churches as well—but they were coming around a long curve in the road leading back to town, and something three-quarters of the way down had caught his eye.

He leaned a little forward in his seat and squinted. There was yellow police tape, which made sense. That was Annie-Vic's house, which was still a crime scene. There was a police car—that made sense, too. There were two state policemen standing guard, which was something Gary Albright should have thought of when Annie-Vic was attacked. Still, there was something. He leaned forward even more, until his seat belt strained and his forehead nearly touched the windowshield.

"Is there something wrong, Mr. Demarkian?" Eddie Block asked. "If you're not feeling well, I could always pull over and let you get out for a little air."

"I'm feeling fine," Gregor said. "We have to stop at Annie-Vic's house."

"At Annie-Vic's house? What for?"

"Because I think something has happened."

Gregor sat back in his seat and bit his lip. By now they were halfway down the hill and he could see it clearly: the red and white ambulance with its lights pulsing convulsively in the grey late-morning light. Another ambulance meant another body, that might or might not be dead.

3

The body was, in fact, dead. It was dead and lying in what seemed to be an untouched heap in the doorway to Annie-Vic's house, while the two men from the ambulance stood around near the gate, one of them smoking. Gregor Demarkian dismissed images of oxygen canisters exploding in flames to concentrate on Dale Vardan, who was on the scene and giving orders, apparently to no effect.

"She has to have gotten here some way or the other," Dale Vardan was saying, poking his finger at the chest of the same state police officer who had talked to Gregor this morning. "You were here. You were keeping watch. You must have seen something."

"But I didn't see anything," the officer said. "I was around the back, I told you. She wasn't here when I went around there and when I got back she was."

"So what about *you*?" Vardan demanded of the other state police officer. "Didn't it occur to either one of you idiots that one of you should be out front here keeping watch at all times? What were you doing, both going back there together?"

"It was gunfire," the first state policeman said in exasperation. "Three gunshots, one right after another. They sounded like they came from a shotgun. Neither one of us wanted to let the other one go on back alone. Who knew what he was going to find?"

"Well," Vardan said, "what did you find?"

The first officer looked away. "Nothing much," he admitted.

"Nothing much," Dale Vardan said.

Gregor stepped forward then. The two state police officers seemed embarrassed to see him, but he had no intention of humiliating them any more than Vardan had already done. It was not a management style he had ever found effective.

Dale Vardan caught sight of him. "Well," he said. "If it isn't the great Gregor Demarkian, the Hillbilly's Friend. I don't know where you've been this morning. I've been responding to a call about a murder. This murder."

"Really," Gregor said. He looked down at the body, but he did not find it immediately recognizable. For one thing, it was lying more or less facedown, although oddly crumpled, almost half in a fetal position. "Who called you?" he asked.

"I have no idea," Vardan said. "It was an anonymous tip. But it was a good one, don't you think?"

"And did you call the Snow Hill Police Department?" Gregor asked. "I know you didn't call me."

"I didn't have to call anybody," Dale Vardan said. "Why should I? You may impress people in Philadelphia, but you don't impress me, and as far as I'm concerned, this investigation has been bungled from the beginning. Right from the beginning. None of these hillbillies know how to investigate a murder that's any more complicated than some stupid redneck getting liquored up and shooting the face off his wife. We should have been called in from the start."

"Possibly," Gregor said. He had been staring at the body all this time. Now he looked at the state police officer he had talked to this morning. "When you went around the back, did you do a search, or did you just check it out to make sure somebody wasn't doing God knows what right in front of your faces?"

"The second thing," the officer said. "We knew we shouldn't be too long away from the front of the house. We're not idiots. We just went around to check and we didn't see anything and the shooting had stopped, so we came around back. And there she was."

"This woman," Gregor said.

"Right," the officer said.

"And you checked to see if she was breathing," Gregor said.

"We did," the officer said, "but it was pretty clear right away that she wasn't. So we were careful, you know. We didn't move her or anything. That's pretty much the way we found her. All sort of twisted up like that."

"Right," Gregor said.

"Bunch of assholes," Dale Vardan said.

Gregor didn't stop to ask which assholes those were. He leaned forward and pulled the body slowly onto its back, holding the left shoulder with his winter-gloved hand to make sure that he would leave no fingerprints. He couldn't imagine that it would matter even if he did.

"She looks familiar, don't you think?" he said. He supposed he was talking to Dale Vardan, or maybe one of the police officers, but he really didn't know.

The body took the last few inches in an undignified plop, and then Gregor realized why it looked so familiar.

It was Shelley Niederman.

PART III

.... our intention is to show that the theory of evolution is not indisputable scientific truth, as many people assume or try to impose on others. On the contrary, there is a glaring contradiction when the theory of evolution is compared to scientific findings in such diverse fields as the origin of life, population genetics, comparative anatomy, paleontology, and biochemistry. In a word, evolution is a theory in "crisis."

—Darwinism Refuted http://www.darwinismrefuted.com

1. Evolution is one of the most strongly supported theories in all of science. It is nowhere near a theory in crisis.

2. This claim has been made constantly since even before Darwin. In all that time, the theory of evolution has only gotten stronger. Prior to the development of evolutionary theory, almost 100 percent of relevant scientists were creationists. Now the number is far less than 1 percent. The numbers continue to drop as the body of evidence supporting evolutionary theory continues to build. Thus, claims of scientists abandoning evolution theory for creationism are untrue.

—Creationist Claims http://www.talkorigins.com

ONE

1

Gregor took one of the two police officers and walked around to the back of the house. Part of the reason for this was practical. Those gunshots bothered him. There was no gun in this case, and the Hadley house was far too close to town to be a suitable site for hunting. It was the kind of detail that made him think, again, of that first kidnaping case, the kind of detail that made him feel that there was something right in front of him that he wasn't seeing. Part of the reason for this was psychological, however, and Gregor was old enough to admit it. He needed to be away from Dale Vardan. It was ironic; it had been his idea to bring the man in to begin with, and he still thought that they needed a state police presence here in light of what had been happening. Dale Vardan, though, being who he was, provided only one advantage: the long-term cover of showing that they had done the right thing when they knew they were getting in over their heads. Unfortunately, the man tended to make the floodwaters surge higher.

The ambulance would take the body to the hospital. Somebody would autopsy it there. Gregor was not worried about the autopsy. He expected to find that Shelley Niederman had been bludgeoned to death, just as her friend Judy Cornish had been, just as Annie-Vic Hadley had almost been.

"It's something to do with the house," he said.

The state police officer, walking beside him, turned. "Did you say something, Mr. Demarkian? I didn't catch it."

"It's something to do with the house," Gregor repeated. "Whatever is going on here. There's something in that house, or about it in some way, that's serving as the catalyst for these crimes. Which means that whoever it is didn't get what he or she was looking for yesterday. That is, assuming that what's being looked for is an object that can be taken in or out."

"I'm sorry, Mr. Demarkian. I'm afraid I don't follow."

"I'm not sure I do either," Gregor said. "What's your name?"

"Ralph. Ralph Tammaro."

"And people call you Ralph?"

"People call me Tammaro, mostly," the man said. "I never much liked the name of Ralph. What do you think is in the house?"

"I don't know, exactly," Gregor said. "My best guess is that it's something in all those papers in the dining room, something Annie-Vic Hadley was working on. I asked Lisa Hadley—that's the old woman's grandniece, I think. Anyway, she wasn't able to tell me anything that was very helpful. Maybe I'll go down there in a minute and look through them myself. She did say there was nothing on the table that had anything to do with Creationism and evolution, though."

"Oh," Tammaro said. "The lawsuit. I keep forgetting about it. I don't know why. It's on the news every day."

"Well, it's going to be on the news even more after this," Gregor said. "If you thought the publicity was bad to begin with, just wait until the cable news networks decide they've got a crazed Creationist serial killer on their hands."

"Is that what this is? A crazed Creationist serial killer?" Tammaro looked doubtful.

Gregor looked up the hill at the back of the house, then down the hill again toward the house and town. There were quite a few trees in back, a little wooded area, but it was in no way a forest or the start of real country. Gregor could see another house farther up the hill, although he couldn't see it very well.

"Let me ask you something," Gregor said. "Did either of you see anybody in this stand of trees? Anybody standing around, anybody walking, anybody running?"

"No, we didn't," Tammaro said. "And I think we would have."

"So do I," Gregor said. "But look at the area here. It's not large, but it's large enough so that it's unlikely that somebody could have fired a gun and then gotten out in time so that neither of you saw anything. Not unless whoever it was was right up against the back of the house, and even then it's something of a climb down to town going this way."

"I'm pretty sure the shots weren't fired right next to the back of the house," Tammaro said. "The reports would have been louder."

"What about much farther way, all the way up to where that house is on top of the hill?"

"No." Tammaro was adamant. "The reports would have been much too faint. We wouldn't have paid any attention to them. Hell, Mr. Demarkian. This is the country. People fire guns. They fire shotguns. They fire handguns. They fire rifles. I know this is pretty close to town, and that's not as usual, but still. I'm willing to bet almost anything that those shots came from the middle of that mess of trees or close to it. And Canton felt the same way."

"Canton is the other officer?"

"That's right. And I've known him a long time. He's a good officer."

Gregor was sure he was. He was also sure that it was not possible for somebody to have fired shots from those trees and made it out clean before Tammaro and Canton showed up. And yet the shots had been fired, and the fired shots had brought the two officers around to the back of the house, and in the short space of time in which they had been back there, a woman had been murdered. And not just murdered any which way. She'd been smashed to Hell with something like a bat, which was not an easy way to kill someone, or a way that was guaranteed to take no time at all.

"Let me ask you something," he said. "The two of you came around back here, and I suppose you spent at least some time checking out what might have been going on."

"Some time, yes," Tammaro said, "but not very long. We were telling the truth to Dale back there, Mr. Demarkian. We really were. We came back here and there was nothing. Not a single thing. And we only looked around a little to make sure that nobody was hiding behind a bush with a shotgun, out to get us, or something. And we didn't see anybody, so Canton went back to the front of the house and I started looking through the wood. We couldn't have both been out here together for more than two or three minutes, tops."

"All right," Gregor said. "That tells us one thing. It's unlikely anybody would have had the time both to murder Shelley Niederman and to get into the house to search."

"Nobody went into the house," Tammaro said positively. "I can guarantee it for the time we were both out front, and Canton can guarantee it for the time he was there. And we weren't gone long enough for somebody to get in and get out again."

Gregor thought about it. "There had to be a second time when nobody was in front of the house, isn't that true? Didn't Canton come back here and get you when he found the body?"

"No," Tammaro said. "He shouted, and I came around the front. And the house is locked up tight. We made sure of it when we came on duty. Nobody was in that house today, Mr. Demarkian, except for you, when you came in this morning and looked around. You could go back in there right this minute and you wouldn't find a single thing disturbed."

"All right," Gregor said. "Then let's go back and look at the house."

2

The front of the house was still full of emergency vehicles and police officers, and probably would be for hours, but they had been joined by a thin line of cable news vans now parked on the road just outside the driveway. Gregor had wondered when that would begin to happen, and now it had. He walked over to the other officer, the one Tammaro had called Canton, and introduced himself. Somebody had put a floodlight on, in spite of the fact that it was the middle of the afternoon. The light hurt his eyes.

"Canton is my first name," Canton said. "Weeks is my last. Nobody ever calls me that. They ought to do something about the way they name children. Nobody ever seems to like their own name."

Gregor actually liked his name just fine, but this was just small talk. Shelley Niederman's body had been taken out of the doorway, which was now in the process of being taped up as a crime scene. Shelley Niederman's body was on a stretcher near the ambulance, in a body bag, as anonymous as garbage put out on the curb for pickup.

"Just tell me one thing, if you could," he said. "When you found her, she was dead. Not when the both of you checked her, but when you found her. Because you were by yourself in the beginning, right?"

"Right. I came back around front because we didn't want the front left unguarded for very long. As soon as I know there wasn't anybody out there meaning to shoot us dead, I came back around and let Tammaro go on investigating. Not that I left him there for long. I came around and there she was, and I called for him before I even started trying to check her out. I don't mean any disrespect for Dale Vardan—"

"You ought to," Gregor said.

"Yeah, well," Canton said. "What I mean is, there really wasn't any time. It had to have happened really fast. And I can't figure out how it did happen. I mean, I suppose we were back there longer than we think were, but it couldn't have been that much longer. If you see what I mean."

"I do see what you mean. Is there any reason why I shouldn't go into the house?"

"You're the chief investigator here," Canton said. "I suppose Dale is going to bitch at you, but I don't think he can do anything."

That was Gregor's assessment of the situation, too. He took a handkerchief out of his pocket and tried the front door. It was locked. He looked at Canton.

"This door has been locked the whole time? I got in there this morning."

"I unlocked for you," Canton said. "We have a key, but we keep the place locked. Just to be safe, if you see what I mean."

"And you locked up after me when I left this morning?"

"Absolutely," Canton said. "I wouldn't forget a thing like that."

"Right." Gregor motioned to the door. Canton came forward and opened up. The door swung on its hinges. The hallway beyond it was dark.

"You always think of the twenties as being such a happy era," Gregor said. "F. Scott Fitzgerald. Bright young things. And yet they built all these houses, and they were all so dark."

Canton Weeks said nothing at all, and Gregor bent down to step under the crime tape and go inside. He turned the light on in the hall. It was the middle of the afternoon, the sun was out, and this house still needed artificial light.

"There ought to be a ghost in the attic," Gregor said.

He went down the hall to the living room, and through the living room to the dining room. The mess that had been made of the papers on the dining room table when Judy Cornish had been killed—or, at least, around the time Judy Cornish had been killed—and that had still been evident when Gregor had looked in this morning, had now been corrected. That must have been Lisa, going through things when he had asked her to see what might be missing. She had protested that she couldn't really know what was missing, and that was true. But he couldn't know, either, and yet he had looked through these papers once, and he was about to do it again. But first he was going to look through the house.

He went through the dining room into the kitchen. It looked as blank and unused as it always had. He wondered if Annie-Vic used it when she was in residence, or if she had someone in to "do" for her now that she was old. He looked into the pantry, which was a big windowless room at the back, lined with shelves that were themselves lined with Mason jars which seemed to hold close to a century's worth of canning. The jars were labeled, with both a description of the contents and the year they were being put up, and some of the years had an almost fantastical quality—1924, 1936. If Annie-Vic had been poisoned by eating ancient home canned goods, he wouldn't have been surprised.

He left the pantry and went into the back hall. There was another door there. He tried it, and it was locked. What was more, there was a small latch bolt near the top, and it was bolted solid. Gregor doubted that it would have been much of a problem for somebody to bust through it, but nobody had, and that meant that nobody had gone out the back door this afternoon.

And if somebody had, he'd have had a good chance of running into Tammaro at the back.

Gregor went back to the dining room. The papers were in neat stacks. He wondered if that was how Annie-Vic herself had left them, before they'd been disturbed by whoever was in here yesterday. He looked at the first stack and saw that the paper on top of it concerned the new teachers' contracts. He thumbed through a few more pages and found more material on the contracts, material on the teachers' pension funds, material on the buying of textbooks, material on the construction of the new school complex, even material on class scheduling for the upcoming school year. Annie-Vic was, as Catherine Marbledale had indicated, concerned with the nuts and bolts of the running of the school district.

He was just going on to the second stack when Dale Vardan marched in, puffing. He would have been like a Gilbert and Sullivan character, Gregor thought, if he had only been funny. Dale Vardan was not only *not* funny, he didn't ever seem to find anything funny, either.

"You shouldn't be in here," he said. "This is a crime scene. You could be destroying evidence and not even know it."

"I think I know how not to destroy evidence at a crime scene," Gregor said. "And as for whether or not I should be here, this is my crime scene, and my criminal investigation, unless I or the town of Snow Hill voluntarily decide to give it up to you, which we are not going to do. Have any of your people managed to remember to search the house this time?"

"Why should we search the house? She was dead on the doorstep, for God's sake, and the door was locked."

"Which only means that somebody locked it," Gregor said. "And there are windows somebody could have gotten through. And then there's that wooded area in the back, the one where your officers heard not one but three gunshots coming from."

"They were imagining things," Dale Vardan said. "For Christ's sake, Demarkian, look at the lay of the land here. They got around the back of the house and there wasn't anybody there, and if there had been they would have seen him."

"I agree," Gregor said, "but that doesn't mean that nobody was ever there. If you people are going to help out here, you should start by searching that wooded area with a microscope. And you should do it now, because whoever killed Shelley Niederman is going to be back, as soon as he thinks he can get away with it."

"So, you know it's a man, do you? Yeah, I'd take it for a man, too. Women don't beat people to death with baseball bats."

Gregor wished everybody would stop assuming that all the murders had been committed with baseball bats. "I was using the word 'he' as a generic. I see no reason why a woman couldn't have committed these crimes. The important question now is why. And the first necessity is to find whatever was left in that wood, before anybody can come and take it away."

"What makes you think you're going to find anything in that wood?" Dale Vardan demanded. "There was nobody there. They would have seen him. I mean, for Christ's sake, they're screw-ups, but they're not brain dead."

"They heard three shots, and shots do not fire themselves," Gregor said. "If you won't get a team of men on it, I'll call the Governor and throw a right royal fit until you do. And don't think I can't do it. The other thing that needs to happen is that this house needs to be searched, top to bottom, again. Right now. That means all the upstairs rooms, all the upstairs closets, and the attic."

"You're out of your mind," Dale Vardan said. "What the Hell do you think is going on here? You know what this is? This is another hillbilly country feud, that's what this is. You get to the bottom of it, you're going to find a couple of good ole boys and some liquor and lots of sex all over the place."

"Annie-Vic Hadley wasn't a good ole boy, and she wasn't a hillbilly. Judy Cornish and Shelley Niederman weren't hillbillies, either. I've never seen a case that had less to do with hillbillies than this one."

"Bullshit," Dale Vardan said. "What's this whole thing about? Bible-thumping idiots, that's what, all worked up because somebody told them they were descended from monkeys. Well, look at them. They look like they were descended from monkeys. They look like they're *still* monkeys."

"That's the thing," Gregor said. "You see all these papers? I looked through them this morning, and then I had Miss Hadley's grandniece look through them again this afternoon, just in case I missed something. You know what's not here? There's not a single thing, not one, having anything to do with Creationism and evolution, or even with the lawsuit."

"Well, Hell," Dale Vardan said. "Our guy took 'em, that's why. There's something in those papers about him and he doesn't want us to see."

"Took them when?"

"Took them yesterday," Dale Vardan said. "When he murdered the other woman. He had plenty of time."

"Then why did he murder Shelley Niederman?"

"Because he's not murdering them for the papers," Dale Vardan said. "He's murdering them because they're Satan-worshiping secular humanists who want to bring that stuff about monkeys into the Snow Hill public schools. Hillbillies, *Mr.* Demarkian. I told you. They're walking advertisements for mercy killing, only it would be a mercy to the rest of us if they'd just all end up dead."

3

It was nearly five o'clock by the time Gregor got back to town, and by then he knew he would be spending another night with Gary Albright.

"It's really not a problem," Bennis told him when he called. "If anything, it's probably a good thing you're out of the way. You'd only get caught up in this fight about the church. Go solve a murder and come back when it's over."

Gregor didn't even want to think about what it meant that that argument was still going on. "Did you talk to Sister Beata?" he asked. "Did you find out anything about Catholics and evolution?"

"Only that Catholics have no trouble accepting evolution, because they've never taken the Bible to be literally true," Bennis said. "Apparently, that's a Protestant thing. She gave me some stuff to give you to read and I put it on your night table. Do you want me to send it to you?"

"No, not really, not now," Gregor said. "I still wish I understood all this, but I've got two murders and an attempted murder on my hands at the moment, so I'll let it wait. I wish I understood people better than I do."

"You understand people better than most people do," Bennis said.

"Which doesn't bode well for the human race," Gregor told her. "Never mind. I have an early dinner meeting, except it isn't going to be so early by the time I get there. And what's worse, there's only one place in town to eat, it's owned by a suspect, and she hates me. Of course, she seems to hate practically everybody, so it's probably nothing personal."

"Maybe I ought to come out there and keep you company."

"If you do, Donna and a bunch of Armenian-American women are going to come with you, and I think I'd go crazy. I'll talk to you later. I've got to go eat a greasy hamburger on a cardboard bun. Let me tell you, it's not true that these little diners are going out of business because McDonald's is underselling them. It's because their food tastes like this."

He flipped the phone shut and put it in his pocket. He was actually standing just outside the Snow Hill Diner. On any other day, he would probably have gone inside to sit down before calling Bennis. On this day he was just tired, and tired of being out in the sticks. He was not a small-town person. He didn't find such towns friendly, and he didn't find them comforting. In his experience, the smaller the town, the more likely it was to be a hotbed of intrigue and resentment. And resentment was the word for what was going on at the Snow Hill Diner and in Alice McGuffie's head.

Gregor looked through the window, past the half curtains and the gold-stenciled lettering. Molly Trask and Evan Zwicker were already sitting in a booth at the back, waiting for him.

Gregor went inside. There was no hostess, as there was at the Ararat back home, and no procedure for seating except to let you seat yourself. There were plastic yellow ribbon magnets reading SUPPORT OUR TROOPS here and there, a few American flag posters, and a big poster of a gigantic bald eagle right over the counter. The bald eagle looked either constipated or angry. It was hard to tell which.

Gregor made his way to the back and sat down across from the two agents-in-place. They both looked thoroughly bored.

"Good evening, Mr. Demarkian," Evan Zwicker said. "We were just talking about your latest murder."

"We were talking about whether or not there really was some kind of domestic terrorism going on," Molly said. "You know, when you brought that up when we first met you, I thought you were being silly."

"I was guessing, that's all," Gregor said, as a girl came over with an order pad. When he looked a second time, he realized she wasn't a girl. She was a middle-aged woman and she looked exhausted. "I'll have a cup of coffee to start, and then I'll look at the menu," he said.

The woman went away without a word. Gregor wondered what she went back to when she left the diner for the night. Then he wondered which side of the evolution/Intelligent Design debate she was on, or if she even knew there was a debate.

"If it makes you feel any better," he said. "I'm now close to certain that there's no domestic terrorism, or any kind of terrorism, happening here. I think what we have is a plain old-fashioned murder, for plain old-fashioned motives."

"I don't know," Evan said. "I was beginning to think things were looking up. At least domestic terrorism would give us something to do. I don't think we've ever been so bored."

"Well," Gregor said, "you could always tell Kevin O'Connor that I thought there was a good possibility of domestic terrorism. In fact, I'd appreciate it if you would say that, because I need you to do something for me. This place simply doesn't have the resources to do the kind of investigation I need. And I don't have them, either."

"What do you need?" Molly asked.

Gregor reached into the inside pocket of his jacket and came out with a folded piece of paper. He had written it carefully when he was still in Annie-Vic's house. He had wanted to make sure to get all the spelling right. He pushed the paper across the table.

"I want you to find out as much as you can about those three things," he said. "Specifically, I want to know everything I can about how those three things are connected to the Snow Hill Board of Education."

Molly Trask opened the paper and looked at what was written there. "Well," she said, "Dellbach Construction. I've seen that name somewhere."

"They're doing the new school complex," Evan told her. "They've got a big sign out there on the road. We pass it nearly every day."

"Ah," Molly said. "But this other thing—this other thing. Isn't this a teachers' union you're talking about?"

"The local branch of the American Federation of Teachers," Gregor said. "Absolutely."

Molly Trask pushed the paper away. "For God's sake," she said. "We can't investigate a teachers' union. Not without authorization from somebody a lot higher up than you. I don't think even Kevin could okay it without getting permission from Washington practically."

"Well, I'm not interested in the union, per se," Gregor said. "I'm interested in whoever the local person is who's doing the negotiating on this latest teachers' contract."

Evan Zwicker shook his head. "It doesn't work like that," he said. "The national office will send somebody out to do the negotiating. That's part of the reason for joining a big outfit like the AFT. They've got lawyers. They've got ombudsmen. They've got professional nego-tiators. If you're saying you think there's something corrupt going on with those negotiations, we have a big deal here."

"Because it wouldn't just be the one guy, if you see what I mean," Molly said. "They've got checks and balances, these unions do. They have to. The Justice Department doesn't trust them as far as it can throw them, so they've all got procedures, ways of checking on their people, that kind of thing. Which means that if something is going on, it's almost certainly going on all the way to the top. They're either clean or they're shot through with corruption."

"All right," Gregor said, filing that one for later. He reached over to the piece of paper and tapped on the item at the bottom. "With that one—I'm not sure just how you should go about it. The school district keeps a textbook fund somewhere. I don't know where. There must be a bank account, bank records, that kind of thing. And the district gets operating money, too. I need the bank information."

"Well, that'll be easy enough," Evan said.

"We may need a warrant," Molly said.

"We can get a warrant," Evan said. "But we might not need one. A lot of districts these days operate with sunshine rules. They publish their stuff at least once every year or two. The first thing we ought to do is look through the local paper and the local records. Everything you want could be right out in public like that, or it could have been sent as a report to every household in the town. Then all you have to wonder about is whether the accountant is honest."

"Can we check that out?" Gregor asked.

"Sure," Molly said. "You know, I hate to say it, but this is the best I've felt since we got here. It really has been boring. I mean, in spite of all the things people say, there just doesn't seem to be any real craziness going on here over that lawsuit. Unless, you know, that's what the murders are about, and there really is somebody willing to kill other people because they believe in evolution."

The middle-aged waitress was back, with her order pad.

Gregor didn't bother to look at the menu, which he had already seen several times in the last two days. He just reminded himself not to order anything fried or with a sauce, and opted for a turkey sandwich on toast with the vain hope that it would not come covered with enough mayonnaise to float the *Queen Elizabeth II*.

TWO

1

By the time the police cars and the cable news vans got back to Main Street, Franklin Hale was scared to death—except that he never thought of himself as scared, so he decided he had to be angry instead. And he was angry, on some level, angry at the way his town was being torn apart by all this crap, and at the way nobody in those cable news vans really cared about anything or anybody that was actually here. That was what Franklin had figured out, long before all this started. The people who ran cable news companies, the people who went to Washington to be representatives and senators, the people who wrote books and articles for magazines—all those people lived in their own special world, where all the people they met and all the people they knew were just like themselves. The other people, the people who made up most of the country, the people left behind in small towns and small cities and second-tier suburbs, *Franklin's* people, well those people might as well not exist. They were only important once every few years, when it came time to vote. Even then, they were more like animals in a zoo than real people, which was why people like Chris Matthews and Anderson Cooper could spend Sunday mornings nattering on about The Mind of the Swing Voter instead of talking about anything serious.

Franklin Hale hated Chris Matthews, and Anderson Cooper, and Bill and Hillary Clinton. He hated Barack Obama and John McCain. He hated Chelsea Clinton and Susan Sarandon and all three of the Dixie Chicks. He hated Barbara Walters and all the women on *The View*. He hated both his senators and his congressman, and most of all he hated every single faculty member of every single university in the Ivy League. But here was the thing—his hate was simply a mental tic he paid very little attention to, as long as all these people stuck to the bargain. That was what was really wrong with the country. It wasn't that hotshots at Harvard thought gay guys should marry each other or that snooty little Hollywood starlets looked down their noses at him because he believed in what God Himself had set down in the Bible, instead of all this Darwin evolution crap. No, that wasn't the problem. That kind of thing had always been true. He remembered it from all the way back in his childhood, the way people like Annie-Vic rolled their eyes at the stupidity of the local yokels, the way people like David Suskind pontificated about the mental weaknesses of the ordinary voter.

No, Franklin thought, that wasn't the problem, that was just life. But up to now, up to just the past twenty years or so, there had been a bargain. Those people lived in their world, and Franklin lived in his own, and neither world told the other world what to do. They had no right, those people, they had no right to come in here and tell him and all the good people of Snow Hill that they had to live the way Hollywood wanted them to live, that they had to think the way Harvard wanted them to think. They had no right to crowd into the nooks and crannies of American life and suck up all the air. That was what it felt like. They sucked up all the air, and more and more, Franklin Hale felt as if he couldn't breathe.

No wonder Marcey was a wreck. No wonder his own home life was an endless saga of pills and liquor and that Ferris wheel of Marcey's mood swings. They sucked up all the air, those people did. They turned the entire world into their backyard, where all the standards were theirs, where all the judgments were theirs, where nothing counted as success unless they wanted it to. That was what was wrong, Franklin knew. If their kind of success was the only kind of success there was, then everybody else was a failure. Everybody.

The cars in front of the police station now included some from the state police. Franklin pressed himself up against the plate-glass window of the Hale 'n' Hardy Tire Shop and watched. There was Dale Vardan, who thought he was God's gift, and a lot of people Franklin didn't know. There was Gregor Demarkian, wearing a good winter coat over what looked like a good winter suit. What was it with these guys, that they never seemed to own parkas, like sensible people. There was Gary Albright. There were half a dozen people from those vans. Franklin hated those vans. He'd seen what they produced, Snow Hill on the news, night after night, the story of a bunch of hillbilly hicks who still thought the earth was flat.

There was a cough behind him, and Franklin turned to see Louise Brooker hovering near a large pyramid pile of snow tires. Why did they have the snow tires out? It was nearly past the snow season—nobody would put snow tires on their car now. Franklin took a deep breath. Louise looked apologetic.

"It's your house," she said. "It's your sister Lynne. It seems that Marcey—"

"Yeah," Franklin said. "She was that way when I left. That's why I called Lynne."

"Yes," Louise said. "I think you'd better talk to Lynne. She seems to think that Marcey may have, I don't know, may have taken, uh, may need to go to—"

"—the emergency room," Franklin said.

"Maybe you'd better talk to Lynne," Louise said again.

Franklin turned back to look at the cars and the vans, at Gregor Demarkian still standing out there in the wind, talking to the newspeople with the cameras set up. Why wouldn't these people wear hats? They didn't wear parkas, they didn't wear hats, they walked around in the cold and never seemed to catch anything. How did Alice McGuffie put it? It was as if they had a secret, and they wouldn't share that secret with anybody else. People thought Alice McGuffie was stupid, but Franklin Hale knew better.

"Franklin," Louise said.

"I don't care," Franklin said. Then he looked up at the ceiling. There was nothing there, except those foam panels they'd put in to help with the noise, but it was as good a place to look as any. He'd told the truth. He didn't care if Marcey lived or died. He didn't care if she went to the emergency room and got caught by every cameraman from New York and Atlanta. He didn't care. It had all been going on and on and on this way for as long as he could remember, and he thought he was done.

"I don't care," he said again. "I don't care what Lynne does about her. I don't care if the whole town knows about it. The whole town knows, anyway. There aren't any secrets in places like this. I don't care."

Franklin could hear Louise behind him, shifting from one foot to the other, hesitating, not knowing what to do. He didn't care about that, either. He looked out across Main Street and wondered suddenly what went on in the head of a man like Gregor Demarkian. They said he'd been in the FBI; that he'd met Presidents, if only in an official capacity; that he was going to marry some rich woman from the Main Line who'd gotten even richer writing stupid novels about elves and unicorns. That was the kind of thing Marcey knew. That was the kind of thing she threw in his face at every opportunity.

"You with your crap about how God wants you to prosper," she would say, spilling lemonade all over the table because she'd taken too much of that stuff to keep her muscles under control. "God wants you to prosper. God wants you to fulfill your dreams. He wants them to prosper more than you, doesn't he? He wants them to get so rich they can swallow you whole."

"Franklin," Louise said yet again, sounding desperate now. "Franklin, you've got to—"

"I don't got to do anything," Franklin said, moving away from the window. "I don't. I don't have to deal with this. Tell Lynne I don't give a shit if I come home and find Marcey dead on the bathroom floor. It's where she wants to be anyway, it's where she's wanted to be for years. I'm going out."

"You don't really mean this," Louise said, "you know you don't. If something happens, you'll regret it."

"No, I won't," Franklin said, and he made his way through the pyramids of tires to the store's glass front door. Everything about the Hale 'n' Hardy was glass. Everything was display. You had to put things out there and make them look tempting. You had to get people in the mood to buy. You had to go after them, day after day, week after week, with a smile pasted across your face and a tone of voice that said that your customer was the most wonderful human being who ever graced the planet, your customer was God, your customer was so wonderful he couldn't really do without this stuff you were selling him, he ought to buy more of it, he ought to buy more and more of it, he ought to buy so much of it that his garage at home was filled with tires he would never use.

Franklin stepped out onto the sidewalk. The vans were still in place, but the cameramen were packing up. Gregor Demarkian had finished talking. People all over the country, maybe even people all over the world, would have heard him speak.

The wind was coming down Main Street like a bowling ball in a bowling alley. Franklin realized he'd forgotten his parka and his hat.

2

Gary Albright had never seen an impromptu press conference or a press conference of any kind, from behind the scenes. He decided that the process interested him very much. If this had been a formal press conference, there would have been a table with microphones. Since this was just off the cuff, Gregor Demarkian had made a point of standing still and with his hands at his sides. The trick was to assume an air of authority, to look like someone official, which Gregor De-markian definitely was. Dale Vardan was also someone official, but he never looked it. He always came off as if he were intimidated by the reporters. The art of looking like you were not intimidated would be a good one to learn.

The reporters had not been interested in asking Gary questions, and Gary had not minded. He was not someone who needed to be front and center. He was not interested in being famous. He watched Gregor Demarkian talk, and then he watched the cameramen put their equipment away, and then he looked up and saw Franklin Hale coming at him across the street.

"Franklin," he said.

Franklin brushed past him. None of the reporters or camera people noticed him. Gary was glad of that. He went into the police station the way he would have gone into the Snow Hill Diner, as if it was the most natural thing in the world, as if the last thing on his mind was doing something important. Gary thought that maybe it was not im-portant. It was hard to remember that other things were going on in Snow Hill these days besides the murders. Maybe Franklin had had a shoplifter in his store. Maybe Marcey had been caught stealing stuff again from the IGA.

Gary looked at the vans. They were nearly all packed up. The re-porters were wandering down the street toward the diner. He won-dered what their lives were like at home. Sarah probably knew something about it, from women's magazines, but it was not the kind of story he paid attention to. He didn't really pay attention to much except sports and the presidential elections. Even the Congress and the Senate couldn't hold his attention for long, although he'd been inter-ested enough when he'd had Rick Santorum to vote for. Men like San-torum didn't last long in politics. Godly men didn't last long at anything that required them to be popular. That was what Christ had promised. He would bring not peace, but a sword, and His disciples would have to suffer and die for His sake. That was something Gary did understand. It was why he had liked the Marines as much as he had. It was not that he wanted to suffer—nobody wanted to suffer. But he knew that the Suffering Servant was the only one that counted.

It really was too cold out here, much too cold, and there was another woman dead. Gary gave one last look around—he had no idea what he was expecting to find, but he was always expecting to find something—and then went into the station. The big anteroom was crowded, because there were so many staties wandering around, doing nothing useful. Gary had to push people to get to the counter.

Franklin Hale was standing at the counter by himself, pounding on it a little. "I want to talk to Gregor Demarkian," he was saying. "I don't give a shit who you think you are. I want to talk to Gregor Demarkian."

"Gregor Demarkian," Dale Vardan said.

That was when Gary realized that Franklin was not actually alone. It was just that Dale was shorter than Franklin and than most of the men around him. There had once been a rule that all state policeman had to be at least six feet tall. The idea was that a man had to be at least six feet to be able to intimidate without actually, deliberately intimidating. Sheer physical presence was a useful weapon in keeping the peace. That rule was gone now, though. It had made it practically impossible to "diversify" the state police. Women were almost never six feet tall, and Latinos weren't very often. Gary hated the whole idea of "diversity," the whole idea that superficial things like race and gender should count more than ability and talent in deciding who would get hired to do a job.

"I want to talk to Gregor Demarkian," Franklin said again.

There was something in the sound of that voice that Gary didn't like. Franklin could get—odd—sometimes. Gary was sure that Franklin never did drink to excess, and equally sure that he never took drugs, but every once in a while it was as if Franklin caught drunkenness and drug addiction just from talking to Marcey on the phone.

"I'm not going to talk to you, Dale, I'm really not," Franklin was saying. "I don't give a crap who you think you are. I want to talk to Gregor Demarkian. Gregor Demarkian is in charge."

Gary pushed through the crowd the rest of the way to the counter and took Franklin by the arm. It *was* one of those times, Gary thought. Franklin looked glassy-eyed. Dale Vardan looked like he was going to punch him.

Gary pulled Franklin away. "He's through here," he said, trying to sound soothing, although that wasn't always a good idea.

Franklin didn't seem to notice. "Asshole," he said, meaning Dale Vardan. "I know what I want. I'm not an idiot. I want to talk to Gregor Demarkian."

Gary got the hinged section of the counter open and pushed Franklin through. "Right through there," he said. "He's using that room next to mine for an office while he's here."

"That's a broom closet," Franklin said. "You put the great Gregor Demarkian in a broom closet. What does he think he's so great for, anyway? Why do any of them think they're so great? Where do they come from, these people? Why don't they go the Hell back home."

Gary pushed Franklin again and they were standing in Gregor Demarkian's makeshift office. Gregor Demarkian was standing behind the desk, looking as if he didn't know what to do next. Gary didn't know, either.

"This is Franklin Hale," he said, pushing Franklin slightly forward. "He's the chairman of the board of education. He wants to talk to you."

"My name is on the lawsuit," Franklin said. "You think it would be the name of the town on the lawsuit, but it isn't. It's *Wackford* v. *Hale,* because I'm the chairman of the school board, like Gary says. I won it in an election, fair and square. I ran against that son of a bitch, Henry Wackford, and now he pulls this. He's only doing it for spite. He's a spiteful person, Henry is. He's spiteful and he only wants to get his own back, and he's an atheist secular humanist and he has no morality and that's what I wanted to tell you. You need to know that. You need to know what you're up against. Except you're probably an atheist secular humanist yourself. I told Gary he shouldn't bring you here."

Gary put his hand on Franklin's arm again. "Come on," he said. "Maybe you ought to go home and rest up a bit. You can tell Mr. Demarkian all this tomorrow."

"Mr. Demarkian," Franklin said. "You all sound like idiots, that's the truth. Mr. Demarkian. Who's Mr. Demarkian, anyway? What kind of name is Demarkian? It sounds foreign."

"It's Armenian," Gregor Demarkian said, sounding helpful. "My parents immigrated from Armenia."

"I told you it was foreign," Franklin said.

"Come on," Gary said, feeling desperate now.

"Just a minute," Gregor Demarkian said.

Gary still had his hand on Franklin's arm. He kept it there. He had never seen Franklin be violent, not even with Marcey, but there was always a first time. Gary didn't like the way Franklin looked. It was almost as if Franklin had a fever.

"Just a minute," Gregor Demarkian said again. "Just let me ask you a couple of things."

"Ask away," Franklin said. "I don't have anything to hide. I'm not even hiding that my wife is addicted to that Oxycontin stuff. Everybody knows it. That's the virtue of small towns, *Mr.* Demarkian. There's nothing to hide. Everybody knows your business."

"It's the accounts," Gregor Demarkian said. "I've got notes on three accounts. The teachers' union pension fund. The operating budget for the school. And the construction money, the money to put up the new schools complex."

"That was bullshit," Franklin said. "New schools complex, like we needed one. That's all these people can think of. Kids aren't learning anything in school, throw some money at it, throw all the money in the world at it. Maybe they're depressed because the don't have a new school. Maybe the teachers need higher salaries. Let me tell you, we had better teachers than they have now and we didn't pay them anything to speak of. What's a teacher, anyway? She's a babysitter most of the time. What's Catherine Marbledale but a stuck-up bitch who thinks she's better than everybody else because she went to college. She didn't even go to real college. She went to education school. *Education* school. Isn't that a crock?"

"So you were going to do what," Gregor Demarkian said, "stop the construction?"

"Hell, no," Franklin said. "We would have if we could have, but it would just have been money down the drain, millions of dollars. Do you think a place like Snow Hill has millions of dollars? We don't, that's the truth, and just raising taxes isn't going to get it for us. Although I'd really like it if the town council raised the taxes on those people in the development. God, I hate those people. Coming in here and swanning around like they owned the place. I'm not surprised a couple of them got killed."

Gary nearly jumped out of his skin. "Franklin," he said. "You can't say things like that in the middle of a murder investigation."

"It's all right," Gregor Demarkian said. "I'm just trying to figure this out. You went ahead with the construction?"

"Yeah, we're going ahead with the construction," Franklin said. "In the spring, when the weather gets better, we're going ahead with it. It's not important, it's just stupid. I concentrate on the important things. I concentrate on saving our schools, because they have to be saved. They have to be."

Gary moved his hand to Franklin's back. This was something he'd seen before, too. "I think I'd better take him home, Mr. Demarkian. He looks—I don't know exactly—but he's been this way before."

"I'm just trying to understand," Gregor said again. "There's nothing happening with the construction now? There's nothing being done on the site?"

"No," Gary said, because Franklin seemed to have lost interest in the discussion. He was looking around the "office." He was looking vague, and vaguely lost. "There's nothing that can be done, with the weather the way it is. If the shell was closed up, maybe, but it isn't. They've been going at it for years and the shell still isn't closed up. Is that what you wanted to know?"

"Well, there are the other two things, " Gregor Demarkian said.

"The teachers' contracts and their pension fund, and the school operating expenses."

"We don't do anything with the pension fund," Gary said. "We contribute to a fund the union has, that's all. And the school operating expenses should be the easiest thing to figure out. We publish a balance sheet in the newspaper every quarter."

"That's not what's important," Franklin Hale said. "Everybody goes running around worrying about the construction, and the teachers' contracts, and are we going to have textbooks and are we going to have supplies. None of it matters. We've taken God out of the schools, that's what we've done, we're raising a whole generation of kids who don't know the Lord. And if we go on this way, Mr. Demarkian, if we go on this way, the Enemy will have won. That's what the Bible says. We have to watch out for the Enemy because he's prowling around us like a hungry lion. He's prowling around us, and if we let down our guard for a minute, he'll be right here inside the house. Evolution, my ass. Atheism, that's all it is. They want to turn our kids into atheists. And I won't let them."

"Come on," Gary Albright said.

Gregor Demarkian had sat down in the chair behind his desk and started to look thoughtful. Gary had no idea what he was finding to look thoughtful about. He hated hearing his own ideas coming out of Franklin Hale's mouth. When Franklin said them, they sounded ignorant and belligerent. They sounded like the kind of thing somebody would say after he'd decided that he'd failed and there was nothing he could do about it.

"Come on," Gary said again.

And then, for an instant, he thought of Sarah and Lily and Michael at home. A man wasn't worth anything as a man if he didn't do what he did for the people who waited for him at home, if he didn't protect them and help them and keep them safe from just that prowling lion. It sounded wrong when Franklin said it, but it was not wrong; it was absolutely right. It was what each and every man had to do with his life, and what each and every person had to make sure he did not forget.

There really was a prowling lion loose in the world, and in the last few weeks it had come to Snow Hill and lain right down in the middle of Main Street.

3

Annie-Vic could not remember, later, how she first realized that she could now open and close her eyes at will. There was a time when she could not, and there was a time when she could, but that was all she was sure about. It felt good, being able to do this thing, even though it was a very small thing. She thought it probably meant that she would be able to do more and more in the days to come. This was something of a relief. She wouldn't admit it if she ever found herself able to talk again, but there had been a part of her that was very worried. There was a part of her that had begun to think that she was dead, and that this was what death was like. Death was being trapped in a body that would not move anymore.

Annie-Vic blinked. Then she blinked again. The thoughts about death had been less than intelligent, she thought. If she had been dead, she would not have been in the hospital. She was very glad that neither Lisa nor Cameron was interested in taking the tubes out of her. They could have killed her, any time they wanted. She wouldn't have been able to stop them. Now that she could make her eyelids move up and down, there seemed to be something different about her sight, too. For most of the last however long it had been—she had no idea of the time that had gone by; she had no idea if she had been like this for hours or days or weeks or months or even years—anyway, her sight had been different. When her eyes were open she had "seen" things, but the seeing was different than this, than normal seeing, which is what she had now. The room was too bright, that was the first thing she noticed. All the lights were on, and they glared.

She tried moving her eyes to the right, not really expecting anything to happen, and was both surprised and elated when the project worked. It worked when she tried moving them to the left, too. She tried moving her head, or thought she did, but that did not work—not quite. Before, when she had tried to move her head, nothing had happened at all. It hadn't moved and she hadn't felt anything. Now when she tried, she felt as if she was pushing against a boulder or as if her head was secured to the bed with restraints. She was fairly sure it wasn't, but that didn't matter. It felt like something. It really *felt* like something.

She tried taking a deep breath. She tried drawing a great ocean of air into her lungs and letting it out very slowly. That worked, too. She could control how fast and how slowly the air went in and out of her. She could feel the air in her lungs and the lack of it when she forced it out. She thought of all the times in her life when she thought she was about to die, about the prisoner of war camp, about a whitewater rafting trip in Colorado when the kayak had flipped over in the water and she hadn't been able to make it turn up. Death was not going to be what she had always expected it to be. Death was also not going to be anytime soon.

She heard the door to the room open and felt someone come in. It was the nurse, and she was wearing those white rubber-soled shoes that never made any noise. Annie-Vic tried to move her head, but that still wouldn't work. She tried to move her arms, but that was completely hopeless. The nurse, the young one who always wore a loose violet tunic with little flowers on it, came over to the bed and picked up the chart.

Annie-Vic looked at the woman. The woman did not look at her. Annie-Vic looked for some time longer, and after a while the woman did look up, the way they do when they sense they are being watched. Annie-Vic stared straight into the woman's eyes, and then looked away, and then looked back again.

It was like watching a delayed-action sequence in a movie. The nurse went very still and then moved in, closer, staring into Annie-Vic's eyes. Annie-Vic looked away and then looked back again. She looked at the ceiling and then looked back. She looked in the other direction and then looked back.

"Oh, my God," the nurse said.

And then she was gone.

THREE

1

The news about Annie-Vic Hadley came in a phone call from Dr. Thomas Willard, so early in the morning that Gregor had a hard time remembering where he was or why it mattered that this woman was suddenly awake and alert.

"Not talking yet, mind you," Dr. Willard said, going off in a spiral of information Gregor had to struggle to retain. "She's not moving much yet, either, but she's definitely awake and out of the coma. She can open and shut her eyes at will. She can follow your movement around the room at will, and she will respond to questions and requests by blinking. That may not sound like much, Mr. Demarkian, but under the circumstances, given her age and what she's been through, it's really remarkable. And that last thing, about blinking yes or no to answer questions, that's an incredibly good sign. It means that whatever happened to her in this attack, it didn't make her mentally incapable. At least not completely. There's some of her mind left. We won't know how much of it for a few days. But still, I didn't really expect the news to be half this good."

Gregor sat up in bed and looked around. He was in the little lower-level guest room at Gary Albright's house. The bed was pushed up against one wall. On the other side of it was a night table with a lamp and an alarm clock, which Gregor had not used, because he always used his cell phone as an alarm clock when he was sleeping away from home. He tried to remember what he had done before he had the cell phone, which he hadn't had for very long. He tried to remember why he had resisted getting one for so long, but he couldn't remember that either. The room was cold, and there was a sharp clicking sound against the windows that probably meant sleet, at the very least. On the wall against which the bed was pushed there was a framed picture of Jesus in a meadow with a little girl in a pinafore.

Gregor ran his hand through his hair. "What about her memory?" he asked. "Have you any idea if she remembers what happened to her?"

"I didn't even try to ask," Dr. Willard said. "And I don't think you should, either, at least not yet. She might start talking and volunteer the information, and then of course we go with it, but for the moment I don't want her unduly tired out. She's been through more than most women her age could survive."

"I know," Gregor said. "But two other women didn't survive it, and I don't know what's going on here. At least, I don't know completely. I'm not sure there won't be somebody else."

"Yes, I understand that," Dr. Willard said. "And I sympathize. But it won't help you to kill this one off after she's just managed to show signs of recovery. Take it slowly. Take it one step at a time. She's been asleep for some hours now. We'll see what's happening when she wakes up."

Gregor thought about it. "Do me a favor," he said. "Get a nurse and put her in that room. Somebody who will stay there and stay awake. Don't leave her alone."

There was a long pause on the other end of the line. "Oh, God," Dr. Willard said. "You can't really think that somebody would come in here in the dead of night—"

"Well, whoever it was tried to kill her once," Gregor said. "There's

311

nothing to say he won't try to kill her again. I'll talk to Gary Albright and we'll try to get somebody up there on a permanent basis, a police guard, something. But in the meantime—"

"Yes," Dr. Willard said. "Yes. All right, I'll find somebody. It didn't used to be like this around here, did you know that? I moved out here from Philadelphia years ago and the first thing I really loved about the place was that you didn't have to worry about crime. You'd be amazed at what we get out here these days, in a rural area like this."

"Yes," Gregor said, although he wouldn't have been surprised at all. He had been in rural areas; he knew what they got. He closed his cell phone and tried to pull himself togther. It was only five o'clock, but when he listened he could hear people moving on the floor above him. Five o'clock in the morning, he thought. Bennis got up at five o'clock in the morning. In fact, most of the adults he knew these days did, and those kinds of early hours were endemic in an organization like the Bureau. But where did that come from? When Gregor was growing up, it was the hallmark of adulthood to stay up late and watch Johnny Carson on *The Tonight Show*. Now the only people he knew who watched *The Tonight Show* were teenagers trying to pretend they didn't still have acne.

He got his legs out onto the side of the bed and counted to ten. He needed a shower. He needed a shave. He needed to move. He especially needed to contact Molly Trask and Evan Zwicker and see if they had found out anything for him. He got his cell phone off the table and opened it. Bennis was number two on his speed dial. Number one was voice mail. There was a reason Bennis had set up the phone that way, but that was just another in the long list of things Gregor couldn't remember this morning.

A second later, Bennis picked up on the other end and said, "Hello?" She didn't sound sleepy.

"You sound wide awake," Gregor said. "I'm not, but I'm supposed to be."

"I've got some stuff to do this morning, and I'm meeting Donna at the Ararat," Bennis said. "Are you all right. You sound frazzled."

"It's a frazzled kind of situation," Gregor said. "I thought you'd want to know, I've had a call from the hospital, and your Annie-Vic is out of her coma! She's not talking yet, and she's not moving much, but she seems to be definitely awake and alert and able to answer at least simple questions by blinking yes or no. It doesn't sound like much when I say it, but the doctor was really excited."

"It sounds wonderful," Bennis said. "The woman is in her nineties and she got bludgeoned. By all common sense, she ought to be dead. I'm glad she isn't."

"So am I. I'm going to be especially glad if she starts talking and it turns out she can remember who beat her up. Because I've got an idea who it has to be, but I don't know that I can prove it, and there are two younger women who weren't as lucky. Are Leda and Hannah and Sheila still mad at Tibor?"

"Well," Bennis said, "they're talking to him again. He might not find that an improvement. Don't worry about it, Gregor. Really. It's just their way. They'll get over it on the day of the wedding and it will be like it never happened. Concentrate on what you're doing."

"I am concentrating on what I'm doing," Gregor said.

"I've got to go take a shower," Bennis said. "Janet sent some new chocolate samples from Box Hill. I'm going to weigh a ton and a half by the time we're actually married. Oh, and I've firmed up the honeymoon. Liz Toliver called and I ended up not being able to withstand the force of her arguments, if you know what I mean."

"You mean she badgered you."

"Well, yes," Bennis said, "but in a nice way, and it's a really spectacular house, and I like Montego Bay. So we'll do that."

"All right," Gregor said. "I don't really care. I'd hole up for two weeks at the local Holiday Inn, if that's what you wanted."

"I want to go take a shower," Bennis said. "Call me if there's any more news about Annie-Vic. It would be nice if she made it through this thing."

"It would be nice," Gregor said.

And that was all. Bennis was gone. He put his phone down. It wasn't just that he never told her he loved her. She never told him she loved him, either. He wondered what it meant, not that he found it difficult to say—he *didn't* find it difficult to say, it just never occurred to him to say it. In movies, couples seemed to express their love all the time. In real life—Gregor wasn't sure what went on in real life. He'd never noticed. It bothered the Hell out of him that he was the age he was, and getting married for the second time, and still hadn't figured out any of this.

He got up from the bed and picked up the clean towel Sarah Albright had left for him. It was easier to figure out who had murdered whom, and he thought he would stick to that.

2

Gary was dressed and standing next to the dinette table when Gregor got upstairs, but he didn't look as eager to get started as he had the day before.

"I got a call from Eddie Block," he said. "The hospital called the station, and Eddie said he gave them your number."

"He must have. Dr. Willard called me," Gregor said.

"He didn't want to wake me up," Gary said. "What is that? He's never cared about waking me up before. Is there news? Is Miss Hadley dead?"

"No," Gregor said, "quite the contrary. She's out of the coma. According to Dr. Willard, she's not talking and or moving, but she's awake and responsive and she can answer simple questions by blinking."

"And they're sure that's real?" Gary asked. "I've heard about people, you know, in comas, and in persistent vegetative states, who look like they're doing that, but they aren't really. It makes people think, well. That they're getting better, when they're never going to get better."

"Dr. Willard said nothing about a persistent vegetative state," Gregor said. "And he definitely sounds sure that she's coming around. Which brings up another issue that cannot be ignored at this point, if you see what I mean."

Sarah had been bustling around the kitchen, pouring coffee, setting a fork and a spoon and a knife down near the place at the table Gregor was standing closest to.

"Sit down," she said now. "You're both ridiculously early. There's no point in leaving for town at this hour of the morning. There's nothing you can do there. I can make you some eggs if you want them, Mr. Demarkian. And some bacon."

Gregor thought fondly of his breakfasts at the Ararat, scrambled eggs, bacon, sausage, hash browns and toast, but he shook his head. "I'm fine with coffee," he said. "And I think getting in a little early wouldn't hurt. We really do have to arrange something to protect Annie-Vic now that she's conscious, because it's not impossible that she remembers what happened to her. And that means—"

"Oh," Sarah said, startled. "Oh, no."

Gary Albright looked a little shocked himself. "I feel like an idiot," he said finally. "I should have seen that right off. Of course, if she's awake, he'll want to come back and finish the job. Or she will. Are you still saying you don't know if it's a man or a woman who's doing this?"

"I'm keeping my options open," Gregor said.

"I'd better get on the line and get somebody out there," Gary said. "We may have to ask the state police for this. I've only got Eddie and Tom. And I can't just deputize a couple of people from town. I don't know who we can trust."·

"If it helps," Gregor said, "I think I can say that I know for a fact you had nothing to do with it."

"It helps," Gary said. "It just doesn't solve this."

"I asked Dr. Willard to put a nurse on duty in there until we had time to provide a police guard," Gregor said. "You've got a little while before you have to panic about this. I don't think anybody knows about this yet, except for us."

"Don't believe it," Gary said. "Lots of people at the hospital have to know, and if they know then their relatives and friends know. Word gets around in a place like this. And I'm not comfortable with just a nurse. She'll mean well, but she won't know what to look out for. I mean, whoever this is just killed a woman maybe fifty feet from two state policemen. He's not stupid."

"No," Gregor said, "but in that last case, he was desperate. Maybe he's been desperate all along. Maybe that's what I got wrong at the beginning."

"Give me a second," Gary said.

Gregor watched as Gary took his cell phone out of his pocket and poked at it. Then he turned to Sarah. She did not look sleepy, and she did not look messy. She reminded him of the mothers on all the television shows of his childhood, the ones who were perfectly groomed all day and all night, no matter what they were doing. At the age of ten, Gregor had been convinced that this was the chief difference between having "real American" parents and having immigrant ones—the immigrant ones were often a mess around the house.

Gary finished up and put the cell phone away. "Okay," he said. "I managed to bypass Dale completely. He's apparently at home asleep. The state police are sending an armed guard right away, and they'll be there twenty-four seven for at least another week. After that, we're going to have to renegotiate. We'll have to call the hospital and give them a heads-up."

"Call the hospital in a minute," Gregor said. "There's been something I've been meaning to ask you. Or rather, there's been something I've needed to know, and for some reason it just occurred to me that you'd know it, because you're on the school board. Textbooks and supplies and that kind of thing."

"Do you mean the school operating budget?" Gary looked confused. "We have one of those. Everybody has to have one of those."

"Who controls it?"

Gary considered this. "I don't know if you could say that anybody *controls* it," he said. "It's got a couple of different aspects. There's a drawing fund. We put a predetermined amount of money in there for specific uses, like chalk and paper and that kind of thing. There's an account for maintenance and repair. There's an account for salaries. That kind of thing. Why?"

"Are any of these accounts large?" Gregor asked.

"Well, the one for salaries is," Gary said. "It has to be. We have forty teachers between the three schools, and they've got a union, so that's not cheap. But we've also got the secretaries, the school nurses, an educational psychologist that serves the whole town, and the janitors—that kind of thing."

"What about sports?" Gregor asked.

"Oh, I forgot about sports," Gary said. "That was a big deal when I was here. It's not so much anymore. And then there's pay to play, which, if you ask me, sucks."

"Gary," Sarah said.

"What's pay to play?" Gregor asked.

"It's just what it sounds like," Gary said. "If you want to play sports these days, you have to pay for it. Not the entire cost, but it's not cheap, and it keeps some kids off the teams because their families just can't afford it. We don't have the money in the budget anymore to fund the teams and fund the academic programs at the same time. And the academic programs have gotten really expensive, because now we've got No Child Left Behind, and it costs a mint to make sure the kids can pass those tests."

"How much is it you have to pay to play?"

"One hundred seventy-nine dollars a sport," Gary said. "It used to be common for guys to play football in the fall, basketball in the winter and baseball in the spring, but not anymore. It costs close to six hundred dollars to do that. And the kids from the hills, you know, a lot of them can't come up with even one of those, although Nick Frapp's people do a good job of raising the cash for at least some of them."

"I thought Nick Frapp's people sent their kids to his Christian school," Gregor said.

"They do," Gary said, "but it doesn't go all the way through high school yet. So if they've got a kid who wants to play football, they'll take up a collection. The hill kids who don't belong to Nick's church just don't get to play. They've got no incentive at all to stay in school."

Gregor nodded. Here was a question for the ages, he thought: Where had all the money gone? When he was growing up people were much poorer than they were now. They had smaller houses. They had fewer clothes, and not designer clothes. Things that came from "dry goods" stores. Even so, in those days, you would never have heard of a public school charging its students to play on its sports teams. The whole thing was crazy.

"Mr. Demarkian?" Gary said.

"Sorry," Gregor said. "I was drifting. What happens to this money that the kids pay into the system? Does it go into this same account for sports activities?"

"The very same one."

"And is that a lot of money? Is there a lot of money in that account?"

"It depends on what you mean by a lot," Gary said. "I'd say there was ten thousand or so in it at the beginning of a school year. Less as you go along."

"And the money churns? There's a lot of depositing and withdrawing?"

"There's a lot of that in all the accounts," Gary said. "There has to be. This is schools we're talking about. At least during the school year, they've got a lot to do."

"And who keeps the records on the accounts?"

"We've got a bookkeeper for the school district," Gary said. "She's sixty-five and been with us forever. Mrs. Carstairs. Then we've got an accountant in Harrisburg."

"And how often are the books audited?"

Gary Albright laughed. "If you think somebody is embezzling from the operating budget," he said, "you can give it up. Franklin Hale is an idiot about a lot of things, but on this he had his head on straight. About five years ago, long before he decided to run for school board, he got the town council to initiate monthly statements. Mrs. Carstairs double-checks everything and then it's all published in the town paper."

"It used to drive Franklin crazy, the money that was spent," Sarah put in. "He's not really very bright about money, in spite of the fact that he runs a business—"

"It's Mike who takes care of the money," Gary said.

"Mike is Franklin's brother-in-law," Sarah said. "He and Franklin own the business together. But Franklin would see this money being spent—at the end of the year the reports would say things like 'fifty thousand dollars for miscellaneous'—and it made him crazy. So he hammered and hammered and got this put through, and now everything is itemized right down to the least little pencil, and it's all published once a month."

"And has the amount of money that's being spent on operating expenses gone down as a result?" Gregor asked.

"It's gone up, to tell you the truth," Gary said. "Franklin really doesn't understand the kind of money a school needs to be properly run. I agree we shouldn't be profligate about it, but he seems to think we should be able to run the schools on the kind of budget that barely made sense in my grandfather's day."

"And some of it is just sexism," Sarah said. "It bothers him no end that teachers make forty or fifty thousand dollars a year when they're women. In Franklin's mind, if it's something a woman does, it should be paid for in pin money. It was one of the reasons why I wasn't sure I wanted Gary to run for school board on the same slate. Franklin has no respect for schools. He has no respect for learning. He's bone ignorant and he's happy to be that way."

"All right," Gregor said, "but does he have control of the funds in the operating budget? Is that something the school board does, hand out that money?"

"We hand out the salaries," Gary said. "In fact, I've been doing it myself since Annie-Vic was attacked. She'd taken on the job of doing it before then. But the other stuff, the supplies and the sports, it's Catherine Marbledale who oversees all of that. It's more efficient that way than if she has to come to us with everything. She hands out the money, one of her assistants keeps the books on it, and it all gets published once a month."

"And Franklin still thinks we're spending too much money," Sarah said. "Last year, he wanted to end the school busses, if you can believe it. We've got kids coming in from miles away, and he wants their transportation left up to their parents, who can probably barely make it to work as it is. He thought it would save on gas money. Honestly, if it was up to Franklin Hale, we'd just abolish the schools altogether and send kids to work when they're fourteen years old. We certainly wouldn't educate them."

"Franklin thinks there are enough pointy-headed intellectuals in the world," Gary Albright said, deadpan.

It took Gregor a moment to realize it was supposed to be a joke.

3

They got in to town "late," as Gary put it, meaning at almost seven thirty, and there was already enough going on to make Gregor sit up and take notice. The news vans were still there. They were such a constant presence Gregor was beginning to think the technicians slept in them. The diner looked as if it might be full to the gills. Gregor saw people in every single booth and all along the counter as they passed. Several of the stores and shops already had lights on in them as well, although Gregor was sure none of them opened before eight, and many of them probably did not open until nine. Down at the end of the street, Nick Frapp's church compound was not only lit up but busy. Parents were dropping off children. Children were running around in between the buildings, heedless of snow and ice and sleet. There was sleet, too. It had been coming down most of the time Gregor and Gary were driving in, and it had only let up slightly. It was the kind of weather that made school districts declare a snow day, but Snow Hill had not. Maybe having "snow" in its name made its people more likely to put up with the weather.

"This is going to be nasty," Gary said as he parked behind the police station. "I hate this time of year. It isn't good for anything. It's not good skiing weather. It's too cold to do much else outside. And the roads are always screwed up."

"Was it this time of year that you . . ." Gregor said. "Ah. I'm sorry. I didn't mean to pry."

"There's nothing to pry into," Gary said. "The story's been, well, everywhere. They even wanted to interview me on CNN, but I turned them down. I didn't want to make a fuss. And no, it wasn't this time of year. It was dead of winter. If it hadn't been, we'd never have gotten that much snow, and if we hadn't gotten that much snow, I wouldn't have ended up lost. I don't usually end up lost."

"I don't suppose you do," Gregor said. "What happened to the dog?"

"Humphrey?" I've still got him. We've just been keeping him out back in the dog house while you're here. I didn't know if you were allergic or something."

"I'm not allergic. I hate to think of the dog suffering in the cold for my sake."

"I wouldn't let him suffer," Gary said. "I love that dog."

"You must."

Gary shook his head. "No, Mr. Demarkian. I didn't do it because I loved the dog. I did it because I was responsible for the dog. And for the girl, you know, she was just a baby. And nobody had taken any responsibility for her yet. Nobody. It's the thing you learn in the Marine Corps, except I learned it before then. I learned it from my family. Responsibility is the key. Or have I given you this speech before?"

"I think you might have mentioned it," Gregor said.

"Yeah, I mention it a lot," Gary said. "Michael told me it's become my 'mantra,' which is a thing from Hinduism. I don't understand where we've gotten to these days, when they can teach Hinduism in the public schools but they can't even mention anything to do with Christianity. We can't even sing Christmas carols at Christmas, and Henry Wackford tried to tell us we should rename Christmas vacation 'winter break' in case somebody tried to sue us. Winter break, when practically everybody in town except Henry himself celebrates Christmas. Even some of the Jewish families get Christmas trees and they don't seem to have any trouble saying 'Merry Christmas' when they pass you on the street. But that's Henry for you. If it was Christians getting killed instead of the evolution people, I'd have said Henry was your best bet for a serial murderer."

"Do you mean he's a psychopath?" Gregor asked.

"Nah, I don't think so," Gary said. "I wouldn't trust him as far as I could throw him, mind you, but I don't think he's Jack the Ripper. It's just that he's seriously pissed. He's pissed because the board is so obviously Christian. Henry doesn't like Christianity. He thinks it's the root of all evil. But he's pissed because he lost at all, to begin with, and he's pissed because he's no longer lawyer for the school board."

"This is Henry Wackford who used to be the chairman of the school board?" Gregor asked, surprised.

"Right," Gary said. "And you don't even have to bring it up. It was an incredible conflict of interest. But Henry was chairman of the school board and the school board had to hire a lawyer and he hired himself and he went on with it for ten years. During which time, by the way, there was nothing for him to do but collect his yearly retainer. Now that there is something for a lawyer to do, we have a firm from up in Harrisburg. We all thought we'd better get somebody who knew how to handle a federal lawsuit."

"Henry Wackford," Gregor said.

They were coming around to the front of the building. Gregor looked up the street. The were lights on deep within the offices of Wackford Squeers, Attorneys at Law, but they weren't just safety lights.

Somebody had to be already in place at Henry Wackford's office.

FOUR

1

Christine had been gone for less than twenty-four hours, and Henry Wackford's life was already a mess. Not that he actually needed Christine, meaning Christine herself. In fact, she was one of the most annoying aspects of living in Snow Hill. She had that thing they all had, that thing Henry had gone away to college to get away from. It wasn't just that she was religious. No. Henry thought he could work up some respect for *seriously* religious people. Thomas Aquinas, say, or Bonaventure—the Middle Ages were full of religious people who were intelligent and thoughtful and attuned to complexity. Maybe that was only possible before science got seriously into gear and started explaining the universe. Henry didn't know. He only knew that religion in Snow Hill was straight off a Hallmark card, full of fuzzy feel-good niceness and floating around in a sea of love and angels. Henry would have hired a fellow atheist to be his secretary if he could have, but he hadn't been able to find one of those. Christine had shown up at the door with her little gold cross on its little gold chain around her neck, and she knew how to operate the computer and had a fair idea of what was supposed to happen with a filing system, and he'd taken her.

Now he looked around the office and there were files everywhere. Either Christine knew better how to handle a filing system, or she had changed the one he had, and Henry was sure it was the latter. He was not an idiot, and he had nothing but contempt for those Hollywood movies about how the secretary moves out and the boss can't wipe his own ass without her help. He was not an idiot, and in the long three weeks he'd been without a secretary before Christine, he'd managed just fine.

He sat down behind his desk and looked at the stack of folders. He had been through them once. He would go through them twice. The folder he was looking for should be labeled Books to Print, and it belonged in the B cabinet in alphabetical order with everything else that was there. He was now more than sure that that file was not in the filing cabinet. Christine had either misfiled it, or relabeled it and filed it somewhere else, or lost it, or something.

He picked up the file on top of the stack. It was labeled Barrington Cross Hunt, and he should have had it put in storage years ago. He remembered Barrington Cross Hunt. He'd been the "village atheist" when Henry was growing up, because nobody in Snow Hill would dare to call old Annie-Vic any such thing. It was to Barrington that Henry had gone when he had first been thinking about starting a chapter of the American Humanist Association, and it was Barrington who had explained to him why it would never work.

"There's too much downside in it," Barrington had said, sucking on a pipe as if it were a baby bottle. "Of course there are humanists here, and atheists and agnostics. There always have been, and there always have been more of them than anybody would guess. But to come out and say that's what you are is a disaster in a place like Snow Hill. Everybody would stop talking to you. You'd barely be employable."

Henry put the folder down. It was only half true, all of that. The town hadn't ostracized Barrington Cross Hunt, and it hadn't ostracized Henry, either. The hostility was more subtle. It was in the way people talked to you, and in the things they said when they knew you weren't quite out of hearing. And there was more, of course. There were the things they said to each other in private, and the things that had gotten two people killed already with maybe a third to come. It was this tightwire act they were all engaged in, this trying to believe things they had to know were not true. Part of Henry didn't believe they did believe them. He thought they only wanted to believe them. That was why they got so crazy when something came along to make what they believed obviously untrue. It was as if you'd knocked the foundation out of one of their houses.

Books to Print, Henry reminded himself. The damned thing had to be around here somewhere. He had to find it, and he had to find it today. He had work to do. It didn't matter if Christine was there to help him do it or not.

Maybe there was some woman in the development who would like a job as a legal secretary. That would be something. Henry loved the people in the development. They were like a promise from another world. Out there somewhere, away from Snow Hill and all the places like it, there was a real world with real people in it.

The sound he was hearing was definitely a knock. It was a very faint knock, which meant it must be coming from the outer office, or maybe all the way from the front door. Christine had left her keys on her desk when she'd marched out of the office yesterday. Maybe she'd changed her mind and wanted to come back.

Henry got up and went out. In the other office, the knocking was louder. When he opened the door to the entryway, the knocking was a pounding. That would not be Christine, that would be a man.

Henry hesitated. There were murders going on here. There were *things* going on. You never know what those people might do. You couldn't count on them, because they didn't rely on their reason. They didn't rely on logic. They relied on fantasies, and all fantasies were murderous in the end.

Henry went into the entryway. Somebody was pounding and calling. Three pounds, then the call. Boom, boom, boom. The a muffled voice that sounded as if it were calling his name. What movie was that from? The original version of *The Haunting*, he thought. Henry had read the book, *The Haunting of Hill House,* by Shirley Jackson, when he was much younger. He didn't read that sort of thing anymore. Ghosts, for God's sake. It wasn't good to encourage that kind of thing anymore. It wasn't good to say "for God's sake." The fundies always jumped on it when you did. Aha! You said "for God's sake!" You must *really* believe in God, even if you're hiding it from yourself.

Henry pulled the front door open. The light was just beginning to get strong on Main Street, but it wasn't that strong. There was no angry mob storming his door with torches. The man on the doorstep—Gregor Demarkian. Henry recognized him from television. He looked past Demarkian and up the street.

Henry stepped back and waved Gregor Demarkian inside. "Sorry," he said. "I'm in a bit of a mess. My secretary quit, and now I can't find anything."

"Your secretary quit?"

Demarkian was in the front hall. Henry closed the door behind him. He dwarfed the place. He made the ceiling look too low, and the hall not as wide as it should have been. Henry thought he was at least as tall as Nick Frapp, or close, but he was bulked out more. He looked like he might have played football.

"It's this lawsuit," Henry said, going back toward the outer office and waving Demarkian to follow him. "It's got the whole town in a mess. And Christine was not exactly on my side, if you catch my drift. It's impossible to find a secretary in this town who would be on my side in this. The kind of people who understand and respect science, and reason, well, if they're in Snow Hill, they tend to move out. And stay out. Which is what I should have done."

"Which one?" Demarkian asked. "Move out or stay out?"

"Stay out," Henry said. "I went to college and law school, and then I came back. Don't ask me why. I mean, I remember my reasoning at the time, but looking back on it from this perspective, I think I must have been crazy. I was on my own, you see. My parents were dead, and I didn't want to go corporate. There's a reason they call them soulless corporations. I don't know. I thought that it would be easier here, to get started on my own, to function on my own. And then there was Mickey Squeers, who'd done the same thing in his time. He took me in."

"That's the Squeers of Wackford Squeers, outside?"

"That's right," Henry said. "He's been dead for years now, of course, but I don't see any reason to change the name of the firm. Or maybe I'm just like Scrooge. Maybe I keep the name so that I don't have to go to the expense of changing the sign. I hate that novella, don't you, Mr. Demarkian? More sentimental treacle. More fuzzy suffocating nonsense that doesn't do anybody any good and that does a lot of harm. We make a point of going on with business as usual at the Snow Hill Humanist Association, right through the holidays. Somebody has to step up and do something, or nothing will ever change."

"Bah," Gregor Demarkian said. "Humbug."

Henry turned, but Demarkian's face was completely blank. He might not have said what Henry thought he'd heard. Henry leaned over and took a pile of files out of one of the chairs and gestured Gregor to it.

"I'm sorry," he said. "Maybe I'm assuming too much. Maybe you're a religious man."

"Not the last time I checked," Demarkian said.

"Then you'll know what I mean," Henry said. "We have to do something about these people. We have to do something that brings this country back to the path of reason and science. We're drowning in a sea of religiosity. We can't be a leader in the twenty-first century if our minds are in thrall to the thirteenth. Never forget: When religion ruled the world, they called it the Dark Ages."

Gregor Demarkian made no response at all to that. Henry sat down and clasped his hands. He was suddenly very nervous.

"Well," he said. "I'm sure you didn't come all the way over here this early in the morning to hear me natter on about fundamentalists and the religious right. Is there something I can do for you?"

The words came out in too much of a rush. Henry swallowed. There was something very disconcerting about this man. He was too still. And Henry didn't really know what he thought about religion. He wished the man would talk.

Gregor Demarkian shifted a little on his chair. Henry twitched.

"Well," Demarkian said, "for starters, I think you know both of the women who were murdered, Judy Cornish and Shelley Niederman. They were both plaintiffs in the lawsuit."

"That's right," Henry said. "Most of the plaintiffs were from the development. I think Annie-Vic and I might have been the only Snow Hill natives proper. Oh, and of course, Miss Marbledale, who is on our side even if she isn't a formal plaintiff. Although we talked about that, back when all this started. We thought it might be an interesting thing if the science teachers sued the school board. But some of them didn't want to."

"Some of your science teachers are sympathetic to the board's position?"

"Oh, no," Henry said. "Some of the other teachers are, the ones who don't teach science, but the science teachers are squarely behind the teaching of evolution. It's not that way everyplace. You wouldn't believe how many science teachers across the country reject evolution and want to teach Creationism themselves. But that hasn't been our problem here. No, the thing is, there's no percentage in it. The science teachers are going to have to go on teaching here, and the town has already shown its willingness to elect a school board that will persecute anybody who doesn't toe the line on its fundamentalist beliefs. Although, if you ask me, that's just because too many of our own people are completely irresponsible."

"Irresponsible how?"

"They don't vote," Henry said emphatically. "I'm serious, Mr. Demarkian. The people in the development, they represent the best hope Snow Hill has of emerging in the modern world. Finally. But they come from places where they don't have to worry about this kind of thing. They come from New York and California and Connecticut, where nobody would ever think of putting Creationist nonsense into the schools. There are barely any people who believe in Creationist nonsense. But we're here, aren't we? And Snow Hill is full of the kind of people who would be more than happy to shove a ten-thousand-year-old earth down the throat of every child within screaming distance. So when the people from the development didn't vote, and the people from town did, well, you see what we got. Franklin Hale and the God-intoxicated stupids."

"So that's why you and the other members of the old school board lost the last election? Because people from the development didn't vote?"

"Exactly," Henry said. "Oh, some of them did, of course. Judy Cornish did. She was a wonderful woman, Mr. Demarkian. She really was. But a lot of them up there just weren't thinking. And they didn't know Franklin Hale or Alice McGuffie either. They didn't realize what they were going to be stuck with if they didn't get out and vote."

Demarkian appeared to be only half-listening. Henry went back to fiddling with the folders on his desk.

"If you're looking around and see one of those that says Books to Print, I wish you'd tell me about it," Henry said. "It's the file I'm looking for. I can't find it anywhere. I used to think Christine was good at filing things, but I guess she wasn't. The damned thing isn't here anywhere."

"I thought," Gregor Demarkian said, "that the reason the old school board was rejected and the new one was elected was essentially a practical issue. People tell me that the problem was your own and your board's lack of attention to necessary details. The teachers' contract issues, for instance. And the new school complex."

"Bullshit," Henry said. "The new school complex? There wouldn't be one if it weren't for me. You don't know what this place is like. They resent every dime they have to spend on education. Every dime. They'd let the schools go without paper and pencils. We've already had to start charging our kids to play sports. The buildings are falling down. They're antiquated and inadequate. It took me six years to get that project approved, and then it was only halfhearted approval. Franklin Hale would end it altogether if he could."

"But the building on the project has gone on for a while, hasn't it?" Gregor said. "It's been something like five years?"

"Because I could never keep the town on track to keep the funding up," Henry said. "We do our school budgets by referendum, you know. Every year, we have to go to the town and beg for money, and most of the time we can't get a budget approved for months. Hell, there have been years we haven't been able to pay our teachers, or anybody else, until practically Thanksgiving because we haven't been able to get a budget through. As soon as there were cost overruns on the project, we were in trouble, because we had to go back to the town and ask for more. And the town never wants to give more. Never. If it wasn't for the state and state law, they'd throw out the teachers' contracts, set a salary scale that looked like it was written for waitresses at the Snow Hill Diner, and refuse to hire anybody who wouldn't work for that. We'd end up with teachers who'd flunked out of ed school, or worse. We'd end up without any teachers at all."

"I thought teachers' contracts were another of those things the town thought your board wasn't handling very well," Gregor Demarkian said.

"They only thought we weren't handling it well because they didn't want to pay the going rate for teachers," Henry said. "Most of these people have no respect for what teachers do. Their idea of education is a lot of rote recitation of what they think of as Timeless Truths: God Loves You, the United States of America Is Never Wrong, Don't Have Sex Until Marriage. Not that many of them listened to their own advice when they were in high school. Marcey Hale almost didn't make it to her own high school graduation, she was that close to showing. It doesn't matter. They don't think they have to make sense. They don't have the decency to be ashamed of their hypocrisy. They weren't ever going to like any of the teachers' contracts as long as the contracts had defined benefit pension plans, and that's not going to change unless the unions go bust. Which they won't."

"All right," Gregor Demarkian said.

"It makes me nuts when I hear people say that they voted for

Franklin Hale because of practical considerations," Henry said. "It's a lie. It's a bald-faced, unvarnished lie. There isn't anybody in this town who doesn't know who and what Franklin is, except for some of the people from the development, and they'd never vote for him anyway because he doesn't want to spend money on schools. But as for the people of Snow Hill, the regulars, the ones who have been here forever—if they voted for Franklin Hale, it's because they wanted what he had to offer, and what he has to offer is religion in the Snow Hill Public Schools."

2

Catherine Marbledale knew this was going to be a bad day, but she had had no idea just how bad before the students began piling out of the school busses at eight o'clock. The busses were late, too. She'd even considered calling a snow day, since there was a sleet storm to provide an excuse for it, but in the end she'd decided to let the day unfold. If you had too many snow days, they tacked on extra school days in June. None of the kids liked that, and she didn't like it, either. It was bad enough trying to teach students who didn't want to learn in the first place. It was worse trying to teach them when they felt that their sacred vacation time had been violated. Sometimes she wondered why she was still doing what she was doing. Back about ten years ago or so, she could have moved on to any private school in the country. She could have taught at Exeter and had nothing to worry about but academically gifted, intellectually ambitious kids. She should have done it. She was delusional to think that she was on a mission from God.

Marty Loudan had come out to the foyer as the number 6 bus began to unload, and he was the one who saw it first.

"Is that a meeting at the pole?" he asked. "In this weather?"

The weather was, indeed, very bad. It was much colder than it had been only yesterday, and there was precipitation on and off. Catherine went up to the big plate-glass windows and looked out. There was indeed a meeting at the flagpole, ten or so students standing in a circle holding hands, their heads bowed.

"They've got a right to meet at the pole," she said. "We hashed all that out a couple of years ago."

"I'm not questioning their rights, I'm questioning their sanity," Marty said. "They've got to be freezing out there. They're going to be sick."

Catherine looked out again. Barbie McGuffie was there, with her knee in a cast and a pair of crutches. Most of the rest were what Catherine thought of as "quiet ones." They came to class. They did their homework. They didn't cause trouble. They didn't perform in that spectacular, singular way that made a student stand out. Catherine didn't think she had had a student with that kind of spark since Nick Frapp. She often wondered what would have happened to him if he'd been born to a different kind of family or in a different kind of place.

"They *are* going to get sick, if they keep that up," Marty said. "I know we're not supposed to break up the meeting until the bell rings, but maybe somebody could go out there and reason with them. You know what kind of trouble we're going to be in if one of them comes down with pneumonia."

"All right," Catherine said.

She wasn't wearing her coat—she'd already hung it up in her office—but she went outside anyway, pausing for a moment on the sidewalk in front of the front doors while the number 5 bus pulled in and unloaded. The number 5 bus came in from the development, and the children piling off were subdued. As far as Catherine knew, none of the students from the development participated in Meet Me At The Pole. It was yet another way the schools, and the town, had divided itself. Catherine bit her lip, and the bus pulled out, and she was looking at the circle again.

She crossed the drive to the circular grassy median where the flagpole was. The flag had not been raised, because it was not supposed to be raised in seriously bad weather, but the circle of students holding hands with their eyes closed did not seem to care one way or the other.

As Catherine drew closer, she could hear the murmuring. They were still on the Lord's Prayer, which was always the first prayer they did. That made her feel a little better. If they were still on the Lord's Prayer, they couldn't have been there long. There was no danger of pneumonia right this second.

She reached the grass and waited. When the murmuring stopped, she touched a student on the arm. It was Tom Radnor, the only kid in Snow Hill these days who was likely to end up an Eagle Scout. Catherine also thought he was probably also headed for the military, maybe with a start in ROTC somewhere small and not very prestigious. He was honest, honorable, likable and morally straight, but he was not—well, Catherine thought, he was not Nick Frapp.

"Tom," she said. "Come inside. It's freezing out here. And there's sleet."

"We can't come inside," Tom said. "We want to pray. School is a prayer-free zone."

"Tom, you know that's not true," Catherine said. "You pray in school all the time. You get a whole table full of people praying at lunch in the cafeteria every day. I see you."

"And we keep quiet," Tom said. "Because that's the deal. We have to keep quiet. We can't be heard praying out loud. Our faith is something we have to hide. Only secular humanism gets to speak out loud in a public school."

Catherine rubbed her fingers against her forehead. She was getting the kind of headache that was going to last all day.

"I wish," she said, "that every single one of you went to Nick Frapp's church."

"Reverend Frapp is an admirable man," Tom said seriously, "but I don't completely agree with him on all points of faith."

"I don't agree with him on any," Catherine said, "but he's got more sense than to work his people up like this. I take it your pastor has been lecturing you all on Godless evolution at Wednesday night prayer meeting."

"There were never any murders in Snow Hill before," Tom said, suddenly eager. "You have to see that, Miss Marbledale. Snow Hill has been here since before the Civil War, and in all that time, I'll bet there hasn't been a single other murder like these we've got now."

"People kill each other in Snow Hill," Catherine said. "They don't do a lot of it, but they do do it."

"Not like this," Tom insisted, and now the rest of the students were out of the circle and crowding around, listening. "People killed each other, sure, but it was mostly stupid stuff. Because they got too drunk or they got really angry and couldn't control themselves. But this is different. You know it is. This is—this is on purpose."

"It's the start of something bad," another student said.

Catherine looked around and saw that this was Brittany Morse. She was fairly sure that Brittany did not date Tom. She looked around the circle. The faces, except for Barbie McGuffie's, all belonged to students who did not usually cause trouble, and that made her uneasy.

"It's cold," she said again. "Come back inside. You can pray in a classroom if you want to, just as long as you're quiet."

"We want to lead a prayer over the intercom," Tom said. "It doesn't have to be an actual prayer. We could lead a moment of silence."

"You know you can't do that," Catherine said. "That's not part of the agreement."

Behind her, another bus pulled up. She turned instinctively to see which one it was, and it was the number 8. When the bus had gone again, she saw that the kids who had piled out were all wearing little ribbons on their shirts, but instead of being yellow for the troops or pink for breast cancer, they were red, white, and blue. She turned back to Tom and saw that he had one, too. They all did, all the students in the circle.

"What is this?" she asked them. "What's going on here?"

"The agreement isn't acceptable anymore," Tom said. "We've all been talking about it for months, now, but after yesterday we knew we couldn't go on with it. We should never have made the agreement to begin with. When you remove the Lord from your life, you bring sorrow on your house."

"Nobody's removing the Lord from your life," Catherine said. "And the agreement wasn't my idea. It's what the lawyers came up with when they reviewed the case law on religion in public schools. You must know that."

"The agreement isn't acceptable anymore," Tom said again. "It's time we took back our school, and took back our town, and took back our lives. And you can't stop us if we don't want to let you."

He turned around and nodded, and suddenly all the students were on the move, across the asphalt drive, across the sidewalk, and through the big plate-glass doors. That was when Catherine realized there were a lot more of them than she had first thought. There were the students from the circle, and the students from bus number 8, but there were others, maybe sixty or more, all wearing those red, white, and blue ribbons.

"Damn," she thought.

And then she ran for the doors herself.

FIVE

1

The most important thing was to go to the hospital to see Annie-Vic, and to that end Gregor piled the bits and pieces of paper he'd started to write on into a manila file folder, put the folder in a manila envelope, and went looking for Eddie Block. He couldn't remember how long it had been since he'd gone about working like that. Even in his last five or so years at the Bureau, he hadn't resorted to the bits and pieces of paper, and in the years he had, his superiors had generally hated the idea. But then, everything about this case, from the beginning, had been an exercise in déjà vu, and he didn't even believe in déjà vu. Maybe it was his time of life, or maybe the wedding coming up. For whatever reason, he had been living the last several days in a time-traveling cloud, and he didn't much like it.

"It's a mistake," he told Eddie Block and Gary Albright as they drove out to the hospital, "to think that memory is your friend. We tend to think that way because there's so much we want to remember—friends, people we love, good times we've had. But in reality memory is a trap, and it's especially a trap when you're trying to solve a case.

New cases are not like old cases, no matter how much you think they are. The human element is always different."

The drive out to the hospital took them through what seemed to Gregor like miles of empty country, empty not only of houses and people but of trees. Who mowed these meadows, stuck in the middle of nowhere, with no houses to watch over them? Somebody must have. If the grass had never been mowed, it would lie much longer in the field, and there would be the beginnings of bushes and trees. The emptiness out here was frightening. Gregor had been in gang-infested neighborhoods in major U.S. cities and had not been as frightened as he was by this. He wondered if he could explain this to Eddie Block or Gary Albright and didn't think he could.

"So what did this case make you think of?" Gary said. "It doesn't make me think of anything. It doesn't make any sense."

"It made me think of the first kidnapping detail I was ever on," Gregor said. "We were looking all over for this guy who had kidnaped his daughter, and he turned out to have gone up to the attic of his wife's house and killed himself and the girl up there. We were in the house for days before anybody thought to do a thorough check. It was negligent as Hell."

"Which is why you made us search Annie-Vic's house after Judy Cornish's body was found," Eddie said.

"I hope I made you do that because I've learned to follow procedure every single time," Gregor said. "But that took a long time to learn. And I've let myself be distracted by memory, and then I realized that I had it backward. The murderer wasn't in the attic. The murderer wasn't in the house at all. And that's the point."

"If that's the point, I'm dead, because I have no idea what it means," Gary Albright said.

"It doesn't matter," Gregor said. "I can't prove it yet anyway. I need some more information. I should have that some time this afternoon."

"And then you'll know who did it?" Gary Albright said.

"I know who did it now," Gregor said, "but it's like I told you, I can't prove it. And I suppose that, if I'm perfectly honest about it, until I have the information I need, I can only speculate that that information does indeed exist. It's possible that I'll go to my meeting this afternoon and find out that I have it all wrong. That nothing of the kind I'm thinking about ever happened."

"But you don't think you're wrong," Gary Albright said. "You think you know who did it."

"I do indeed."

"And it isn't one of us?" Gary Albright said. "It isn't somebody trying to get rid of evolution, or anything like that?"

Gregor wanted to chide him for saying "one of us," as if the parts of Snow Hill that were not Christian did not really belong to him, but that was another discussion. "No," Gregor said. "It's not somebody trying to get evolution out of the public schools. It's got nothing to do with evolution or Creationism or Intelligent Design. That particular controversy was a gift our murderer had no reason to expect. Because, from what everybody has told me, when Franklin Hale ran for the school board and got his friends to run, he didn't say a single thing about wanting to bring in Intelligent Design."

"He didn't even say it to me," Gary said. "I had no idea that that was what he was thinking of. I was floored. He might have told Alice."

"He might have," Gregor agreed. "If you're interested to know, we can find out later. But it isn't important to the case. The only thing that is important is the way in which the controversy worked as a blind to let our murderer get away with—well, murder. That, and the fact that the killing of Shelley Niederman was completely gratuitous. I have no way of knowing if she knew what the murderer was afraid she knew, but I do know she didn't know she knew it."

"How do you know that?" Eddie asked.

"I know because we talked to her, and she didn't tell us anything," Gregor said. "She was sitting outside the Hadley house in that car, completely distraught, and she couldn't think of a single reason why Judy Cornish would want to go into that house. And I think that if

338

she had known, she would have said something. She had no reason to shield the murderer, and there was no reason to shield herself, either. She hadn't done anything wrong, and Judy Cornish wasn't doing anything wrong."

"She could have thought it over and remembered something later," Gary said.

"She could have," Gregor agreed. "But that still leaves us in the same place. If she knew something that she knew implicated our murderer, she wouldn't have gone running up to the Hadley house when the murderer called her."

"*Called* her?" Gary Albright looked stunned. "You mean got her on the phone and asked her—to what exactly?"

"To meet at the Hadley house so that they could talk to the officers on duty," Gregor said. "Of course, the sensible person to talk to would have been me, but my guess is that the party line was that I couldn't be trusted, because Gary here hired me, and I was obviously on the side of the Creatonists. Because right up to the very end, Shelley Niederman believed that Judy Cornish had been murdered because she didn't want to see Intelligent Design taught in the public schools."

"Nobody was proposing to teach Intelligent Design in the public schools," Gary said. "I told you about that, Mr. Demarkian. All that we wanted to do was to put a sticker in every biology textbook that said that not everybody accepts Darwin's theory, and that Intelligent Design is another theory, and that if they want to know more about it they can go to the library and get a book. That was it. And we were going to get the book *Of Pandas and People* and put maybe five of them in the school library for students to check out. Nobody was trying to indoctrinate anybody, except the evolution side is trying just that. They want to force-feed our kids their point of view and ban any other point of view. That's what they want."

"Exactly," Eddie Block said.

"The point remains the same," Gregor said. "Shelley Niederman sincerely believed that she and Judy Cornish and others were being persecuted because they accepted the theory of evolution, and because they were part of a law suit to forbid the *introduction* of Intelligent Design into the public schools. Is that better?"

"I suppose so," Gary said. "But you know, Mr. Demarkian, we're not wrong. We didn't want all that much. We weren't asking to actually teach Intelligent Design. We just wanted to acknowledge that there was a different point of view. And they won't even let us have that. Separation of church and state? What is this, anyway, but the establishment of a state church? Their church. The church of evolution, or whatever it is. Dogma decided from on high, and no disagreement allowed or you get burned at the stake for heresy."

"I don't think anybody is burning anybody at the stake," Gregor said.

"Look at that," Eddie Block said. "There's something going on at the hospital."

2

What was going on at the hospital—or rather, in front of it—was a press conference. Dale Vardan was standing in front of a bank of microphones, the lights from dozens of television cameras pointing straight at his face, and waving a sheaf of paper in the air. Gregor was reminded of old Joe McCarthy, waving his papers and declaring that there were exactly two hundred and fifty-seven card carrying members of the Communist Party in the State Department. Gregor thought Dale Vardan was most likely to be exposing hillbillies, but he got out of the car and tried to listen. He wondered what the hospital was going to do if emergency vehicles started arriving.

"Where is the emergency room, anyway?" Gregor asked Gary. "Isn't he blocking something with all this nonsense?"

"It's around to the side," Gary said, staring at the microphones. "It's got it's own separate entrance."

"I am here to announce," Dale Vardan said, "that we are ready to make an arrest in the murders of Judy Cornish and Shelley Niederman. Earlier this morning, I sent officers to the home of Alice and

Lyman McGuffie, owners of the Snow Hill Diner in Snow Hill, Pennsylvania, where the murders took place. Mrs. McGuffie is a member of the conservative faction of the Snow Hill Board of Education and of the Snow Hill Baptist Church. All of that is public knowledge. What was not known until it was uncovered by our investigation is that Mr. and Mrs. McGuffie are also members of the Sword of God Covenant, a radical religious movement dedicated to bringing the United States of America under the rule of what they call 'Godly men.' By that they mean members of their own movement. In order to achieve that end, they are also dedicated to destroying any person or persons who oppose them."

"For God's sake," Gary said. "What is this idiot talking about?"

"Listen," Gregor said.

"Mrs. McGuffie was seen both entering and leaving the Hadley house on the day Judy Cornish was killed," Dale Vardan said. "The house is not far from the Snow Hill Diner, where Mrs. McGuffie was supposed to be at work. Mrs. McGuffie left the diner, walked up a small hill to the Hadley residence, went inside the house and stayed there for some time. Then she came out again and went back to the diner by the same route. We have witnesses to both her going and coming, and witnesses that place her at the house at, or near the time, of the murder."

"Do you have the murder weapon?" one of the reporters in the crowd called up.

"No," Dale Vardan said. "We do not have the murder weapon as of yet, but we're confident that we're going to find it. I have men searching the Hadley residence, the McGuffie residence, and the diner. We think the most likely place for it to be is in the Hadley residence, since none of our witnesses saw her carrying it."

"Hasn't the Hadley residence already been searched?" another reporter asked.

Dale Vardan looked smug. "A cursory search of the premises was done on the day of the murder under the direction of the local police," he said. "But the search was inadequate, and no useful evidence was found. I am now personally heading up the investigation into these crimes, and we are making rapid progress."

"What about Gregor Demarkian?" yet another reporter said.

"I have no information on what, if anything, Mr. Demarkian is doing. He is not assisting me or my men and was not a part of this morning's arrest."

Up until then, Gregor hadn't been sure that Dale Vardan had spotted him. Now Dale looked directly at him and smiled, and Gregor sighed. The only thing he wanted, absolutely, was to get into that hospital without being swarmed by reporters, and he knew it wasn't going to be possible. Dale Vardan was going to make sure it wasn't possible.

"There's Mr. Demarkian now," Dale Vardan announced, pointing in the direction of the Snow Hill police car and its three occupants. "If you've got something to ask him, ask him. I'm sure he'll be more than happy to take your questions."

3

Gregor was not happy to take their questions, and he wasn't happy about anything else that happened to him for the next half hour or so, but he lived with it, because he had to live with it. He'd been in messes like this one before.

"The great detective," Dale Vardan said to him at one point, when they were both away from the microphones. "It's all a bunch of bullshit, that's what it is. There's not a damn thing a great detective can do that solid police work can't, and that's what I've got to offer, Demarkian. Solid police work. And once I started using it, it didn't take me any time at all to figure out who did it and get those people safely locked up in jail."

"That's where you've got Mrs. McGuffie?" Gregor asked. "She's in jail?"

"As we speak," Vardan said. "And her husband with her. They're domestic terrorists, that's what they are. They're no better than Timothy McVeigh. And we're going to get the death penalty for both of them."

The morning might have gone better if there had been better news about Annie-Vic, but there wasn't. The news wasn't exactly bad, of course. Dr. Willard had been quite right. Annie-Vic was awake and alert, which was a vast improvement over what she'd been like when Gregor first arrived in town. She followed them with her eyes. She looked directly at them when they talked to her. Unfortunately, she was still unable to move any of her limbs, and she was still unable to talk. Unless a miracle happened, and she was able to communicate by using her eyelids to deliver Morse code, they weren't going to be able to get anything like testimony from her yet.

"Maybe we should try that Morse code thing," Gary suggested. "I mean, she's the kind of person who would know Morse code, don't you think? She was probably in the Girl Scouts when she was a kid. Everybody in Snow Hill does scouts. She probably had every merit badge in the book, too."

"I couldn't possibly agree to an experiment of that kind," Dr. Willard said. "Even if she could do it, it would leave her exhausted."

Gregor couldn't believe that anybody had taken him seriously. Still, Annie-Vic's condition had improved even in the few hours since Dr. Willard had talked to Gregor on the phone, and that meant there was reason to hope it would improve even more, to the point of making it possible for her to name her attacker. Once they had that, all the rest of the evidence would be just back up. That was the kind of assurance Gregor liked when he was winding up a case, and he almost never got it.

They drove back to town at a slower pace than they had driven out to the hospital, and on the way Gregor contemplated, once more, the emptiness of rural areas. If somebody attacked you out here, you could scream for hours without anybody hearing you. It was like that scene in that movie *Fargo*, where the bad guys kill a policeman and a couple of high school kids on a lonely stretch of road, their guns going off full blast, and it didn't matter. There was nobody to come to the rescue. Gregor hated the thought of there being nobody to come to the rescue. He had no idea why he was always thinking of the need for rescue, but he did.

When they arrived back in town, the place was insane. The reporters and their mobile news vans had come back from Dale Vardan's press conference—and why had he held it in front of the hospital, anyway? Even if he wanted to highlight the fact that Annie-Vic was awake, he didn't have to go all the way out there to do it. The vans were now parked close to the Snow Hill Diner, which had a big CLOSED sign hanging in its window. Gregor could see faces behind the glass nevertheless. They were probably employees, caught short by the news that the McGuffies had been arrested.

Eddie Block parked the car behind the station and Tom Fordman came out, looking harassed.

"It's like some kind of riot," he said. "It's unbelievable."

"We saw Mr. Vardan's press conference," Gregor said.

"I saw it too," Tom Vardan said. "They carried it live on CNN. Alice and Lyman killed those two women at the development? Is that supposed to make sense to me?"

"When did they arrest them?" Gregor asked.

"It couldn't have been half an hour ago," Tom said, "and you should have seen it. They practically sent a SWAT team. Bunch of state police cars pulled up in front of the diner and about twelve guys got out and went in with their guns drawn. It was like a military operation. The next thing you know, they're hauling Alice and Lyman out in handcuffs and Alice is completely hysterical. She's screaming and pulling. She's got her hands cuffed behind her back, so she can't punch anybody, but she bit an officer—"

"Bit him?" Gregor asked. "How the Hell—"

"It was a her," Tom Fordman said. "The officer, I mean. And I don't know how. She wasn't careful enough and Alice bit her, and then all Hell broke loose. It was like a television show or a movie, maybe. I'm not making much sense myself."

They all went into the back door of the station together, and as soon as they did Gregor could hear the noise. There were people in the big outer office, lots of them, and most of them sounded angry. Gregor, Gary, Eddie, and Tom came around the corner in the corridor that led to the front of the station and Gregor saw them: some reporters, lots of ordinary people. One of the ordinary people was a pastor of some kind. He was wearing a clerical collar.

"This is outrageous," the man in the clerical collar was saying. "This is completely unacceptable. Alice and Lyman McGuffie are two of the finest, most God-fearing citizens of this town, and the idea that either one of them ever killed anybody is completely absurd."

There was a young woman behind the counter, looking embattled, but it wasn't Tina from a couple of days before. She saw Gregor and Gary and the others come in and rushed over to them, looking frazzled.

"There's something else that's just come in," she said, grabbing Gary's arm and trying to whisper, but whispering was hard. There was so much noise that real whispering wasn't going to work, but raising her voice meant risking the possibility that the people on the other side of the counter would hear her, and Gregor thought it was obvious she didn't want that.

"We've got another problem," she said, leaning as close to Gary's ear as she could. "I've just had a call from Miss Marbledale. There's trouble up at the school."

"What kind of trouble?" Gary asked.

"Some kind of sit-in," she said. She looked confused. "What's a sit-in, exactly? It sounds like a kind of riot, but that doesn't make any sense. Miss Marbledale says that Tim Radnor and a lot of other students are in the office and they won't let her or anybody else in and they're using the intercom. It doesn't make any sense. I mean, Tim Radnor?"

"I'll go up there," Eddie said.

"You'd better take Tom with you," Gary said. Then he put his head in his hands. "I can't believe this," he said. "I really can't believe this."

The young woman shook her head. "I really can't believe it, either," she said. "But there's more. There are two people in Mr. Demarkian's office who say they're from the FBI and they've got an appointment, except it was supposed to be in the diner and now they can't go there.

I'm sorry if I did the wrong thing, but I just couldn't think of anything else to do with them."

"It's all right," Gregor said. "I'll let you people work on the sit-in and go talk to them."

"This is outrageous," the pastor said again. "This is religious persecution, that's what this is, and you're not going to get away with it. We're going to sue. We're going to take it all the way to the Supreme Court."

Gregor let Gary take care of the rant and retreated to his closet of an office.

4

The entire town of Snow Hill might be panicking, but Molly Trask and Evan Zwicker were not. They were sitting on the only two chairs in Gregor's "office," drinking coffee, and playing games on their cell phones. Gregor wondered if these were their personal cell phones or phones the Bureau gave them. Then he realized that he'd been out of the Bureau for so long, he didn't know what kind of cell phone policy it had.

Molly looked up when Gregor walked in, but Evan stayed staring at his phone intently and saying "Damn!" Molly coughed. Evan looked up and blushed.

"Sorry," he said.

"Nothing to be sorry for," Gregor said. "You were bored. I don't blame you. Were you here when the McGuffie's were arrested?"

"We were sitting in the diner when the cops came in," Evan said. Then he shrugged. "It was a light and sound show. They were being as conspicuous as possible. And they were getting a lot of help. That woman can really scream her head off when she wants to. Was all this your doing, Mr. Demarkian? You didn't tell us anything about it."

"It didn't have anything to do with me," Gregor said. "I didn't even see it coming. It was the work of a state police detective with an ego. Did you bring me the information I need?"

"Absolutely," Molly said.

She stored her cell phone in her pocket and sat forward. Gregor wasn't sitting at all. Two chairs was as many as the "office" could hold, and nobody was jumping up to offer him a seat. Molly reached into the pocket of her jacket and came up with a sheaf of papers.

"You'll be glad to know," she said, "that you turned out to be right. We checked the operating budget, the pension fund, and the construction. The operating budget and the pension fund are both clean, at least on this end. If somebody is embezzling from the pension fund, they have to be doing it at the union national end, and I'm willing to bet they're not. The AFT has good controls for that sort of thing."

"And the operating budget?" Gregor asked.

"Well," Molly said, "a lot of money goes through there on a regular basis. Wages and salaries, though, are the biggest item, and we double-checked the bank accounts. Everything adds up. We did consider the possibility that there might be a phantom employee, but we double-checked that, too, and apparently not. The rest of what goes through that budget is large in the aggregate, but small in each individual withdrawal. And we mean small. There's stuff under five dollars on that list, and nothing over about a thousand at a time except for the sports stuff. And we checked out the sports stuff, and at least from a first-time overview, it looks clean, too."

"So," Gregor said, "that leaves the construction."

"Yes it does," Molly said. "And the construction is very interesting indeed."

She stood up, leaned across to Gregor's desk, picked up another sheaf of papers and handed it across to him.

"Look at those," she said. "Dellbach Constuction."

"Those" were page after page of disclosure documents, all in very tiny print. Gregor looked up at Molly.

"Never mind," she said. "I'll tell you. First, those are the documents Dellbach Construction had to file when it went after the job for the schools complex. If you look carefully, you'll see some interesting stuff. For one thing, according to the sworn statement, Dellbach

Construction only came into existence a month before it bid on this project."

"Only a month?" Gregor asked.

"Exactly," Molly said. "And it gets weirder than that if you look beyond the disclosure documents, because not only did Dellbach Construction not exist until a month before it got the project, it doesn't really exist now. It's a holding company. It subcontracts the work out in bits and pieces, never the same subcontractor for two phases in a row, never a phase that lasts more than six months, several phases that last only six weeks or so."

"And the money is completely screwy," Evan said. "We both spent a lot of the night trying to figure it out, and we know somebody is embezzling something—"

"Somebody is embezzling a lot," Molly said. "At least five million dollars over the last five years."

"Yeah," Evan said. "But we don't know how. And that's worrying."

"But the real kicker is at the bottom of the first page," Molly said. "Take a look at line fourteen. That's the line that says 'ownership.' That's who owns Dellbach Construction."

"And who owns it?" Gregor said, scanning down the page.

Then he saw it. Right there, next to the word *ownership,* was not one name, but two.

Catherine and Margaret Marbledale.

SIX

1

Somewhere along the way, somebody had put a needle in her arm. That was the last thing Alice McGuffie remembered at all clearly, and it was pickled in emotion. Everything was emotion. Somewhere underneath this haze they had put her in was what she felt, and what she felt was hot and red and angry, where it wasn't scared to death. She hated that man, that Dale Vardan. She had always hated him, and everybody in town hated him, too. She had been waiting for years for the secular humanists to come for her. All across the nation, the secular humanists were making martyrs out of good Christian people, and they were doing it right here in America, which had been founded as a Christian nation and meant to be a City on a Hill. Alice could not, for the life of her, remember what the phrase "City on a Hill" actually meant. She'd heard it a million times in church over the years, but the truth about church was that she just didn't pay that much attention to the sermons. It was hard to keep your mind on anything that went on and on like that. The pastor liked to quote from people, too. They were always people Alice knew she was supposed to recognize, but almost never did—Plato, Aristotle. It made no sense to her to bring up people like that in church. They had "never had the chance to hear the Gospel of Our Lord Jesus Christ." The pastor said that. The two guest pastors they had had over the past year said the same thing. What good were they, then? For the Christian, Christ was all in all. The pastor said that too. Alice didn't see why they needed to know about these people who had lived a long time ago and who hadn't believed in Christ and who had said things that sounded crazy and stupid. Maybe there were secular humanists back there, too. Maybe they roamed the countryside like a lion waiting to devour you. The words were all getting mixed up in her head. She couldn't make herself concentrate. She had never been able to make herself concentrate. Maybe that was the problem.

She was lying in a cell in the county jail; that much she knew. She did not know what had happened to Barbie. Barbie was back at school when all this had happened. Did Barbie even know this had happened? She must, by now. She must be home alone, or maybe social workers had come and taken her away. Social workers were what Alice McGuffie feared most after secular humanists, but she thought that a lot of social workers were secular humanists as well. It was unbelievable, the way the secular humanists had managed to get themselves into all the nooks and crannies of government. They had managed to get the law on their side. They had managed to get the courts. Maybe the social workers would take Barbie and claim she was being "emotionally abused." That's what they called it when a child was being raised in a Christian home. Christianity itself was "abuse," and if you could claim "abuse" you could kidnap the child and take her way somewhere, where all that Christianity could be trained out of her. Maybe the social workers would claim that Alice could no longer "provide a safe space" for Barbie, because she couldn't provide a safe space for anybody, because she was in jail. "Provide a safe space" was like "emotional abuse." It was a phrase that could mean anything or nothing. It existed only as an excuse, to make it possible for the social workers to take the child away. Social workers were dedicated to taking children away from Christian parents because they hated Christianity and they hated parents. They wanted all children to be raised up as secular humanists.

Everything was spinning, and her head hurt. One entire wall of the room she was in was bars. A woman in a police uniform was sitting on a chair just on the other side of that, reading her way through a magazine. Alice wondered what the woman was like. She didn't understand it: The police in Snow Hill weren't secular humanists. There was Gary Albright, who went to her very own church, and Eddie Block, who went to the Methodists. Even Tom Fordman went to church, to the Lutheran one, and he was like lot of men, uncomfortable at services and not happy about being asked to show his love for Jesus in public. But they all loved Jesus. Alice was sure of that. Most of the teachers in Snow Hill loved Jesus, too, except for the science ones, and Miss Marbledale. Where did all these people come from, people like this woman on the other side of the bars? Where did they find them?

It was like that movie she had seen once very late at night on television, *Invasion of the Body Snatchers*. It was in black and white. It starred this man Alice recognized because she'd seen him in a million old movies, but whose name she could never remember. She thought of him as "the man with the jaw." He had a big jaw, but that didn't matter. What mattered were the pods. There were pods in the basement, and when they popped open people popped out—bodies, not real people—but their bodies looked like the bodies of real people, they looked like people you knew.

She was really very dizzy. She was so dizzy she didn't think she could stand up. She hadn't tried to stand up, though, so she didn't know. She didn't want to try to stand up, because then she would have to look at it all: the bars, the woman in the uniform, the corridor where the other cells were. She was alone in this cell. She didn't know why. From the noise she could hear, the other cells seemed to have lots of people in them. She was glad she wasn't with lots of other people. She didn't want to see people. She didn't want to talk to people. She had no idea what she would say.

"Hello. I'm Alice McGuffie. I'm being persecuted by secular humanists."

It was the kind of joke they would make on those late-night television shows. Alice hated those late-night television shows—David Letterman, Conan O'Brien. Who were those people? Why did they think they knew so much? She didn't understand half the things they said. They were always talking about things that made no sense and then everybody was laughing. Alice couldn't see what there was to laugh at. Lyman couldn't see it, either. Maybe there was nothing to laugh at and they were tricking people—people who were too embarrassed to admit they didn't understand what was going on. That was what happened with the Emperor's new clothes. Nobody wanted to say the Emperor was naked because they thought everybody else could see his clothes. They didn't want people to think they were stupid. Alice had spent her entire life trying to keep people from thinking she was stupid. They thought it anyway. It was like she had a brand on her forehead. It was all Catherine Marbledale's fault, and the fault of people like Annie-Vic, and the fault of secular humanists. There were secular humanists under the bed. There were secular humanists in the refrigerator. There was no refrigerator. What was she thinking of?

She was lying on a very narrow cot that was shoved right up against the wall. Alice thought it might be bolted into the wall. She didn't want to look. She had a blanket on top of her that felt like horse hair. It was rough, and the few times she had opened her eyes she had seen it was gray. There was a sheet under her, but no sheet on top of her. She always had a sheet on top of her at home. Maybe this was what they did to you in prison. Maybe they took away all your sheets. Maybe they would execute her, and first she would have to lie on a gurney somewhere and sing at the top of her lungs to keep from being afraid. She was afraid, though. She was so afraid all her muscles had gone rigid, so that none of her joints had been able to bend. Then they had given her that shot, and everything had melted. It was melted now.

She opened her eyes and stared straight up at the ceiling. The ceiling was filthy. It was as if nobody had ever cleaned it, not in all the years it had been up there. How long ago had this jail been built? Alice didn't know. She didn't pay much attention to the news, except for things going on locally, and nothing much ever went on locally. This would be something going on locally. Everybody in town would watch it on television. They would buy newspapers and read about it. Maybe it would be in a magazine somewhere. Look at the crazy Christians. Watch them kill everybody. Her head hurt. The pain was far away, on the other side of a barrier of fuzz. Her mouth was dry.

"There was a picture of me on the dining room table," she said. The words came out as clear as the sound of her television. There was no fuzz at all.

Over on the other side of the bars, the woman in uniform stood up and turned toward Alice. Alice could feel her looking.

"What did you say?" the woman said.

"There was a picture of me on the dining room table," Alice said again. "So I took it. I brought it home and I put it in my sewing table."

The words were not crisp anymore. They were going in and out of blur. She was very tired. She wanted to go back to sleep again.

"I don't think you should be worrying about your sewing table now," the woman in uniform said. "There are other things to think about now."

If she didn't force herself to speak, she would fall asleep again. The woman in the uniform was making a note. She would probably pass it along to other people in uniform. Alice watched all the cop shows. She liked cop shows. She liked thinking that there were people out there who lived in terrible places full of crime, while she was safe and happy right there in Snow Hill.

If she didn't concentrate, she would forget. If she didn't concentrate, she would drift back into space and the secular humanists would be there, they would be there, they were always there, they were all around us. They were that devouring lion. That's what they were.

"Listen," Alice said.

"I'll listen if you want me to," the woman in uniform said. "But you've had a very powerful sedative, you know. You ought to get some rest."

"Listen," Alice said again. Then she made one last, great effort. She pushed by the barrier of fuzz that was all around her. She pushed by the flitting ghosts that were really memories, because you couldn't have ghosts of people who were still alive. They were there all around her. They were waiting for her to fall asleep.

"Listen," she said for the third time, and then it worked. She was in a place where she could talk. She was in a place where she could think. The ceiling still looked dirty. The walls of the cell looked dirtier. There was a toilet screwed into the back wall, right out in the open, as if they expected her to relieve herself like that where anybody could see her.

"I want," she said, "to talk to that man. I want to talk to Gregor Demarkian."

"What?" the woman in uniform said.

"It was a picture of me and I took it," Alice said, and then she fell back to sleep again.

2

It was the arrest of Alice and Lyman McGuffie that made up Nick Frapp's mind for him, but he'd been on the verge of making it up on his own for an hour or more before that. He had been thinking about it all night, in fact, and the more he thought about it the more sure he had been that, in the last analysis, it was civilization that mattered.

"Civilization," his old philosophy professor had said, "is not something we have. It's something we do."

Philosophy professor. Dr. Raydock. Dr. Raydock was always in trouble with the university administration because he wasn't quite Christian enough, he wasn't quite with the program. It was not the kind of thing Nick had understood before he'd gone to Oklahoma, but it hadn't taken him long to learn. Civilization is something we do, Nick told himself now, and that was right. It was absolutely right.

And if you stopped doing it, you found yourself howling in the wilderness.

He stuck his head into the main office where yet another one of the church women, Marianna Beck, was filling in as church secretary.

"I'm going to go out for a bit," he said.

Marianne looked up and pulled a drawn face. It didn't entirely hide the excitement in her eyes. "Isn't it terrible?" she said. "Alice McGuffie, of all people. I never would have believed it. But then, you never know with people, do you? Especially people like the McGuffies. Kept themselves to themselves. Like my mother always said, you've got to watch out for people like that. You always know something is wrong when people are too quiet."

Nick didn't think Alice McGuffie had ever been quiet for an hour in her life. He thought she might even talk in her sleep. He let it go and went downstairs and out the door onto Main Street. The town was quieter now than it had been the last time he'd seen it. He'd come out to watch with everybody else when the police cars came and the police raced into the Snow Hill Diner. People were saying it was just like a movie, and they were right, but not in the way they meant it. It was like a movie because it was so completely exaggerated. Men in black uniforms with rifles slung over their backs, to arrest Alice and Lyman McGuffie? It was like taking out a kitten with a bazooka.

Nick went down the street to the police station. He had seen them all come in, Gary and Tom and Eddie and Gregor Demarkian. He went up the front steps and let himself into the building. The woman behind the counter was working at something on a computer. He cleared his throat and waited. She looked up and then looked annoyed.

"Is there something I can do for you?"

"I'd like to talk to Mr. Demarkian, if I can," Nick said.

"I'll see what he's doing," the woman said. "We're in the middle of a murder investigation, in case you didn't know. Do you have information about the murder investigation?"

"Maybe," Nick said.

The woman looked suspicious, but she got up and went to the back. A second later, Gregor Demarkian emerged, looking rumpled.

"Reverend Frapp," he said. "Good to see you. Why don't you come on back?"

Nick gave the woman a smile, but she turned away from him. He followed Gregor "on back," and found himself in what he was sure was supposed to be a utility closet. The utility closet had a desk and two chairs. Nick sat down in the chair that was not behind the desk.

"This is interesting," he said.

"It's adequate, believe it or not," Gregor Demarkian said. "Although I have to admit, it makes me feel a little claustrophobic. Do you really have information for me, or did you just want to talk?"

"Did you authorize the arrest of Alice and Lyman McGuffie?" Nick asked. "Was that your idea?"

"No," Gregor said. "We seem to be beset by a state police detective who thinks he knows everything."

"Ah," Nick said. "So it was a Dale Vardan special. All right. I didn't think it was you, but I thought I'd better ask. Have you ever been to Holland?"

"Holland?"

"I went last year," Nick said. "I don't travel much. There's too much work here, with the school and church and everything, but I went last year to a conference. And it's Holland I think of when I think about all of this. About Alice and Lyman. About the teaching of evolution in the public schools. About the murders. Because that's what Holland is all about these days, you know. It's about death."

"Excuse me?" Gregor Demarkian said.

Nick threw his head back and stared at the ceiling. He wondered if this room would feel so small if it was being occupied by people closer to normal size than either he or Demarkian were.

"They have all these things," Nick said. "Abortion. And what they call 'assisted suicide.' They kill off their children and they kill off their old people and they just don't see it. They don't see that they're sinking into an orgy of death. They think it's freedom. And in the end, you know, that's my bottom line. If you wake up one morning and find out you're collaborating with death, you ought to understand that you're doing something wrong. In the end, that's the difference I see between people of faith and people without it. When people of faith collaborate with death, they know they're doing something wrong. When people without it do, they often don't even realize they're collaborating. I don't really think it matters whether you're a Protestant or a Catholic or a Hindu, for that matter. I think there are probably many ways to God, but the reason I know God exists is because people who believe in him feel guilty about collaborating with death and people who don't not only don't feel guilty, they don't even realize there's an issue."

"And you think that's true of me?" Gregor said. "That I collaborate with death, and don't even see the issue?"

"No," Nick said. "But I think you're unusual. You're unusually intelligent. You're unusually thoughtful. And you're unusually free of that thing so many people have of needing to prove to themselves how wonderful they are by proving that everybody else is awful. And for unbelievers, that's usually trying to prove they're smart by 'proving' that anybody who believes must be stupid."

Gregor Demarkian looked puzzled. "Is this going someplace?" he asked.

Nick nodded. "Just call it the background to what I'm going to say. Four of my parishioners came to me last night to tell me that on or around the time that Shelley Niederman was murdered, they saw Franklin Hale go up to the Hadley house by that path through the woods at the back of Main Street."

"Did they," Gregor Demarkian said.

"But I've got more than that," Nick said, "because I saw Alice McGuffie come down that same path just before we heard about Judy Cornish's murder. But I didn't just see her go down. I saw her go in."

"Into the house?"

"Exactly," Nick said. "If you want to come over to the church later, I'll show you the view from my office window. When the leaves are on the trees, I can't see anything, but on days like we've been having, with the cold, and the trees bare, I can see anything all the way up there, and I saw Alice go in and not come out again for at least fifteen minutes."

"That is interesting," Gregor said.

"Here's the thing," Nick said. "I'm not the only person with a view up that hill Several other people have a good line of sight there, all the buildings that line that side of Main—"

"Which doesn't include either the Snow Hill Diner or Hale 'n' Hardy."

"No, it doesn't," Nick said. "But consider this. Judy Cornish was up there for no more than a couple of minutes before she was killed. From what I hear in town, Shelley Niedeman was up there for forty-five minutes or so, and she was killed. But Alice wasn't killed, and it doesn't look to me like anybody has tried. And nobody has tried with Franklin, either."

"So what do you make of that?" Gregor asked.

"Well," Nick said. "I don't make of it that somebody is killing over plaintiffs in the lawsuit, and I don't think that's what you make of it, either."

"No," Gregor said. "I don't."

Nick got up. "I hope I've been some help," he said. "You don't know how much I've enjoyed having you here. I'm still amazed that I ever got to meet you. I hope you'll drop by before you leave."

"Maybe I will," Gregor Demarkian said.

Nick walked back out to the big front room, nodded to the sullen woman at her computer, and made his way to the street. Sometimes he wished he had gone about living his life another way, that he had understood what Oral Roberts University was, or that after he'd graduated he'd made his way to someplace bigger, more exciting, more full of possibilities for the realization of ambition. On days like today, however, he had no doubts. There were very few men in the world lucky enough to make a significant difference in the lives of other people, and he was one of those men. There were few shacks in the hills these days, at least around here, and they sometimes went four or five months without the police being called in to break up a "domestic dispute." He had ten-year-olds in his religion class who could read their way through Martin Luther's *The Freedom of a Christian* and explain what it meant. He had more who could identify Plato and Aristotle and Gandhi and Leonardo da Vinci.

Nick couldn't remember when he had first realized what was going on out there, something that had to do with books but, more important, had to do with minds. People had lived and died in the world who thought about all the same things he thought about, who wanted to understand what it meant to be a human being and how to be a good one, who looked at the manifest tragedy of human existence and turned it into El Greco's *Crucifixion* and Dante's *Divinia Comedia.* It was a seven-thousand-year-old conversation, a way of talking to the dead and having them talk back to you, and everything was better when you were a part of it. Even pain and suffering were better.

He walked back down Main Street to the church, only half realizing that he'd come out without his coat, again. They would build a high school soon, and Nick had already planned its curriculum. It would be a Great Books curriculum, and it would include all the books that mattered, the pagan ones and the Christian ones and the beautiful ones and the ugly ones. He would take these children of moonshine artists and grandchildren of coal miners, these one-step-away-from-going-barefoot-to-a-backyard-privy teenagers, and turn them into the next generation of American scholars. They would not be scholars in the new sense, holed up in universities and writing endless articles about the place of food in the novels of Jane Austen. They would be scholars the way John Adams had been a scholar, and Thomas Jefferson, and George Washington. They would be men and women who lived in the Great Tradition the way fish lived in water.

It was a good thing he had come home to stay. Nicodemus Frapp did not experience the world as purposeless or random. He felt the meaning of it in his bones. The meaning of it for him was this, and he came back and back and back to the fact that he could never have been as happy as this doing anything else.

3

Catherine Marbedale was tired. She was tired in the ordinary sense, because it had been a bad day, and it was going to get worse. The student protestors were out of her office now, and the microphone was back in the hands of the people it belonged to, but there had been news cameras up here and not only local ones. The trial was going to start in a matter of days, and everybody was here, everybody wanted a chance to show the world what a backwards hillbilly place Snow Hill was. There were going to be protests. The parents from town would demand to know how she dared to try to stop their children from praying. The parents from the development would demand to know how she dared to let those other students "marginalize" their children by putting on a sectarian religious display. It went around and round and round, and next year it would go around again, and that's why she was tired in the other way.

It hadn't been what she'd wanted for herself, all those years ago. She hadn't imagined that she would take a job in some godforsaken small town and then just sit there, year after year, getting older and grayer and weaker in the process. For a while she thought it would be enough as long as she and Margaret got away to Europe for the summers. They could walk through Florence and Madrid and Athens and see the art and talk about books. It was almost as if they were children again. Catherine Marbledale remembered her childhood. She remembered going to the library with Margaret and taking out all the best books, *Anna Karenina* and *David Copperfield* and *Pride and Prejudice* and *For Whom the Bell Tolls.* She didn't know how long it was before she discovered that you weren't supposed to read like that, jumping around among the different time frames, paying no attention to literary history. She didn't care. It was the best way to read, and she hadn't read that way in many years.

She had the door to her office closed. The secretaries were out there, dealing with things. She thought they could deal with them a little while longer. She thought about Florence again, and about

Athens, about walking up the steep hill to the Parthenon and down again, and stopping at a little place on Nikis Street to have galatoboureko and coffee.

She pulled her phone to her and picked up the receiver. She wondered how long phones like this would last. Everybody had cell phones now. It was close to one o'clock. Margaret would be in her office. Margaret was always in her office. Catherine punched the numbers in, and Margaret picked up on her cell phone.

"Are you alone?" Catherine asked.

"I am," Margaret said. "I've been watching you on the news this morning."

"It's over now," Catherine said. "I have a headache, but I was wondering . . ."

"About what?"

"About money," Catherine said. "Remember, a couple of years ago, we talked about it? There would come a time that we couldn't handle it anymore. That we couldn't go on fighting a war we knew we were never going to win?"

"And you've come to that point," Margaret said. "Because of the protestors?"

"It's not the protestors," Catherine said. "It's everything, really. It's the lawsuit, and the school board, and the fact that nothing ever gets done unless I do it. It's having to live day after day with people who are just so damned proud of their ignorance they glow. I don't know. I take it you don't feel the same way."

"I feel the same way," Margaret said. "I'm just not quite as close to the end of my rope as you are."

"Well, I'm at the end and beyond it," Catherine said. "And I've been sitting here ever since they let me back into my office, thinking that if I have to do this for one more year, I'm going to have a breakdown. I can't fix people, Margaret. I accepted that long ago. I can't fix people, and I don't want to live with the people I can't fix."

"So?"

"So I was thinking it was about time for me to bail," Catherine

361

said, "and I was just wondering, that being the case, whether we have the money for me to do it. I know I should be better about these things, Margaret, but you were always better about these things than I was."

"I, at least, look at our bank statements every month. You want to know how much we have in the retirement accounts?"

"That was the idea," Catherine said. "Yes."

"At the end of last month, it amounted to five point eight million dollars."

"That's more than I thought," Catherine said.

"It's less than it could have been, if you hadn't insisted on sticking to government bonds," Margaret said.

"I wanted to be safe," Catherine said. "It was so complicated. Getting the money and getting it put away, I mean. And I didn't think we'd ever have that chance again."

"I think we can retire, if we want to," Margaret said. "We can't stay in five-star hotels and eat out of the Michelin Guide, but we can definitely retire."

"That's good," Catherine said.

And suddenly, she felt much more relaxed.

She could take anything now, because she could see the light at the end of the tunnel. She could see the end of her misery.

She could taste escape.

SEVEN

1

Gregor Demarkian did not go to see Alice McGuffie in jail. For one thing, it was too far a drive at a time when he had a lot to do much closer to home. For another, he knew almost everything she had to tell him without asking, and he didn't like the idea of asking her. There are some people in this world who are always in a state of crisis, no matter what is happening to them. A mildly offhand remark in the supermarket is interpreted as a gross insult, or a racial slur, or the first step in sexual harassment. A driver who won't get out of the way so that the people behind him can pass is an example of incipient road rage, or deliberately attempting to prevent our heroine from getting to work, because he's always been jealous, even back in the third grade. It went on and on, with no good ever coming of it, and often a lot of harm. Its practitioners were male as well as female, every possible color, every possible nationality. Gregor sometimes thought that some nationalities—the Armenian, for instance—practically turned it into an art form. It didn't matter, because what it came down to was that it was tiring, and he avoided that kind of person, and the events they generated, when he could. Fortunately, there really was nothing Alice

McGuffie could tell him that he didn't already know. He listened to her brother when he called and agreed to take a look at the photograph Alice wanted him to see, and that was that.

"It won't kill her to sit in jail for a few hours," Gregor told Gary, Eddie, and Tom, as he spread papers out across Gary's desk. He'd given up on using his own desk. The space was too cramped, and he needed room. "My guess is that she has a picture of the building launch. Would there have been any reason for her to go to that?"

"Sure," Gary said. "She was president of the PTA when that happened. Say what you want about Alice, she's very concerned about her kid's education. Why would she think it would be important to see a picture of the launch?"

"Because there's somebody who's not in it," Gregor said.

"Who's not in it?" Eddie asked.

"Catherine Marbledale," Gregor said. "She should be in it. She's the principal of the high school. But my guess is that she's not in it."

"And that's important?" Gary asked.

"In a peripheral way, yes," Gregor said, "but not in the way Alice thinks it is. You've got to understand that all of this, from the very beginning, was about money. And if Annie-Vic Hadley hadn't been elected to the school board, nobody would ever have gotten hurt. Except the taxpayers of the town, of course. They'd have been out several million dollars with nothing to show for it. But there'd have been no reason to go running around town, bashing people on the head with baseball bats. Note I said bats, plural. I'm fairly sure they were each of them disposed of as soon as possible after the event. There'd be no point in keeping them around."

"I want a case like on *CSI*," Eddie Block said. "You know, there's a forensics lab, and they take a hair, and they get everything, name, rank, serial number, DNA, phone number, last known location—"

"Why was it Annie-Vic who had to be elected to the school board?" Gary asked. "Wasn't it the case that anybody new who was elected to the school board would cause the same problem? I mean, just because you have one group of people hoodwinked doesn't mean that you're going to be able to pull the wool over the eyes of the new ones who come along."

"I wish they'd call in and tell me that they've found it," Gregor said, looking at his cell phone as if it were personally responsible for the delay. "And I wish they'd find that woman, just in case. Never mind. No, it couldn't have been just anybody. Look who else was elected to that school board. There was you, Gary. Was there ever any danger of you pulling out the files on that construction project and looking them over?"

Gary Albright considered this. "I don't think so," he said. "I don't really have that kind of time, and I explained that to Franklin when he asked me to run. I could come to meetings. I could do a reasonable amount of homework. But I couldn't take on a major project. I've got work here. I've got my family."

"Exactly," Gregor said. "And you would have had the brains. But you know, even if you did decide to get involved, my guess would be that it would have taken a long time before you figured out anything was wrong, and even longer before you figured out what. You're not a trained accountant, or anything close."

"Annie Vic isn't a trained accountant," Eddie Block said.

"No, she isn't," Gregor said. "But she manages her own investments. I don't know how many times people told me that. She manages her own investments, and she's good at it. So she must have at least a rudimentary idea of how deals are done, and what disclosure forms mean."

"I know what a disclosure form means," Gary said.

"You might, but I'll bet you don't know how to read one," Gregor said. "And then who do you have? Alice McGuffie and Franklin Hale. Franklin Hale runs a business, so there should be some expertise there. And there probably is. It's just that Franklin Hale doesn't seem much interested in looking into the practical aspects of running the schools in Snow Hill. There's no sign in any of these papers I have that he's ever so much as asked to see the operating budget. I called the secretaries down at the high school. Not a single one of them has ever had a request for any information from him, *except* for information about the biology curriculum. He wanted to see lesson plans. He wanted to see textbooks. He did not want to see budgets and disclosure forms."

"None of us realized he was so single-minded about the evolution thing," Gary said. "When he ran for the board, his campaign was all about competence, not evolution. He talked a lot about the construction project then."

"That was because he knew he couldn't win an election in this town saying he was going to get evolution out of the schools," Eddie Block said. "Even most of the people who've lived here all their lives wouldn't have voted for that."

"And why not?" Gary asked. "Does that make sense? I don't mean getting evolution out of the schools. I mean not letting anything else in. We didn't vote to remove evolution from the curriculum. We didn't even vote to let Intelligent Design into the curriculum. We just wanted to put a book in the library—"

"All right," Gregor said. "Enough. The fact remains that Franklin posed no danger to anybody, because he wasn't looking into any of the financials and probably wasn't going to. Alice McGuffie posed no danger to anybody because no matter how often she might have looked at the paperwork, she'd never have the first idea of what she was seeing. Her husband might, I admit. He runs a business. But why would she show it to him? The only reason Alice McGuffie cared about the money the Snow Hill schools were spending was that she resented any money being spent on schools at all. She would have looked at a bunch of numbers and complained that they were too high, but she'd have had no idea of what she was seeing and no interest in learning. Franklin Hale may have gotten himself elected to the school board to get evolution out of the public schools, but Alice McGuffie got herself elected to the school board so that she could stick it to all the teachers she'd hated since she was in high school."

"Middle school, probably," Gary Albright said.

"The thing is," Gregor said, "the one person on that board who did care about the financials was also the one person on that board who would know what she was seeing when she saw it, and that was Annie-Vic Hadley. And there was no way to distract her. She didn't care about the evolution and Intelligent Design debate, except that she was willing to lend her name to the lawsuit. After that, from what I can tell, she paid no attention to that at all. I looked at the papers on her dining room table three times. The first was when Judy Cornish was killed. The second was when I walked up to the house the next day and the officers offered to let me in to look around. The third was just after Shelley Niederman was killed. And in between those times, I had Annie-Vic's grandniece Lisa look again. And all those times, all I found, all Lisa found, was financial paperwork on the Snow Hill school accounts. That was it."

"Nothing on the lawsuit?" Eddie Block said. "That surprised me. She didn't keep any material on the lawsuit?"

"She probably did," Gregor said. "When Judy Cornish was killed, the papers on the table were pretty badly messed up. I think the papers on the lawsuit, whatever Annie-Vic had, were taken away in order to make it look like the killer was interested in the lawsuit. Eventually, somebody would have mentioned the fact that Annie-Vic had a lot of material on that. If we'd followed the plan, we'd have gotten suspicious and started looking into people who might hate or resent the woman because she was part of the lawsuit. In fact, everything about the way all this was set up, right from the beginning, was meant to direct our attention to that lawsuit. Because that was the one direction we could look in that our murderer was sure would not help us in any way."

"But I still don't see how it makes any sense," Gary said. "How long could somebody keep this up? School boards are elected. They come and go. Eventually, there would probably be somebody with a real accounting degree on the board. Somebody from the development, maybe. And then what would happen?"

"Nothing, if that day took long enough in coming," Gregor said. "Look, the paperwork was sloppy. It was so sloppy that Molly Trask, who's a rookie agent, knew what was wrong with it the minute she saw it. It was a question of getting your hands on the paperwork and fixing it, or fixing some of it and making the rest of it disappear. And once it was gone it was gone, because the Dellbach Construction Company does not exist. It's a post office box in Harrisburg. Eventually, after everything was tied up, it would just vanish, and the chances were good that unless our murderer got enormously stupid, nobody would ever be able to pin anything on anybody."

"You'd think it would be harder to get away with than that," Gary said. "You see all these things on Court TV—sorry, Tru TV. Anyway, you see all these things about the FBI going after fraud perps. You'd think it would be harder than that."

"If our murderer had wanted to steal fifty million dollars instead of just five, or if there had been multiple sources for the income, it would have been harder than that. But this was a very simple case. It was like raiding a cookie jar. It was not particularly sophisticated from an accounting standpoint, and it didn't require a lot of fancy footwork to be kept out of sight. Unless somebody went deliberately looking for it, the chances were good that nobody would ever guess."

"And Annie-Vic went looking for it," Gary said.

"She saw the disclosure form and knew there was something wrong, and then she went looking for it," Gregor said. "Exactly. And if she'd died when she was attacked, nobody else would have had to. You would have filed the case under 'unsolved' and put it down to juvenile delinquents in your head. Her family would have come in and boxed up all her stuff and put it in storage. Our murderer would have had all the time in the world to clean up the garbage, and that was that. As long as Annie-Vic was alive, those papers stayed put and anybody with access to them became a danger."

"But Shelley Niederman didn't have access to them," Eddie protested.

"Our murder thought she did," Gregor said. "Or maybe I'd better say that our murderer had no guarantee that she hadn't, and it was better safe than sorry. So Shelley got a call from somebody she trusted.

She went up to the Hadley house for what she probably thought was a meeting. The officers were diverted to the back by—"

Gregor's phone went off.

"There it is," he said. "That's Molly and Evan. Thank God."

2

They came trooping back to the Snow Hill Police Department, not just Molly Trask and Evan Zwicker, but two state police officers of the small platoon that had been left at the Hadley house.

"No more chances that two of us go missing at the same time again," one of the officers explained to Gregor that morning, back when he'd told Tammaro and Weeks to find out what was in those woods behind Annie-Vic's.

Gregor did not blame Dale Vardan for this one, although he still blamed Dale for a lot of things. Even Dale's belligerent opportunism was serving some good today, though, and so he let it go.

Molly had the evidence bag when she came in, and she laid it down on Gary Albright's desk in front of Gregor.

"There it is," she said. "Or, I should say, they are. There are two of them. There was one about fifty feet or so behind the house. The other was right at the back. On the lawn. It was close enough to the house to have started a fire if something went wrong."

"What are those?" Gary asked, holding up the evidence bag and looking at its contents in the light. "Are those caps? Like for cap pistols?"

"They're caps," Gregor said, "but not for cap pistols. They're what special effects departments used to use to make the sound of rapid gunfire. They're probably three or four hundred times as powerful as a cap pistol cap."

"And all you have to do is light them," Molly said, "because they're primed to a delay when they go off. And they're really loud. And they sound so much like real gunfire, I've never met anyone who can tell the difference if they haven't been told."

"But why two of them?" Eddie Block said. "It looks like they each make, what, three or four shots? Why put one so close to the house?"

"Oh, I know that," Molly said. "To get the officers to come on back. I'll bet there are more of these around somewhere, unpopped ones, just in case those two weren't enough to get the officers to come looking."

"Very good," Gregor said. "There were two officers posted guard, both of them had to be away from the front of the house when Shelley Niederman arrived. Our murderer put one of these sets in the woods, then another closer to the house. Our murderer went around one way and the officers came around the other, and a few minutes later Shelley Niederman arrived and headed for the front door."

"It was an awful risk to take," Gary Albright said.

"It was," Gregor admitted. "But there's a lot of risk taking here. Judy Cornish died because the house wasn't empty when she went inside. That was a bigger risk than the one with Shelley Niederman. For one thing, there was Shelley Niederman, sitting out there in that Volvo the whole time the murder of Judy Cornish was going on. But it was the only thing that could have been done, under the circumstances, so it was done. And that's how we got here."

"And we can make an arrest?" Gary Albright asked.

"Not quite yet," Gregor Demarkian said. "There's one more question I need an answer to. After that, you can arrest away."

3

There was actually more than one question Gregor Demarkian needed the answer to, but those other questions did not need to be answered before they made an arrest. There were always loose ends at the close of cases, always things he had to keep hounding people for after the main action was over. In this case, he would want to know something of what happened to Alice McGuffie after her several hours in jail. He wished he could look inside that woman's head and see what had finally sparked that small bit of intelligence, the one that made her realize that that picture she had had something important to say. He wondered if she knew what it was that was important there and decided she probably did not. Alice McGuffie's hatred and resentment of Catherine Marbledale were so deep and so hot, she would have done anything she thought would get the woman in trouble. It frightened him, sometimes, how much bad emotion there was in the world, as if human beings could never completely accept happiness as a state of mind. So much of what went wrong everywhere, so much of crime, so much of violence, so much of murder, was just this: that human beings cared only about other human beings, and half the time that care was expressed as a wish for annihilation.

He wasn't making any sense, and he knew it. He was tired, and he wanted to get this done in time to catch Dale Vardan unawares. Or something. That was a wish for annihilation, too. Even so, he had a life waiting for him. He had Bennis, and the wedding coming up, and Tibor and Donna and a dozen other people he hadn't spoken to in days. He had a world where he felt comfortable.

Now he looked up and down Main Street from his vantage point at the police department's front door and felt suddenly wonderful that he did not live in a place of this kind. The diner was still closed. The mobile news vans looked deserted. Even Nick Frapp's church complex seemed to be devoid of people for once. In a day or two things would be back to normal here, but Gregor did not think they would be any better. The problem here was the people themselves, and he didn't think that would change no matter how long Nick worked at changing it. People had to want to change, and even then they usually didn't.

He crossed the street and went up the block a little to the offices of Wackford Squeers, the faux old-fashioned sign hanging in the air next to the door. Gregor could see through the front window to the empty receptionist's desk. He wondered why the secretary had quit and where she had gone when she left. He walked up to the front door and opened it. It wasn't locked. Secretary or no secretary, Henry Wackford was open for business. Gregor supposed he would have to be. Appointments don't cancel themselves just because secretaries quit.

Henry Wackford's office door was closed, but Gregor could hear him in there, walking around, talking to someone, or maybe just to himself. There was nobody waiting in the outer room. Gregory looked at the pictures on the walls. They were bland pictures, reception area pictures, nothing that would offend anyone anywhere: There was a scene of horses in a field. There as a landscape of an old mill over a river. Gregor thought he had seen these same pictures in hundreds of places. He thought he might be wrong.

He listened to the talking coming from Henry Wackford's office and decided there was only one voice. There was no client in there. Henry Wackford was talking to himself.

Gregor went up to the door and knocked. The talking stopped, abruptly. The door was opened. Henry Wackford looked disheveled and sweaty. It made him seem older.

"Mr. Demarkian," he said. "What are you doing here?"

Gregor walked past him into the office. The pictures on the walls here were no less vapid than the ones in the reception area. Here, though, there were the diplomas, the degrees, the awards, and there were quite a few of each. There was a time when Henry Wackford must have looked like the next big thing.

"There was a lot of promise here, in the beginning, wasn't there?" Gregor asked.

"I don't have the faintest idea of what you're talking about," Henry Wackford said. "Christine's gone and I'm up to my neck, so if there's something you need—"

"A confession would be nice," Gregor said. "Gary and his boys ought to be here in a minute or two, and a confession isn't strictly necessary, since I know who and how and why pretty thoroughly at this point, but a confession would be nice. It saves time."

"A confession to what?" Henry demanded. "To murdering a couple of women I barely know?"

"Oh, it's a lot worse than not knowing them," Gregor said. "You murdered Shelley Niederman for no good reason at all. It was Judy Cornish who was the accountant before she decided to have children and stop out to raise them. Shelley Niederman was a dance major in college. She wouldn't have known a disclosure statement from a restaurant menu even if Judy tried to tell her about it. You went to all that trouble. You killed a woman you had no need to want dead. And you hanged yourself when you did it."

"I'll repeat," Henry Wackford said. "I have no idea what you're talking about."

"Of course you do," Gregor said. "You know what your big mistake was? You put Catherine Marbledale's name on that disclosure form. I suppose you thought it was clever. After all, Miss Marbledale and her sister had just come in to a nice pile of money that nobody knew about, but you did. I wonder how you did."

"I know no such thing," Henry Wackford said. "Catherine Marbledale came into money? When? How?"

"About seven years go, I think," Gregor said. "But you did know this, Mr. Wackford. You had to. It was the only reason to put that woman's name on that disclosure form instead of making one up out of thin air. The social security numbers didn't matter. You could have made those up, too. But just so that you know I know, Catherine Marbledale and her sister Margaret won the jackpot in the New Hampshire state lottery. It was a small jackpot, but it was big enough. And New Hampshire is one of only three states in the country that allows winners to remain anonymous, so there was no publicity. But you knew. I don't know how you knew, but you did, and we can find out how later. We can find out anything if we know what we're looking for."

"What difference does it make if Catherine Marbledale won the lottery," Henry asked. "These murders weren't about money. They were about religion. And you know it. Those people are dangerous, Mr. Demarkian, and you know it. They're one step away from being a mob with torches out to burn the heretics at the stake."

"The difference it makes," Gregor said, "is that Catherine Marbledale was the one suspect in this case who could not have killed Shelley Niederman under any circumstances and might have had a hard time killing Judy Cornish. But with Shelley Niederman, it's just impossible. There's been nothing but trouble up at the school for the last few days. There's been a fight. There was a sit-in this morning. Miss Marbledale hasn't been able to run out and get a cup of coffee, never mind set up a meeting with Shelley Niederman, plant delayed-action caps at the back of the Hadley house, and then commit a murder. Never mind the problem with the car. Somebody would have seen her car."

"Maybe somebody did."

"But you didn't need a car," Gregor said. "It took me a while to get geographically oriented, but you're right at the bottom of the hill from the Hadley house. All you had to do was go out your back door and go up, on foot. And nobody would have seen you. The buildings would have shielded you from the sight of anyone on Main Street. You called Shelley Niederman and told her—what? That you had information about Judy's death, but you needed her to confirm it? Or that you had proof of the conspiracy to kill all the supporters of evolution involved in the lawsuit? It doesn't matter. You just had to get her up there. It didn't even matter if the cops saw her there. The caps would go off and sound like gunshots. The officers would go investigate. All that mattered was that they didn't see you, and you were sure that they wouldn't, the way you had it set up. Are we going to find the caps in your office, in your car, or in your home?"

"You don't know what you're talking about," Henry said.

"Sure I do," Gregor said, "and it doesn't even matter, because Annie-Vic is awake and she's alert, and there's a good chance she'll be able to identify you as the person who beat her up. You left a living witness, and that's always a bad mistake."

It was one of those odd moments. Gregor had had a number of them in his career. The air seemed to become almost palpable. It rippled and warped. Henry Wackford had been standing next to his desk. The desk was still piled high with file folders. There were a pair of expensive pens in a brass pen holder. There was a wallet lying out on a green felt blotter.

Henry Wackford sat down.

"You don't know what you're talking about," he said again. "You don't know what it's like, being stuck out here, living with these people. Welcome to Snow Hill, Pennsylvania. Stupidity is our business, and our passion. We've got so much of it, we're giving it away cheap."

"The women you killed weren't stupid," Gregor said, "and it wouldn't be an excuse if they were. And you're not nearly as intelligent as you think you are."

"I'm intelligent enough to know that I'm not going to give you a confession," Henry Wackford said. "And I've been around the law long enough to know that you're going to have a Hell of a time proving any of this if I don't. Reasonable doubt is a wonderful thing."

"Ah," Gregor said. "But you keep forgetting. You left that living witness."

Henry Wackford smirked, and shrugged, and turned away, so that he was looking out his back windows.

There were two state policemen out there, armed.

EPILOGUE

Nothing makes sense except in the light of evolution.
—Theodore Dobzhansky

1

On the day Gregor Demarkian married Bennis Hannaford, the sun was shining, the air was crisp with spring, and forty-two Armenian-American ladies of various shapes and ages were running around like chickens with their heads cut off, trying to make sure there was enough food. It was eight o'clock in the morning. The wedding wasn't due to start for three hours. The reception wasn't due to start for four and a half. It didn't matter. The street had been closed off at both ends, leaving a six-block stretch in between. Police officers had been dispatched to patrol the perimeter so that no incident of any kind could mar the proceedings, except for the ones the guests created themselves. Photographers had taken up their stations on the side streets, hoping to get pictures of some of the people who were supposed to have been invited. This was the greatest thing to happen to Cavanaugh Street since the boys had come home at the end of World War II, and the Armenian-American ladies wanted to be ready.

Gregor stood at the window of his apartment and looked down on it all, feeling vaguely put out because he seemed to be expected to go without breakfast. Normally, he would have gone down the street to the Ararat, but the Ararat was closed. It would be open—but not for business—later, because that was where it had been decided that the buffet would be set up and the bar would be in business. This made a great deal of sense, but it played Hell with his routine, and Gregor didn't like things that played Hell with his routine.

Of course, if that was the case, it was a mystery as to why he was marrying Bennis Hannaford of all people, but he'd given up trying to figure that out years ago.

He pressed his face to the window pane, trying to get a better look at what was going on. He failed. He turned around and went back through his living room to his kitchen. Father Tibor Kasparian was sitting at the kitchen table with Russ Donahue. They both had cups of the coffee that Gregor had made earlier. They both looked unhappy.

"Is this any kind of a mood for you to be in?" Gregor asked them. "I'm getting married in a couple of hours."

Tibor and Russ looked at each other. Tibor said, "Krekor, this is not coffee. I think maybe it is coal sands."

"Sands you can extract coal from," Russ said helpfully.

Gregor went over to the cabinet and pulled out a box. "Bennis left these," he said, putting the box on the table. "They're kind of like tea bags but for coffee. You just boil water in a kettle, I've got a kettle around here—"

"I'll get it," Russ said. "It's a good thing you're getting married, Gregor. You could kill yourself with that stuff."

"Does Bennis make coffee?" Tibor asked.

"I'll bet anything she knows how to get it delivered," Russ told him.

Gregor sat down at the kitchen table and took the glass Russ passed over to him. It wasn't true that his life was going to change radically after today. He and Bennis had been together for years. They didn't actually live in the same apartment, but they might as well have. Now there was the town house they had bought up the street, so there would be that change, and new furniture, and things like that. But it was all trivial, all of it, except that it wasn't. Sometimes Gregor wondered why he had been so insistent that they had to be formally married—but he never wondered for long, and he always knew for certain under his skin.

The water in the kettle was boiling. Russ passed out coffee bags. Tibor looked hopeful.

"The whole thing is going to take forty minutes," Russ said. "They're planning it like Napoleon just got a re-run at Waterloo. Does this make any sense to any of you?"

It didn't make any sense to any of them, but the coffee was finally drinkable, so they concentrated on that.

2

They were in Gregor's living room an hour later, trying to think of things that would keep them from being nervous, when the subject of the case came up. Of course, they would have had far less cause for nervousness if the phone hadn't been ringing every ten minutes or so, delivering messages so strange they might as well have come from the moon.

"I'm sending Tommy over for the garlic," Donna, Russ's wife, had said at one point. "Bennis says it's in a white mesh bag on top of the microwave. Just give him the whole bag and send him back right away. We don't have any time."

"What's she need garlic for?" Russ had demanded. "She's helping Bennis dress, she isn't doing the food. Is she warding off a vampire?"

"And why does it take them three hours to get dressed?" Gregor said. "Bennis can be dressed and out of this apartment in the morning faster than I can. Have any of you actually seen this dress?"

"I haven't even seen the maid of honor's dress," Russ said, "and I paid for that. And there's something I'd like to know. What kind of a dress costs forty-five hundred dollars, anyway?"

"Bennis's cost almost ten," Gregor said. "It's a Caroline Herrera. Whatever that means."

"Donna's is one of those, too," Russ said.

"You said you would tell me about the murders," Tibor said. "We cannot do this, you must know that. We will all make ourselves crazy."

"Just don't lose the rings," Russ said.

Gregor stretched out on the couch. In the end, he thought, women always behaved like women. It didn't matter if they had been tomboys in their childhoods, or if they had joined the army and spent six years in the military police. Give them a wedding, and they took forever to get anything done and spent hours making up and getting dressed, and had little nervous breakdowns about whether earrings matched or bows were put on straight. Even Elizabeth had been like that, and he had known it, no matter how hard she had tried to hide it. That had been a wedding on Cavanaugh Street, too. It had been a long time ago.

"Whatever are you thinking about?" Russ said.

"I was thinking I'd already been married in Holy Trinity Church, once," Gregor said. "It's funny, but I'd never thought of it before. It's what we should have told Leda and Sheila and Hannah when they were so upset that Tibor wouldn't marry us in the church. I've already been married once in that church. Well, in the old church before it was blown up, but the same one, ah, institutionally. If you know what I mean."

"To your first wife," Russ said.

"To my first wife," Gregor agreed. "A long time ago. Leda and the rest of them would have understood that, you know. They were even there when I married Elizabeth."

"It's all right, Krekor," Tibor said. "We reached a compromise."

"I know," Gregor said. "But I never thought of it, and I should have. There's something—I don't know—off about the idea, I guess. Getting married twice in the same place to two different people. Even Bennis would have understood it."

"Bennis did not want to be married in Holy Trinity Church," Father Tibor said, "but she was not the one giving us the problem."

"No," Gregor agreed.

Then he drifted off a little. It had been a long time since he had thought of Elizabeth. When he had first come back to Cavanaugh Street, he had thought of her every day. Of course, she had been newly dead then, and newly buried, and he had come here only because her grave would be near, in the Armenian-American cemetery just on the edge of the city.

Then and now, he thought, but it was harder to get his mind around than that. His life had changed so drastically since the days when he and Elizabeth were both growing up on Cavanaugh Street. Cavanaugh had changed drastically, too. Time is the measure of change. That's what they had taught him at the University of Pennsylvania. He could close his eyes and see Cavanaugh Street exactly as it had been then: the tall tenements with their railroad apartments; the women on their knees scrubbing the sidewalks because the street cleaners never seemed to bother; the tiny storefronts offering shoe repair and check cashing. The Ararat had been in its usual place, but it had been small, too, with tiny windows and bare floors. Gregor had been away in the FBI, living in Washington, D.C., when the Melajians had done the remodeling. He had no idea when the tenements had come down to make way for the town houses. Someday, he thought he ought to ask.

"*Tcha*," Tibor said. "Krekor, if you do not make small talk, we will make you get into your tails. Then you won't be able to sit down without getting them wrinkled."

3

People started arriving just after ten. Some of them caused a lot of fuss and had to be ushered onto Cavanaugh Street with a police escort.

"That's Liz and Jimmy," Russ said, from his new place looking out the window. "And Mark and Geoff. In tuxedos. Has Geoff hit puberty yet? You should see him in a tuxedo."

"He was telling us about the phony construction company," Tibor said. "Listen."

"I was thinking it was about time we all got dressed," Gregor said. "If we're late, I think Bennis will probably kill us."

"No she won't," Russ said. "That's because she'll be late. I think that's a Rolling Stone. I mean it. He looks embalmed and he's brought a girl who looks younger than—well, younger than legal, quite frankly."

"The phony construction company," Tibor insisted.

"Well," Gregor said, "there's not much to say. Henry Wackford wanted to get out of Snow Hill for good. And the reason he wanted to get out was exactly what he said it was, because he hated the people there. Because he thought they were all stupid. You name it. What threw me off in the beginning was that he wasn't faking any of that. He wasn't even faking his announcements of how the Christian fundamentalists were out to murder everyone who wanted to keep evolution in the public schools. He really believed that."

"He must have been a very stupid man," Tibor said.

"I don't think stupidity is his problem," Gregor said. "What's that thing Bennis is always talking about? We all have narratives we use to shape our lives. Christianity is a narrative. She claims to have one of her own she won't tell me. Well, this was Henry Wackford's narrative."

"Still," Russ said. "He knew there weren't any Christian fundamentalists committing violence in this case. He was committing the violence himself."

"Well, yes," Gregor said, "but as I understand it, logic is not a big element in these narratives. Anyway, what he did was actually very simple. When the town finally agreed to build the new schools complex, they put him in charge of the project. And he invented a construction company, and awarded it the contract. Then he subcontracted the actual work out to various firms, always being careful never to use one firm for very long. That's why the construction was taking so long. There was very little continuity. Not that he minded, of course, because the longer the project went on, the longer he could skim money off the top of it. And he would have been all right, really, except for two things. The first one was Annie-Vic. The second one was that silly impulse he had to put the Marbledale sisters on the disclosure forms as owners of Dellbach Construction."

"And he did this because they won the lottery?" Tibor said. "When people win the lottery in Pennsylvania, they are all over the news."

"I know," Gregor said. "But they won it in New Hampshire, and New Hampshire allows winners to remain anonymous. Still, he knew about it, somehow, and he thought it would be a good blind if push ever came to shove. Then something entirely different tipped me off. That woman I was telling you about, Alice McGuffie. She had a picture of the ribbon cutting on the project. She was there, because at the time she was president of the PTA. Henry Wackford was there, because he was chairman of the school board. Catherine Marbledale should have been there, both because she was principal of the high school and because she was supposedly head of Dellbach Construction, but she wasn't there. And her sister Margaret wasn't there either. Margaret wasn't there because she had no reason to be there. Catherine wasn't there because she was down with the flu, but Margaret should have been there. If you own a company like that that has just been awarded a major project, you make sure *somebody* attends the ribbon cutting. And nobody from Dellbach did. Alice McGuffie thought that the fact that Catherine Marbledale wasn't in that picture was proof that Catherine Marbledale was guilty of something, but she had it backwards. It was proof that Catherine Marbledale wasn't guilty. That, and the other thing."

"What other thing?" Russ asked. He was still at the window.

"The fact that Catherine Marbledale couldn't have killed Judy Cornish without being seen," Gregor said. "But that's not the funniest thing about all this. You know what's the funniest thing?"

"What?" Russ said. "That's Senator Casey out there. Did you know Senator Casey was coming?"

"I think Bennis gave a ton of money to his campaign," Gregor said.

"I want to know what the funniest thing was," Tibor said.

"Ah," Gregor said. "Well, that had to do with Henry Wackford's secretary, Christine Lindsay. On the day before we arrested him, she quit. Not over anything illegal he was doing. She wouldn't have understood that. In fact, Henry Wackford tended to hire secretaries who were not necessarily too bright because he didn't want them prying into anything he had going. She quit over the lawsuit, Darwin, and all the rest of it. And after she was gone, Henry went looking for the copy of the disclosure form he'd kept for himself. It was in a folder he'd labeled Books to Print, but when he looked through the files, he couldn't find the folder. The two times I talked to him, he was engaged in a frantic search for the thing, and he never did find it. Because he had to keep that disclosure form out of sight. Anybody at Snow Hill who looked at it would have realized immediately that there was something wrong."

"So what happened to it?" Russ said. "Did she take it to the police?"

"No," Gregor said. "She'd actually removed it nearly a month before. She had no idea there was anything wrong with it. She just knew it said it was a file of things to print, so she'd taken it and everything in it to the printers. It was still waiting there when Gary Albright made the arrest. He picked it up later. She'd seen the number one hundred seven on the folder, which was there for God only knows what reason, but she decided that was how many copies needed to be made, so she made them. Gary ran her down at her married sister's house in Lehigh and she told him she'd just assumed this was material needed for the new school board. She'd never thought anything of it, and she certainly hadn't read any of it."

"This was perhaps a good thing," Tibor said. "If she'd read it, he'd have had to kill her, too."

"I don't think so," Gregor said. "She isn't all that bright, so I don't think she would have figured it out, and she's very deferential to authority, at least according to Gary. If her boss told her something, she'd probably believe it. And all that was good, because murdering Christine Lindsay would have blown the cover story. Christine is not a fan of Darwin. She's very devout, very devoted to her church, and publicly Christian. It would have been hard to pin any murder of her on crazed fundamentalists looking to rid the land of Darwinism."

"And the old lady?" Tibor said. "She is going to be all right?"

"She's going to be fine," Gregor said. "Bennis knows her, do you know that? Annie-Vic went to Vassar. Anyway, she's up and around, recovering much faster than she should at her age, and writing an article on her experiences for the *Vassar Quarterly*. Then she says she's going to spend the summer on an ecotour of the Amazonian rain forest, but I think they're trying to talk her out of that."

"Who's that?" Russ demanded. "That's the tallest man I've ever seen in my life. He's taller than you are."

Gregor came to the window. "Ah. That's Nicodemus Frapp. He wasn't one of our suspects anymore, so I didn't see any reason not to invite him. He's a very interesting man."

"You invited a suspect?" Father Tibor said.

"Look at that," Russ said. "That's Oprah Winfrey. That's *Oprah Winfrey*. She's got more security than the President of the United States."

4

It was at the last minute, when he was already dressed and ready to go, that he went into his bedroom and locked the door behind him. Russ and Tibor were also ready and dressed, but they were out in the living room, looking down on the crowd from the windows, trying to spot people they knew. There would be plenty to spot, because Bennis was like that—a best-selling author, a former Main Line debutante. She knew people.

Gregor sat down on the edge of his bed and leaned over to open the bottom drawer in his dresser. Bennis knew about this drawer. He'd made a point of telling her about it. He had not shown it to her, because he never looked at it himself. Mostly, he didn't want to. He did want to now.

The drawer stuck. It was part of an older piece of furniture. He tugged until he got it open and then reached in for the single thing it contained, a long cardboard box. He put the box on the bed and took the lid off it. He took out the framed photograph of Elizabeth he had always kept on his desk when he was at the Bureau and reached for the small album just underneath it. It was his wedding album, the first one, and he hadn't looked at the pictures inside it for a very long time.

Time is the measure of change, he thought again, but then he thought of something else, one of the things that had been part of the packet about evolution he'd insisted on reading when he got back from Snow Hill: *Nothing makes sense except in the light of evolution.* There had been evolution here, all right. He had evolved from a young man to a middle-aged one, from a poor man to a "comfortable" one, from an ignorant boy to something he liked better.

But he knew this: if Elizabeth had lived, he would have stayed married to her. Even if he had met Bennis under whatever circumstances, he would not have left his marriage. He had been in love with Elizabeth then, and in many ways he was in love with her now. It was supposed to be impossible to find a love that lasted forever, but he had done it.

What struck him was that he was sure he had actually done it twice.

He flipped through the pictures one after the other: Elizabeth in the wedding dress she had bought at a "good" department store; himself in a rented tuxedo; the long bar at the place they had rented for the reception; his own mother and father, and hers. It was odd to think how many of the people he had grown up around were already dead. It was odd to think that Elizabeth herself was dead, and that he had once sat on this very bed in this very bedroom and talked to the pictures of her, and thought that she might be talking back.

He took one more look through the pile and then put everything back into the box and the box back into the drawer. He closed the door and stood up. Things happened, and then other things happened, and in no time at all your life was something you had never expected it to be. That was not all bad. In fact, a lot of it was good, at least in his case. Even so, you needed to keep control of it. You needed to make sure you did not forget, just because living got in the way.

"Culture," one of his professors at Penn used to say, "is our conversation with the dead."

Gregor didn't know about culture, but he did know about life, and there were plenty of conversations with the dead in that.

5

Twenty minutes later, Gregor Demarkian was standing all the way at his end of Cavanaugh Street, just a few feet away from the police barriers. Tibor was at his side, holding the rings in one hand and looking uncomfortable. Russ was at Tibor's side, still looking through the crowd for people he recognized. At the police barriers themselves, in the place where a priest would have stood if they were in a church, was John Henry Newman Jackman, mayor of the city of Philadelphia, and, as he would tell anybody who would listen, on the way to being President of the United States. John was confident about only two things. One was that he himself would be President. The other was that Gregor and Bennis would last forever. That one was all Gregor cared about.

Down at the other end of Cavanaugh Street, where Russ and Donna had their town house, there was a stir, and Gregor realized that this was it. They were going. There was a band somewhere. Gregor had no idea where they had been placed. There were folding chairs stretched out for blocks on both sides of the street. There were flowers, and ribbons, and a little girl, no more than four years old, with a basket full of rose petals.

A second later, Gregor saw the bridesmaids, Donna in that expensive dress Russ had complained about. It was a very beautiful dress. Bennis did not seem to be of the opinion that bridesmaids ought to look ugly. After Donna came Linda Melajian. After Linda Melajian came a woman Gregor didn't know—a cousin, the last female member of Bennis's family alive and young enough to be here. Bennis's brothers would be in the crowd somewhere. Gregor thought he would deal with them later, or just get Chris in a corner and pretend the rest of them didn't exist. Especially the one who was just out of jail.

Then there was Bennis, all the way at the back, with a huge bouquet of flowers in her hands. She was not being walked down the aisle by anyone at all, which made sense, but made Gregor feel a little disoriented. She was wearing a spectacular dress, the top part of which seemed to be made entirely of off-white beads that sparkled in the sun. She had her hair up and back. She was wearing pearls that had belonged to her mother. That was because "wearing diamonds before dark is tacky." She had told him that. Gregor felt dizzy. She was, he thought, a remarkably beautiful woman, and the beauty had not drained away because she'd passed the age of forty. He was finding it a little difficult to breathe.

Then she was standing right next to him, and handing the bouquet to Donna Moradanyan Donahue. John Jackman picked up the book he'd been holding in one hand and said:

"Dearly beloved, we are gathered here today—"

It was the Episcopal wedding service. Why was he using the Episcopal wedding service? John was a Catholic. Gregor had been baptized in the Armenian church. Bennis had been an Episcopalian once, but Gregor was sure she wasn't one anymore. At least, he'd never seen any sign of it.

Gregor looked over to Bennis, who was staring straight ahead, ignoring him.

And then she turned her head very slightly, bit her lip to control a grin, and winked at him.

ACKNOWLEDGMENTS

Months ago, in the middle of working on the long series of correc-
tions and cuts that I do in the final phase of writing a book, I told my
editor that I was going to need at least four or five pages for the ac-
knowledgments section. I needed them not because of all the people I
had to thank, although I have a lot of people to thank. I needed them
because I wanted to rant, without being compromised by the filter of
a character's point of view, on the American obsession with the theory
of evolution.

Comes time to write this final word, and I find that I don't have a
rant left in me. All the things I knew to be true when I started writing,
I still know to be true. In fact, my knowledge has been perfected, because I have read my way through books and articles not only by scientists and others supporting evolution, but by scientists and others
supporting everything from Intelligent Design to young earth Creationism. I've read Behe as well as Prothero, Johnson as well as Eugenie Scott. I sat down with books called *Evolution: What the Fossils Say
and Why It Matters* and *Evolution: A Theory in Crisis* and pasted them
full of Post-It notes in an attempt to compare and contrast them. I
spent hours on the Web sites of TalkOrigins (www.talkorigins.org)
and The Discovery Institute (www.discovery.org). I went to see Ben

Stein's movie *Expelled: No Intelligence Allowed* and then read through the information debunking it at the National Center for Science Education's dedicated site, *Expelled Exposed* (www.expelledexposed.com).

So what do I know to be true?

First, I know that evolution is a fact. There is also something else, called the "theory of evolution," which attempts to explain this fact, but evolution itself remains a fact. It's the same with gravity—there's the fact of gravity, but there is also the theory of gravity—and with the germ theory of disease. It is a fact that germs cause many diseases, in spite of our habit of calling that fact the "germ theory."

Second, I know that evolution is not what most of the people fighting it are really fighting. Oh, some of them are. There are still a few young earth Creationists out there who believe that the Bible gives them a time frame for the creation of the earth. The dating always seemed to me to be a little squishy—nowhere in *Genesis* does it say anything about 10,000 years—but there are people who believe that proof of anything else would make their religion untrue, and who fight that anything accordingly.

Most people who reject evolution, however, are not young earth Creationists, and evolution itself is not their problem. What is their problem is far more complicated. It begins with the question of whether or not science is a suitable judge of all human values. And here, they have my sympathy. There's been a fad recently in some quarters to declare that something is either scientific or it is "superstitious," either scientific or not worth anything. It is a view that blocks a lot out of human experience besides religion: literature, for instance, and art, and all those areas where human beings have traditionally worked to learn to understand themselves. I still think Shakespeare knew more about human psychology than Freud. He knew light-years more about human psychology than the present run of psychological "experts" who testify in our courts and make our educational policies.

But the problem is this: fighting the "scientization" of everything by denying the fact of evolution is a recipe for defeat in the long run. Evolution really *is* a fact, and it's a fact that isn't going to go away.

What's more, it's a fact about which more and more supporting evidence piles up every year. Trying to pretend it doesn't exist will not return literature, art, philosophy, and religion to their position as authorities on human living and human morality. It will just make all those things look silly, outdated, and wrong.

If you're still not convinced, start by heading over to the National Center for Science Education's Web site (www.natcenscied.org). They're the only organization in the world dedicated to defending the teaching of evolution in public schools, and they've accumulated a vast array of materials to help you understand evolution and the American debate about its place in education. The deputy director there, Glenn Branch, gave me great help finding all kinds of things (like a statement of the theory of evolution for one of the epigraphs) that I was having trouble finding on my own. I want to thank him and all the people he works with, and especially NCSE's director, Eugenie Scott, for all the work they do on behalf of science education.

I'd like to thank a lot of other people, too. First, Carol Stone and Richard Siddall, who introduced me to Edelweiss, and who kept my life viable throughout the writing of this book in ways too numerous to list. They're good friends of a kind and degree that most people never have the privilege to have. I'm lucky to have met them.

I'd also like to thank my agent, Don Maass, and my editor, Keith Kahla, and all the people at St. Martin's Press who have worked on these books over the years and on this one in particular.

And finally, my sons, Matthew and Gregory, whose contributions to my life have been vast and incalculable, and whose primary mission is to remind me that it's not good for me to sit at the computer so long when there's the latest superhero movie to see . . .

—*Litchfield County, Connecticut*
May 2008